LAFOURCHE PARISH PUBLIC

0 0533 0072 2485 0

P9-CDY-640

8/2014

PRAISE FOR CAMP UTOPIA

"Ruden has created the most unconventional and unforgettable of heroes. Cynical, vulnerable, often misguided, and always delightful, I dare you not to fall for Bethany as she fights, steals and flails her way through fat camp and beyond. This book is delicious."

—Miriam Gershow, author of *The Local News*

"*Camp Utopia* is a poignant, laugh out loud story about the redemptive power of friendship and forgiveness."

—Donna Cooner, author of *Skinny*

"In her smart and funny debut novel, Ruden examines weight and self-doubt, friendship, anger and transformation in a story reminiscent of Louise Rennison's Angus, Thongs, and Full Frontal Snogging. If you've ever questioned your looks or had a toxic relationship with your bathroom scale, read this."

—Suzanne Morgan Williams, author of the award-winning *Bull Rider*

"*Camp Utopia & the Forgiveness Diet* is a laugh-out-loud romp through Bethany's journey to—and escape from—what she derisively calls "fat camp." But to call the book humor is to diminish it, because Ruden's debut novel is more than merely funny. It skewers our cultural obsession with the superficial, lampooning everything from fad diets to reality television and self-help gurus. And Bethany's inner journey from bitterness to forgiveness is one that will resonate with all readers.

Read *Camp Utopia & the Forgiveness Diet* for the laughs, reread it for Ruden's profound insight into the transformative power of forgiveness."

—Mike Mullen, author of *Ashfall*

Camp Utopia

by Jenny Ruden

© Copyright 2014 by Jenny Ruden

ISBN 978-1-940192-31-4

All rights reserved. No part of this publication may be reproduced, stored in a
retrieval system, or transmitted in any form or by any means – electronic,
mechanical, photocopy, recording, or any other – except for brief quotations in printed
reviews, without the prior written permission of the author.

This is a work of fiction. All the characters in this book are fictitious,
and any resemblance to actual persons, living or dead, is purely coincidental.
The names, incidents, dialogue, and opinions expressed are products of the
author's imagination and are not to be construed as real.

Published by

◤ köehlerbooks™

210 60th Street
Virginia Beach, VA 23451
212-574-7939
www.koehlerbooks.com

Publisher
John Köehler

Executive Editor
Joe Coccaro

This book is dedicated to fathers and daughters everywhere, though to my daughters and their father, I dedicate it a little harder.

CAMP UTOPIA AND THE
FORGIVENESS DIET

JENNY RUDEN

VIRGINIA BEACH
CAPE CHARLES

Lafourche Parish Library

I want to be the girl with the most cake.

~Courtney Love

NOW ROUTING TO
YOUR DESTINATION

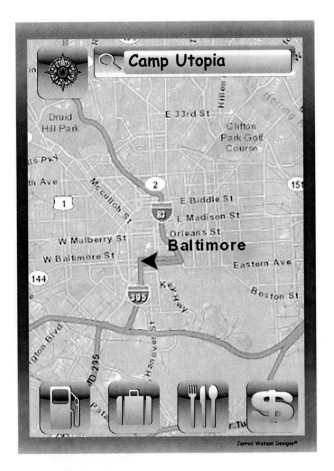

1

HE HEARTS ME

THE NIGHT BEFORE Utopia, TJ and I had a goodbye dinner at China Hon. Everything about the evening was romantic. Magical. Perfect. All that stuff that happened between us last year? Forgotten.

Right after TJ fetched beef and broccoli from the buffet, he guided me by the elbow, saying, "I have a better idea." Then he sat down in a horseshoe booth across the aisle and patted the space beside him. "Let's sit here tonight. That way you can sit next to me."

So we sat in the same booth, next to each other, our thighs brushing lightly like they do in all the Delilah Rogers romance novels I read. TJ looked at me deeply then back to his plate, where he speared a green stalk of broccoli.

He sighed. "I don't think you need fat camp. I think you're beautiful just the way you are. Especially now that you gained back all that weight you lost last year." He squeezed my hand. "Face it, Bethany Stern, you put the Bee in obesity."

"That's sweet, TJ, but I really should go to Utopia. I know it's far, and it will be hard not to see each other all summer, but I'll write to you every day."

"You should *not* go," he argued, feeding me a sliver of beef from his chopstick. "We should stay together. I mean I'm eighteen and you're sixteen. We can make our own decisions." He moved closer to me, the heat between us like a blazing nether-world. "It just doesn't feel right, Bee. You not watching me grad-uate. You missing my *American Envy* audition." He stopped, lips poised in front of mine. "This is our last summer together. Don't leave."

After hearing this confession, I became so overwhelmed I couldn't even finish my fried wontons.

"But, TJ, we're neighbors." I ticked off all the obstacles in our path. "You're gorgeous. I'm not. You're graduating in two weeks, and I'll only be a lowly junior. You're a magician and an athlete, and I'm athletically—and magically— challenged. The place we live,"—I gestured to Baltimore outside the restaurant's curtains—"why, it's practically a ghetto. Nothing good ever hap-pens here." Then I got all-out impassioned. I pounded my fist on the table. The silverware jumped, and the waiters stared. "We've been best friends for eight years, TJ. Let's not ruin it by becom-ing lovers."

"Oh let's," TJ replied, scooching even closer to me, his hot breath on my neck. "Let's!"

I climbed on TJ's lap and, behind me, he cleared the bone-white dishes off the table in one magician's swoosh. He leaned me back on packets of duck sauce and rice debris while the wait-ers screamed, "You two need hotel! Get out China Hon!"

TJ then carried me—yes, carried me—out of the restaurant, the doorbells jing-jangling behind us. We drove to a remote Maryland beach and scrumped as the passionate surf unreeled behind us.

The End.

Yeah. That was how it was supposed to happen.

2

HE HEARTS ME NOT

SO HERE'S WHAT really went down the night before fat camp. The bells on China Hon's front door jingled their same greasy song when TJ and I walked through them. Outside, Baltimore was a sweltering inferno. Inside, China Hon felt like a boiling pit. When the waiter seated us at the table closest to the dingy aquarium and across from the noisy kitchen, I thought I should really ease up on the romance novels. Maybe if I read Russian tomes about suffering and famine, it wouldn't bother me that TJ's red polo shirt sported a bird poop stain near the collar. And maybe the restaurant's plum-colored carpet would look downright chic with all those duct tape X's over the rips. I'd bet a good dose of practical, serious books would prepare me for the vinyl seats that stuck to the backs of my sweaty legs. And who knows, right? Maybe I wouldn't get so gut-twistingly disappointed when TJ looked right at me and didn't talk me out of Camp Utopia, as he'd done in my imagination, but attempted to talk me into it.

"It's supposed to be beautiful, Bee, and isn't the camp located at California University of the Pacific?"

I nodded, unimpressed.

TJ straightened his collar. "That's one of the best colleges in the country."

I stared at the restaurant fans spinning lopsidedly on the

ceiling.

"Besides," he went on, "the camp's website didn't look bad. It's pretty posh. Famous people go there."

"I'll hate it," I said.

"How do you know that?"

"I just know."

TJ chirped this part, like a bird. "You could meet great people, see the country, and fall in love."

"You sound like the brochure."

"And who knows," he said, snapping open a napkin theatrically, "you might even lose weight."

There we have it—even more reality hovering between us, like the steam from the egg roll I just split open.

Before we visited the buffet table where vats of food bubbled, TJ appeared some chopsticks from behind my ear, and then, a dollar. He kept appearing objects (a penny, a shell, a tampon—WTF?!) until I smiled. Maybe most boys gave up magic tricks by age nine, but TJ wasn't most boys. TJ had skill. Finesse. Magic was like a fever he caught and never let go. While other people suspected he had a knack for magic, even for dove training, only I knew how obsessive he was about it—and how professional. Magic tricks were the one thing he reserved for me.

He rounded the buffet and claimed beef and broccoli, his favorite. I slopped some lo mein and chicken fried rice on my plate. As we made our way back to the table (no booths here), all the things I wanted to say inched up my throat. Now would've been a good time, for instance, to bring up the unfortunate fact that I loved him, still, even after everything that happened between us last year. I might mention the three thousand miles that separated Baltimore from California. Or I could ask him, "Don't you want me to stay?"

But when I caught sight of our table, I noticed that my drink, originally a Sprite, had turned a putrid yellow. Liquid smoke tumbled from the glass.

"Now isn't that interesting," noted TJ, nodding toward my beverage.

I swallowed the words crawling up my throat and decided to play along. Truth be told, I never got tired of his illusions. "How strange, TJ," I said in my best TV voice. "I thought for sure I ordered a Sprite."

"That's definitely not a Sprite, Bee," TJ replied. "That looks dangerous."

Fog funneled around our table and drifted over my thighs in an icy cloud.

"Dare me to drink it?" I asked. He knew his lines. I knew mine. Our exchange was like a dance.

TJ shook his head. "I wouldn't swallow that if I were you."

I reached for the glass brimming with a liquid so yellow it could've been pee.

TJ feigned surprise. "Oh my goodness, ladies and gentlemen," he said, signaling to a nonexistent crowd. "Will she drink it? Will she really drink it?"

I swirled my glass, and raised it high. Smoke swooshed from my cup. "A toast," I said.

In response, TJ lifted his normal cola-colored drink.

"To your *American Envy* audition," I said, a little emotionally. "To your summer."

TJ cocked his head. "And to your utopia," he replied. "May it be everything you imagine."

Our cups tapped each other's, and I hastily swallowed. "Blech!" I exclaimed. "Can I drink this stuff? I mean, it's kind of sour-tasting."

TJ appeared to ponder this. "The doves never showed any toxic reaction to the powder. I'm sure it's fine. I mean, does it taste poisonous?"

And even though it tasted really bad and was probably radioactive, I drank it. Every last bit. "Not at all," I said, trying my hardest to enjoy it. I mean, I wouldn't see him all summer. I figured it was the least I could do.

3

AMERICAN ENVY

WHEN TJ AND I got back to my house after dinner, my heartbreakingly beautiful sister, Jackie, motioned us to her closet. She pried it open slowly to reveal Doug, her boyfriend, hiding inside.

"Shhhh," he shushed.

"He's going to help us drive across country," Jackie whispered. "Don't tell Mom, OK? She would freak if she knew I was bringing him to California. She doesn't even want him in the house!"

Doug grinned moronically beneath my sister's color-coordinated hangers. If you wanted to know the truth, I didn't want him in our house either. A cross-country road trip with the guy kind of made me want to stick daggers in my eyes.

"It was supposed to be just me and you, Jackie. This was our road trip."

"Sorry," Jackie replied. "Plans change."

"Mom will murder you if she finds out."

"But she won't find out, right?" She elbowed me hard. "Right?" She looked to TJ. "Right?"

Then my sister flitted around her room like perfection itself, gathering camping equipment and condoms—tossing them to Doug. Even though my sister was twenty and I was sixteen, neither of us had ever been west of Maryland. Months ago, Jackie begged my mom for the chance to drive across country and bum around California for the eight miserable weeks I'd be bumming around fat camp. But months ago a road trip with Jackie might have actually been fun. Not now. Now Jackie was a real pain in my ass.

"I'll need help driving," she said, touching the dance costumes and majorette uniforms she'd long since retired. "All those bridges and freeways, I might get lost."

"Doug can't even drive," I reminded her.

Jackie's boyfriend cleared his throat. "I can read a map though," he said.

"Who needs a map?" I asked. "Ever hear of GPS? Every phone's got it." Jackie and Doug ignored me. "Doug's always wanted to see California, and you'll be at camp, remember? For eight whole weeks. You're going to get so skinny," she tittered, crisscrossing the cord around her hair dryer. "You must be jazzed."

Jazzed? Sure.

Eventually, TJ and I resigned ourselves to the dark basement because, in all honesty, the springy sofa and dark-paneled walls provided more comfort than my sister and Doug ever could. Besides, *American Envy* started at eight. TJ's main ambition in life was to perfect a magic routine that would land him on the show. Convinced it was his only shot out of going to community college, TJ had been practicing forever. First came card tricks. Then there were the doves he trained to burst from stranger's hats and sleeves. Let's not forget the color-changing microorganism he'd used on my Sprite earlier. Recently, though, TJ brought it to a new level. Now, it was all about illusion. Specifically, levitation.

TJ and I watched *American Envy*, just like last Sunday night and the one before that. We critiqued the voices, dance moves, and talent routines.

"She can't sing!" I screamed at some girl loud enough for my mother to tell me to keep it down.

Always more forgiving, TJ said softly, "She wasn't that bad."

"Oh come on. She was terrible."

Once in a while a contestant appeared who was just tears-streaming-down-your-face talented, and we would toast each other with our *Rockstars* and say, "There it is." We always cheered for the people from Baltimore no matter how bad they were.

But there were no Baltimoreans on the show this fat camp eve. No talent either. Tonight was a rerun. The real envy didn't come until fall when the new season started. In this episode, talentless rich kids crooned crapfully and danced like the floor needed humping. As minor consolation, an eight-year-old magician stumbled onto the stage. His act was predictably lame. In the end, Eugene Gold, Envy's meanest judge, imparted this to the boy: "Find another pursuit, young man. A magician you'll never be." In spite of himself, TJ smiled a little.

This made me appreciate TJ's talent even more—how when he did an illusion he made it look so easy, like you, the person watching, were responsible for making it happen. Like the magic resided in the observer, not the dumbass bird he trained to fly out of your hair. Thinking about his skill made me want to kiss him. Thinking about kissing him made me want to sleep with him, and thinking about scrumping him only reminded me that tomorrow morning I was headed to fat camp. I tried not to think about Utopia, the evil fat farm at the excuse-me-I'm-a-genius-at-California-University-of-the-Pacific. Instead, I held out for a miracle—a giant boulder to fall on the minivan rendering it impossible to drive. An escaped unabomber, murderer, cannibal terrorizing cross-country drivers. A rapidly spreading eye disease that made fat people look thin. Anything to keep me here. Away from Utopia, next to TJ.

4

SLEIGHTED

AMERICAN ENVY ENDED without a miracle. No boulder. No cannibal either. There was only an infomercial TJ and I were obligated to view because the couch had sucked the remote under one of its cushions.

The commercial featured a giant fish bowl filled with multi-colored scraps of paper. Xylophone sounds tinkled in the background. At first, I thought the commercial was for some kind of craft, like moon sand or a Chia Pet. Then a voice blasted out from the TV:

DO YOU NEED TO LOSE WEIGHT?

I was lifting scratchy cushions, rummaging for the remote. When I heard the voice, I turned around.

HAVE YOU TRIED EVERY DIET AND FAILED?

On the screen that glass bowl glittered again, rainbow swirls of paper spinning around.

I WANT TO HELP YOU, the voice roared.

No doubt I had heard various diet infomercials a million times, but never during prime time and never one quite as hypnotic. I couldn't look away. TJ seemed rapt too. We studied the screen where the fish bowl overflowed with paper like jewels.

PAY ATTENTION. THESE NEXT FIFTEEN MINUTES COULD CHANGE YOUR LIFE.

There was something about this voice. Like a magnet.

"It's not about food," a lady wearing a giant sunhat said. She lounged beside a pool, the glittery bowl positioned next to her sandaled feet. "I weighed two hundred pounds and thought it was about food."

Then the woman stood, dropped her towel, and twirled in a gold bikini. "But I discovered it's about forgiveness," she said.

"Hey!" TJ said. "My boss went on this diet."

I shrugged. TJ's boss at Rent-My-Ride went on every diet.

YES, the voice intoned, *IT'S ABOUT FORGIVENESS.*

That was when the room darkened a notch. It was dusk, and Baltimore had just breathed its last streak of sunlight against the pavement outside. The city's gutter smells and sounds drifted past the open basement window. I should've told TJ to go home. It was getting late. And it was hot—too hot to even have the television on, which seemed to breathe fire. But I couldn't talk or move. Even TJ didn't get up to excuse himself and walk to his row house across the street.

Like my sofa had been slicked with paste, we watched this commercial as intently as we had *American Envy*. Five minutes. Ten minutes. Fifteen entire minutes. There were testimonials from people all over the country. Men and women held up size 20 pants, size 24 skirts, 3XL sweats. Then they pirouetted in something slinky, showed off their skinny jeans, patted their flat tummies.

"The Forgiveness Diet," they all chimed, was how they did it.

THAT'S RIGHT, said the voice. *WITH OUR PROVEN THREE-PART SYSTEM YOU CAN DROP THAT UNWANTED WEIGHT. INSTANTLY.*

On the screen, a middle-aged guy stood before the ocean.

"Hi, I'm Michael Osbourne, and I invented The Forgiveness Diet. At twenty-seven years old and three hundred pounds, I was carrying too much weight and too many burdens. I decided to write everyone's secrets on a piece of paper. All mine too. Then I put that paper inside a bucket. Enough, I said to myself. It's time to forgive them.

"Before I knew it, the weight vanished. And yours will too. You can read about my innovative approach to mercy weight loss in my new book. If you call now, we'll even throw in your very own Forgiveness Jar to get things started. For free. Free!

Call now to find out more about this amazing opportunity. Come on, what do you have to lose?" The corners of his mouth lifted as if attached to strings. *"Except weight."*

He turned and ran out into frothy surf.

A phone number flashed across the screen.

"Maybe you should buy the book," TJ said shyly.

"Why?" I asked, still staring at the television.

"Because my boss lost mad weight. And fast!"

I rolled my eyes. TJ's boss was always trying to thrust TJ onto better things. Like herself. He nudged me gently. "If it worked you wouldn't have to leave for camp tomorrow. You could see me graduate. Watch me audition."

"You mean you don't want me to go either?"

"I mean you could stay here. Just buy the book."

"I don't have a credit card," I said.

"What about PayPal? Order the e-book."

"No e-reader."

The fish bowl, on the screen again, brimmed with folded papers. Fat people walked up to the jar, kissed their papers, and dropped them inside. As they skipped off it appeared they lost the weight before our very eyes.

"You can do that," said TJ. "Just write down the names of people who have pissed you off."

"I'm sure the book has some kind of specific directions. There must be more to it than that."

"Maybe not," said TJ. "My boss said she just had to forgive her boyfriend for cheating on her and forgive her fingers for stealing change out of the rental cars, and she lost like ten pounds." TJ stared at his Converse. "Bee, you have a lot of people to forgive. Maybe all that pissiness is stuck inside you making you big, like that voice said. It makes sense in a way."

I bristled. "It makes absolutely no sense."

TJ removed his glasses and rubbed them on his shirt, a ritual he only performed when something bothered him. "You could make it like a bucket list. Write everything down like in those long letters you used to write."

"Those letters sucked. You're crazy."

"Your letters were amazing. Just write it true. Then put it in a Cool Whip container." He replaced his glasses. "You could start with that night, you know. When we almost—"

"Shut up, TJ."

"What?"

"It will never work."

TJ sighed. "It worked for all of them," he said, nodding toward the television.

YOU CAN NOT FAIL the voice bellowed. *GUARANTEED.*

Then the commercial ended.

"I mean you don't want to go to fat camp, right?" TJ asked. "This might be your only hope."

"But it's just an infomercial," I said. I looked back to the television where a woman discussed a very absorbent paper towel. I dug around behind the sofa, felt the hard plastic of the remote, and pushed the rubber button. The television buzzed off. "How am I supposed to get thin by tomorrow?"

TJ walked to the basement stairs and sat on the third step. Behind him moonlight dripped in the window. It had to be one hundred degrees in my house, yet there was no sweat on his forehead. TJ never sweated. When he opened his mouth, he spoke slowly, as if I were retarded.

"Look, Bee. Remember that guy who levitated on *American Envy* last season?"

Here we go, I thought. "How could I forget when you bring it up every other day?"

TJ's eyes darted around the room, and he lowered his voice, conspiratorially, "Well, I finally figured out his secret."

"Yes, TJ. It's called Hollywood. It's called camera tricks."

He stood up on the step and spread his arms wide. Then he brought them together in front of him like he was praying. He put his chin down near his collar and prepared himself for what looked like a swan dive directly into the coffee table.

"It's called the Balducci levitation. You stand at an angle," he said, rocking on the balls of his feet. "So from where you're sitting it looks like I'm floating, but really, my foot is just on my ankle, see?"

We had that *American Envy* episode on DVR. For weeks TJ was over my house pausing it, flipping his head upside down in front of the television, trying to determine if the contestant had some sort of fan contraption crammed in his pants.

TJ stumbled off the step and landed, face down, on our shag carpet, which was the exact color of a tennis ball.

"Didn't it look like I was floating a little?"

"No." I said. Then, "Well, maybe slightly."

He studied his shoes like they were to blame. "I'm still practicing," he explained. "My point is that instead of trying to figure out how the Levitator couldn't do it, I tried to work out how he did."

"I don't understand how writing down secrets and forgiving people will make me thin."

"You don't need to understand how it works." TJ stood and stepped closer to me. "You only need to know that it's possible." When he reached behind my ear, I expected he would flick out a silvery coin or, if he was feeling mysterious, a gardenia. But he didn't. He smoothed my hair back behind my ears and looked directly at me.

"You never believe what's right in front of your face."

"I believe in you," I said.

He leaned in. "Don't believe in me," he whispered. I could see the red indentations his eyeglasses had pressed into his nose. "Believe in you."

TJ dropped his hands from my face. When he brought them up again, they held a crumpled ball of paper. I started at it curiously, then I touched it with the tips of my fingers.

"Open it," he said.

Once in a while, he could still surprise me with a magic trick.

"Go on," he urged.

I slowly uncrumpled the paper.

It read: *I forgive my dad for not seeing me.*

"Where did you get this?" I asked, my voice tight.

He shrugged. "It was behind your ear."

"TJ!"

"You're full of magic, Bethany."

"Tell me how you did this. Seriously."

But TJ had slipped into illusionist mode where every movement was choreographed and every smile insincere. He might explain later how he'd managed to write this on a restaurant napkin when I wasn't looking. He might cop to how he'd found purple ink, my favorite, and how he'd made the handwriting look identical to mine. Exactly like mine. Maybe he'd admit to somehow crawling into my future ahead of me, but not now. Now he only kissed my forehead, lustlessly. The way you would kiss a cat. "You could forgive him," he said, referring to the slip of paper, "your dad, for ignoring you at Chuck E. Cheese's."

"Stop," I said.

He plucked the paper from my fingers. "You could forgive me too," he continued, "for everything. You know. Last year."

I could, I thought, *but I won't*. Leave it to TJ to present it like an option. An option about as viable as a diet based on forgiveness.

"So if you won't try the diet then will you at least write to me every day you're gone?" he asked as he readied himself to leave. "Not just texts, e-mails too. Long, epic ones."

My phone vibrated in my pocket. I pulled it out and read the text he'd somehow sent when I wasn't looking. *You my girl.*

He'd never told me how he'd managed that trick either.

Not that it mattered. Tonight, just like every other night, I'd fall for him all over again. I'd believe I was his girl. I'd accept that someone so extraordinary could have a thing for me—someone so ordinary.

And fat.

So fat.

From:bumblingbee@yeehaw.com
To: Toby Jacobson <voodooyou@abracadabra.com>
Subject: twas the night before fat camp...

dear TJ

i never stopped writing you emails. i only stopped sending them. i bet i've written u fifty this past year. That's almost 1 for every pound I gained. Not that u noticed.

That's what's called a lead-in, TJ. u taught me that. Like in ur magic shows when i'm supposed to bait you with a well-timed, "Now, TJ. Where did those magical doves get to?" or, "Hey, TJ, is it just me or is my Sprite foaming?" I'm still giving you lead-ins. Only in real life u never answer.

At 7 AM tmrw I leave for Utopia. I really hope ur awake. I hope u flag down the minivan. Barricade urself in front of it. I hope u call Jackie a traitor and punch Doug in the face. Then I want u to get ur bullhorn and tell everyone up and down Falls Road that ur sorry about last year. Sorry about what happened between us. Of course I'll forgive u. Forgive u everything. I'll let u take me back to your room. Lean me back on ur bed. Let u kiss my face and neck. My bra unhooks in front, TJ. know that.

I will tell u everything. like how when I was thirteen I started imagining u … Naked. Always @ the most inconvenient times too. Homeroom, fire drills, American Envy marathons. Then the tingles started. Tingles tingled places I never imagined tingling. ur shoulder blades underneath ur shirt, jutting out like wings, it does things to me. Makes my knees weak. Makes me sneak in the bathroom and fan my red face. And u reading ur trick books and biographies, TJ, I swear it makes me swoon more than anything else. More than ur grunts when u swish basketballs into the net. More than when u cup doves in ur hands like a secret. Something about ur gold-rimmed glasses, shirt off, belt threaded thru loops, a thick book fanned in front of u well, it kills me.

See what happens when I write to u? I guess that's why I stopped. I'm too afraid of where I'll go. Maybe you are too.

~bee

PS: you dumbass…I still freaking love you

PPS: I am still sorry re: the doves

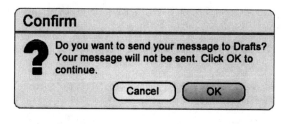

5

WHAT I'M PACKING

IT WAS STILL dark outside when Jackie flung open my blinds the next morning.

"Operation Fat Camp," she barked. "Let's go."

I hadn't even packed. Guessing as much, Jackie scurried around my room, her ponytail swinging violently. She opened drawers and snatched shorts and tank tops. She grabbed my cell phone from the nightstand and tossed everything in a duffle bag. When I rolled over, my eyelids growing heavy again, she hauled me out of bed by my ankle.

"No you don't," she warned. My sister, who weighed one hundred and five, maintained a freakish strength. When I finished brushing my teeth, she shoved my still-wet toothbrush in the bag.

Mom was already downstairs making breakfast. On the table sat a plastic jug of orange juice, whipped cream in a can, and sliced strawberries. She slurped coffee from her favorite Zyprexa Pharmaceuticals mug.

"I used real butter too," she said, presenting me with a plate of waffles. "And real syrup."

Mom hadn't eaten sugar in ten years—at least not in front of me. She was the kind of woman to make a big show about asking for lite or fat-free everything, even though she didn't need it and even though that stuff's been killing lab rats for decades.

I studied the succulence before me. "Wow. You should send me to fat camp more often."

She sighed like someone let the air out of her. It was her *don't-start* sigh.

I looked at the giant sunflower plate crowded with waffles, syrup, butter, and bacon. Bacon. Sure everything was burnt, but it didn't matter. It looked delicious. Dreamy. You can imagine just how dreamy if a waffle-less, bacon-less, butter-less summer stared you in the face.

For whatever reason, just then, Delilah Rogers, my all-time favorite romance author, popped into my head. She had granted only one interview during her career, and in it she said something that, as I plowed my fork into a heap of waffles, made a lot of sense. "Brains are great, but if a woman really wants things to go her way she should try hysteria."

Things definitely weren't going my way. The old Honda Odyssey waited for me in the street, its trunk opened like a vortex. A glossy Utopia brochure and U.S. map rested beneath Jackie's keychain on the entry table. And my mom? Well, she couldn't get me out the door fast enough. Underneath her Zyprexa Pharmaceuticals bathrobe, I bet she rocked a cocktail dress.

No. Things definitely weren't going my way. Maybe Delilah had a point. I mean, I always envied her hysterical female characters who super-glued themselves to the legs of their lovers and did not let go. The soft-haired heroines who leaned back in the arms of their fanged boyfriends and ordered, "Bite me." Those were the best. Maybe I needed to dig in my heels.

"How's breakfast?" Mom asked.

"It'd taste better if I wasn't headed straight into the hellmouth." I pushed my plate away then pulled it back. I loved waffles.

My mom shook it off.

"It's called Utopia, Bethany. How bad can it possibly be?"

"Why don't you go, and then tell *me* all about it," I snarked.

"If I needed to go, I would," my mom huffed, pulling the bathrobe belt tight around her narrow waist.

"Who said I need to go?"

She didn't respond. She just gave me "The look." It was the same look she gave our neighborhood, Jackie's old report cards, waiters out of Diet Dr. Pepper, Doug. The same look she gave my dad before he got sick of it and left. It was her signature expression of pity mixed with disgust.

Faced with "The look" now, I willed my jiggly thighs and ankles to slim. I tried to appear slender in my shorts, but the chub seeped out over the button. I felt my mom eyeing the roll. She was about to mention that last year these shorts fit. She was going to say, "You were so motivated to lose weight before. What happened?" Next she'd get into how she searched my room for food and, much to my embarrassment, found it. But she was oddly quiet this morning. She didn't even bring up her whole *but you have such a pretty face* shtick.

"If you let me stay here, I'll go back on my diet. I'll join a gym." I stared at the butter pooling inside a waffle square. "I'll try harder."

Mom sat down across from me. She looked tired, spent—nothing of the I-Have-It-Together-Superwoman she thought she was and every bit of the single mom she happened to be. She pulled a napkin from the dispenser centered on our linoleum table and dabbed her eyes. "I just want good things for you."

"Good things don't happen to fat people?"

"No," she replied. She sniffed once. "Just look at your father."

Not even seven in the morning, and she was bringing him up. "Dick only wanted to read books and do crosswords. Never understood what teamwork meant. Or sacrifice. He had no drive."

"No ambition," I chorused in my mom's sales pitch tenor. "Couldn't even finish optometry school. Needed someone to hold his hand the whole time."

She looked at me, trying to figure out whether to be proud or offended that I knew her speech better than she did. "That's right," Mom said. "He was definitely an overweight and unhappy man. You don't want that kind of future, do you?"

Not that this could be verified, mind you, given I hadn't actually seen my dad in two years. Unless you're inclined to count when I ran into him at Chuck E. Cheese's, and he ignored me. Forget about that for now, though. Ancient history. My point is that in my dad's occasional e-mails or too-late birthday cards, he presented himself as exceedingly happy with his new wife and new kids in Ellicott City.

I started to say something, but then the smoke alarm went off. My mom had burned the waffles.

"Perfect," she said, which was what she always said when life stepped in to remind her that I was fat, Jackie was dumb, or that we basically lived in a dump.

Perfect. Perfect. Perfect.

6

VANISHING ACT

JACKIE BARRELED DOWN the stairs and dumped the duffle bag by my feet. "I even packed you a nice blouse in case they have a dance or something."

Blouse. She never used to say words like that. She never used to dress like a Mormon either. This fine morning, my sister wore capri pants and a matching white "blouse" of her own. Her outfit was tasteful, modest. It did little to conceal the fact that everything about her body was flawless down to the neat circle of her navel whose piercing she'd removed last month. Looking thirty-five instead of twenty, Jackie poked a finger in my belly. "You'll so love being thin," she said, like she held the patent on skinny. "You must get tired of lugging all that weight around." She tied the strings of her pants in a dainty bow. "Don't you?"

You're wondering what happened to Delilah's plan—the one that involved hysterics? The plan was very much in effect when I said, "Carrying a few extra pounds is nothing compared to hauling a loser boyfriend everywhere. Or a baby."

Jackie tilted her head at my insult, more curious than hurt. "I wouldn't know anything about that."

Of course she wouldn't.

I looked from my duffle bag to the car keys and back to Jackie's sensible shoes. My mom's coffee pot belched and hissed. *This is actually happening,* I thought. Sixteen years old on a Monday morning in June, I, Bethany Mitzi Goodman Stern, straddled a vector aimed right at fat camp.

One. Final. Plea.

"Please don't," I tried. "I've lost weight before. I can lose it again." Now I was crying. I thought about throwing myself on the floor and kicking around in circles like the three-year-old I used to be. I knew if I did, though, my sister and my mom would only join forces, lift me up, and ever so calmly throw my too-big-butt inside the minivan. After all, they were used to my tantrums considering I used to have them all the time. In fact, according to my mom and all the psychobabble she endorsed, the only thing that ever snapped me out of them was to completely ignore me. If my family wanted me to shut up, then they need only pretend I was invisible. What can I tell you? Years later, and it was still their modus operandi.

My mom and sister packed up the minivan obliviously while I howled, cajoled, bargained, threatened, and then, finally, gave up.

In no time at all, we were standing outside as the sun peeled back a layer of sky.

"Mom spent five thousand dollars," said Jackie. "The least you can do is kiss her goodbye."

"This wasn't exactly my idea," I reminded them.

"You can always come home," my mom said, like someone held a cue card in front of her. "But at least try it. Try it before you decide to hate it. Promise?"

Massive lie in three ... two ... one ... "Sure."

Jackie started the car like it was the most natural thing in the world, like we were Magellan and Columbus leaving Baltimore for brighter waters. I leaned back in my seat and looked at TJ's row house, every inch of it still in sleep. I couldn't see the cages that held his doves, but I knew they were asleep too. What lucky winged bastards they were, privileged to hide up TJ's sleeves, the object of so much of his attention.

If this were a Delilah Roger's romance novel, I'd unlatch my seatbelt, run across the street, dig up his house key buried in a fake rock, and crawl next to TJ in his bed. "I want to stay with you," I'd whisper. Better yet, he'd somehow gotten my e-mail and had chained himself to the minivan the way tree-huggers chain themselves to two-hundred-year-old sequoias.

But there was nothing romantic about my story.

"*Bon Voyage*," Jackie said, pronouncing it voy-*idge*. She waved at my mom and pulled away from the curb. "Off to brighter waters."

I opened my window for one last whiff of Baltimore: Fishiness mixed with cinnamon from the defunct spice factory. We'd been waking up to that fishy/spicy aroma since my dad walked out, which landed my mom back here, in Baltimore, twelve years ago. It was the last place she wanted to be. It was the last place anyone wanted to be.

"But I like it here," I said, my eyes filling with tears all over again. Yes, I loved my neighbor, but I loved Baltimore too. Sure it stunk when the wind blew up from Dundalk, and yes, the accent was goofy, but it was home. My home. And, according to Dorothy and other great minds, there's no place like it.

I opened the glove box for a tissue, but instead a cyclone of Jackie's condoms poured out. Natch.

My sister drove for two blocks then pulled into an alley where Doug was waiting for us. He opened my door and directed me to the backseat.

"What? I can't even ride shotgun in my own adventure?"

"Negative."

From the backseat I watched my house, TJ's house, China Hon, and the rest of my world disappear like a vanishing act. Now you see it.

Poof.

Now you don't.

7

NUCLEAR

JUST LAST NIGHT I was sitting in my basement with TJ watching *American Envy* and now, twelve hours later, my sister merged the minivan on I-70 West. I felt like I was stuck inside a riptide that had sucked me out of my house and was about to slam me down at fat camp. Well, not if I could help it. What I needed was a plan. One that would get me back to TJ as quickly as possible. The task before me was daunting, no doubt. Maybe, I decided, checking the time, what I needed was brunch.

Chinese food would do nicely, but it was early morning. It looked like Colonel Carolina's Fried Chicken would have to do. I had a weakness for their nuclear orange macaroni.

"I'm hungry," I said.

Doug sighed, but I was used to extensive sighing whenever I said I was hungry.

"You're kidding me, right?"

"No. I'm quite famished."

Then Jackie and Doug debated my hunger.

"It's nine o'clock in the morning," said Doug. "She can wait."

"She's so upset though," whispered Jackie. She tapped her thumbs on the steering wheel. "I promised her she could eat whatever she wanted as long as she didn't tell Mom you were coming with us."

Doug gasped. "That's idiotic. She should get used to not eating."

"Do you two realize that I'm sitting right here?" No answer. Evidently they did not. "I want chicken—of the Colonel Carolina variety."

"How do you expect us to find that?" asked Doug.

Before we could plug it into our phones, Jackie angled down an exit and discovered a Taco Hut/Pizza Plaza/Colonel Carolina drive-thru window. Praise Jesus! There were cameras in the driveway and bullet holes on the menu, but whatever. They had chicken and fiery orange macaroni. I uncrumpled the fifty dollar bill my mom instructed was for emergencies only and handed it to the employee.

"By the way," said Doug, collecting my change and my chicken bucket, "this is how you got fat in the first place." Then he tore open the bag that contained my neon macaroni and shoved a handful of my French fries in his mouth. "I'm just putting it out there."

Jackie touched his knee as a reminder that we weren't that far into our trip yet, then Doug touched Jackie's knee. I realized I would have to watch their squeeze-me-stroke-me marathon for days. The overflowing condoms at Doug's feet reminded me that I'd be forced to listen to their guinea pig sounds all night too. Bonus: We only had one tent.

"Just hand me the bag, Doug," I said.

Doug did not hand me the bag. Instead he dug his hand inside of it and removed a biscuit. My biscuit. Then Jackie, who was driving, reached confidently into the bag still centered on his crotch and said, "Come on, Bethany. You can share your food with Doug." She held the fries up and chewed them slowly, like someone was filming a porno of it. From the backseat, I saw the downy hairs on her neck swirling up to her ponytail. "Doug's right you know," she started. "This is the time to adopt new eating habits, and you aren't off to the best start."

You could positively smell the hormones—thick and pungent—in that car. Jackie and Doug were so excited to be driving to California that they forgot what initiated the expedition in the first place: *me.*

"I just want my macaroni, guys. Please?"

Then Doug leaned over and kissed Jackie, a sloppy one on the lips. Like I wasn't even there. On and on the kiss went. And on. Did I mention that the only person who ever kissed me was dreaming in his bed right now? And the last time he kissed me—really kissed me—was a year ago? Now you can imagine how uncomfortable it was to view this tongue fest, which clearly violated about a hundred traffic laws. I stuck my face right between them, so close I smelled the gardenia perfume Jackie dots behind her ears every morning, so close I saw the razor bumps sprouting on Doug's chin.

"Macaroni?"

They broke apart, a string of saliva between them, then Doug groaned. I guess he was estimating how long until he could be alone with my sister. He had assumed this was their road trip all along—never mind that the inevitable end was Utopia. I could see this epiphany crash into him—his small mind grappling with the fact I'd be there for every state, every mile, sticking my face between theirs. He must have been thinking about something bad because instead of offering me the bag like a normal human being, he hurled it back so viciously it exploded all over the backseat.

"There's your macaroni," he said. Then: "You fat pig."

He muttered that last part, loud enough for me to hear but quiet enough for Jackie to convince herself I didn't.

"Dooooouuuuggg?" That was Jackie's attempt at annoyance.

"What? Your sister's the one with all the demands. Give me this. I want that. She's worse than a baby."

Jackie, who had a thing for babies, tried her hand at empathy. "She's only sixteen, Doug."

"Sixteen isn't three. At sixteen I had a job. I went to the gym. All she does is chase that fairy magician around hoping he'll pop her cherry."

Oddly enough, he turned around to offer me the plastic fork. The macaroni he'd propelled; the utensil required civility. "We all know you like a good romance, so here's yours, Bethany." He waved the fork like he was conducting an orchestra. "TJ isn't interested in anything but birds, so maybe you should start eating like one, and he'll notice you too."

What was worse than his words was the smile. Doug grinned almost sweetly. "I'm only trying to help, Bethany."

Jackie smacked him playfully. "They'll help her at camp."

"Your mom spent too much money for that, and it's not like she even wants to go." Doug loved cataloguing how people spent their money, because he never had any of his own. "Take my mom. She went on that new diet. The forgiveness one. Downloaded the e-book for ten dollars."

"Really?" Jackie interrupted. "Did it work?"

"No," I said. They'd forgotten I was there again.

"As a matter of fact," Doug said, raising his voice. "She forgave my dad for ..."

Spawning you?

"... losing his job and for Internet porn, and she forgave the cat for rubbing his butt on the carpet, and she was telling me how she didn't feel hungry lately. Like she could walk by Wawa and be like, meh. It only took a day."

There were times I hated Doug with a fury so thick it practically suffocated me. Now was one of them.

"Did she forgive you for being a worthless pothead? A tagalong loser that wasn't even supposed to be in this car?" I grumbled.

"What did you say?"

"Nothing." I muttered. "I was only talking to myself."

"Just remember, you wouldn't even be in this car if you weren't so fat. Start with that fact, little girl."

Then he pitched back my lemonade in this way that resembled some version of friendly, like I could easily catch it, which, of course, I couldn't. It crashed to the carpeted floor of the minivan, spilling ice everywhere.

"Doug," Jackie whined. "Stop!"

The windows and the seatbelt, already coated with little orange noodles, were now completely soaked. So was the front of my shirt. And my flip-flops. They would be sticky *forever*! Fries limped along the seat and floor. I wiped my face and looked at Doug, who had been dating my sister on and off for two years.

"I thought you'd catch that," he said.

He faced forward, baseball cap low on his forehead. His light brown hair peered out from under it, all full and curly.

Just then, I wanted to burn those little hairs. Watch his corkscrew curls jump in alarm. Smell the fine ends singe. Crackle. If only there were a blunt object in the backseat, a lead pipe or even a chunky shoe, I was sure I could bring myself to clunk him over the head. But before I could wrap my hands around his neck,

Jackie slammed on the brakes.

"Perfect," she said.

In front of us were orange barrels, giant dump trucks, and cranes. The van wriggled into a construction zone and stopped between a knot of cars. Jackie turned off the engine and flung off her shoes. "This will be awhile," she said.

Doug rolled down his window, and the smell of boiling tar swept in the car. He pivoted the side mirror in order to better see his reflection. His words echoed in my mind: *If you weren't so fat, you wouldn't be here. If you weren't so fat, you wouldn't be here.* Well, I'd show him! I concentrated on the reversing ding of trucks and the cacophony of jackhammers as I picked the macaroni from my hair. What I needed was an assassin. A hit man. Construction men gathered around a steaming pile of tar. I eyed each one, trying to determine which one might be up for knocking off Doug. One knelt down below a billboard. He shaded his eyes with his palm and seemed to look right at me. Maybe him.

Above his head, slanted on the side of the rocky mountain, was an electronic billboard. Letters comprised of orange dots urged drivers to PLEASE FORGIVE OUR MESS over and over again. That message PLEASE FORGIVE OUR MESS scrolled continuously above his orange hard hat like a marquis—as soon as the S disappeared, the P flashed across. PLEASE FORGIVE OUR MESS. I looked to Doug, who now checked his phone for alternate routes. Doug: so in love with my sister that he'd forgotten she deserved much better.

Suddenly the minivan felt hot, crowded. Its doors seemed to contract, squeezing me tighter and tighter, pulling me closer and closer to Utopia. The sun beat down with no mercy. Macaroni curled all over the seat. Pink lemonade baked into the carpet. My eyes took in the construction zone, the wavy heat lines twisting above the asphalt.

This bus was hellbent on fat camp, there was no stopping it. However, one couldn't go to weight loss camp without weight to lose, right? Just like TJ'd said, I had a lot of people to forgive. I had a lot of weight to lose. The Forgiveness Diet made sense in a cosmic collision of desperation and marketing kind of way. It had to have worked for someone. Why not me?

Who knew, right? Maybe The Forgiveness Diet was based

on scientific fact. For every one person you forgave, you lost three pounds. Or thereabouts. Doug had to be worth ten pounds alone. Of course afterward, I'd have to maintain the loss, but forgiveness enhanced the results the way certain spices enhanced flavors. Maybe it sped up the whole process. Given my sitch, rapid was key. I eyed the chicken bucket on the floor. It looked delicious. I would try this Forgiveness Diet. Let's see how tasty Colonel Carolina looked afterward.

I didn't have any glass fish bowls like they had in the commercial, so I emptied out the Colonel Carolina bucket by eating the chicken in it. The infomercial blipped in my brain. What were the instructions again? There had been that surfer, his slicked hair glistening in the sun.

All I had to do was write down the names of the people I needed to forgive and what they needed to be forgiven for, and the weight would just vanish.

Did this mean I had to forgive Doug for being a model douche?

So be it. I grabbed a yellow napkin from the bag. I fished out a Zyprexa pen from the seat pocket. I wrote: I forgive Doug for bringing Jackie down.

True that. For the past two years she'd been saying, "I'm going to dump him," but it never happened. Now she didn't even bother saying it anymore. I crumpled up the napkin and flicked it in the bucket. *That wasn't so bad*, I thought. *I can do this.*

I wrote down the people who had pissed me off. I scribbled every offense, every misgiving, and mean thing. Out it bubbled—everyone's trespasses. Everyone's screw-ups. *I forgive my mom for being embarrassed by me.* Bam. *I forgive Terrel Bailey, Wendy Schmidt, Allison Continelli, Jeremy Connoll, Merry Rodesky, Piper Fleish, and every other loser at Magnet who calls me Beth Aint Thin Ny.* Done. *I forgive Victoria's Secret for their too small bras. I forgive food for tasting so good.* I wrote down my father's oversight in Chuck E. Cheese's. TJ's blunder. Even the secret Jackie made me swear on a Hebrew Bible I wouldn't tell. You bet I wrote it down. It took a long time too, writing everything. Maybe an hour. Maybe more. Long enough that I had to shake my cramping hand a few times. *Just look at them all*, I thought, after I was done piling the napkins around me. *No wonder I'm so fat.* And then I did what the commercial said. What TJ had said. I forgave them. Everyone.

"I forgive you," I said, kissing the napkin scraps tenderly before dropping them in the Carolina Chicken bucket. Then, just to be safe, I forgave them again.

With the construction zone behind us, Jackie steered the minivan past billboards advertising Lap Band surgery and Burger King. Her tanned legs flexed on the gas pedal. Truckers leaned on their horns when they glimpsed her graceful profile and clear skin. Such a beautiful girl, my sister. Everyone said so. I could see it—especially now that I'd forgiven her.

Did I think The Forgiveness Diet would really work? Well, after I'd finished, I didn't feel so hungry anymore. That was good. Then I thought about TJ. Sometimes he would rig things around the house and out of nowhere an umbrella would blossom or the stereo would serenade me or I'd find a token in the hood of my sweatshirt. My eyes would get all wide, and he'd laugh and start to tell me how he did it when I'd put my finger to his lips. "Don't."

When you've been head over heels for a magician for as long as I have, you learn pretty quickly that anything's possible—even some crazy diet.

Like last year, when TJ's doves were stolen from their cage, he came over to my house totally panicked. We all staged a funeral for the birds because we didn't think they'd last one minute in Baltimore city. TJ wouldn't give up. After countless flyers and Internet postings, I said, "Let's face facts. If given the choice between a cage and the sky, which would you choose?" We were eating ramen noodles in my kitchen. TJ lifted his bowl and drank the broth. "I'd choose here," he stated matter-of-factly. "I'd definitely come back."

"Why?"

"For you," he said, slurping his soup. "I'd come back because you're here."

And when he said things like that, random things tossed out to the universe while he glugged ramen noodles or shuffled his cards or drove the humps of Dulaney Valley Road so fast our butts lifted from the seats, I believed him. I mean, how could I not?

Two weeks after the dove robbery, when TJ's determination

showed signs of wavering, we saw them. His two doves, a little ruffled and greasy, were perched on top of the streetlight. When he opened the cage door, they flew right in like we'd invited them. "Now that's magic," TJ said, gloating. "For real."

That's what I was thinking about after I'd forgiven everybody and returned the bucket to the sticky floor. TJ's life philosophy: It didn't matter how magical shit happened. It only mattered that it did.

8

BLACK EYE IN THE BUCKEYE

I FELL ASLEEP just as our van headed into the cool, inky darkness of a tunnel outside of Pittsburgh.

I woke up in Ohio.

"Is there any chicken left?" Jackie asked. She was still driving and had reached her right hand behind her to tap my knee. "Bethany, hand me the chicken bucket. I'm hungry"

Half-asleep, still dreaming about TJ's doves balanced on the streetlight, I felt around on the minivan's floor, and gripped the bucket. Eyes still closed, it was out of my hands and into hers.

"What's in here?" Jackie asked, all innocent.

I sat up straight. "Wait," I said. "No!"

"Where'd the chicken go?" my sister asked. "Did you eat all of it?" Alternating between looking at the highway and trying to gauge what was in the bucket, the van swerved a little. "Are there papers in here? What did you do?"

Situated in that trippy territory between wakefulness and sleep, I watched it all happen. First Jackie's hand plunged in the bucket and withdrew a ball of napkin now separated from the others. "Now what's this?" she asked. Calling on driving skills I never knew she even had, she steadied the wheel with her wrist and, using her fingers, straightened the napkin. From the backseat, I watched every ounce of color drain from her face. She swallowed.

"What?" asked Doug. "What does it say?"

Jackie inhaled. Exhaled. She concentrated on the high-way ahead. "Nothing. It was nothing. Bethany and her stupid games." She crinkled the paper again and squeezed it. Squeezed hard enough her knuckles turned white.

Doug reached for the bucket on Jackie's lap, and Jackie's hand snatched his wrist. "No way," she said. "You don't want to read it."

Not the best thing to say because now Doug had to read it. Read them all. He ripped the bucket from her lap and Jackie screamed. And then I screamed. Then Jackie angled across four lanes of traffic and squealed the Odyssey onto the shoulder. Then the van rocked when she flung it into park and the door ding ding dinged because she didn't even bother to close it when she flew out her seat and began chasing Doug around the car. Doug laughed. Yes, laughed. He thought it was funny, a game. Until he grabbed a different napkin from my spilled-all-over-the-highway forgiveness bucket and unfolded it, gently, like something delicious steamed inside.

Later, after they had read everything, ev-er-ry thing, af-ter Doug had unfolded most of the napkins, and formed the words with his mouth, I couldn't help wondering if TJ's boss and Doug's mom and everyone else who'd tried The Forgiveness Diet had this kind of experience. They say losing weight is hard, but good God. *This hard?* When Doug's voice cracked not on the word "baby," but "mine," I thought the price for being thin, well, it was sky-high. When Jackie finally climbed back into the van, defeated, tears streaking down her cheeks, she flung her head on the steering wheel. The horn blared. Then she looked in the rearview mirror—where she saw me.

Of course she crawled over the seats in one deft maneuver and beat the holy mother effing Jesus out of me. Did I retaliate when she smacked my face with the heel of her hand? Nope. Did I fight back when she whacked me with her industrial-sized straw purse? No. Did I even yelp when she twisted my hair around her fingers so hard I heard the roots give?

Not at all.

Why?

Well, I'd forgiven her.

I felt lighter when Jackie liberated that knot of hair. *After all this*, I thought, wiping the tears that poured from my stinging, tender eye, Doug in the front seat weeping like the baby he never knew, *this forgiveness crap just might work.*

9

EXIT RIGHT

THE NEXT WORDS Jackie said to me were at California University of the Pacific. "Just think. By the time I pick you up, you'll be beautiful." She hadn't spoken to me since Ohio, the state where she threw my forgiveness chicken bucket out the window, climbed in the backseat, and nearly killed me. She did ask if I had to pee once in Kansas, but that didn't really count. It wasn't a sentence in the traditional sense. Doug had been just as mute. When he flushed the toilet (twice) while I showered in a Colorado motel, he didn't apologize. When Jackie accident-ly-on-purpose stepped on my face inside our tent in Reno, she smiled but didn't laugh.

Now that we'd arrived at C.U.P., my sister's words were dumb anyway. Even if I were thin I wouldn't be beautiful. She knew it. I knew it, but I'd kept quiet anyway. I was just glad she was finally talking to me after what was, without a doubt, the singular worst road trip in the history of all humankind. Ever.

She lifted my duffle bag from the trunk and placed it by my feet. Doug, who still refused to speak to me, waited in the car. Jackie didn't turn the engine off; she just let the van idle in front of a dormitory building and said, "Here we are," like I was twelve, and she was dropping me off at the mall.

A lumpy fog wrapped itself around all the trees and hovered over the stiff grass.

"Wow," Jackie said, eyeing a scene so spooky it looked like one of those haunted log rides. "This place just oozes intelligence."

Jackie wouldn't know oozing intelligence if she slid in it, but now was not the time to point that out. I'd caused more than enough trouble already.

Instead I turned to face the immaculate, sprawling campus that housed, according to their website, the best weight loss camp in America. Looking around, I felt every last one of the two thousand eight hundred and forty-four miles I'd just traveled. The air was cool and damp—nothing like Maryland air. Even the trees looked different here. The classroom buildings were mission-style, old, and very impressive, if you were into that kind of thing, which I wasn't. The campus was quiet and a thick fog rolled around like a special effect. MontClaire Hall rose in front of me, a white building about three stories high. There were four long rows of windows, many of which were open, so that old curtains sailed out. Directly behind me a fountain gurgled. It was a busty mermaid with a stream of water curving from her tail and pooling along the blue-tiled bottom.

"Have fun," Jackie said through her clenched teeth.

"A blast," I offered and tried to smile.

When she patted me on the head and said, "Just call me if it's unbearable," I had the sudden urge to bite her hand. Her eyes narrowed. "But I know you'll love it here. Right?"

Right.

This chilly morning my sister wore a white-pocket T-shirt and khaki shorts, both of which she'd pressed on the travel ironing board she'd brought along for that purpose. Goosebumps trailed her arms and legs. Obviously she was prepared for the California with peach flamingos and year-round surfing, not this foggy and cold imposter.

"It'll get better," she said, looking down at her clogs. I didn't know if she meant fat camp would improve or life generally. Perhaps she was suggesting she would get better. Either way, I knew now would be the moment for apologizing.

"About that stuff I wrote," I started, but Jackie held her hand up.

"You were right about some of it," she said. "About Mom,

for one." She lowered her voice. "And Doug." She looked back at the minivan, where Doug sat, then returned her eyes to me. "He does bring me down."

I smiled too soon, mistaking this attempt at conversation as forgiveness. "But it's not your job to point that out."

I should have continued with *I hadn't meant for you to see those papers. The commercial insisted I write down everyone's secrets and forgive them. I'm sorry for spilling yours, Jackie.* Though the words were balanced on the tip of my tongue, my mouth would not open. Something coiled around our feet as insistently as that fog. Something that I might call hatred, but won't. Whatever it was had changed things between us. I never felt further from my sister than I did at that moment standing on the threshold of fat camp.

"See you in eight weeks," she said.

I watched her drive off into a vaporous cloud. Neither of them waved goodbye. Hell, neither of them turned around. Before she peeled out of the university's gate, Jackie tapped the horn twice, which instigated an eerie echo that to my ears said, WEEP! WEEP!

10

WHAT BLOWS IN UTOPIA

I SAT OUTSIDE and listened to the mermaid fountain drip water behind me and watched a family of ducks fluff up their feathers. Beyond the quad, golden-yellow hills humped like mounds of Country Crock. Paths wound around everything, neat and orderly. A few geniuses walked on them, heads down, backpacks clunky with books, sandaled feet aimed forward. Even the quivering birds in the trees seemed to sing out ACT scores. *Well, well, well,* I thought. *So this is college.*

Sitting on the edge of that fountain, the curled edges of fog starting to burn, I sipped the mocha with extra whipped cream I'd just purchased from a coffee shack. I must've looked like a freshman because the first person to speak to me needed directions.

"Excuse me, but I'm looking for Utopia," a guy screamed over his truck's engine that rattled like emphysema. "Ever heard of it? Utopia?" His rusted-out hoopty had the inconspicuous conspicuousness of a vehicle smuggling drugs, fruit, or immigrants into the country. It was not the kind of transportation I'd envisioned for the students at California University. "We're lost," continued the driver. He pointed his thumb at the girl sitting next to him. "My sister forgot the directions."

Was it that obvious I was en route to fat camp?

Aiming my drink toward the signs sprouting from the manicured grass that read, *Utopia this way* ⟩⟩⟩, I stated the obvious. "I think it's right over there. You know, where the signs are pointing."

That was when the passenger, a kid by the looks of her, smacked her forehead. "I told you this was it, *estúpido*. You never listen to me." Then she climbed straight out of the truck's window, turning around only to yell, "*Hasta, 'mano*," before tearing off through the grass.

The truck fell silent, and I wondered if he'd turned off the engine or if it had simply died.

"Sisters," said the driver. "*Jodiendos*."

Let's hope that word summed up sisterhood accurately, because I nodded, indicating I had sibling problems of my own. The driver scratched his head, and a few long strands of hair slid down to cover his eyes. He moved the bangs away and looked at me for a beat. Maybe he was embarrassed to pull away—afraid when he tried, the truck wouldn't start? He cocked an elbow out of the window. "So," he began, "you wouldn't happen to know where Copernicus is, would you?"

I sipped my espresso. "I'm pretty sure he died a few centuries ago."

The dude grinned crookedly. He looked younger than a college student, maybe around my age. He had dark hair and dark eyes, and his words kind of jumbled together when he spoke. "Good point," he mused. "I guess I'll just ask somebody else. It's a big campus. Someone'll know." Of course three people walked by, and he didn't ask any of them. He just sat there. Something told me he felt as out of place as me. Maybe he was letting his truck warm up or whatever it required before moving. In the meantime, I checked my phone.

Hey Bee. Guess what? I can levitate a full three inches off the ground! ISYN. So, are you in Cali? Is it beautiful??

I wondered how to answer TJ honestly when the truck parked in front of me distorted my view. Mr. Busted-Truck fiddled with a stereo button and loud angry-boy music swelled in the quiet morning. "One more thing," he said to me over the stereo. "Before you go to class or whatever, I thought I should mention something. Well." He shifted some unidentifiable truck part. "You'd look a whole lot better if—"

Oh Lord. Not this. Not now.

"Not that you look bad. It's just that."

If this guy said what I thought he was about to say, I would absolutely die. Just frickin' kill me.

"Well," I heard the squeak of a clutch. "It's just that you have. You have trash in your hair. I thought I should let you know."

Then he took off. Finally.

So much for college encounters. The boys here seemed just as eager to point out a flaw as high schoolers. Oh well, at least he wasn't on the verge of recommending a diet. Absorbed in the toxic black cloud the truck imparted, I felt around in my hair because, well, I had to check now. Sure enough, up around my forehead, I felt something sticky. I wondered why, for the last hundred miles or so, no one had bothered to tell me something was stuck in my hair. My trip replayed in my mind, only now every scene featured a giant chunk of gum in my hair, and Jackie and Doug pretending not to see it.

I finally separated the tangle and saw it was a faded yellow piece of paper, dirtied with tar. When I smoothed it out, I reunited with the Colonel Carolina Chicken napkin I could've sworn tumbled down the highway in Ohio.

I forgive my sister for killing Doug's baby.

Just arrived, I texted to TJ. *In paradise.*

11

FLIP-FLOPS

WOULDN'T IT BE great if college life continued to speed right by me while I stayed frozen in time on the curb? Here I'd wait, with my mocha, for the next eight weeks until my sister fetched me. Oddly enough, though, now that I'd landed outside the place everyone thought I should be, I figured I might as well see what the fuss was about.

I followed the signs pointing me toward Utopia. Bypassing bleary-eyed intellectuals with sweatshirt hoods around their faces, I squished through some grass—not a dandelion in sight— and leaned into the open back window of MontClaire Hall.

Inside a tall redhead stared directly at me. She enthusiastically waved me into the dormitory's common room with hardwood floors, a fireplace, one prehistoric television, and three Odwalla juice vending machines.

"Hi there!" she said in a raspy voice. I dragged my duffle bag behind me like a corpse. "You looked a bit lost staring in the window like that. I was pretty sure this was where you belonged."

I didn't realize she was insulting me until I was already inside and plopped down in a circle full of Utopians.

Twenty-five girls gathered in the common room of Mont-Claire Hall. Most of them sat on top of their luggage, checked their phones, or looked absorbed in the reading material the loud-mouthed redhead had distributed. I recognized one girl from the noisy truck outside; she now sat on the floor picking at her black nail polish. The other girls looked like girls everywhere: big sunglasses, flip-flops, tan lines on their shoulders. Truth be told, I'd expected them to be fatter. Oh well, I reasoned, maybe they were *returning* campers.

Finally the redhead bellowed, "We're waiting for one more." She licked her finger and leafed through papers on her clipboard, "In the meantime, let me introduce myself." She smiled with all her teeth. "I'm Miss Marcia, and I'll be your counselor."

Something about Miss Marcia reminded me of Timothy Tinsel, host of *American Envy*. Maybe it was her unchecked enthusiasm as she rattled on about her fat camp experience nine years ago in Pennsylvania. Maybe it was her easy smile. It was probably because when she turned around to retrieve a folder she'd dropped, I observed a gigantic marijuana leaf tattoo on her back.

"*¡Dios!*" said the girl from the truck, who must've seen it too.

Miss Marcia pulled her shirt a little lower and continued. "I'm also a lifeguard," she said.

I supposed that meant we'd be required to swim here.

"As soon as the last camper arrives, I'll divide you into teams," she went on. "Five groups of five ..." Before our counselor could finish, MontClaire Hall's door swung open and there, framed in the doorway, stood a tall African-American girl with a long, expensive-looking weave. Miss Marcia consulted her clipboard. "You must be the girl from Boston," she said, making a checkmark on a folder.

"Cambridge," the newcomer's velvety voice returned. "And SFO had a fog delay." Next she removed a silver stylus from behind her ear and tapped at her cell phone. "So sorry to keep you waiting. I'm almost always punctual." Then she sat down next to me and hugged her legs to her chest. "Hi," she whispered.

Miss Marcia peered around the circle of girls. "Well, now that you're all here, let me welcome you to Utopia."

12

DIGITS

THE NEXT FORTY-FIVE minutes seemed to last eight days. We learned about Utopia's expectations, rules, commitments, schedule, blah-blah-blah. After that we endured yet another speech about the organizational flowchart of Camp Utopia. There were the owners of the camp, Belinda and Hank, who we'd meet later. Miss Marcia was the next in charge. She counseled all twenty-five girls and some guy, Courtney, managed the boys. We were divided into teams and my team consisted of Atlanta, Santa Fe, Cambridge, and Hollywood. Miss Marcia tapped each of us on the head like it was game of Duck Duck Goose. "And you." Tap. "You must be Baltimore. We call you by your city and not by your weight." She said this like I should be grateful. "First things first," said our counselor waving a hand toward the scale, "I'll need your digits."

Well, they certainly didn't waste any time.

I swallowed the coffee taste pillowing in the back of my throat as Miss Marcia stood on the scale, which was now positioned in the center of our circle. It was a fancy piece of electronic equipment, and Miss Marcia threw around words like "state-of-the-art," "cutting-edge balancing technology," and "calculates to the tenth of an ounce." I wasn't listening all that closely. Instead I studied the machine's rather large LED display that, as soon as Miss Marcia stood on it, illuminated a slim number in satanic red.

"OK," said Miss Marcia. "It's accurate alright."

The girl from the truck raised her hand. "You mean everyone sees our weight?"

Miss Marcia nodded her head. "Yes," she said and stepped off the scale. "The owners like to instill a little bit of competition among teams."

The girl crossed her arms. "No way, *verdad*. No thank you. My own brother doesn't know my weight. Don't you have a curtain or something?"

Miss Marcia sighed. "It's a necessary part of Utopia," she said almost apologetically. "It's why we're all here."

The young girl rolled her eyes.

Miss Marcia continued. "It's just a number," she looked at a file. "Santa Fe. It doesn't mean anything. Come on up."

"In front of strangers?"

"These aren't strangers," said Miss Marcia. "These are your team members."

"Yes," said a voice I hadn't heard yet. It belonged to a thin girl. A pretty one. "We're on your side."

Then the girl with the black nail polish and bad mouth sighed and crossed her arms. Finally she stood up, walked to the scale, and got weighed. Three more girls followed, including the beautiful one. Then I heard one word.

"Baltimore."

"Baltimore?"

Who was this Baltimore chick, and why was she taking so long? Oh wait. Right.

Here's what I thought about in the eleven steps it took to get to the scale. First, I thought: *Damn.* Then: *Why did I have that macchiato?* Finally: *Wait. It had been seven full days since I'd tried The Forgiveness Diet. Seven days since Jackie whacked me with her clogs, and Doug took a vow of silence. I thought: Maybe it worked.*

Six steps in, I wasn't looking forward to getting weighed, but I wasn't dreading it either. I was kind of curious. TJ had been so adamant about The Forgiveness Diet and that commercial—so, miraculous. Now would've been the perfect time for good news. If the diet kicked in then I could send Jackie a quick text, have her turn the car around, and pretend like none of this ever happened.

So far, on our team, we had a 168.4, 183.1, 159.9, 190.7, 146.2. Now in front of the scale, I slid out of my flip-flops and prayed. *Universe*, I thought, *let the diet have worked. Feature me on the next infomercial.* I was practically rehearsing my lines: *I was on my way to fat camp when BAM I was … Thin. Thin. Thin.*

I stepped up and sucked in my stomach. Red numbers appeared on the scale's neck, blinked twice, and steadied. It was a large red number and, unfortunately, it was the one that had greeted me before I left.

I weighed exactly the same.

Miss Marcia called out my weight a little too loudly for my taste, then scribbled in a file. "You can step down now, Baltimore," she said. Yet there I stood, still glaring at that red-hot number. "Go ahead and step off, Baltimore."

Finally I de-scaled. I sunk one foot and then the other back inside my flip- flops. My eyes fell on each one of my teammates sprawled near my feet: Cambridge, the girl's whose flight was delayed; Santa Fe, who rocketed out of her brother's truck earlier; some chick named Atlanta who sported a giant Bumpit in her hair; and one called Hollywood, who wasn't quite as thin or beautiful as Jackie, but was damn close. Looking at them I realized the unthinkable had happened. I was the heaviest girl at Utopia. The fattest person there. The fattest person at fat camp.

Brilliant.

The girls didn't ohh and ahh or anything when I stepped off the scale, but there was a tension so palpable you could have stepped in it. Hollywood with her chunky light-brown curls and triangular purse whispered to Atlanta next to her. They both laughed. Something told me it was my still illuminated number on the scale they were giggling about.

Miss Marcia weighed the rest of the girls of which (surprise!) I still remained the fattest. Then she stacked our hospital-blue files and climbed on top of a metal desk. She secured her hair with a pencil.

"Let me tell you a bit more about what we do here," she said.

Just then a black bird slammed into the window behind her. A few of us startled as its limp body slid down with a suctiony squeak. Miss Marcia prattled on unawares about this being the BEST WEIGHT LOSS SYSTEM IN AMERICA. CONSIDER YOURSELVES LUCKY, she screamed. This will be THE SUMMER OF YOUR LIVES.

13

THELL PHONE

AFTER MISS MARCIA'S lengthy speech about the best place on Earth, aka Utopia, it was time for our Motivation Orientation, which was scheduled, just like everything else would be. Now the male campers shuffled in, all five—count 'em, *five*. They wore baseball hats and T-shirts that pulled tight across their bellies. Watching them file past, I ached for TJ. If only he were here as opposed to the chubby boys slouching toward us. Not a magician in the bunch, that much was clear. One guy looked my age, but the rest couldn't have been beyond the eighth grade. The boys settled on a scratchy sofa, then two old people glided to the front of the room and introduced themselves as *the owners*. They laid slender hands on Miss Marcia's shoulders and began their speech about *how much better life is when you're thin*.

"My husband and I were campers at Utopia thirty-five years ago. It's hard to believe we were catastrophically overweight once, but we were. We bought Utopia fifteen years ago and moved it here, to California University of the Pacific." They looked around, full of pride. "That first long-ago summer at weight loss camp changed our lives. Not only did we meet and later get married, we decided to help others."

The woman looked at us like there was an applause sign above her head. "Given the prevalence of childhood obesity, we felt it our calling."

The boys tapped their feet while a few kids clapped. The owner woman, Belinda, wore a lime green shirt and a white jean skirt. Her jewelry looked like it was recently excavated from an ancient archeology site. She had short, spiked white hair. Her husband, Hank, wore a jogging suit in navy blue and white. Something shiny hung from his neck. Something that looked a lot like a whistle. When he spoke, he lisped, which was distracting.

"This is the Cadillac of weight loth programs," he started. "You *will* lose weight here." *Is he staring at me?* "Many of you are a long way from home, but science has proven that young people, when lifted from their environments, often thoar. We're here to help you thoar. We will do whatever it takes to make your journey a thutheth." He pulled out something from his back pocket. "Including confithating your thell phone." Thirty groans bubbled up. "It's polithy," he said. "No dithractions."

He grinned hugely and peeled a black lawn bag from a roll.

"Commitment," he urged, snapping the trash bag out like a Fruit Roll-Up.

My fellow team member, dainty Hollywood, gathered phones and other tech from her purse. "All of them?" she asked.

"All of them," Hank advised. "You have acceth to the computer labs, and we've provided each of you with an e-mail addreth. You can check e-mail onth a day and, of courth," Hank laughed, "you can write letters." He crossed his arms. "Anyone ever heard of a letter?"

Hank was the kind of guy who believed kids should smile even as their tongues were being ripped out. That much was evident with his No Thellphone Polithy. I couldn't imagine anyone in my generation agreeing to it. Mind telling me why, then, all these Utopians powered down their phones beside me so, so willingly? Even pretty Hollywood dug out gear from her designer luggage happily, inquiring about rollover minutes and voice mails.

Not I.

Phonelessness just wasn't an option. How exactly would I text TJ? Or e-mail him? Or send him pictures? Or perform any of the ten thousand other tasks I did in a day that required my phone?

Good thing Hollywood had a cell phone tower up her ass because gathering all her electronic equipment afforded me time to formulate a plan. I shoved my phone deeper inside my pocket just as everyone else emptied theirs. Had the others known about this? Did my mom cleverly omit this factoid in her Utopia pitch?

What I needed was a hole. If I could tear a hole, say, in my shorts with my fingernail I could secure my phone inside my underwear. When Hank and Belinda got to me, I'd just say I didn't have a cell phone because I was part Amish. I knew Belinda and Hank would cop to a bag search, but I was sure they'd draw the line at a strip search. My phone would be safe in my underwear. No question.

I worked my fingernail into the crumb-lined pocket of my shorts. As soon as Hollywood had dumped at least four phones into the garbage bag, Hank shook it, and three other girls deposited theirs. Then, from behind me, I heard that smoky rich voice.

"Who knew these had calories in them," it said. Cambridge, who weighed 190.7, strutted up to the owners as if she were made of feathers. When Hank widened the lips of the garbage bag, she paused. "It's just that ..."

Hank shook the bag. "What?" he asked. "It'th juth what?"

"Oh, never mind," she said and powered down her phone.

"We are not doing this to harm you," said Belinda. "We'll keep your phones safe."

Cambridge shook her head. "It's not that. It's just that if I didn't know any better, I would venture that this is a violation of our civil liberties." She held her phone between her thumb and index finger, but did not drop it inside the bag. "I mean, even prisoners have the right to make one phone call, yes?" She began walking away, still clutching her silver phone. Hank followed her, the nylon of his jogging suit sveet-sveeting. "Prisoners aren't minors, for one. And your parents signed away your rights on the enrollment form," he said to her back. "Thorry."

"I'm almost eighteen, sir," Cambridge enlightened Hank.

"But not yet, Ms. Nelson."

Cambridge shook her head. "Not quite yet." She looked at her phone like it was meaningless. Then she tossed it over her shoulder, and all together we watched its graceful curve until thunk—perfect shot—it landed in the trash bag.

By this point everyone's phone was in the bag.

Except mine. Mine was nearly through the hole I'd dug in my pocket. *Just a little bit more. A bit more.*

Just as I had almost pushed my phone through the ripped material of my pocket, edging it close to my underwear's elastic band, I heard a song bubble up. It was faint and muffled, but insistent. In no time all the girls were humming the theme from *American Envy*. Everyone turned toward the garbage bag rattling in Hank's hands. Only I knew better. The song was not coming from the bag. It was emanating from my underwear. Miss Marcia tilted her head. "Baltimore, you're ringing," she said. "Hand it over."

"I have a medical condition," I returned. "I need my phone for emergencies."

"Policy," Belinda snapped.

"My boyfriend needs to be able to reach me."

"And he can," said Hank. "By e-mail." He shook the garbage bag. "Phone, mith."

Miss Marcia looked at the files like she wanted to make a red mark on mine. "This is a test of your commitment," she said.

I removed the phone from my pocket. Then Belinda pried it from my hand.

"She's busy," she screamed into it before powering it down.

I had no idea who was calling. In my mind it was Jackie phoning to tell me she'd forgiven me for monumentally screwing up her life. "I'm on my way back now," she was about to say. "How about a caramel macchiato?" Perhaps it was Doug calling from the side of the road, stranded. "I am a douche." Then again it could've been my mom, "You're right, Bethany. No one's perfect. Let's get some Chinese food and fully-caloric soda." And of course it could have been TJ. "I love you, Bee. Come home."

The caller was never revealed, though, because Hank carried our phones off like dirty laundry.

"You have to respect the program," Belinda iterated.

"Commitment," Hank said for the hundredth time before knotting the bag and dropping it on the floor.

Miss Marcia referred to her clipboard and Hank nodded. "Of course there's more to life than losing weight," Miss Marcia hollered. She glided on those long legs of hers up to the front of the room. She pulled a tape measure from her back pocket. "There's inches too."

The owners assembled the campers in a line. They continued on their harangue about the healthy, thin person who lived buried beneath our fat. How that person was suffocating, and Hank brought his hands up to his neck in a strangulation gesture. "Trust me," he gasped. "You will never want French fries again once you taste how good being thin feels." He gave a thumbs-up. "It's tight."

Jesus. They must have had a book: *Motivating Teens for Dummies*. Some kind of manual that gave pointers for blowing sunshine up the American teenage behind. I refused to believe that these not-even-all-that-fat people were buying into this until I looked around and realized that indeed, they were. In fact, when Hank and Belinda left, the campers cheered. Clapped. Sang. Wooted. They stomped like they were downright ecstatic to be rid of their cell phones and text messages.

As I watched these Utopians, I had that feeling I always got during spirit week when everyone was forced to be upbeat and the teachers dressed up as homeless people and the cheerleaders donned bullwhips and lacy bustiers. It was the feeling I had during pep rallies and football games. The feeling I got walking down the narrow aisles of the school cafeteria waiting for TJ to catch my eye, and pat the space-he-never-saved next to him. The awareness that somehow I was still outside the window, hands cupped over my face, looking in.

The uncomfortable truth slipped in once again that I didn't fit in anywhere. Even at fat camp. I knew watching the other campers lean toward one another, excitement boiling out of their exfoliated pores, Miss Marcia wrapping a tape measure around middles and bust lines, that I had been right all along. I would hate it here.

From: Bethany Stern <bethanys@utopia.com>
To: ellenstern@zyprexapharm.com
Subject: RE: ARE YOU THERE YET?

Dear Mom,

Of course I got your e-mail, so please stop sending the same one 500 times. I'm here. I'm here. I'm here. Golly gee, it's frickin fantastic. Just as u promised. Thanks for spending all that money to get me out of the house. It's worth every penny. I'm already a shadow of my former self!

I hope you earn that big bonus this summer without me and Jackie around to mess things up. Maybe you can spend quality time w/ur boyfriend too w/out having to explain why you can't keep butterscotch krimpets in the house or why jackie's boyfriend hides in the closet (oops).

Don't worry about me, mom. I'll be fine. There are public weigh-ins here and everything. AND when they wrapped the tape measure around my stomach some kind fellow in the audience actually mooed. What a peach! Pls sign me up for next yr. Better hurry.

PS Jackie h8s me now too.

PPS u both need zyprexa.

PPPS If u see TJ tell him I love him

Urs,

~bee

14

CELLMATES

AFTER THE COMPUTER lab, Miss Marcia led us to a cinderblock stairwell where study-abroad opportunities were posted for Greece and Thailand. Phone numbers were listed on tear-away sheets. French Lessons. Yoga. Discounted Textbooks. I was about to tear one down for NEW YORK STYLE PIZZA: FREE DELIVERY when Miss Marcia warned, "Before you go to your rooms, I want you all to know that we've never had a problem with fighting. It just doesn't happen here at Utopia." Why she directed this at me, I had no idea. But that's what she said. She said this was a place where girls stayed up all night and talked about how beautiful they were going to be. Never mind that I hadn't stayed up all night discussing whose figure I wanted since third grade while snugly zipped in my Barbie sleeping bag. She had to be kidding, right?

Wrong.

The boys were shipped off to another dormitory on another area of campus. The Utopian girls were housed on one complete floor of MontClaire Hall, two or three girls to a room, with adjoining rooms connected by a bathroom. Needless to say, Miss Marcia and her long legs held private accommodations down by the stairwell a bit closer to the younger campers.

My dorm was in the middle of the hall next to a sun-bleached patch of tile where presumably a vending machine once sat. On my door were the words "Baltimore, Cambridge, and Santa Fe" written in puffy bubbly letters and festooned with curly ribbon. The room next to ours housed Hollywood and Atlanta.

I swiped my Utopia card into the slot and a loud click followed. The red light blinked to green, and I pushed the door open like a coffin lid. Keeping with themes, our dorm rooms, like everything else at this *prestigious* academic institution, were fancy, old, and probably haunted. There were hardwood floors, dark-mahogany desks with scholarly green lamps on them, and a wall of built-in bookshelves. The ceilings were high; in the dusty corners cobwebs drooped like lace. On one side sat wooden bunk beds and on the opposite side a single metal bed.

We agreed that since Cambridge was the oldest, she should be permitted to pick her bed first. She gravitated toward the top bunk like it had a magnetic field. In the bathroom, I reveled in the claw-footed tub and complimentary fluffy towels when Santa Fe asked, "I wonder how many geniuses sat their butts on that very toilet?" She stopped. "Lighten up. I'm going to SEE YOU PEE!"

I tried not to laugh, but couldn't help it. Who starts a university with the initials C.U.P. anyway? Lame.

Santa Fe walked back into our room and flopped down on the metal bed next to the window. That left me with the bottom bunk.

We all three busied ourselves in silence. Santa Fe removed an electronic device from her suitcase that beeped a few times. She rapped it on the wooden desk, cursed, and it dinged some more. Cambridge hummed a song on the bunk above me. I dumped my duffle bag out on the bottom bunk and pretended to fold my underwear.

The silence was tense. I'd bet prisoners felt like this when assigned a new cellmate. Reaching into the empty pocket space where my cell phone once lived, I shuddered. Of course if I'd had it, I would text TJ. It felt strange not to be narrating everything to him. I knew he'd be curious about my roommates and, pathetically, I wondered if he'd find any of them pretty. Cambridge especially. She leaned toward preppy, sure, but there was a strength there I'd bet he'd find appealing. Or maybe Santa Fe. She had a foul mouth and didn't look older than twelve, but she was funny. More than likely, though, he'd swoon over the one they called Hollywood. Her waist measured the smallest even though her boobs were by far the biggest, which, back in the common room, it seemed all the boys had noticed. And she'd noticed their noticing.

The phone in our dorm room had been removed as well as the mini-fridge. Everything smelled of mildew and smart people. As my roommates unpacked around me, I frantically searched my mind for something to say. But it was Cambridge who spoke first, her voice jazz itself.

"Anyone hungry?"

"I am," I replied quickly. "I haven't eaten since breakfast."

Her hand reached down from the top bunk and in its grasp was an espresso mocha frappe drink, the kind in glass bottles with three times the caffeine that's recommended. I hesitated. Was this some kind of test?

"Go on and take it," Cambridge said. "My dad sewed them into the lining of my suitcase so they'd get past the bag check." She swung her head down and smiled. "He's an expert at hiding things."

I opened the bottle. Just then Santa Fe asked, "*¿Tienes más?*"

Almost instantaneously, one thunked beside her. "I shouldn't drink this," Santa Fe said, but she did drink it, and thirstily, like she had just crossed a desert. While she drank, I concentrated on her *Hello Kitty* shirt with a bleeding bullet hole centered in the cat's forehead.

"Help yourself, girls," Cambridge offered. "There's plenty more. He stuffed all kinds of things in here. Candy. Granola bars."

"What about you?" Santa Fe asked Cambridge. "Aren't you going to have anything?"

"No thanks," Cambridge replied. "I really shouldn't."

"Me neither," replied Santa Fe, downing the last drop, "considering I'm diabetic."

Bummer. That electronic device was a blood sugar monitor not an iPod. I hoped its beeping wasn't a warning.

"*No te preocupes,*" said Santa Fe. "It's under control." She was lying on the striped, vinyl mattress with her shoes on—hot pink high-tops with black laces. If memory served right, she weighed 180, which wasn't that bad, but she was short, maybe five foot, and she carried her weight in her gut. She had nice legs, skinny ones, and her black hair oozed behind her like an oil slick. "My condition is constantly monitored by my brother," she said matter-of-factly. "So let's keep the candy our little secret, OK?"

Cambridge mimed zipping her lips.

Santa Fe lifted her arms upward in an effort to smell her armpits. "I got the Utopia scholarship this year," she said. "I'm Hispanic and Native, and I've got diabetes to boot. I was their dream come true."

Cambridge tossed her a cellophane bag filled with a pink wig. "Sorry to hear that. That's a lot of boxes to check on an application."

Santa Fe ripped into the bag. "Cotton candy! Thank you!" she sang out. "Anyway, Utopia is fine with me. It beats sweating in New Mexico all summer."

I glugged my drink. "I've always wanted to visit there," I told her. In fact, I'd nearly asked Jackie to drive through New Mexico before our road trip took its most unpleasant turn. Santa Fe laughed and wrapped a tail of cotton candy around her finger. "I don't live in Santa Fe. Counselor Carrot Top couldn't pronounce Albuquerque, or spell it either, so I went with Santa Fe. Sounded exotic."

She launched her espresso drink into a metal trash can then belched a few bars of what I was pretty sure was a Shakira tune. "*Perdón*," she expressed. "Thanks so much for the candy, Cambridge. You sure you don't want to sample your own goods?"

Cambridge sighed. "It seems that since I'm here, I might as well try and lose a few pounds. That's what everyone is expecting anyway."

"True, true" observed Santa Fe. "But you can't start a diet in the middle of the day. Tomorrow is the official first day, *verdad*? What happens in Utopia stays in Utopia."

Cambridge fondled a box of Goobers. "I don't know about that."

Santa Fe continued kneading the cotton candy like dough. "*Entra más profundo*, friends. That's what my brother's always saying. You have to fall in deep inside a situation to understand it—or something like that."

"Your brother seriously followed you to fat camp?" asked Cambridge, confused.

Santa Fe rattled the window's curtain and stared at the campus below. The sun was out now, its light settled on her face and shiny hair. She looked so young. Thirteen maybe. Her navy blue braces glittered when she smiled. "No, he's at genius camp. When I got a scholarship to fat camp, he didn't want me to be alone. He applied to all of CUP's summer programs. You can imagine my surprise when he walked in one day talking about some string theory cha-cha, blah-blah-blah-ing about rocket science math camp, waving his acceptance letter around like some girl's panties. Me and Mom couldn't believe it. He's smart, alright, but a real slacker."

She looped the cotton candy around her neck like a necklace. "By the way, I'm Liliana Delgado," she said. "I almost told you guys not to laugh at the name, which means thin one, but I forgot where I was. Anyway, if I can ever get out of Albuquerque, I want to design clothing for thick tweens one day. I'm a mad seamstress."

When she unzipped a leather carrier, I assumed she was removing the blood sugar monitor again. Only this time she whipped out a deluxe bedazzler. She reached for the curtain and fired a few rounds at the old crusty material. Twenty silver studs materialized. "Check it out."

I admit it was a nice touch.

We all laughed as Cambridge produced candy from her bag as easily as TJ pulled cards from his sleeve. I could get used to this: lazy mornings, bedazzling curtains, clean towels in the bathroom. Cotton candy. What a life. Why, at California University of the Pacific, we'd even have a refrigerator and cell phone. Likewise, if we visited a vending machine during the night, it wouldn't result in a penalty of the fifty push-up variety.

Just as Cambridge dug deeper into her Mary Poppins bag, promising us a box of Milk Duds, I heard the clonk, clonk, clonk of heels in the bathroom. Within seconds, our door swung open revealing Hollywood, who didn't even have the courtesy to knock.

15

HOLLYWOOD

WE HAD BEEN in our rooms for less than twenty minutes and already our suitemate had changed outfits. Hollywood now wore a dark-pink velour sweatsuit with a ruffle on the butt. Tiffany hearts dangled off her wrists and neck like rabies tags.

"I brought this over," the starlet informed us and presented a jar the way Vanna introduced a puzzle. "It's our forgiveness bucket. I thought we could join forces. Forgive everyone we can think of and give our team an advantage."

Her beautiful smile only underscored how idiotic she looked standing in the center of our room with a fishbowl. This was no Carolina Chicken bucket either—the jar looked official, a glittering one like in the commercial. "The Forgiveness Diet says inspiration is important for weight loss."

"I tried that diet," I blurted. "How long before it works?"

Hollywood rolled her eyes. Evidently she was asked this question a lot.

"The entire city of Los Angeles is on that diet. It will work if you work it. I'm already down eighteen pounds."

Eighteen pounds! Where was my eighteen pounds? Maybe I did it wrong. No question this girl followed the directions. I bet Hollywood had even bought the book!

"Have you?" I started. "Um. Like the stuff you put in a jar. The directions said ..." This was ridiculous. I could barely speak a sentence. Oh, forget it. "How long did it take for the diet to kick in, Hollywood?"

Cambridge sat up in bed. Her legs dangled to my left. "Don't tell me you actually think it'll work."

"Well ...," I replied. "No?"

"It totally works," snapped Hollywood. "My father endorsed it."

Cambridge laughed. "My father endorses a lot of bullshit too. That doesn't make it effective."

Hollywood's neck turned pink. Then red. Less than two minutes, and we'd already pissed her off. "How do you know it doesn't work, Cambridge," Hollywood asked. Each word was like a slap to the face. *Have. You. Tried. It?*

"Please," Cambridge returned. "I'm not that dumb."

Liliana, picking at her nail polish nervously, interrupted, "The chick who won *American Envy* last season went on the diet. She lost ten pounds in two weeks. My brother saw her on a commercial. He said she looked like she could use a feeding tube."

Last year's *American Envy* winner was a bit of a sore spot back home because she'd beat out The Levitator.

Hollywood sighed. "She lost twenty-five pounds on The Forgiveness Diet, not ten. And your brother's wrong—she looks great."

IMHO, last year's winner, didn't really need a diet at all. It was Eugene Gold, the meanest judge, who brought much media focus to the singer's butt, which he'd termed *harpoonable*.

"What about you, Santa Fe?" asked Hollywood. "Have you tried the diet?"

Our roommate flicked a layer of nail polish into the radiator vent. "I think I'll try it tomorrow," she said. She lowered her chin and stuck out her tongue in order to sample the cotton candy looped around her neck. "Tomorrow is a much better day for forgiveness."

This not-so-secretive lick did not go unobserved by Hollywood. In fact, Hollywood was now examining Liliana like a menu written in a foreign language. Her petite nose crinkled. "Is that candy around your neck? You brought cotton candy to a weight loss camp?"

Liliana let go a whistle. "Now how did that—"

"But why?" Hollywood asked. "Don't you want to lose weight?" She looked from Liliana to Cambridge, then her eyes settled on me. "Don't you want to lose weight?"

This was a fantastic question that none of us attempted to answer.

"Don't you?"

In the silence that followed, I waited for Hollywood to draw a chalk line between us. Not that she needed to. It was *très* obvious that our team was a tad divided. Just in time to even the score, Atlanta, the girl with the giant Bumpit in her hair, walked in.

"They brought in CANDY?!" Atlanta balked, her hair jolting.

"My brother did it," Liliana confessed. "Gabriel gave me the candy. You can throw it out. No big deal."

Hollywood softened—a little. "Your brother's stupid," she said. "This is an opportunity to be taken very serious."

"Serious*ly*," Cambridge corrected. "Camp officially starts tomorrow anyway. Let's just drop it, OK?"

Hollywood returned her gaze to the forgiveness jar. "I was just trying to help. I want our team to win."

What I gathered from this girl in the whole hour I'd known her was not only did Hollywood like to win, she needed to. Some girls just have a scent about them that makes them naturals for sports or tiaras or homecoming courts. She was one of them. She was pretty with her honey-brown hair, big green eyes, and what seemed a more than adequate bra size, but she was also organized. Her sweatsuit was immaculate, so was her luggage, which she'd neatly piled in a corner during orientation. Even all those phones she had forfeited to Hank's trash bag seemed disinfected with Purell. I hated myself for liking her outfit, for caring about that stuff, but I did. She was definitely the thinnest on our team too, which lent her a certain authority, which she wielded like a professional.

"Take it from me," Hollywood started, "the diet works."

Atlanta made a noise like a drain sucking up bath water. "Oh, come on guys. Do it for the weight loss! I forgave everyone I could possibly think of. It was so easy."

Hollywood crossed her arms. "She was motivated."

Atlanta smiled wide, pleased with the compliment tossed to her like a dog biscuit.

"How about I just leave the jar here for a bit," Hollywood coaxed. She placed it gingerly on our dresser. "In case you get inspired." Then Hollywood's eyes centered on me. First my face. Then my stomach. "Think about it."

Only as soon as Hollywood and her sidekick turned around to leave, a sound bubbled up. It was a pinging, a tinkling noise—like a Disney song. Like a ringtone. Then, very casually, Hollywood withdrew a violet rhinestone cell phone from her pocket.

"Hi," she squeaked, smiling perfect pearls of teeth. "I met the others, yes. They seem OK." She shot us a dirty look. "I guess." She continued blabbing, her purple phone glittering like a crown. After a breathy, "Oh. OK. I love you too," she clipped it shut.

"Where did you hide your phone?" Liliana asked in a voice that she tried to keep measured.

"Oh. I'm allowed. We worked out a deal."

"What kind of deal?" Cambridge asked.

I was too stunned to speak. Hadn't she thrown all her phones into the garbage bag downstairs like everyone else?

"It was my dad. He knows people. A lot of people," she said, and smiled. "He knows I can't live without my phone. What a stupid rule."

If I didn't hate her before, I sure did now. Judging by the looks on my roommates' faces, they did too. It wasn't because she was beautiful either. It wasn't because she was the thinnest. It was because Hollywood got to keep her cell phone.

Miss Rules-Don't-Apply-To-Me winked then—one shadowed eyelid clamping down like a crocodile's jaw—and placed the phone in her pocket. "You can type your forgivelets in my dorm! I have my laptop too." She stood up and fondled the recently bedazzled curtains. "Just promise me you'll put someone in the jar!"

Thank God Cambridge discovered the Milk Duds right after Hollywood left.

"Ten bucks says she's stuffing her hole with candy right now," said Liliana as a glob of Milk Duds paraded down her throat.

"But her ph-ph-phone," I stuttered. How did she get to keep

her phone?

Liliana shrugged. "I heard that her dad dropped her off in a helicopter."

Cambridge finally relented and sunk a Milk Dud on her tongue. "I know the type."

Yeah, we all knew the type, which is why none of us were surprised that Hollywood secured her spot as Utopia's queen in less than two hours. Campers relinquished their autonomy the way I liberated peas from fried rice. It was no shock either when, the next day, Miss Marcia asked us to pick a team captain, someone who could manage the ITINERARY and keep us motivated, Hollywood stood up and accepted the nomination from Atlanta like a People's Choice Award. She was just thrilled to be in charge of the schedule and would do everything in her power to make sure we campers were where we needed to be when we needed to be there.

"Great!" Miss Marcia screamed, bestowing the multi-paged ITINERARY in her hands like a bouquet of roses. "Everyone, this is your captain."

From:jacqueline.stern@dancedancedancestudios.com
To: Bethany Stern <bethanys@utopia.com>
Subject: Re: SORRY SORRY SORRY

dude, I get it. you're sorry. You can stop with all the emails. Geez, Bethany.
It's only been three days! Is it really that bad there? Is that Hollywood girl re-
ally the spawn of Satan? Bethany, you're so dramatic! She can't be that bad.
I mean, isn't she overweight? Aren't you all bonding? Are there any BOYS?

Anyway, I have a story for you. Do you remember seeing a weird papery thing
up in the corner of the minivan on the drive out here? None of us were speaking to each other at that time, so I don't know if you'd noticed it. Anyway, I saw
it soon after I dropped you off. Come to find out it was a nest! I showed it to
Doug, and he checked his phone and told me it was a hornet's nest. Then he
climbed in with his lighter and gets ready to torch it when I start to feel bad,
right, because I don't SEE any hornets and I'm like, stop, Doug. Let's just wait.

So we're near San Francisco and we get out at this scenic view point near the
bay bridge. Then, when I get back in the van, there's like 25 BUTTERFLIES fluttering around and Doug goes, "Dur. I guess they weren't hornets." So I climb
in and open the doors and the windows and they start to fly out—all black
and yellow and white. I start crying because it's so pretty. Then I remember
that book dad used to read us about the caterpillar that wouldn't stop eating.
And how, at the end, he wakes up as a butterfly. Do you remember it? It was
my favorite book! Anyway, my point is I love California! and I forgive you! so
stop apologizing, ok?

See you in 7 weeks!

xoxoxo

jackie

16

FRENEMIES

FOR ONE WEEK the campers and even Miss Marcia crowded around Hollywood and asked her how she got her hair that way (she rolls it in Diet Coke cans every night), her skin so clear (no eggs), her teeth so white (Dental Spa), and everyone looked away when her phone cheeped delicately—"Hi, Daddy."

It didn't matter one iota that Cambridge went to a private school so competitive you had to get on a waiting list before you were even born. No one cared that her dad was a professor or that her mom traveled around the world. No one mentioned Liliana's brother—some kind of rocket scientist—either. All that mattered to everyone at Utopia, with the exception of my dorm room, was Hollywood, whose hair dryer whirred like an alarm at five every morning. Hollywood, who after one week, had Utopians following her like she was Twitter. Needless to say, after one week I couldn't stand her. My feelings about her beloved California were pretty much cemented too. I thought the place sucked. It was foggy and cold. What a rip.

But there I was. Since I had no cell phone and no family member who would aid my escape, I had no choice but to wait for The Forgiveness Diet to kick in—and Hollywood promised me it would. All the campers except Cambridge were on it now, and given where I was, I figured I'd try. So I did. For one week. I tried to listen to Miss Marcia and the other girls. I attempted

to imagine how life would be as a skinny lawyer, a lithe marketing executive, a thin fashion designer. I wondered how great life
would be to be bony in Manhattan, anorexic in Beverly Hills, or
slender in Santa Fe.

I even tried to take part in their nightly discussions about
beauty—and they were nightly. I never mentioned the fact that
when I lost weight last year, no one even noticed. Well, maybe
they did a little, but the world kept on spinning. School was just
as lonely, TJ just as cryptic. "Don't I look better?" I asked him.
"You look a-ight, Bee." The same "a-ight" I always got.

Early one foggy camp morning, when Hollywood saw me staring down a muffin a student had absently left on the fountain's
edge, she said to me, "Don't even think about it, Baltimore." Had
she not been there, I must confess, I would have picked it up—all
nonchalant—like it was mine. Would have peeled off its crinkled
skirt and plopped it straight into my mouth. But she caught me.
And I was pissed. She snatched the muffin—a banana walnut, I
think—and dumped it in the nearby trash bin.

"It's not like I ate it," I said.

"But you were thinking about it." She planted her hands on
her hips. "Look, I'm just trying to help you, Baltimore. I am trying to be a friend." She looked almost sincere. It was six in the
morning and our luscious captain had on makeup. Eye shadow.
Lip gloss. Mascara. Her skin was flawless. I was already breaking out in those annoying sweat zits along my forehead. My armpits were damp, and we hadn't even started our power walk.
What I wanted was a muffin. A banana walnut muffin. I looked
at Hollywood tapping a furry pen on the ITINERARY she had
laminated. I wanted to kill her.

"I think if she wanted your help she'd ask for it." Did I just
say that out loud? Hollywood's eyes widened like dinner plates.
"What did you say?"

Everyone turned and stared at Cambridge, who was leaning
over in a stretch. When she pulled herself up, she faced Hollywood.

"I think Baltimore is just a little hungry, Hollywood. Relax."

Hollywood gathered the gray hoodie trimmed with faux fur
around her face. "It's only week one. Don't you think she could
at least pretend to be motivated?"

I didn't see how anyone could be ecstatic about waking up at five o'clock in the morning. Not to mention the whole running thing. Sure I knew people did it. Rumor had it the city of Baltimore held a marathon catering to such individuals. I just didn't happen to be one of them. I enjoyed staying inside, under the covers, until my mom would beat on the door and tell me the sun was shining, as if I cared.

"She needs to lose forty pounds," said Hollywood to Cambridge. "At least."

"I'm not sure that's for you to determine."

Then Hollywood reminded us, "But she's the heaviest one here. She's our best shot."

"At what?" I asked.

But she didn't answer. This was a conversation she wanted to have with Cambridge, not me.

Miss Marcia walked over. "What's going on here?"

Hollywood dropped it, but not before she shot me a look of pure ice. My transgression, her look read, was not forgotten. In her mind, she stuck a lavender Post-it on my head with the words: DANGER, DANGER.

For one week Hollywood's face was the first I saw in the morning. Even before mine. As predictable as the roly-poly fog she swung open our door, sashayed in, and thrust apart our curtains.

The ITINERARY mandated a jog or power walk by the water before breakfast. That was the worst part of the day—and the rest of the day didn't get much better. Question: If you saw twenty-five fat people running toward you, would you laugh? Apparently it was pure comedy to every summer school student on campus stumbling home in the morning. Even Liliana's brother, Gabe, shivering out by the lake in his skull cap and black sweatshirt—even he laughed a little as we waddled past. Hollywood told us this was meant to provide incentive, but it only made me feel like an ass.

Afterward we devoured cantaloupe and naked wheat bread in the dining hall. We ate in shifts. Usually girls ate first, then boys. This was designed so that Belinda and Hank and Miss Marcia could monitor campers' meals closely. Calories were controlled substances here at Utopia.

Given Hollywood made us swear off egg products, the boys got the omelet chef every day while we plowed through lumpy oatmeal or Greek yogurt. After we stacked our breakfast dishes on the conveyer belt, we met in MontClaire's common room for a goal-setting meeting. Here, Hank and Belinda discussed being fat and how satanic it was, warning about our pending deaths should we not shed pounds. Then we had dance class and cheerleading. Next was lunch—more wheat bread with one tablespoon of peanut butter, no jelly, an apple and twenty-four pistachios. Let me not forget the salad bar complete with everything except dressing, cheese, eggs, croutons; so, essentially, a table with lettuce and carrots. After lunch we swam, and I don't mean delicately dipped our toes in either. I mean we *freestyled* laps back and forth in an Arctic-temperature Olympic-sized pool. Yes, I actually got in a bathing suit in front of these people. It was purple and it had a skirt. A skirt.

After the Ultimate Water Challenge portion, there was another meeting where guest speakers sambaed in to gloat about their thin lives. Sometimes I don't think any of them had ever been fat. After that, we ate dinner, which for seven straight days, *seven straight days,* was a baked chicken breast, French cut string beans, one baked potato with spray-on butter that looked orange, and one sugar free Popsicle in either red or purple.

After dinner, the male Utopians gathered with us in Mont-Claire Hall. Rumor had it that in addition to the omelet chef, they got two chicken breasts for dinner. Tampa Bay confessed they played a lot of basketball and were not forced to swim after meals. As a group we were supposed to encourage each other but that never happened. When it was time for nighttime yoga, all the boys competed for a spot directly behind Hollywood, whose face, I was beginning to notice, wasn't all that pretty. When Belinda dragged Hollywood to the front of the room to demonstrate her perfect downward dog, a male voice called out, "Now that's what's up."

Before bed they made us recite a prayer like we were in Alcoholics Anonymous—something about a lack of carbohydrates and a higher power. Then we went back to our dorm rooms and rubbed our sore quads. Every muscle trembled. By day six, zits clustered along my forehead, cheeks, chin, and back. I tried telling Miss Marcia that I had my period. I told her if I swam one more lap, or power walked around the campus, my ovaries would fall out. Our counselor looked concerned, but Hollywood intervened.

"Menstruation is no excuse," she said. "They don't postpone the Olympics for it."

Like this was the Olympics.

"True," Miss Marcia barked. "No excuses."

Granted, this all sucked of the highest variety. None of it, however, rivaled the astonishing loneliness I felt at night after so many days without TJ. I missed him as much as the delightful cream-cheese crab puffs China Hon served on Sundays. I imagined him levitating over the gum-caked sidewalks of Baltimore, cupping a gray dove under a handkerchief. Days ago he'd tossed his graduation cap into the rafters of Baltimore Magnet High School. And I'd missed it.

As if to compensate, most nights Cambridge threw down some Fiddle Faddle or Lemonheads from her seemingly bottomless stash, but it didn't help. Not a Chinese buffet in sight. No banana walnut muffin. No TJ.

From: Bethany Stern <bethanys@utopia.com>
To: Toby Jacobson <voodooyou@abracadabra.com>
Subject: sleepless in utopia

Dear u:

It's been 384 hrs since i've seen u. most of those hrs I've spent swimming, power walking, aerobicizing, or avoiding Hollywood's frosty stares. But @ night we are blessed with 2 hrs to watch TV or stretch our muscles or whatever.

Usually i watch Liliana bedazzle items around our room. sometimes her brother will come by and throw sugar-free gum thru the window. Cambridge usually reads literary novels that have been assigned by her boarding school. Eventually my roommates fall asleep & i spend the next 8 hours thinking about u.

I think about b'more too and how squished together everything is. i try to name all the exits off 695 in order—memba how u used to quiz me on that? then I remember more stuff, stuff that happened between us and stuff that didn't.

Do you remember that party @ Chuck e cheese? When u did the magic show and MY DAD was there & I kept saying he saw me and u kept saying he didn't. remember how afterwards, u drove me home the back way & we got a snowball in Catonsville (exit 12) & u wanted to change the color of my tears but u were out of powder & you wanted the birds to fly outta my hair but they were locked in their cages & u wanted to appear some quarters frm my ear but u didn't have any change & we were just 2 normal people sharing a snowball. u weren't a magician & I wasn't fat & you kept saying my dad didn't see me. then u let me put my head on ur shoulder & u held my hand & kept saying if he'd known it was u he woulda said something. No one would ignore u, Bee. No one would walk away.

remember how I believed you?

instead of levitating, I wish u'd concentrate all your efforts on disappearing. i know u say it's impossible, but maybe u'll discover some kind of rabbit hole or some glitch in the universe & u'll snap ur fingers in b'more and then particle by particle u'll assemble in utopia. First ur hands & then ur face. U'll hover by my door. Then by my bed. Then u'll crawl in my bed. Then u'll…

Love,

Bee

PS. Sorry re: the doves.

PPS. If u do appear in utopia, can u disappear me out of it? #jussayin

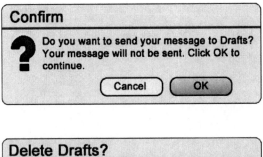

17

WEIGH DAY! WEIGH DAY!

AFTER SEVEN DAYS of aching muscles, quivering sit-ups, and a dark rumbling hunger, we were rewarded with an extra half-hour of sleep. The idea behind it? An extra thirty minutes of sleep might provide the strength to confront Sunday, our official Weigh Day. Weigh days occurred publicly on that same demonic scale. The goal was to see which team shed the most weight, so we could promote this hellhole in a TV commercial. But by day seven, a prime time spot on cable TV was no match for, say, chocolate lava cake with caramel icing. And after one week, that was all I wanted.

Hollywood remained the skinniest and the most revered. This glorious Sunday she wore a pink T-shirt pulled tight across her bodacious chest. It read "Captain Thin." It was unclear whether the camp provided her with the shirt or if she took certain liberties. Needless to say, she continued to take the role very seriously.

"Thank you," she said when we all shuffled in, knuckling our crusty eyes, "for getting here on time." Like we had a choice. She was the one who hauled our asses out of bed. "The Forgiveness Diet emphasizes the importance of punctuality." Even Miss Marcia, our counselor, rolled her eyes. How could someone be this pleasant in the morning? So sunny? I decided right then if this were some crazy M. Night Shyamalan film and Utopia was a deserted island where our plane just happened to crash, I would eat Hollywood first. Just saw off her leg, pearl anklet and all.

The campers gathered in the common room of MontClaire Hall. Boys included. Our collective stomach growling could have been measured on the Richter scale. As Belinda and Hank tried to encourage us, I imagined dousing them with syrup. Butter. Eating them alive.

"Now keep in mind," said Belinda, who sported a pink shirt that was a raspberry pie, a strawberry tart, the fluffy exterior of a Hostess Snowball, "everyone loses weight at a different rate."

"Yes," echoed Miss Marcia. "Back when I was a camper, I only lost four pounds my first week," she said. Only.

Without further ado, Miss Marcia fanned out our files like a deck of cards and Belinda plucked one out. Tabitha Calliope Nelson.

Cambridge eyed the scale cautiously. "I don't like these things," she said. Miss Marcia reminded her that this was an opportunity and, "We're here to help you, not judge you." Cambridge groaned. "Here's to getting it over with," she said, stepping on the platform.

Despite all the Laffy Taffy, espresso frappes, and peanut storms she'd supplied, Cambridge had lost weight. I snuck a peek at Tampa Bay. He grinned. I had a feeling those two had burned a few calories together. There was some kind of chemistry between them. Regardless, Cambridge was down three pounds. She looked more relieved than happy. It was Hollywood who cavorted around like an epileptic, screaming, "Take that!" to the boys. Whenever someone from the boy team was weighed, I watched Hollywood tense. Then she'd count on her fingers, squeeze her eyes shut and calculate.

In no time at all, every file had been fished out from Miss Marcia's fingers by Belinda, except one. So far everyone had lost weight too. Tampa Bay led with a whopping seven pound loss. Only one girl from our team needed to get on the scale. The only thing that camper had to do was drop more than one pound. When my team realized the stakes, everyone relaxed. Even Hollywood. Once everyone saw who was remaining, certainly, they thought, she would lose a pound. I mean really. Out of everyone.

I stood up in front of my team, the boys' team, Miss Marcia,

Hank, Belinda, and all the other Utopians. I walked up to the scale in my flip-flops. Thwak—thwak—thwak. Fifteen days ago I tried The Forgiveness Diet. I forgave everyone I could possibly think of. I even forgave my dad. Not to mention TJ, who begged me to forget him. To move on. I let it go. For the past seven days at Utopia, I swam in a skirted swimsuit. I power walked and ate chicken breast. I sacrificed my phone to a Hefty bag.

When I stepped on the scale, I heard hhhhhhhhhhhhhhhh-huuuu as everyone drew in breath. I knew Hollywood writhed behind me, tapped her nails on her sparkling phone. I was her money shot. Her MVP.

Then, from Hollywood I heard this: "Are you frickin' serious?" Followed by this: "Not even a whole pound!"

It was safe to assume that my loss was not as significant as everyone'd hoped. When I looked over my shoulder, Hollywood's pink mouth hung open in an enraged O. "Tell me you're retaining water, Baltimore. Tell me." She was trying to control herself, but an angry redness crawled up her neck and ears. "I want a do-over," she said to Miss Marcia, snapping her fingers. But a do-over was useless because I was still on the scale, my .8 weight loss ablaze behind me.

It was Miss Marcia who shushed her. "All bodies are different," she said, directing this to the crowd. "And some lose weight a little slower."

"And just how slowly is that?" Hollywood spat.

When I went back and sat, Cambridge and Liliana congratulated me anyway. I couldn't see Hollywood, but I felt her eyes burning into my back. If my shirt smoked, I would not have been surprised.

"Don't worry about a thing, Baltimore," screamed Miss Marcia. "I'll bet your loss next week will be Tree. Men. Dus."

From: Bethany Stern <bethanys@utopia.com>
To: inquiries@forgivenessdietllc.com
Subject: URGENT: REPLY REQUESTED

Dear Forgiveness Diet Inventor,

I am curious about the advertisement featured on national TV after American Envy two weeks ago. I followed the directions on your infomercial and have been eating next to nothing.

I am hungry, so hungry that I would eat this f%4#*ng computer if it wasn't delivering this e-mail, which I hope won't be ignored. I am exercising so much my bones hurt.

At exactly 11:06 AM on Sunday I tried The Forgiveness Diet. Fourteen days later I have not seen results. I ask you: WHEN CAN I EXPECT WEIGHT LOSS?

Sincerely,

Bethany (an obviously undervalued customer) Stern

From: donotreply@forgivenessdietllc.com
To: Bethany Stern <bethanys@utopia.com>
Subject: RE: URGENT: REPLY REQUESTED

Dear Dissatisfied Consumer:

We here at The Forgiveness Diet LLC regard your concerns and opinions with the utmost gravity. A qualified dietician will evaluate your query within seventy-two hours. You may anticipate a thoughtful reply within four to six weeks.

In the meantime, thank you for purchasing The Forgiveness Diet*. You are one step closer to a body transformation. Our website is teeming with information including a detailed FAQ section where most questions can be answered. We appreciate your patience and look forward to your metabolic success.

Sincerely,

The Forgiveness Diet Staff

www.theforgivenessdiet.com

*Results on website and commercial are not typical. Most participants see mild results within 8-10 weeks after using the patented 3- part system. As with any change in exercise or diet, consult with your physician first. The Forgiveness Diet LLC and its claims are not FDA approved and should be instituted at own risk.

18

INTENSE

AS YOU CAN imagine, things were tense my second week at Utopia, and Hollywood watched me like a hawk. Every time I lifted my fork to my mouth, she was there breathing down my neck. She began wearing fuzzy slippers and swooping in without the alert of her clonking heels. "Baltimore!" she'd sing like an *American Envy* contestant. "I was just checking in!"

For the most part, I ignored her. At least I tried to. Liliana took her pretty seriously even though her brother told her not to. Liliana's rocket science bro stood outside our window at night and told Liliana not to lose weight so quickly. "It's supposed to be a slow process," Gabriel said, rattling off equations about calories and heat conduction. He made the most ornate paper airplanes and shuttled them through our window. He'd stuffed them with diabetic candies too, which I ate. Her blood sugar, Liliana said, was fine. Better than ever. She wanted to get on Hollywood's good side anyway. She was convinced our captain was connected to the fashion industry somehow. With her brother groveling below like some scrawny Romeo, Liliana sat on her bed in bedazzling yoga pants. She shouted at Gabe to settle his algebraic butt down. "For shit's sake, *hermano*, get a girlfriend. This is college."

Then there was Cambridge. She had her own agenda, but by week two I still didn't know what it was exactly. We finished off her supply of goodies the night after weigh day. She was sure her father would send more, but so far he hadn't. This worried me more than it did her.

"Maybe they are searching our mail," I wondered out loud.

"I certainly wouldn't doubt it," Cambridge agreed, twisting her hair while she spoke. She was bent on having a head full of dreadlocks by the end of the summer. She wanted to go back to Miss Tidy Twats Prep (her words, not mine) with a new look. Cambridge—who was built a lot like me with big legs, a thick waist, and broad shoulders—had no apparent need for sleep because, by our second week, she was sneaking out at night. She futzed around the dorm—all distraction and flushed cheeks—until eleven or so, then she'd say, "Pshew! I could use some air," and creep out barefoot. I knew Tampa Bay waited for her outside. He was a bit of a hipster, I guess, but he had nice teeth when he smiled, which he never stopped doing whenever Cambridge walked into a room.

From our dorm's window, I'd watch her snake her way between the bushes, lamps, and emergency call boxes, her backpack thunking against her shoulders. When she came back to our room, always pretty late, Liliana would be sleeping and I'd be thinking about TJ.

"You're thinking about that boy again, aren't you?" she asked one night.

"Guilty."

She looked at the photo I'd brought of him. I had it on my desk leaning against a Delilah Rogers romance. It was taken last summer after I dropped a few pounds and TJ and I were eating at China Hon. The waiters snapped it just as TJ pulled a violet out from behind my ear. The way he regarded the camera, the way I smiled at him, we looked like a couple. A real one. Or at least a possible one.

"He's good looking," Cambridge said, kneeling down by the desk. "But is he a good kisser?" she asked. "I'm all about a good kisser. I can't stand those pointy tongues. Or the Dirt Devil who wants to suck out your tonsils. No, kissing really is an art form. "

I wasn't sure how to respond. TJ and I kissed for the first time the summer before ninth grade. I was thirteen. For months I had asked him about kissing: Had he thought about it? Had he done it before (I knew he hadn't). Might he be interested in trying it? With me? He was noncommittal and mysterious, the way he always is. Then, one night, we were outside, and he was showing me a card trick. He kept flubbing it too, holding up a card.

"Is this it, Bee?"

"No."

"Yes it is."

"No it's not. I know my own card."

TJ grabbed another card. "It's this one, right?"

"Ummm. No? Sorry."

We were on his back porch. The sky was all purply-pink.

"When I looked at you just now, it looked like you were balancing the moon on your head."

I flexed my flabby muscles. "Maybe I was."

TJ looked back at his cards. "You can do it now."

"Do what?"

"Kiss me."

Still he didn't look up from the cards, and I thought he probably should, but what did I know. I was only thirteen. Anyway, I was sitting Indian-style and so I uncrossed my legs and then leaned across the milky glass table, a bull's-eye hole in the center for an umbrella between us. Just before my lips touched his there was this low rumble in my throat, like a growl. The kind of noise a dog makes when it's stretching.

"What was that," TJ asked, still not looking at me.

"My stomach," I said, "I must be hungry."

But it wasn't a hungry noise at all. It was desire—what Delilah Rogers called longing. I knew I'd love kissing TJ before I even got to do it. I wanted to live inside his mouth, even at thirteen, just crawl inside a molar and stay. I held back though, just brushed my lips against his, the way it happens when you're kissing someone for the first time. He looked at me then and held up the Joker.

"This it, Bee?"

"Yes," I lied. "That's the one."

"He's a wonderful kisser," I told Cambridge now, knowing it was true. "Gentle."

Cambridge stared at the photo. "Gentle is good."

When she stepped on my mattress to climb up to her bunk, she mumbled an apology. Once she was up there I tried asking her about where she'd gone and what the campus looked like at night and what it was like kissing a boy like Tampa Bay, but she changed the subject, letting it go at, "It feels good to do something I wouldn't normally do. You won't tell anyone, will you?" She shifted in her bed. "Everyone thinks I'm perfect."

From our respective bunks, we chatted until eventually the conversation shifted to food because, surprise, it always did. If you were stranded on an island and could only eat one kind of food for the rest of your life, what would it be?

Liliana, who turned out to not be sleeping at all, would say, "Chocolate."

"Frappuccinos with extra whipped cream," Cambridge added.

"Chinese food. Duh."

But what if you had a choice between the man of your dreams and the meal of your dreams. What if you were going to die the very next day? These dilemmas went on and on, until Hollywood, who never bothered to knock, slithered in.

"I really think you should go to bed now, Baltimore," she instructed. "The Forgiveness Diet says that the teenager needs at least nine hours of sleep and the overweight ones need even more. If I were you I'd aim for twelve hours."

By now it was week two, and I wanted to poison her. I really did. "Well maybe you should stop waking me up at five every morning and let me sleep."

"Fat chance," she replied, sniveling. "You need a wake-up call more than anyone."

Cambridge and Liliana, who positively lettered in insults, launched them at Hollywood like missiles.

"Hollywood, isn't there a parade somewhere requiring rain? Some toddler's Halloween candy in need of razorblades?" Liliana would ask her. While I seethed in my bed, thinking of brilliant comebacks later, Cambridge had an entire arsenal ready for deployment. She whipped them out until Hollywood left, yelling after her, "Watch out for flying houses! Wouldn't want them landing on your implants, now would you?"

19

GAINING ACCESS

TWO WEEKS LATER, and I still hadn't received any replies from The Forgiveness Diet. I was beginning to think I had been right all along. It really was a scam. Sure everyone was on it and losing weight. Obviously the campers were into it, but even the CU-Pids were toting around little fishbowls forgiving-off their college students fifteen. Lord knew I didn't feel any lighter but, according to scientists, miracles can happen. So I waited some more.

No mail from Jackie. Nothing from TJ. Neither of them were writer types so I wasn't exactly surprised. I did get e-mails from my mom asking me how things were going. What was I supposed to say? Love it here, Mom. Thanks for forcing me into fat camp. This is a dream come true! She did say she missed me, but I doubted it.

Just as my fatcampsucks-o-meter was in overdrive, something good happened. We were preparing for our Ultimate Water Challenge when I spotted a flat gold card sticking out of Miss Marcia's pocket. Thinking it was an American Express, I could hardly stand my luck. While our counselor splashed around in the pool, calorie-reducingly, I decided to investigate. As I got closer to her shorts, now piled in a heap on the grass, I saw the word "Mailroom" written in Sharpie marker along the card's edge. *Close enough*, I thought. I pretended to stretch deeeeeeply before jumping into the pool. I leaned right over and snatched the key. I stuffed it in my towel and vowed to give it back later.

Later turned out to be never.

They doled out mail like our food, with stinginess and caution. We'd only received letters once when Miss Marcia shoved them under our doors during a scheduled fifteen minutes of "down time." I got a philosophical card from my mom complete with setting sun image and lame bullshit about inspiration vs. perspiration. Cambridge received notes from her private school, but still nothing from her dad. Liliana didn't get a single letter, even though Gabe said their mother was sending them. Either way, it seemed illogical that twenty-five girls away from home hadn't received more mail. I had a feeling Belinda and Hank were stashing it somewhere. And I was right.

The mailroom turned out to be the Chemistry Department's teaching assistant's headquarters located in the MontClaire Annex, a portable tacked on to the backside of our MontClaire Hall. Inside were a few rows of cubicles and a long wall of inboxes. Next to names of future chemists were slots with camper names scrawled on masking tape. I was a bit surprised to see a padded envelope angled in my box. Inside was a note from my mom written on Zyprexa Pharmaceuticals stationary.

Bee~ This came today. Typical Dick. Late again. ~Mom.

Looky here, I thought. *A present from Richard Goodman, aka my father. And wow! Only eight weeks late this year. A new record.*

Dear Bee: Sorry this is so late, but I wanted to wait for the latest model. Your mom told me you love to read and I thought you'd enjoy one of these new e-readers. Happy 17th! Dad

I decided to play "How many insulting things I can find in one note."

First clue, I'm only sixteen.

Great. An e-reader. Too bad it didn't come with a side of fries.

Moving on.

I wasn't surprised to see Hollywood's (aka Amber S. Gold's) box full. I was, however, a teensy bit amazed when I found a lonely piece of chocolate tucked inside a letter. It melted under my tongue bitterly as I read a note in slanted handwriting. Daddy Dearest must have been in a hurry. *Shhhhhh*, it read. *I'm missing my princess. How is it there? Are you making progress?* His address was 3206 Canyon View Drive, Hollywood Hills, CA 90210.

Then there was Liliana. Her mom wrapped up sugar-free chocolate wafers and diabetic hard candies. *Your quinceanera, mija, is more than a year away. Certainly one candy won't hurt.* Atlanta (Parker Mendell) didn't have any food, but her letters were sliced open and dubious sentences had been high-lighted: *We tried calling, but ....*

No one's mailbox rivaled Cambridge's. Cardboard boxes and pastel envelopes overflowed out of the slot and into one of those giant mail-hauling bins beneath it. Gifts were piled high; glittery cards with the words *I'm sorry, Please Open* were scattered about. Looking at all those packages and envelopes and goodies, I could hardly believe it. Utopia wasn't just holding our mail—they were hiding it. Intercepting it. Granted the parents probably should not have been smuggling in food. So much food. Bad food. But still.

Re: The Food.

What I said to myself:

Do not even think about the crunchy caramel corn with al-monds. Forget the chocolate-covered coffee beans. Pay no at-tention to the fancy crackers and cheese.

Avoid bliss. Deny rapture. Instead note the other items of importance in the room: The scale living next to a ficus plant in the corner. Next to a copy machine. Note a tall filing cabinet.

File cabinet duly noted.

I rattled the file cabinet that first night, completely expecting it to be locked, or to have those red laser beams criss-crossing inside. Not even. The drawer pulled out a bit noisily, but eas-ily, and inside all our files sat. The exact same files Miss Marcia toted around and made notes all over.

That first night I told myself I wouldn't eat anyone's food—ex-cept Hollywood's. I sat next to the file cabinet on the floor eating the dark chocolate our team captain's father had sent. I also said I wouldn't read anyone's file even though the drawer yawned open torturously. I was very righteous about it. *No*, I thought, *you are not this cunning, Bethany. Or this nosy. This is absolutely none of your business and this food is not even yours.* That's what my brain said. And I actually listened to it for once. I walked back to our dorm room with my e-reader and pretended everything was fine. I had just felt like stretching my legs. My roommates didn't buy it. Since when do I elect to exercise? But I wasn't sure if I could trust either of them yet. I felt fairly confident that Cambridge would be cool, but you can never be too careful.

Predictably, though, the third night I found myself in the mailroom I'd read everyone's file and downed about half of the care packages. My brain said:

Do not eat this gorgeous peanut butter cup, Bethany.

Ignore its scalloped edges. Bypass the Wheat Thins. Just say no. Get yourself some water.

Only fourteen hours 'til breakfast. Remember TJ. Remember The Forgiveness Diet ...

But then the voice got real quiet. This might have been due to the fact it was drowned out by the sound of my own crunching. A more intelligent person would have listened to her brain. I knew I should've, I just didn't. I like to eat. I love to eat. I'm embarrassed by this, which, for whatever reason, makes me hungrier. You try rattling a package of Sno-Caps in the face of hunger. Let me know what happens.

Next were the files. They were more addicting than the sweets. Well, as addicting. On each application parents had to write why their kid needed fat camp, then the camper had to write why they thought they needed to go. Tampa Bay's parents wrote, *We need Simon out of the house for at least eight weeks, as we are divorcing. He is also overweight. This will kill two birds with one stone.* Simon wrote, *I need to be better at ball.*

Hollywood's dad wrote, *Though I maintain some serious reservations about sending my daughter to Utopia, she needs help. She says she's better, but I'm not sure. She needs to learn how to eat again, in a healthy manner. I'm confident in your reputation as well as mine that these concerns will be addressed.* Amber Gold wrote, *I want to be a size 2. Pleeeeaaaassssseee. Think of the PR!*

Utopia required campers to send a picture, so in everyone's file a photograph was paper-clipped to the inside flap. Hollywood stood on a wooden pier—the ocean rolling out behind her. Her hair was down and wind-blown, natch, but the sexy surfer guy, who stood next to her, didn't seem to care. Hollywood was looking down at her bare feet, her palm covering her eyes, trying to talk the person out of taking the picture. *Not now*, I could practically hear her. *Not wearing this.* Her shirt was folded into a halter—its bottom tucked through the neck. Her belly pushed out a little.

In the other files, most campers stood outside a McMansion, smiling aquafreshingly. Some were by a pool. Cambridge did look just about perfect in her private school's navy blue jacket with gold-threaded lettering. She wore equestrian pants, a riding cap, a crop by her side. Someone had printed *Tabitha and Ace 2013* on the bottom. Who was Ace? I looked behind Cambridge toward the multicolored leaves and saw, in the background, a giant white horse. Cambridge had a frickin' horse? Liliana's picture, though, took the cake. She stood outside her brother's truck in the craziest outfit I'd ever seen—a short denim skirt with rainbow feathers—*feathers!*—sewn across the bottom. Her bangs were dyed a ballpoint red and her dizzy black and white socks stretched to her thighs. She was positively adorable. Hanging out the truck's window, just barely noticeable, was Gabe—saluting the camera with his middle finger. No doubt that brother of hers was a troublemaker. He wasn't bad looking, though, and in a parallel universe where I didn't happen to be in love with a magician in Baltimore, I might have even called him cute.

On *my* application, my mom wrote, *This picture should speak for itself.* In the place where I'm supposed to write, she did loopy handwriting that didn't look like mine at all. It read, *To attend Camp Utopia would be a dream come true.* In my photograph, I stood next to Jackie outside our row house. Doug had taken the picture last spring.

"Look pretty," he'd said, "if you can."

Miss Marcia made little notes on my file: *Motivation? Anger? Only .8 loss!!!!* Then yesterday, under comments, she wrote: *Funny.*

20

CRABBY WITHOUT YOU

SATURDAY NIGHT. DAY fifteen of fat camp. Day five of Operation Mail-Snatch. When I walked into the mailroom, I noticed a postcard slanted in my slot. Figuring it was from my mom, I let it rest there and inspected the other campers' mail. A few cheesy letters from Hollywood's dad alongside a DVD set of last season's *American Envy*. A few more packages had been added to Cambridge's storehouse including a sign that read, *I'm sorry,* made entirely from chocolate -covered espresso beans.

Finally I made my way back to the postcard in my slot. On the front was a fake-looking red crab, Baltimore city towering behind it, and the words: "I'm Crabby Without You" on the bottom. I flipped it over: *Big Bee—You skinny yet? JK. I'm guessing they nabbed your phone. There has been much progress on my levitation. I passed the AE prelims in B'more last week. I'm going to AE NYC tryouts next Friday. Do they let you watch TV there? I'm hoping I make the cut. My dad is even praying for me LMFAO! I've been thinking about the smack that went down between us, it's all good, Bee. I hope you forgave me. Did the diet work??? Love, TJ*

I knew I should have been freaking about *American Envy*. That was TJ's dream. And I know I'm biased, but TJ has skill. Like *American Envy* skill. Yet when I read the second to last word, a bead of sweat darted down my armpit. And then another. I took a deep breath and picked off the espresso-beaned "S" in sorry. My hands shook as I tore off the "O." I moved on to a box of Whole Foods chocolate-covered graham crackers. I read TJ's card again. I must have stared at it for forty minutes. L-O-V-E. L-O-V-E. L-O-V-E.

TJ's just not the kind of guy to use the word lightly. "You my girl," was about as sentimental as he got. He always thought about things. That's what made him an expert magician: deliberation and execution. Like that first night I kissed him. I knew he'd picked that moment for a reason. It's just how he was. Wanting to get it all right.

Of course my brain said, *It's just a word. His pen must have slipped. Get a grip, Bethany.*

Yet some other voice—who knew where it came from?—was calling to me. And it was loud. Loud like Miss Marcia's. It screamed: HE WANTS ME. HE WANTS ME. HE WANTS ME.

Did it matter to me that it was Saturday night and I was sneaking around like a stalker, eating chocolate-covered espresso beans addressed to someone else, which, I'm thinking, was some kind of felony? Did it matter that last summer, when the "smack" went down, when the words, "I love you" flew out of my mouth like a man shot from a cannon, TJ'd just sat there. Silently.

It didn't matter a bit. Something made him use the word love now, on that postcard. Perhaps absence does make the heart grow fonder. I dipped into some trail mix priority-mailed from Cambridge's apologetic father. *Yes indeed*, I thought mightily, basking in yet another indulgence. *TJ totally misses me.*

I stayed in the office looking at the postcard until the sun stretched its yellow self across the horizon. Then I cut across the quad back to the dorms where a hair dryer hummed from Hollywood's room.

"Baltimore, where have you been?" asked Liliana when I eased open our door. "Today is Sunday, girl. Domingo."

21

POWERING DOWN

HOLLYWOOD LED US downstairs to MontClaire Hall's common room, where the boys had already gathered. The garbage bag with the life jackets and balls spilled next to the sofa. The files fanned across the desk. The scale had been positioned in the center of our circle, and Miss Marcia stood in front of it, all of us bending our necks like sunflowers to check out her long, long legs.

This Sunday our team captain got weighed first.

"I'm so nervous," Hollywood said calmly. Her hair was brushed; the ends curled up suggesting she hadn't been awake for an hour getting it precisely that way. When she stepped on the scale she looked, unfortunately, a little thinner.

Affirmed!

According to the traitorous scale, Hollywood had peeled off another four pounds from some place that didn't need it. No doubt her father would be ecstatic.

Next up, Liliana Delgado.

She sashayed up in her sweatsuit and star-studded socks. Obviously the sugar-free diabetic candy Gabe tossed to her hadn't touched her game. She was down three pounds. Liliana hip-hopped back to her spot in the circle. Next, Miss Marcia fished out Atlanta's file. Though Miss Bumpit's bouffant was looking a little tired these days, it got a jolt of electricity when she screamed annoyingly over her two-and-a-half-pound loss. Clearly we were on a roll.

The boys' team, scattered across the floor, seemed nervous. Even Tampa Bay, whose parents were probably fighting over who got the couch this very minute, looked tense, worried. Cambridge squeezed my hand. "Me and Tampa Bay had some marshmallows two nights ago," she whispered. Then Miss Marcia plucked her file, and Cambridge sauntered up to the scale.

Check that out. She and Tampa Bay must've burned those extra calories in some imaginative way because Cambridge's red number was three pounds less than last week's.

"That's a total of seventeen pounds for your team, girls," said Miss Marcia, beaming. We were rocking her world. You could tell. Our counselor perched next to the scale holding one last hospital-blue file. My file. The one I'd shoved back in the cabinet a few hours ago, careful not to smear any chocolate on it. Miss Marcia crossed her arms. "Your turn, Baltimore."

Sure, I should've been worried, but I wasn't. I was still swinging on the cloud TJ whisked over when he sent that postcard. You know the one. In my happy pink universe, things could not have been better. So what if I'd just burned through a dozen chocolate-covered graham crackers? I felt light. So light I knew The Forgiveness Diet had finally kicked in. I could've positively floated away on my wispy-light featheriness. Soared right out of MontClaire Hall and chillaxed in a fluffed-out sky. TJ signed it L-O-V-E. Let the record show, people. I was still his girl.

Miss Marcia stood behind the scale, her pen poised on my file. She nodded.

As I steadied on the platform, no one made a noise. Nothing. If gravity made a sound pressing down on Earth, I could have heard it. I'm talking silence, and not the good kind either. The funeral kind. It was Hollywood's voice that shattered it.

"Jesus CHRIST!" she screamed. "What. The?"

I did not look.

"Do you have some change in your pockets?" asked Liliana. "Or some weights?" God bless her for trying.

Hank and Belinda, who I never even saw arrive, now shot up like the couch had burst into flames. Only they weren't running to silence Hollywood. They were running to check the scale.

The owners had me step off then step on again.

More silence.

It was safe to assume the number was not what they expected. Obviously The Forgiveness Diet had not delivered yet. Maybe the care packages I accidentally consumed might've had something to do with it. I turned around to explain to the campers about the mailroom, how the very owners who stood beside me were blacking out letters like we were in prison, and holding our care packages hostage!

Only just as my mouth made efforts to open, Hollywood's beat me to it.

"You fat bitch," she hissed like it was a line she was supposed to deliver. She was far enough away that Belinda and Hank couldn't hear her, but close enough that I could. "Don't ... make ... us ... lose," she warned me, a little louder this time.

"Amber," Miss Marcia snapped. "Is there something you'd like to share?"

Hank and Belinda reset the scale while Hollywood addressed Miss Marcia. "Isn't there some rule about gaining weight? Some intervention?" She tried to say this as innocently as she could muster, but it came out like a whine. "I don't think she even wants to be here."

"You don't know what you're talking about," I mocked. "This is a dream come true."

"You're lying," Hollywood shot back, louder still. "I'd bet it was you hiding cotton candy that first day." Captain Thin actually stomped her feet. "I bet you're still hiding it. My dad says he's sending me stuff, and I think you're stealing it. I want you off the team or I will sue your f—"

"Enough!" Miss Marcia interrupted.

Near me, Hank and Belinda seemed more flummoxed by my weight gain than Hollywood's tantrum. "It has to be the scale," said Belinda, tapping a square fingernail on the display. "Maybe we should measure her."

Miss Marcia sighed. "Put your arms out," she instructed before wrapping the tape measure around my waist. Unfortunately, though, that number wasn't any good either.

On the floor in front of me, Hollywood rapidly approached core meltdown. Her breathing was ragged and quick. She looked possessed. "Have you even been doing the diet?" she asked. "By the size of you, I'm guessing you have a lot of people to forgive. Like an entire city."

"Hollywood, calm down," coaxed Miss Marcia. She looked at me the way you would a crushed dog on the highway.

"Calm down? Are you serious? I want a lawyer because this poor heifer is making us lose."

Did she really call me that? Judging by the muffled laughter from the boys, she had indeed. Her green eyes burned into mine. "Look at your clothes. Fashion Bug PLUS called and said you can keep them! Oh, let me guess your phony boyfriend likes them." She rolled her eyes. "He's probably not even real. I'd bet you Photoshopped that picture in your room."

"Hollywood!" warned Hank.

"Like anyone would ever look at her."

There were twenty-five campers in the room hearing this. And maybe because of all the fog, everything she said seemed deafening. Her voice was shrill.

"Come on. No boy would ever want her."

"Amber Gold. Thop."

"I got a postcard," I said belatedly, pathetically. Just then I desperately wanted to collect that postcard and shove it in her face. But as that scene played out in my imagination, I knew Hollywood would only laugh at it. It was, after all, only a crab. Only a word.

She cackled. "A postcard?"

"He signed it 'love,' " I said, my voice trailing off.

"Don't they have mirrors in Baltimore? Have you looked at yourself lately?"

"Thop it!" Hank yelled, but it was really hard to take him seriously when he spoke like a Loony Tune. "Enough with the inthults!"

It was Belinda who ended it. She waved her arm laden with bracelets and said, "You're treading on thin ice, Amber Gold. Don't make me call your father, because I will."

At that, Hollywood flinched. We all saw it.

"It's not about winning," ordered Miss Marcia.

"Yes it is!" blasted Hollywood.

Of course it was about winning. At least to Hollywood it

was. Which was why I wasn't surprised to see Hollywood, right then, reach into her pocket. As Belinda made her way over to her, I saw angry Hollywood's arm cock back. Then seconds later, something hit me. Literally—something knocked me on the side of my face so hard my teeth rang. My eyes were closed so I didn't see anything, but when I opened them, a certain lavender rhinestone cell phone pivoted on the floor beside me. It spun around cleanly, artfully, like a pinwheel. *She must really have an arm*, I thought, *because that was hurled with incredible velocity*. Then something wet slipped down my mouth. When I wiped my lip, I saw blood. A lot of blood. First my lip tingled. Then it throbbed.

After that, Belinda, Hank, and Miss Marcia tackled Hollywood. They pounded her with their fists. Hank slammed her heart-shaped face into the floor again and again.

Not exactly.

Instead we all collectively watched that violet cell phone spinning on the floor. Hank blew his whistle and everything— even time—seemed frozen inside a magic trick. The campers looked at their shoes or their hands like something very important had happened inside them. Ever so slowly, cell phone still pirouetting, lip still pulsating, I slid my feet into my flip-flops. One small step at a time, I stumbled toward the door. Holding my lip that hammered, and swallowing my iron-tasting blood, I tried not to cry. And by some mercy, I didn't.

Walking to the door seemed to take fifteen years. When my fingertips finally grazed the door's metal handle, and Hank's whistle finally quieted, I knew one thing for sure: I was done. Done. The deepest part of myself—that part that doesn't even have a name, that part that's a red hot lava—boiled up and howled at me: *Leave. Leave. LEAVE!*

"Take that, mudder-fubbers," I said, making sure the door hit my ass like the easy target it was on the way out. "I'm ou-wa here. I'm leab-ing Uto-ia."

Bumblingbee: TJ?

Voodooyoo is offline.

Bumblingbee: R u there, TJ? IM me.

Voodooyoo is offline.

Bumblingbee: I need to talk to you. PLS IM ME.

Voodooyoo is offline.

From: Bethany Stern <bethanys@utopia.com>
To: inquiries@forgivenessdietllc.com
Subject: WARNING! WARNING! UR DIET IS A SCAM!

Dear Forgiveness Diet Inventor,

newsflash, ur diet is fake. Too bad I learned this @ fat camp, but hey, u take ur chances. You should stop leading ppl on with ur dumb forgiveness hocus pocus. It's a lot of crap, and what's worse, u probably know it. Being fat sucks, it absolutely sucks, so don't make it any worse with ur phony claims.

Forgiveness MY ASS.

Sincerely, Bethany (another dicked around customer) Stern

Bumblingbee: TJ WTFRU? You wont believe what just happened.

Voodooyoo is offline.

Bumblingbee: someone threw a PHONE AT ME

Voodooyoo is offline.

Bumblingbee: AND CALLED ME A POOR HEIFER

Voodooyoo is offline.

From: Bethany Stern <bethanys@utopia.com>
To: inquiries@forgivenessdietllc.com
Subject: WARNING! WARNING! UR DIET IS A SCAM!

I hope u die a long, drawn out painful death. Then I hope u are buried in a sewage plant next to all the other crap in the world. U SHOULD B ASHAMED OF URSELF. every single person I meet I'm gonna tell them what a liar u are. And by the way, I hate ur guts. And another thing. I hope you get REALLY fat.

Bumblingbee: TJ! WAKE UP. WAKE UP. IM ME.

Voodooyoo is offline.

Bumblingbee:TJ I HAVE TO GET OUT OF HERE. RIGHT NOW. IM ME.

Voodooyoo is offline.

Bumblingbee: TJ????!!! PLEASE. WAKE UP!

22

CHECK YOURSELF

THE ONLY PERSON who could've possibly made me feel better after the Hollywood scene in MontClaire Hall was TJ, so I trudged to the computer lab. All he had to do was admit that he'd signed the postcard intentionally—that whatever it was between us, whatever happened that night, had meant something. That I meant something. Of course if he happened to show up, kill Hollywood, and fashion me a pair of earrings from her eyeballs, I wouldn't exactly complain about it.

Hollywood could bring you down alright. Just look at me, shaking all over like a proper wuss in the computer lab, pinching myself to keep from crying. It felt as if she'd thrust apart the hemispheres of my brain and seen straight through me. Well, eff her. She was wrong. I knew if TJ heard the humiliation in my voice, the hurt, he'd come get me. He L-O-V-E-D me. I was almost sure of it.

As for those Utopian punks who didn't have the decency to walk me to the door, screw them. I had violent images of steamrolling them inside MontClaire Hall. Kung fu-ing through the window like a scene from *The Matrix*. But I couldn't face them, not after what just happened. Instead I sat in the computer lab with the cardboard boxes of recycled paper and the hum of printers, where the whiteboard hung a little off- center, and willed the tears not to fall. But—and you knew this was coming—gravity is a bitch.

I cried in front of my computer, wanting desperately to send my draft messages to Fake Forgiveness HeadQuarters, USA. I wanted a response, compensation, a refund. I wanted someone to admit that the fault lie within the diet's fine print, not within the mailroom and the calories I had consumed there. I alternated drafting scathing e-mails to the diet racketeers and desperately IMing TJ for so long my fingers cramped. I must have refreshed my inbox five hundred times, waiting for a reply, yet when an e-mail finally dinged in, it wasn't from either of them.

From:rgoodman@mdk12.library.us.edu
To: Bethany Stern <bethanys@utopia.com> on behalf of <bumblingbee@ yeehaw.com>
Subject: Gift

Dear Bethany,

Hi, Bumble. I was wondering if you received your birthday present. I don't know if your mother gave it to you because I mailed it several weeks ago and still haven't heard. Sorry it was so late. I've been busy finishing up at the library and Penny and I are overwhelmed with the boys too.

What are your plans for the summer? I thought maybe you and Jackie could come over and swim one day. Penny and I got one of those giant pools from Costco. The boys are terrified to go in it, so it's just sitting out there, populated by mosquitoes and frogs.

I could pick you both up one Saturday. Or maybe Jackie could drive you over? It's been a long time since I've seen you. I assume you are still in the same house?

If you got your gift, I hope you like it. It's neat because I can make recommen-dations from my e-reader straight to yours. Anyway, I recommended that new diet book. Have you heard about it? The forgiveness one? I'm on it now. So far I've forgiven Penny for her cooking. Ha ha ha! (sorry lol lol lol)

Let me know about swimming, ok? And please let me know about the e-reader. Hope to hear from you soon. PS Click on the recommendation below and it should take you to the website

~Dad.

From:rgoodman@mdk12.library.us.edu) thought you might like:

The Forgiveness Diet: Discovering Rapid Weight Loss through Mercy

Written by Michael Osbourne, PhD

Ratings: 4,898

Please visit readerresources.com to view this recommendation. 40,000 titles are ready for download and thousands more are added every day.

Just when I thought the day couldn't get any worse. Now my own father recommended The Forgiveness Diet. Ridiculous. My mom always told me he wasn't too bright, but really. Was this the best he had? Just seeing the word "Forgiveness": the insinuating F, the gullible G, well, it brought the tears down even harder. Faced with those unanswered IMs and that heartless, blinking cursor, I started typing, the letters springing under my fingertips faster than they'd ever sprung. If Richard Goodman wanted to know if I got his little gift, then fine. He'd asked for it.

From: Bethany Stern <bethanys@utopia.com>
To: rgoodman@mdk12.library.us.edu
Subject: RE: Gift

Dear Dick aka my father:

As a matter of fact, I DID get your gift. Thanks for the e-reader. It's exactly what I wanted. Not really. I steal books from the school library every chance I get—especially the inappropriate ones, the ones the PTA is always banning for SEXUAL content. I rip out the metal strip and shove them in my backpack. Then I hide them under my bed (next to the Rolos, chocolate gems, and butterscotch krimpets) until l8 @ nite when I read them & think of TJ.

So YES. DAD. I GOT YOUR BIRTHDAY PRESENT. Except my birthday is APRIL 16th and, forgot to mention, I'm 16. Not 17. Stick that date in your e-reader & then SHOVE IT UP UR ASS. Mom was right: you really are clueless. No wonder u flunked outta optometry school. How STRESSFUL life must be 4 u now @ a LIBRARY!

Looks like u'll have the pool to urself this summer given that I'm @ FAT CAMP! Love it here, btw. Starving couldn't b better. My stomach enjoys resting against my spine. I so heart mean bitches like Hollywood who call me a whale and throw phones at my face. This is the stuff of summer, right?

Jackie won't be able to make it either b/c she's 'finding herself' (scrumping her bf) while I stay here and starve. Besides, she's no longer speaking to me, asshat, I mean, DAD b/c I wrote down: I forgive Jackie for killing Doug's baby, JUST LIKE THAT F%^*ng DIET BOOK TOLD ME TO DO. Did I mention that Doug (baby's daddy) was in the passenger seat?

The diet? Flippin genius. Check this out: I lost 10 lbs the minute after I 4gave Doug for bringing Jackie down. Dropped another 15 lbs, pop, when I 4gave my english teacher for telling me I could be frickin famous author if I ONLY LEARNED HOW TO SPELL. A whopping 8 lbs gone after I 4gave TJ for THE INCIDENT last year another 12 lbs when I 4gave u for basically * scratches my head* fu**ing me over w/ur Chuck E Cheese salad bars and diet books and annual emails and for the trainwreck of my life that basically started when u derailed. so yes I tried ur diet and no it didn't work. Im still fat. Still fat. Still fat. Next year DEAR DAD. On my b-day. Get me a puppy.

~Bee

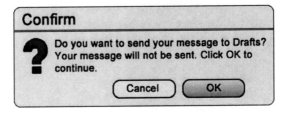

23

AUTORECOVERY

"NOT THAT IT'S any of my business, but are you OK?"

That was the girl sitting near me. Her long blond hair was pulled up on top of her head like a soufflé. It looked a bit greasy, like it might require a shampoo. She addressed me sideways while www.shroomerytips.com blinked on the computer screen in front of her. When she finally turned around, I noticed she had pierced dimples. "I mean, your lip is bleeding for one thing, and you seem really upset."

When I waved my hand as if to say *oh, this is nothing*, she looked doubtful. "Are you sure you don't need help? You've been crying and cursing in front of your computer for at least an hour."

My lip still felt numb from its collision with a certain lavender cell phone. I'm sure a ginormous bruise blossomed on my cheek. This girl probably thought I had escaped from a mental institution. Yet when she took hold of my wrist and turned me toward her, just that tiny gesture followed by the words, "It's OK, you can tell me," well, I lost it. I sighed and flung my head down on the keyboard. I didn't want to look at her face when I said the following into the springy-lettered darkness:

"I hate Hollywood. I hate Utopia, and I hate my life." The girl released my arm and a series of bracelets jangled on her wrist. My chin hit the space bar. "I gained a pound." I pulled the keyboard from under my head, and rested my cheek on the cool desk. "I gained a pound at fat camp."

Finally I faced her. Her chair was swiveled toward mine. "By the way," I said, "my own dad recommended I try The Forgiveness Diet for my seventeenth birthday." My eyes fell toward her dress, a sky-blue hippie ensemble. "He forgot I was only sixteen."

She closed the windows on her computer and offered me her undivided attention. "I'm Olive," she said, dimples sparkling. "I'm a summer school student retaking Macroeconomics."

"I'm Bethany. I'm here for Utopia." I pointed in MontClaire Hall's general direction because the computer lab had no windows. "The fat camp."

Olive's big blue eyes widened. "Did someone punch you in the mouth there?"

"You could say that."

"But why?"

I didn't want to end the conversation because maybe this girl had some divine insight into my current situation, but my eyes wandered back to my computer where they greeted this ever-so curious icon.

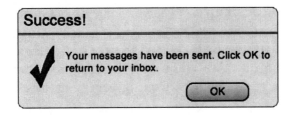

What was going on here? I hadn't sent any e-mail. I had merely drafted an e-mail. I checked my drafts folder, only when I did, there had to be some kind of mistake. Where a (10) blinked innocently a minute ago now there was a (0). OK? Where exactly was the NOT OK button? I checked my sent folder and yes, there they were. Every one of the my increasingly vicious, curse-ridden messages to The Forgiveness Diet in addition—in addition!— to the one e-mail the computer did the extraordinary favor of sending to my dad.

Yes.

"I didn't know C.U.P. had a camp here," Olive continued beside me. "Wait. Why are you turning white? Do you feel alright?" She looked at my computer. "What happened? Can you hear me?" She snapped her fingers in front of my face. "Did you lose something? Did your computer freeze?"

My mouth dried out as if it'd been vacuumed and sealed. I imagined hurtling through the twilight of cyberspace, chasing a winged envelope, screaming, "Come back here!" Almost every single thing—think about it—almost every single thing in the universe is reversible except an e-mail. An e-mail! The one thing that can never, ever be unsent.

"These computers get freaky," Olive said and bumped the keyboard with her fist. "There. I unfroze it." She waited for me to thank her. When that didn't happen, she checked out the wall clock. "Crap," she said, wheeling back to her computer and logging off. "I was totally supposed to meet someone fifteen minutes ago. Look, I hate to do this." She pulled out a little pad of paper from her Guatemalan bag. "Here's my e-mail and my phone number if you need anything. I'm twenty and will tell you that sixteen is pure hell, but it will get better." She placed her hand on my shoulder. "Don't let people treat you badly. It sounds stupid, but it's true. If they did that to your lip, don't go back there. " Her hand squeezed my shoulder. "Oh, and I don't know if you lost something on your computer, but you can get it back. There's an autorecovery on these machines. Just ask the lab attendant. No worries."

She left in a flurry, her blue dress ballooning out in all directions.

An autorecovery? What about autodelete? What about delinquent e-mail obliterator? Or a time machine? Autosave! What did she know anyway? Hippies—always looking for the silver lining.

I tried to calm myself. OK, I soothed. Richard Goodman aka my father only sent me e-mails once or twice a year. Maybe that meant he only checked his e-mail as often. He acted like the e-reader was a teleporter or some other sci-fi invention reserved for future generations; this meant he was more than likely technologically illiterate. Most old people were. He'd never see my e-mail. Straight into the SPAM folder, I'd bet. Pshew.

The clock in the computer lab had a loud tick—like the kind on a game show. It seemed bent on reminding me that it was only nine in the morning. Utopians were having "free time," which meant engaging in sportlike activities that did not involve food. I thought of Hollywood twirling a jump rope, her full lips blowing a perfect egg of bubble gum, her breasts corralled in her Captain Thin shirt. *Not a chance*, I thought. I wasn't going anywhere.

Convinced my misfired e-mail slumbered in my father's SPAM folder, I surfed the Internet because, let's face it, I had no plans for the day. I Googled *American Envy* and checked Timothy Tinsel's season updates. He was quoted after a preliminary judging as saying, "I don't want to give anything away, but I am extremely excited about this season of *American Envy*. We found a promising magician who vanished during his act! We searched for ten whole minutes until finally he materialized in the audience applauding his own disappearance. There were also Siamese twins in Philadelphia who harmonized like angels. We cried just hearing them."

I searched for clips on ViewTube, but only uncovered footage from outside the Baltimore *AE* preliminaries, a line of teenagers snaking all the way from the harbor to Timonium. I zoomed in close, but didn't see TJ. I would have given anything for just a glimpse of him then. I even used Google Earth's street viewer and honed in on his row house, wobbled the scene to his aluminum front door that screeched whenever the wind blew. If only Google Earth could have slinked up the stairs, the worn-out carpet, his family pictures lining the hallway, creaked open his bedroom door, and focused on TJ, reading Houdini's biography on his bed, his glasses (he hated that he needed them) positioned on his nose. But Google Earth couldn't do all that. No one could.

I read my horoscope, which predicted a happy ending to a "tempestuous" morning. I visited Delilah Rogers's blog where she promoted a new book and finally, I wound up at a magic eight ball site where I tossed my questions out to the universe.

Is Hollywood evil?

>>>>Favorable outcome.

Did my mail go to my dad's SPAM?

>>>>>>Unlikely prediction.

Does TJ love me?

>>>> Magic Eight Ball Must Rest.
Up yours, Magic 8 ball. You didn't read the postcard.

Eventually Google carried me back to Baltimore—back to
TJ. I Google-Earthed the brick circles of Fells Point, the purple-
cloaked Raven's stadium. The harbor was flecked with sailboats
like marshmallows. I could nearly hear the metal trash cans
scraping down Falls Road. If I thought it might've gotten me
home, I would have clicked my own blistered heels together.

I wrote an e-mail to Olive, thanking her for listening to me.
A few more students wandered into the lab. A few wandered
out. Then I heard it. The bzzzmmp. An e-mail. Maybe it was The
Forgiveness Diet people.

Or not.

From:rgoodman@mdk12.library.us.edu
To: Bethany Stern <bethanys@utopia.com>
Subject: Re: re: Gift

Jesus Christ, Bethany. Where did that come from? Did you really write all that?
Did your mom hack your account? IS THIS YOU, ELLEN? Jackie was pregnant?
Bethany's at a fat camp? Who's Doug? Where's Utopia? What in God's name
is going on?

Sweat drenched my back. I looked around for a trash can
because I honestly thought I might puke. Richard Goodman, aka
my father, read the e-mail. He got it. He got it. Thankfully, in the
midst of puke-rising panic, I had an idea. In hindsight, it was a
stupid idea, but someone with a better one didn't happen to be
there.

From: Bethany Stern <bethanys@utopia.com>
To: rgoodman@mdk12.library.us.edu
Subject: Please Ignore Emails from this Account

Dear Mr. Goodman,

Our records indicate that several unsuitable messages have been sent from camper accounts, this being one of thousands. If you have experienced any e-mails with questionable content, please disregard them. Please forgive us for any discomfort this may have caused. Our server was recently hacked by hackers from space.

Sincerely,

The staff

Given the circumstances, it wasn't half-bad. I mean computer glitches were blamed for 99% of the world's problems anyway. Accounts were always getting jacked with. Identities stolen. It was believable. Right?

From:rgoodman@mdk12.library.us.edu
To: Bethany Stern <bethanys@utopia.com>
Subject: Re: Please Ignore Emails from This Account

Nice try, Bee. That letter was a little too personal for a hacker. And I don't think your mother would admit to the half of it. I see, however, your mother's been successful in poisoning you and your sister against me. I never FLUNKED OUT of optometry school, by the way. I DROPPED out. Your mother couldn't stand to be married to someone whose main ambition in life was to stamp dates on cards or direct researchers to the almanacs. It always had to be BIG and IM-PRESSIVE with her and, let's not forget, PERFECT. Ashamed of you? She was ashamed of me. I could never provide her with the soccer mom fantasy and TALK SHOW life she was sure she deserved. Forget WATERCOLOR classes and mah-jongg lessons and synagogues off Stevenson Lane that we could never afford ...

Before I signed off, Wadooomp. Another e-mail.

From: rgoodman@mdk12.library.us.edu
To: Bethany Stern <bethanys@utopia.com>
Subject: Re:Re: Please Ignore Emails from This Account

Bethany,

Forget I said that. Forget what I said about your mom. I'm sorry. Tell me everything that happened. Start at the beginning. Tell me about Jackie and Doug. Tell me about THE INCIDENT. Tell me about your forgiveness jar (ouch. Next year I'll get you a gift card). Please. I want to know everything.

I concentrated on the loud-ticking clock, focused my eyes on the lab attendant, the students next to me, the flickering fluorescent light bulbs, anywhere but the e-mail. Good God. Someone put in a call to FEMA because my life was nothing short of a natural disaster. And here's what's worse. Not that I'd just been knocked in the face with a cell phone. Not that I fell for an idiotic diet commercial, not even that my dad had just read my fire-breathing dragon of an e-mail. What's worse than all that was that it was only ten o'clock in the morning. The day was still impossibly young. I hadn't even had breakfast yet.

Lafourche Parish Library

24

CARE PACKAGES

I KNEW UTOPIANS would be in the SUC (Student Union Complex) playing pool and video games like last Sunday afternoon, but it was still risky to be out where any camper or counselor could see me. Walking over to MontClaire, I'd aimed my eyes downward so intensely I nearly fell into the mermaid fountain when I passed it. Luckily, I arrived at the mailroom without incident and once inside, things looked quiet. I'd never been in there during the day, and now the sun slanted in the windows and dust motes swirled in front of the computers. Thankfully, the gifts and cards and food remained undisturbed in their slots. Only the scale had been returned to its rightful position by the plant. I made a beeline toward a candy-sized box, hoping to score my breakfast of champions, when, off to my right, a desk chair swiveled.

"I have been looking for you everywhere," said Cambridge. She sat up straight, her legs crossed. "Liliana and I checked the nurse's office and the library too. I had a suspicion you'd be here, though."

Cambridge sure looked natural behind that TA desk. The poster that claimed "Chemists Do It On The Table Periodically" and the Einstein bobbleheads all seemed to suit her. She only needed a lab coat.

"How did you get in here?" I asked, still shocked to see her.

She held up a keycard identical to the one in my pocket. "Tampa Bay swiped it off his counselor a few days ago."

Because I still wasn't sure whose side she was on, I tried to play it off like I'd just stumbled upon the stacks of cards and gifts.

"Wow. Remember when I said they were stealing our mail?"

Cambridge laughed then sipped from a Dr. Pepper (non-diet) can. "I'd say that's affirmative." Both of us surveyed the piles of loot scattered around the mailroom. I wondered how she managed to sit so close to her personal pile of gifts yet seemed so disinterested in them.

She pushed off the desk and spun her chair a bit. "So right after you left, Liliana cussed out Hollywood in Spanish. Called her a *pendeja* and some other stuff that involved her mother. I just thought that might make you feel better."

"It doesn't make me feel any better. Sorry."

OK, so maybe Cambridge had scored a point for tracking me down, but I wasn't about to forgive her stellar faux pas of ho-humming after Hollywood launched her phone. And even though it did make me feel slightly better knowing Liliana had my back, it didn't matter much considering she was only thirteen.

"Someone should have stopped Hollywood," Cambridge said now, pulling her legs underneath her in what I now knew was a lotus pose. She wobbled a little on the TA's desk chair, spinning herself faster and faster. "I don't know why nobody did anything. I don't know why I didn't do anything. I should have and I'm sorry."

I stared at my shoes so she couldn't see my tears. "I don't want to go back," I said, my throat thick. "Utopia sucks." Cambridge spun round and around, the chair edging closer to the cubicle's portable walls. Her hair whizzed out like fuzzy caterpillars.

"I can't say I blame you," she said.

Finally she stopped spinning, and her hair beads clacked together noisily. "Whoa," she said, looking a little dizzy. "So, Baltimore. What's your plan exactly?"

"I'm over Utopia. I'm going back to Baltimore."

Cambridge cocked an eyebrow. "Really?"

"As soon as I find a phone, I'm calling TJ. He'll be here in five days. Four if he drives at warp speed."

"What about in the meantime?" Cambridge asked. "Where will you stay? How will you eat?"

"I have other sources," I stated matter-of-factly. I didn't tell her that my sources involved the Tabitha Calliope Nelson care packages overflowing to her left. "I won't starve," I assured her. "Besides, I wouldn't worry about it. Just go back and tell Miss Marcia you never found me. Tell her you think I bled to death."

She was quiet for a beat, and I figured she was performing the basic arithmetic it took to put together her opened care packages and my weight gain. She leaned back in the chair, laced her hands behind her head, and looked either deep in thought or utterly premenstrual. I figured she was pissed at me for eating her food. I should have exercised some self-control for once.

"I'm sorry I ate your care packages," I started. "The crackers and marbled cheese. The Moose Crunch and an instant coffee packet or two. Or five. I can go to a store. Order you more from the Internet."

"That won't be necessary." She pointed to her mailbox. "Can you hand me those cards?"

I gave them to her, and she shuffled through them the way my mom did a stack of bills.

"Aren't you gonna open them?"

"No."

"What about the packages? Aren't you hungry?"

"No."

"There's a whole big box from Harry & David. I'm sure there's some kind of caffeine in there. More Moose Crunch."

"You're welcome to it, Bethany." She removed a letter opener from the desk drawer.

I knew I should not have been thinking about food, especially Cambridge's food, but now that I was AWOL, I should eat while I had the opportunity. That was my rationale anyway. The first box I ripped into was a Harry & David wicker basket filled with crappy pears. Thankfully these pears were complemented by caramel popcorn and peanut brittle. Behind me, I heard Cambridge slicing envelopes. A few ten dollar bills, escaped and she stacked them beside her.

"Your dad is definitely generous," I said, pinching off a triangle of peppermint bark.

"He's generous with apologies."

I motioned to her piles of cash. "Money too."

"Same thing."

I held up a bag. "You sure you don't want these chocolate-covered espresso beans? I really don't like coffee beans so much. Well, they're OK, but you're more than welcome. This is your food."

Cambridge rifled through the basket, squishing crimped paper through her fingers. "I'll tell you a secret, Baltimore," she said, laying the money in little heaps. Holy G's! Those weren't tens, they were hundreds! There had to be five piles, maybe more. Cambridge snapped them out, licking her thumb first. "Every summer, since I was thirteen, my mom goes abroad and me and my dad go to the Cape. Just me. Just him. And Whitney."

"Whitney?" Maybe that was the name of her horse.

"Whitney, his mistress." Cambridge had a way of looking directly at you when she said something important, making sure you didn't miss a word. "But this summer my mom didn't want us at the Cape. She said I should stay in Boston and volunteer for my community service credit. Obviously my dad had concerns about this." Cambridge continued stacking bills. "So my dad told my mom, 'I think Tabitha is getting too heavy. I think she should attend one of those summer weight loss camps before her senior year of Barrington.' Then my mom asked me if that sounded like something I would enjoy. I told her I didn't know." Cambridge then shook out the envelopes one last time before piling them up. "My dad, on the other hand, thought I'd enjoy it immensely."

I remember Cambridge's picture in her file. How fancy she'd looked in her riding clothes, the sunlight dappling the fall leaves behind her. How different she looked now, her shorts splotchy with dirt and her loafers downsized to red tennis shoes. She was still beautiful, mind you. Just grubbier.

"You're at fat camp so your dad could scrump his mistress?" I didn't mean to be so crass, but damn. Only Delilah Rogers could write her way out of that plot.

"In a manner of speaking, yes," Cambridge said. "I'm here

so he could go to the Cape house and resume his summer as planned, with Whitney." She tossed the unread cards and envelopes in the trash.

"Why didn't you say something?" I asked.

She folded the piles of cash and stuck the wad in her bra. "I would never do anything like that," she said, smiling falsely. "I'm the perfect child."

"Nobody's perfect," I said.

"Thanks," she replied. "I'll alert the media."

I didn't know why she was telling me this, but it suddenly made sense why she ignored the cards and food. She was furious. You'd think that would make her eat more, but even in her rage Cambridge was calculated, rational. And smart. So smart! She wouldn't need the expensive grade-grubbing classes to boost her ACT score by two points (I would). She was quicker than me, quicker than anyone I knew, and she saw things that whizzed by everyone else. Yet she didn't flaunt it. And I liked her for that.

"Does your dad like, know you know?"

Cambridge patted the cash in her bra. "I think he knows I know."

I felt a little stupid for eating her food, and guilty, I guess, but there it was, out of its cellophane, detached from its baskets, naked without its foil wrappers. Did I mention how much I love caramel popcorn? Honey roasted peanuts? As I shoveled them in it was more than apparent Cambridge, my roommate, wasn't a sucker. And I was.

"So that's my story," she said, tossing me a pear. "What's yours?"

Just before I could show her TJ's postcard, or get into my e-mail debacle or highlight the ways my life resembled a steaming pile of crap, a phone rang. It was that same irksome tinkle of a Disney World ringtone that Hollywood had. It ought to be illegal to have a ring that prissy. Some absentminded grad student must've left their phone in a desk drawer or something. Only the ring became louder, probably because Cambridge stood up and pulled a phone from her pocket. Hollywood's purple phone. "If you'll excuse me," she said, "looks like I have a call."

She brought it up to her ear and sang out a, "Good afternoon. Thank you for dialing Utopia, a camp unrivaled in starving teenagers. I mean offering healthy choices for today's youth." She spoke with confidence. "I'm deeply sorry, sir, but we have confiscated your daughter's phone due to extenuating circumstances. After several warnings, your daughter performed a scene worthy of her motherland, and our policy mandates repercussions. In light of this, we took her phone. It's only fair. Should you have any questions, please direct them to ..." Cambridge disconnected. "Now what were you saying, Bethany?"

I tried to talk, but couldn't. I sounded like Hank. "Hoo-Huuu-Haaa. Isn't that Hollywood's?"

Cambridge winked at me then, a smile lighting her face like a star. "It's yours now."

I had my doubts at first, but now I knew. Cambridge was a thief, and I could trust her completely.

25

HEARTBREAKING

"HEY, TJ. DID I wake you?"

"Bee? I saw that crazy area code. No, I'm just tired. I keep having these crazy dreams every night. You're in them."

"For real?"

"I had this one and I was on *American Envy,* and I vanished myself back to Magnet, right? I was wandering around thinking, *What am I doing still in high school?* And then Mrs. Garonzik was all *Toby Jacobson, you never turned in your Spanish journal,* and I was panicking. You know how she gets in your face?"

"Were you in her classroom with all the bullfighting posters?"

"We were in Vomit Hall. I kept trying to tell her that I was in the *AE* finals and I made myself disappear back to Baltimore by mistake. And you were there trying to convince Mrs. Garonzik that she wasn't even seeing me."

"I wonder what it means."

"I seriously never did turn in my journal, but it doesn't matter now. I'm officially a graduate."

"Sorry I missed it."

"No worries. How did you get a phone, or did they give you one phone call like in jail?"

"Actually, Utopia is a lot like prison."

"Lame. Hey, did you get my postcard? Unbelievable about *AE*, huh?"

"Not so unbelievable, TJ. You have skill."

"If you were here, I would levitate. I showed your mom yesterday, and she was screaming. You know how she is."

I laughed even though I felt like crying. Even TJ's voice could turn me inside out.

"My dad thinks I'm auditioning for *Paranormal Activity* part twelve."

"Well, he might think differently when you win."

"Maybe." TJ yawned. "Girl, it's all kinds of lonely. How many more weeks you got?"

My eyes moistened. "About that."

"What? What's happened?"

"Things are a hot mess. This girl Hollywood, she hates me. She threw her cell phone at me and busted my lip. She called me a poor heifer. And no one did anything." My voice began to shake. "Nothing! I think her dad is a shareholder. Or a movie producer. So I kind of ran away. No, I officially ran away. And this girl. My roommate. My friend. She's with me. She let me borrow the phone she stole. And then, well, Richard Goodman kinda had a breakdown. He bought me an e-reader."

"Your dad? Dang. This should be a reality show."

I inhaled deeply. "I want to come home, TJ. Do you think Rent My Ride would let you borrow a car for a week or so? I would drive myself, but I can't."

"You mean you're leaving Utopia?"

"Yes. If you can come pick me up."

The tears came before the words.

"I can't do that, Bee."

Tears fell harder.

"I have to go to New York and after that, who knows? I want you to come home, Bee. But I think you should stay."

"Ask your job! They let you drive cars all the time."

TJ laughed. "To Glen Burnie. Not California. You aren't crying, Bee. Are you?"

"It's fi—" I swallowed a hiccough. "I'm fine. I can't believe you want me to. You want me to stay here."

"I think you should."

"Why? Because I'm fat?"

"Partly. And partly because—"

"What?"

"All that stuff, Bethany. You know—what happened between us. It's nothing you did. It's not you. Please don't cry. It's just that how it is in your head, Bee. It's never gonna be that way."

"I just need a ride home, TJ."

"It's more than that. There's some serious stuff I need to tell you, but I can't do it now."

"So pick me up and tell me on the way home."

"I miss everything about you. But it's not gonna be like what you got in your head."

"So you won't come get me?"

"You're killing me here." I could hear a horn honking.

"You're in a rental car now, and you just can't head west for a few days? Take me home?"

"No. I can't. I'm sorry."

"I can't believe you'd leave me in Utopia." By now I was sobbing uncontrollably.

"Please don't cry, Bethany. Are you still there? There's a cop behind me. Can I call you back? Bee? You gotta let me go—"

26

REVELATION

SOMETIMES, IF NOTHING was on television, TJ and I watched the Jesus channel. This worried my mom—a Jew—and thrilled TJ's dad—a born-again—whenever we tuned in, but we didn't care. We found the channel entertaining.

Our favorite program featured this one preacher, and every single time we flipped past, every single time, he was crying. If he happened to be dry-eyed, we'd count the seconds until he opened the floodgates. The highest we ever got was five. The preacher TJ called "Friar Crier" sobbed without embarrassment. He was always talking about how weeping was good because it got you to see the light.

When that phone call ended, I wept like Friar Crier on the Jesus channel. Big holy sobs that doubled me over. Fat, wet tears slipped down my cheeks like rain. Friar Crier could not have been righter. I'd finally seen the light.

TJ didn't love me. He never would. He never did.

Of course the only thing worse than seeing that light in the mailroom, right in front of my fat camp roommate, was this. Everyone else had seen it first. Even Hollywood.

Cambridge was very civilized as TJ scooped my heart out with a shovel. She didn't get all *there, there*. She just sat on the floor next to me and undressed a Hershey's Kiss, which I ate. I lay down on the floor, still sobbing in spite of the chocolate, wanting really to just go to sleep and wake up in a different story. Preferably one that did not involve fat camp or a boy who thought I should stay there. I couldn't tell you how long I sat on the floor. One hour? Five? All I knew was Cambridge stayed with me the whole time. When I'd cried myself out, she stood up and thrust out her hand. "I think you need a drink," she said.

I studied her long fingers and the pink skin of her palm. I realized it was the most anyone had offered me in a long time. I put my hand in hers, and she eased me off the floor, out the annex door, and into the bright campus.

"I know this place," Cambridge said, skipping out into the flowering afternoon. "With frappuccinos so good"—her eyes fluttered in ecstasy—"so good, they'll break your heart."

27

QUICHE

THINGS LOOKED PRETTY bleak after my conversation with TJ, but it was hard to dwell when outside the sun glimmered like a stone fired straight out of Liliana's bedazzler. Sure, the love of my life brushed me off (again), but with Cambridge scaling hills and paths like a field guide, the promise of a frappuccino pulling her forward, my tears had no choice but to dry.

The library café was definitely going for an Emo theme, with hardcover books tossed around like they could afford to use them as decoration or coasters. There were a few geektastic students stuffed in their very own periwinkle barstools, wearing black-rimmed glasses and sipping from mugs. It could have been any coffee shop in Baltimore, with its small stage in the center and a chalkboard full of drinks: Tennyson Tea, Robert Frosty, cuppa Joe Heller, etc.

Even more beautiful were the glass-covered cases crammed with lemon pie, scones, blueberry muffins, buttery croissants, and the rotund bagels that called to me in sugary voices. The quiche was as thick as wedding cake. Cambridge ordered two vanilla frappuccinos with extra whipped cream, triple espresso, and an extra shot of caramel. I knew how pretentious it sounded to order quiche, so I let Cambridge do it for me. She added a chocolate chip scone for good measure, and the tray swayed under the weight.

We sat down in a corner booth because we didn't want to risk a run-in with any Utopians. "Forgot to mention," Cambridge said, positioning the quiche in the table's center and shaving off a sliver, "Tampa Bay might have discovered this place a few times without me because he gained three pounds. I wanted to tell you sooner. Our teams are still tied." She took a bite. "Oh my, this is good." She pushed the plate a little toward me and dabbed her mouth with a napkin. "I mean if you wanted some good news, it's possible we could still win."

I didn't care if we won. In fact *we* seemed like a historical pronoun. There was no *we* as far as I was concerned. I stared at the quiche before us: so much like an omelet on one hand, a pie on the other, yet not exclusively either. All life begins as an egg. That was TJ's line. He often delivered it as he juggled half a dozen of them for kicks. An hour ago he'd torn my heart out, and here I was thinking about him again. How long, I wondered, until that went away.

Just then I saw a figure lean out from a table near ours. My heart lurched.

"Oh crap," I said, wishing for a newspaper to hide behind. But it was too late. He'd spotted us.

"I thought that was you, Tabitha," said Tampa Bay, walking over. "Mind if I sit down?" Before we could answer, he squished down next to Cambridge, tapping her with his ample behind. He stretched and draped one arm over her shoulder, where it lounged like a slaughtered beast. "I knew I'd find you here." He stuck his finger (his finger!) in our quiche, then he smiled at Cambridge. "I've been searching for you everywhere."

For solving the world's most obvious mystery, he looked rather pleased with himself. Then he scooched closer to Cambridge, pinning her against the booth. He went back to our quiche, this time with her fork, moaning in boy pleasure with each bite. Cambridge swigged her frozen beverage while I waited for little cartoon hearts to shoot out from Tampa Bay's eyes.

"What are you doing here?" she asked him.

"Looking for you," he replied. "I told the counselors I felt sick. They think I'm at the nurse."

"No one followed you, did they?" I asked.

For the first time since he sat down, he looked directly at me.

"Damn. What happened to your lip?"

"Weren't you there when Hollywood threw her phone at me?"

"Oh, right. That was messed up."

From his file, I knew Tampa Bay liked to play ball. There was a report card in there too. Lots of C's, only one A in guitar. Then there was the whole parental divorce thing. I could ruin his day right now if I wanted to and, in a way, I really wanted to. I didn't like the way he looked at Cambridge, and I didn't want his finger in my quiche! But he seemed so visibly smitten with my roommate and her fuzzy, coiled hair, I couldn't do it. Our last bite of quiche, what did he do? He held it up to Cambridge, cupping his palm under her chin as she ate it. "Good, huh?" he asked, like he wanted her approval first.

"Well," he said, "I gained weight too. It just means we gotta work double time next week, Bethesda."

"Baltimore."

"Right. Baltimore. You just have to do better next week. No B-F-D."

Sure.

"Well," I said, taking my cue. I knew when I wasn't wanted. "This has been beyond fun, but I really have to get going."

Tampa Bay looked relieved, while Cambridge looked confused. "Do you have a place to hide?" she asked.

"Not exactly." I thought about my options. "I'll see if my sister will pick me up."

"Doesn't she hate you?" asked Cambridge.

"Yes, but it doesn't hurt to ask."

Tampa Bay adjusted himself in the booth and tugged at his baseball cap. "Why don't you just go back to Utopia and stop eating so much?"

Why do the most obvious answers sound the least appealing?

Cambridge slid her empty cup to the table's edge. "Before you do anything rash, maybe you should just think about things. Perhaps a little sabbatical from camp might do you well."

Tampa Bay gripped the tiny fork. "What's there to think about? She should just go back and kick Hollywood in the teeth. Then lose some weight. Am I right, Tabitha?"

Cambridge was silent. As was I.

Tampa Bay pointed out some of Utopia's highlights. "This place is great, and the people are alright. They want to help you achieve your goals." He had now moved on to our chocolate chip scone. "I mean my counselor, Courtney, he has helped me so much. Two-pointer? I got that. One-on-one? Done. The food sucks, but if you sneak out once in a while, you'll live. And just think how much hotter you'd both be if you dropped thirty or forty pounds." He zeroed in on Cambridge. "Tabitha, you especially. You'd be smokin' if you lost weight. You must know that. I mean *perfect*." He wolfed down our scone like an afterthought.

Cambridge ignored him. "I know a place you could hide, Baltimore. A place they'd never look."

Tampa Bay dropped the fork. "Why are you complicating it? Just. Go. Back. It's perfectly simple."

Cambridge pulled her hair back and fastened it with a plain rubber band. She had this habit before she did anything requiring strength: swimming, aerobics, getting weighed, eating. Then, to my surprise, she stood up in the booth and stepped over his lap.

"No, it's not," she spat. Her hands were planted by her sides. "I'm almost as tired of being perfect as I am of being hungry," she said. "I never wanted to come here in the first place."

Tampa Bay shredded a napkin into tiny pieces. "Then why did you?" he asked.

Cambridge seemed to consider this. "Good question," she noted.

"Well go then," said Tampa Bay, changing tactics. "Go show her the hiding place. But come back, right?" Tampa Bay continued. "Please come back, Cambridge." He was begging! "I want to see you again. You know, at night. You never even took your bra off with me."

"Is this about my boobs" asked Cambridge, pointedly.

Tampa Bay shook his head no, which, as I understood it, meant yes. "You are just so worried about everything. Worried about becoming valedictorian. Worried about sneaking out of camp at night. I just want to see you more. "

Cambridge jumped from the booth and was next to me now. When she turned around to leave, Tampa Bay stood so suddenly that the café workers stared.

"I didn't intend that to be mean," he whined. He raised his voice a notch. "Just come back later. I don't care about your boobs!"

He said something after that too, but I couldn't hear him. We were already walking toward the door. Cambridge, not even turning around to deliver her golden insult, hissed, "You'll have to remember my ass, Simon, because you ruined any chance of seeing my spectacular breasts."

From:rgoodman@mdk12.library.us.edu
To: Bethany Stern <bethanys@utopia.com>
Subject: waiting…

Dear Bethany,

You haven't written me back and I can't say I blame you. I really wish you'd elaborate on your e-mail. I think I've read it a hundred times. I don't understand some of the things you wrote and I'd like to. I know you think I've forgotten all about you, but I haven't.

For example.

I met your mother in speech class at Catonsville Community. When I saw her deliver her two minute impromptu, she was so poised. I was from Catonsville. She was from Pikesville. We were twenty years old and had no shot. Naturally she convinced me otherwise.

After we separated, looking back at the life we had together became painful. I told myself that you & Jackie were better off without me. This assumption was costly and stupid. You don't have to tell me you forgive me or that it's ok. You don't have to tell me anything. But if you did, I would gladly listen. I had no idea you were at a weight loss camp. I don't know who TJ is either.

I will tell you, however, your English teacher was a moron. Spelling is overrated. A good story comes down to voice and character. You've got all that (and then some). Trust me, I'm a librarian. I would know.

Please write me back.

Yours truly,

Dad

28

CARDIO

RIGHT NOW THE campers would be drying off before heading back to the dining hall for rubbery chicken breast with string beans and spray-on butter. Me and Cambridge? We were in the state-of-the-art fitness center located on the other side of campus. I must've missed the speech, but Cambridge told me Miss Marcia had "encouraged" campers to use the facility during their free time. With just one swipe of our Utopia cards, these three levels of cardio equipment, two Olympic-sized indoor pools, and racquetball courts were all ours. Props to Cambridge for the suggestion. It was, as she informed me pushing through the turnstile earlier, counterintuitive.

We settled on the sofa behind the elliptical machines and watched TV. After a few too many dirty looks from the cardio crusaders, Cambridge and I took the elevator to the third floor, parked our butts on some beanbag chairs, and now shared a peanut butter chocolate banana protein smoothie.

Somehow the day had slipped by, and outside the windows the sun crawled down the skyline. "I guess I should be heading back now," Cambridge said as we both watched, somewhat sadly, the smoothie-maker wash out blenders and sweep the floor. "I wouldn't want to miss my sugar-free popsicle." I laughed at that, but then realized Cambridge was probably right. It was getting late, and I was sure Miss Marcia or Belinda or Hank had noticed our departure.

"Do you think Tampa Bay said something? You dogged him pretty hard earlier."

Cambridge leaned back on her beanbag. "Oh, he wouldn't do that." She looked at me. "You know what? I've never run away before, and it feels kind of good. It's fun."

She did look relaxed in her squishy chair. She'd even slipped off her shoes. "After your conversation with TJ, I feel bad about leaving you too."

Even though I wasn't sure, I said, "Don't worry about me. I'll be fine."

Cambridge picked at her dreads. "Would it be weird if I stayed with you? Just for the night? We can both go back tomorrow and explain everything."

I shrugged. "Tomorrow's not looking so good either. For me anyway."

Cambridge flexed her bare feet. "I bet you'll feel differently in the morning. That's how it is. I'll go back to being me. You'll go back to being you. But tonight I want to take a hot shower, eat energy bars, and sleep on one of those dreamy sofas in the cardio room. I don't want anyone to know where I am." She smiled. "You ever feel like that?"

Did I ever. Still I worried a little. Miss Marcia would notice I was gone, but she might write it off as mortification. She wouldn't push it. But with two of us MIA, it looked bad. Real bad. That in mind, the best thing to do would be to thank Cambridge and send her on her way. Figure out my own sitch. The more I thought about it, though, the more I realized how much I enjoyed having her there. Besides, what if I accidentally locked myself in the sauna room? More terrifyingly, what would I do without the smoothies and chocolate chip scones she'd been financing all day? It wasn't like *my* dad had slipped me a few hundreds. Underneath all that, though, I liked her. This girl had seen me at my absolute worst, and she didn't get freaked about it. I guess you could say that an invisible thread had crossed between us—and knotted. In a few short hours, she'd become the best thing to come out of this lousy, no-good, craptastic day. Someone make a note on my file: *I had a friend.*

Cambridge took the smoothie and shook it to loosen the bits

on the bottom. "So is it OK if I hang out with you just for to-night?"

"Absolutely."

To celebrate, we ordered a last-call protein smoothie—no banana. We finished off four energy bars before heading down to the locker room, which by six thirty on a Sunday night was deserted. Steam licked our ankles while a whirlpool sloshed in the distance.

I was about to tell Cambridge that if Jackie agreed to come get me, she'd probably be willing to give Cambridge a ride home, at least as far as Baltimore anyway. Only before I offered, a tune startled both of us. I wondered why the gym was clogging the locker room with the theme to *Rocky*, but then I remembered that I'd changed Hollywood's ringtone. We both looked to my bra.

"You should answer it," said Cambridge, nervously.

I looked at its dazzling blipping lights in my hand. "Camp Utopia," I offered timidly.

"Oh shut the hell up with your Camp Utopia," said Liliana. "I knew Cambridge stole that phone. I saw her grab it, that sneaky *culebra. ¡Dios!* Hollywood's thong is in a bundle: How am I gonna call Papi? Where's my lawyer? You two are in a shit cyclone. I can't even tell you."

"Hi, Liliana," I said. "How did you get a phone?"

"My brother tossed his up to me. He can't stop laughing. He says you two got *muchos huevos!*"

"We have big eggs?"

"Balls! Anyway, Miss Marcia is all wondering why you're taking so long at the nurse's office. She's about to put the campus security on your ass."

"We're thinking of something," I said, trying to think of something.

"Girl, I already did. I told her the nurse gave you a painkiller for your lip. She thinks you're in here with Cambridge now, all sleeping peacefully. I asked for privacy and she said, 'of course, of course.'" I heard muffled noises as she yelled something down to her brother. "But you gotta be back by tomorrow morning, *es-cuchame?* Hollywood knows something's up. I locked the door to our room." I pictured Liliana leaning out the window, her butt covered in jewels. I missed her. "And another thing, *putas*, if you're in the neighborhood, stop by and visit."

Before I hung up, I thanked her for defending me.

"You can thank me with chocolate, *sabes*? Seriously, where are you? Is there candy there? I'll be waiting by my window. Chock. Oh. Lat. Tay. Come now."

In the end, it looked like Cambridge's wish was fulfilled. We had the night off. Thank God our youngest roommate with the big huevos had covered for us. Cambridge and I watched a few more reruns of *American Envy* before hitting up the vending machine. There, in order to thank Liliana for safeguarding us, we bought her two chocolate chip energy muffins. They were gluten free and made with Splenda, but it was the best we could do, given the circumstances.

29

FAN CLUB

WHEN WE GOT to MontClaire Hall, Liliana's brother, Gabe, was wobbling on his skateboard beneath our dorm's window. We tossed a few beads from Cambridge's hair at him until he saw us. He shook our hands like we were celebrities. "You ladies caused some historical stuff right there."

"Look at her blushing!" said Cambridge, pointing at me. "But it really was all Bethany's idea."

We threw the paper bag filled with Liliana's chocolate muffin up to her window, where it thudded back down on the sidewalk. Gabe picked it up and sent it past Liliana's head like a missile. In exchange, she threw down two pairs of underwear and our pajamas.

"Let me get this straight," she said, digging into the bag, "you never actually went to the nurse?"

I shook my head.

She tore at her muffin like an animal. "Well, Tampa Bay confirmed the story."

"What story?" I asked.

"The one I made up. He said he saw you in the nurse's office and said you were really hurt. Miss Marcia was sweatin'!"

Cambridge jabbed me with her elbow. "I told you he wouldn't rat us out."

Liliana whispered hoarsely, "Even Hollywood fell for it.

Yuck! This muffin tastes disgusting. Is it diabetic? Did you think I wouldn't notice?" She threw half at it at Gabe. "Did you tell them to get me sugar-free, you bastard?"

"We have been staying at the gym," I apologized. "It's all they had."

"The gym?" Gabe laughed hard between us. "Brilliant."

Hollywood's curtains were drawn, her room dark and silent. Beauty sleeping, no doubt. It was after midnight. Part of me hoped we wouldn't wake her, but another part of me wished we would. That same part of me really wanted to throw a rock at her face. Or a grenade.

Liliana tossed the rest of her muffin in the bushes. "Make sure you guys are back in the morning for our power walk. And please bring me some real chocolate."

"You can't have real chocolate," Gabe warned.

"Will you get off my ass?" Liliana pushed a little further out the window. "Hey, Bethany, why don't you show my brother a good time? Introduce him to chocolate and maybe a few other things. He would really like that. *Right*, Gabe?"

"Shut up, *'mana.*"

"What do you say, Bethany?" asked Liliana. "Go show Gabe some things."

What kinds of things did she mean? "Like fondue?"

Liliana laughed so hard and loud I really thought she'd wake up half of Utopia. "Yes. By all means, go have a fondue with Gabe. He could use one." She pulled her curtains closed and told us she had to go—she really had to go and piss herself now.

Cambridge and I traveled a little farther down the path while Gabe skated circles around us. The sky was dark and a few stars blinked above MontClaire Hall. "What should we do now?" Cambridge asked. She turned to Gabe, teeter-tottering on his skateboard. "What have you been doing at night?"

He cleared his throat, tugged at his band T-shirt with the word "SPOOGE" spray painted across it. "Well, sleeping, mostly. Sometimes homework."

"Don't you guys party in math camp?"

Gabe chuckled. His shoes, silver and black Vans, shimmered a little in the night. "It's robotics and rocketry camp. Not exactly a frat house over there." He looked at me. "What do you want to do? I mean, tonight."

I sure as hell did not want fondue, if that's what he was getting at. "I need to really figure some stuff out, you know."

Looking a little embarrassed, he pumped his back leg off the skateboard and pushed down the path. Cambridge and I walked back to the gym, the moon rising like a sucked-on peppermint above us.

From:rgoodman@mdk12.library.us.edu
To: Bethany Stern <bethanys@utopia.com>
Subject: still waiting

Dear Bethany,

Other stuff I remember.

Because I wore glasses, your mom reasoned, I would be a natural expert on eyesight. A future in optometry would earn a lot of money for our family. It was a respectful career. I'd get to wear a white coat. The program director at UMBC sat me down and told me how fascinating the eye is. After two classes, I found it complicated and boring.

Jackie was a toddler, and you were a baby then. I didn't care about lenses and corneas. What I liked was hanging out with you two kids and reading books. God, how you both loved one called IF YOU WOKE UP WITH WINGS. Do you remember it? It was about this ravenous caterpillar that eats six watermelons, seven cabbages, and then goes on to consume fifteen carburetors and then an entire neighborhood. Everyone gets tired of waking up to missing cars and depleted pumpkin patches, and the neighborhood prepares to confront this nuisance. Only then the caterpillar wakes up as a butterfly, and says, very self-righteously, "I was growing wings."

I read that book so often to you girls that I didn't even need to look at the words. I could recite it from memory. Still can. I've forgotten your birthday, Bethany. More than once. But I do remember some things. Please write me back. Tell me about Utopia. I checked out the website. Looks nice!

Yours truly,

Dad

From: ellenstern@zyprexapharm.com
To: Bethany Stern <bethanys@utopia.com>
Subject: Oversight?

Bee,

I'm supposed to get an update from Hank and Belinda with a chart of your progress. I did not get one tonight. I'm sure there was an oversight somewhere. How did this week's weigh-in go? I'm sure it was meaningful! I was also wondering if you've heard from your sister. I keep trying her cell phone, but she doesn't pick up. I'm beginning to worry. If you hear from her, tell her to call me right away.

Write soon...Mom

30

TREMOR

MONDAY MORNING AT the gym. Tennis shoes squeaked, headphones leaked out techno. The whirlpool slopped in the background. University girls jogged around in sports bras and thongs like any other ordinary day, I guessed, but here's the thing: I still didn't want to go back to Utopia.

Cambridge stretched on the locker room's bench. "We have to be back by power-walk, Bethany. Come on."

There was a part of me that really believed I might wake up and think, *OK, enjoyed the night, now it's time to head back to fat camp.*

"Not happening," I said, rubbing my crusty eyes and wishing desperately for toothpaste. "I can't do it, Cambridge. I'm sorry."

"Bethany, be real. Where are you going to go?"

"I'm going to call my sister."

"And you seriously think she'll pick you up?"

"I seriously think she might."

Cambridge washed her face and shook her dreads out. "Do you realize the consequences of this?" she asked, looking like a TA again. "You're making a very bold decision."

I told her yes, I was aware of the consequences, and I'd have to charge the phone soon, especially if she planned on calling me on it, but this was my decision. I was standing by it.

"At least walk me back, OK?" she asked. "Walk me as far

as the fountain." I could tell by the way she dawdled in front of the steamy mirror and tied and retied her tennis shoes that she hoped I'd change my mind.

Walking back to MontClaire Hall was like swimming through marshmallow fluff. The fog hung densely, and the campus stood eerily quiet. In the distance, birds cawed from unseen branches. Though we were late, hurrying was impossible given how cloudy everything looked. By the time we made it to the trickling mermaid fountain, Miss Marcia's words boomeranged around us: "Where're Cambridge and Santa Fe? Did you get Baltimore?"

Hollywood's voice stopped me dead in my tracks. "I tried. They locked the door last night."

A rustling sound from a clipboard followed. "That should have been your cue to apologize to her."

"Why on earth would I do that? You know who my father is."

Miss Marcia sighed. "Not everyone wants to be a size two, Hollywood."

"Well not everyone wants to be a size twenty-two either. Plus, I think the black girl took my phone. Maybe it was the Mexican. I bet they ordered pizzas all night. That's probably why the door was locked."

I couldn't see her through the fog, but I didn't have to. As horrible as Hollywood was in my imagination, she was worse in person. All around us, her voice echoed.

"I'll just make them run harder today."

"Hollywood," Miss Marcia hissed, "I think you might be taking this captain role too seriously." MontClaire's main door squeaked open.

"Where are your roommates, Santa Fe?" asked Miss Marcia. "I haven't seen them since yesterday."

Poor Liliana. We shouldn't let her squirm like this. I nearly pushed Cambridge out from our station behind the tree, but she wouldn't budge.

"*No escuchas.*"

Hollywood inquired sharply, "Baltimore? Cambridge? *¿Donde?*"

"*No hablo Inglés.*"

"Where are the other girls, Santa Fe?" asked Miss Marcia.

Someone coughed. I thought I heard the shuffling of feet.

"Ummm," said Liliana. She was a very bad liar. "They wouldn't wake up. They're still sleeping. Must've been those painkillers. Knocked their asses down, *verdad.*"

"Were they in bed this morning?"

"*No comprendo.*"

"Did they even come back, Liliana?"

"*¿Qué?*"

"Good riddance," said Hollywood. I'd bet you a million bucks she flipped her hair here. "Dead weight anyway. Let's get started with the run, ladies."

"The run? Forget the run, Hollywood," Miss Marcia's voice rang out loud and panicked. "We are missing two campers."

"Obviously you are missing them more than me," said Hollywood, her voice bent down in a stretch.

This was the exact moment we stepped through the fog and said, "Liliana! Girls! Campers! We missed you. Let's run, run, run. We're back and ready to work harder than ever."

Only that moment never happened.

What did happen was my stomach growled so intensely the earth shook. At least I thought it was my stomach when then the tree swayed, and the bikes chained to racks rattled. Then the ground, well, it rolled—not dramatically, but it vibrated a snitch. Not ever having experienced the sensation except when standing on the sidewalk while a semi darted past, I was convinced it was the end of the world.

"Did you feel that?" Cambridge whispered. Before I could answer, we both looked at the canopy of leaves quivering above us as if a breeze tickled them. Only there was no actual breeze. Then a deep sound growled below our feet. Cambridge went to scream, thought better of it, then pulled me away. We ran aimlessly through the fog, the earth grumbling. We hurried past the duck pond that shifted and splashed, until we found ourselves in the library café again. The barista said, "That was a four point two, easily."

Then a bzzz, bzzz, bzzzz, zip. Darkness.

"There goes the electricity," said the cashier, like this sort of thing happened all the time. "The generator should click on in a few."

In an inky black, the earth now quiet beneath us, I barely got the words out, "What. Was. That?"

I heard Cambridge breathing heavily beside me. "I'm no seismologist, but I think that was an earthquake." She paused to catch her breath. "For a minute there I thought the world was ending."

"Me too."

"I know it's ridiculous, but here I thought the ground was going to crack open and lug me down into its gut, and I was going to die." She exhaled. "I was going to die at Utopia. During a power walk." She grabbed my elbow and squeezed. "My life flashed before my eyes like in the movies."

"It's OK," I said. "I think the earthquake's over."

"No," said Cambridge, "you don't understand. When my life flashed before my eyes, it was so quiet. And serene."

"So?"

"It was boring, Bethany. A total yawn." Her voice was thick, like she might be crying, only it was too dark too tell. "I've always done everything right. I've never even had detention." She loosened her grip on my elbow. "I should have taken off my bra with Tampa Bay."

"That's what you were thinking?"

"Well, yes. You have to do the stuff you're afraid to do. And I haven't done anything."

"Example?"

"Like everything. I want to try every single thing."

We heard a loud metal click followed by a whining whir. The café stirred to life. Cambridge faced me in this new light, which was somehow brighter than before. Her shoes and calves were splattered with mud. Hands on her hips, eyes shiny with tears, she pulled her dreads back and wrapped the rubber band around them. Then she looked at me, serious as a heart attack, and said, "I'm not going back either."

31

TWO TO GO

THE THING ABOUT California earthquakes was that life there went back to normal about twenty seconds after the last aftershock trembled. Lights flickered on. Conversations started up again. Coffee resumed its drip. But for me and Cambridge, we needed some time to adjust. We tiptoed through the café, found a table, planted our feet on the floor, and gripped the table's edges just in case the earth took to wobbling again. Given we were both from the East Coast, we kind of assumed that things—things like the ground—stayed put. Not so. Now the world seemed doughy, much like the still-warm chocolate-drizzled croissants and blueberry scones on the plate between us.

"I want to drive across the country," said Cambridge. She drank her frappuccino with gusto. "I want to see the whole country. I want to make dinner reservations and be late. And then," she said, smiling like a fool, "I want to eat non-organic food. Mashed potatoes and gravy. I want to purchase tobacco products and smoke them." She bit into a croissant. "I want to talk on my cell phone while I drive."

Did she just say drive? Of course! I'd almost forgotten she was older than me by a couple of years.

"So let's do it," I said. "Let's rent a car and drive across the country!"

"Erm," Cambridge started. She bit her cheek. "I was speaking metaphorically. I actually can't drive." She cast her eyes downward. "You don't really need a car in Boston or boarding school, and my mom's always been a mite overprotective, so I never learned." She dunked a cloud of whipped cream into her coffee. "I thought you said Jackie'd come get us."

"My sister's kind of a long shot," I admitted.

Cambridge nodded toward my bra where, tucked inside, the cell phone ran low on power. "This seems to be the summer of the long shot. Give her a call."

I swallowed a decadent bite of scone and glugged my iced coffee. I steeled myself and touched the phone. "What if I just text her?"

"Absolutely not. You need desperation in your voice, not emoticons."

"I'll use extra exclamation points."

"Not the same thing."

"Did I mention that she despises me?"

"Several times, but she's still your sister." She fixed her gaze on me. "There aren't too many other options here, Bethany. Call her."

Luckily someone picked up on the first ring. Only thing was, it wasn't my sister.

"Doug?"

"Is this you, Bethany? What the hell are you calling for?"

In the background I heard thumping bass. "I wanted to talk to my sister."

"Jackie can't talk right now. What do you want?"

Knowing Jackie never left her cell, I tried again. "Put her on the phone, Doug."

"What part of *she can't talk now* don't you understand?"

I looked to Cambridge for guidance. She mimed note-writing.

"Fine, Doug. Can you give her a message then?"

Doug's silence went on for at least fifteen seconds. "A message. That's great. Yeah, I'll give her a message."

Cambridge fanned her fingers around her heart, urging me to amp up my emotions.

She mouthed *speaker*.

"So where is she?" I asked, clicking the speaker button.

"Bethany, are you calling for a reason? What's your message? I'm not exactly over the whole road trip either. You were a complete shit with your little heartbreak jar. You ruined my life."

I could not deny these things, so I didn't.

"Whatever," I said, hoping that Doug had the brain cells to remember a message. "Can you just let Jackie know that things aren't so good here." Dramatic pause. "The nurse told me I have a thyroid condition, and I need to leave camp right away. It's rather severe. Jackie needs to come get me ASAP." Across from me, Cambridge went on with her charades. She begged me to cry—to sob like I had yesterday in the mailroom—but I knew where this was going.

Doug laughed. "Your thyroid? Nice try, Bethany." The bass quieted. "Your mom paid so much money for that place! What is your problem?"

"Will you just tell her?"

I tried to listen for Jackie in the background—her voice or laughter. Maybe she was asleep or driving. The more closely I listened, the more slurpy, sniffling noises I heard. Wet sounds. Maybe Doug had a cold. "Are you writing this down, Doug?"

"You know," he replied and his voice seemed caught in the bottom of his throat, "I'm even going to miss you too. I mean, I'll miss her more, but you, you were always with her, and you always said this crazy stuff that made us crack up. She really did want you to lose weight," he said. "She used to talk about it all the time. How she wanted you to find some guy who would appreciate you." He sucked back some serious snot. "God, you were always so hungry, Bethany."

Cambridge looked at me confusedly.

"Doug. Why are you saying this? Where is my sister?" This definitely wasn't funny anymore. "Put her on the phone, Doug."

"She left," he said. "I don't know where she is. She said she's done with me."

"What? She left? Left you where?"

Beneath his words, now softer, I heard him laugh. "On the side of the road in California. She kissed my cheek and everything. Before she drove off she gave me her phone. Told me to keep it. This is the first time I actually answered it."

I was silent. Dead silent.

Doug sighed. "Your thyroid's OK? You were just bullshitting, right?" he asked. "I'm sure Jackie will pick you up in five weeks, but I don't know where she is now," he said, and his voice sounded like an old man's. "She was so happy you were at Utopia. She knew you'd love it. Do you love it?"

Maybe because he sounded so sad and so lost and so nostalgic, I lied. "It's not that bad," I found myself saying. "This is a dream come true."

"Well, if she comes back," said Doug, "I'll be sure to tell her you called."

Cambridge lunged for the phone, probably to tell Doug what we'd both figured out: Jackie wasn't coming back. For any of us. I held the phone above my head as Doug's words clattered around the café. "Just hang in there," Doug bartered as Cambridge clawed my arm. "Forget about that diet too." He was quiet for a beat, and even Cambridge looked at the phone I held like a torch above me. "It's a fraud ..." The phone beeped three times. Low battery. "My mom gained everyth—"

"Well, that ends that," I said, clamping it shut. "Phone's dead."

Cambridge dug at the syrupy residue cemented to her glass. "What is it with your family and cell phones?" she asked. "Your sister gives hers away. One hits you in the face."

Damn right. How weird that Jackie's journey had somehow paralleled mine. Maybe at the exact moment Hollywood's phone hit my face, Jackie slapped hers in Doug's hand. I was done with fat camp. She was done with him.

"Do you think your sister's OK?" Cambridge asked.

I thought long and hard about that. When I replied, "Absolutely," I meant every syllable. After all, dumping Doug wasn't proof that Jackie'd gone crazy. It was proof that she'd finally come to her senses. "But I don't think she'll be picking us up."

Cambridge aimed a finger at a row of computers whose sign cautioned FOR LIBRARY RESEARCH ONLY. "Tell you what," she said. "Let's research our predicament. Check the Internet. Reference a few books. Certainly we aren't the first girls to run away from fat camp."

Cambridge steepled her hands. "There's always a precedent."

While my fellow fugitive roommate combed the Internet and electronic card catalogue for precedents, I opened the e-mail that had just wadoomped into my inbox like a scroll from a carrier pigeon.

From: olivekretchky@cup.edu
To: Bethany Stern <bethanys@utopia.com>
Subject: Quake

Bethany~

I woke up at six with the earthquake and was worried about you. Are you feeling better? Did you ever unfreeze your computer? I hope so. I should have stayed and talked more yesterday, but I had some business to take care of. If you need help, I live in Poindexter, 10B. It's located on the North side of campus, near the bookstore. You should stop by.

Olive

32

RSVPs

"Who's with you?"

I worried this might happen. Once Olive stuck her head out her Poindexter dorm and learned there were two of us, she hesitated. "This is Cambridge," I said as gently as I could. "My roommate. She, um, she ran away too."

Thankfully, Olive opted for C. U. P. hospitality. "Must be Guantanamo over there," she said, ushering us in. Once inside her room, Cambridge presented Olive with the shot glass we'd bought at the bookstore—along with our new wardrobe of C.U.P.-branded gear and a phone charger—on the way over. "For your troubles."

"Thanks," replied Olive. "But I don't drink."

Olive wore the same blue dress as yesterday, but she'd changed her dimple piercings to emeralds. Her dorm room was about the same size as the one we'd shared with Liliana, only somehow she had scored a single. The girl had a thing for plants. In heavy ceramic pots, hanging in baskets from the ceiling, blossoming from plastic jugs over her headboard and desk, various types of foliage crept and curled. Her dorm smelled smoky, leafy, and moist, a tang underneath it—maybe fertilizer. In the window, she'd hung an Indian tapestry, making the place dark and cool.

Cambridge and I inched out of the doorway, but hadn't fully

entered her room. There was something sacred about it.

"How'd you manage a single?" Cambridge asked, checking out the Post-it notes stuck up and down Olive's walls.

"The university keeps assigning me roommates, but they never last. One couldn't stand that I smoked cigarettes," Olive said, and then lit a long brown one to prove it. "Another one didn't like all the wildlife, and the last one was moody, period. She said I snored."

Cambridge pulled down a paper. "Usually, you have to be an athlete or bipolar to bunk alone. I'd count my blessings if I were you." She examined the Post-it. "These are good. Are you an art student?"

"No, I'm studying horticulture. I'm trying to learn how to tattoo for extra money, because my financial aid got cut. I'm on academic probation now." She sucked on her cigarette until the tip glowed. "So what's up with the camp mutiny?" she asked, eyeing us both. "I mean, are your parents coming to get you?"

I looked at Cambridge's red shoes with the white laces. I willed her to speak for me—to say something intelligent in her prep school words and make it appear we knew what we were doing, but she only asked Olive for a smoke.

"Well," I began, "that's not really an option. Our camp counselors have no clue where we are, but our parents don't either. You see, Olive, how should I phrase this?" My eyes rested on leaves of a fern tickling her head. "We're screwed."

Cambridge piped up. "We're looking for a ride, preferably one that would take us across the country, but we're not real particular."

Sitting at the chair in front of her desk, Olive pulled her bare feet under her and picked at her toes. "I don't have a car on campus," she said. "We aren't allowed. What about a bus? San Francisco has a huge Greyhound station, you know. You could probably mooch a ride from a student into San Francisco. Some go on the weekends, so you might have to wait awhile."

Cambridge plopped down on Olive's rumpled bed. "That's a good idea, Olive. Do you think we could. If we ..." Cambridge smiled diplomatically. "If we could crash here with you. Just for a night or two. "

I tried to look pathetic. "Or longer."

Our "maybe" hostess flicked her cigarette in an Aquafina bottle, where it sizzled. "Oh, I don't know," she said. "The last thing I need is more illegal activity in my dorm room, and I'm pretty sure harboring minors is illegal."

Cambridge blew a fluttering smoke ring. For a nonsmoker, she was a natural. "I'm not a minor for much longer."

"But I am," I volunteered. At least I was being honest. "For two more years, anyway."

Cambridge twisted sideways and unzipped the new California University of the Pacific fanny pack we'd just purchased at the bookstore. "We'll pay you," she said, holding a fifty between two fingers.

Even though Olive looked at the bill the way I have leered at a plate of crab and cheese wontons, she said, "I can't take money from you. You're kids."

Cambridge tapped the Post-it. "Just imagine I'm paying you for a service you haven't rendered yet."

"And what service is that?"

"Say I wanted this tattoo. How much would you charge me?"

"Cambridge!" I blurted.

"Relax," she said. "I'm speaking metaphorically."

Olive shook her head. "I've only practiced on fruit anyway."

"Say I trust you."

Olive rolled her eyes. "Hundred bucks."

Cambridge dropped the bill in Olive's already outstretched hand. "Then consider this a down payment."

When Olive's fingers closed around the money, she sighed dejectedly. "You can stay for a little while," she said. "Only until you find a ride. And you need to be actively searching!"

Even though she accepted the money halfheartedly, she still accepted it, which meant we could stay. It took every ounce of restraint not to scream with joy. Olive had two whole beds and a laptop! She had a dorm fridge and a Tupperware container of brownies!

Our hostess slid the cash into the pocket of her blue dress. "But I have two conditions."

"What conditions?" I asked, hoping they involved eating all her brownies and using her computer.

"First, I have to go out tonight, and when I do, you guys need to stay here. Don't answer the door or leave the room. Got it?"

Cambridge's eyebrow arched. "Where do you have to go?"

Olive twirled her dimple rings. "The drama department is having a par—" She stopped. "Gathering. It's extremely important I attend."

When Cambridge suggested, "Why don't you bring us with you?" it sounded almost rational. Even Olive appeared to consider it. For three seconds.

"Not a chance," she replied, latching her front door. "You girls are locked in. I have Rock Band on my computer and movies on demand. Have at it." She paused in front of her closet, looked at us hard, and said, "And now for the second condition," and then swung open the closet door.

When I saw the red lights suspended from the metal poles and the strange plants and vines winding around the bottom, I full-on gasped. Where normal people lined their shoes, glass terrariums and clay pots were piled high. The smell of dirt was suffocating. "You have to promise me you won't say a word about anything you saw here," Olive instructed. She aimed a water bottle and began spritzing her plant life. "Not one word. Promise me."

"I swear," I said.

A few flies could have set up camp in Cambridge's mouth. "No trouble at all," she replied mechanically.

"Swear to me," urged Olive.

"I swear," repeated Cambridge, but it came out more like a question.

33

PRODUCT PLACEMENT

RE: OLIVE'S FOREST.

For much of the afternoon, I ignored it. So what if the nice hippie had an emerald city growing in the dorm closet? Perfectly normal. She'd said she was studying horticulture after all. Extra credit, I assumed. And the people knocking on her door? Wanting the brownies she kept stored in the Tupperware container on her desk? Maybe Olive had a lot of friends and a weakness for Betty Crocker. No harm in that. For much of the day, I used her computer and pretended all sophomores had rain forests blossoming next to their bathrobes. And when an Internet search of her local flora confirmed what any half-witted troglodyte already knew, I zipped my mouth. She agreed to let us stay, so why start in with questions about her gardening club? Bad manners. Instead I resolved to take her advice and find a Greyhound bus out of town. Only when I gingerly lifted a chocolate square from the Tupperware bin, Olive snatched my wrist. "Do you have thirty-four dollars?" she asked.

I shook my head.

"Sorry," she said, spritzing a poppy plant behind my ear. "No freebies."

"Thirty-four dollars for a brownie?"

Spritz. Spritz. Spritz. "Thirty-four fifty. To be precise."

I couldn't stop myself. "Jeez, Olive. What do they have in

them?"

Olive twirled her dimple piercings. "Just a vitamin supplement. I'm selling them to, uh, raise awareness."

"What kind of awareness are you raising?" Cambridge's inquiring mind wanted to know.

"Um, environmental."

Cambridge dragged on her cigarette. "Environmental? Must be quite the supplement for people to dish out that kind of money."

Olive nodded. "My brownies, um, make people not tire so easily if they, you know, want to study all night." This girl was a born saleswoman, no?

"And exactly what ingredient does that kind of enhancing?"

Olive counted her cash. "Just a little something I discovered in the woods."

By the way she turned from us, we both knew Olive was done talking about it. So I went back to the Greyhound website. It took a bus twenty-two days to get from San Francisco to Baltimore, Maryland. TWENTY-TWO DAYS?! We could walk faster. The good news was I'd return home around the same time fat camp ended anyway. I could simply pretend I lost weight. "What, Mom?" I could say. "You don't see a difference?"

Using the mouse, I followed the Greyhound's cross-country route through Nevada, across to Utah, Colorado, down to New Mexico, then across Oklahoma, Kansas ... Just think! All the places I could see with Cambridge. Not Jackie and not Doug. It would be a real adventure this time, without secrets and emotional breakdowns. I was about to book two seats when Olive turned on the TV.

"Oh my God!" she cried. "Come look at this."

Cambridge and I turned our attention toward the television. There the campus station aired a promotional tour of the university. I didn't see the problem until I caught sight of the bottom half of the screen.

White letters. Blue background. Infinite loop.

Full vegetarian lunch served in Copernicus 1:00 PM ... University fireworks display set for July Fourth 9:00 PM Mont-Claire Hall ... One African-American teen and one Caucasian teen missing from weight loss camp. Last seen in gymnasium.

Contact campus security 5510 with info ... Full vegetarian lunch served in Copernicus 1:00 PM ...

In case we couldn't read, Olive did us the favor of repeating it out loud. Then her eye started twitching. "Did you see that? Did. You. See. That?!"

I could barely say the words: "Holy f—," before Cambridge got up and turned off the TV.

"Who watches public television anyway?" she said and lit a cigarette. "Don't worry about a thing, Olive."

Nice try, Cambridge. "Don't worry?" Olive asked. If there'd been a trapdoor beneath me and Cambridge, Olive would've already pulled the lever. "DON'T WORRY?" She peeked behind the tapestry in the window. "Campus security will be all over this."

I wanted to argue with her, but hell, I'd just seen the evidence. Not only had we run away from Utopia, people were actually looking for us. Chances are this would not end well. Knowing this, Olive dropped her cigarette in a water bottle. "You two need to be out of here by tomorrow morning." She picked at her toes again. "Sorry."

Cambridge sat in the window and the tapestry, fat with wind, billowed behind her. "Can't you give us a bit more time?" she asked, exhaling a column of smoke. "Time enough for us to figure out a proper course of action?" Cambridge reached into the fanny pack and removed another bill. "No one watches the crawl," she assured her. "We'll be discreet," she added. "Pretty please."

Olive fondled the lid to her brownies. "No way. There's too much at stake. I have so many customers in and out of here too," she started. "They'll see you."

Right then, as if this were some perfectly orchestrated drill, someone knocked. All three of us stopped, completely unsure of what to do next. After a few tense seconds, Olive snatched the bill from Cambridge, opened the closet, then whispered, "Get in there, you two. Go."

Hidden behind Olive's closet doors, our feet separated by terrariums, I allowed myself to panic. True, my anxiety had started long ago, but now, hidden in the hot cramped red-lit closet of a drug dealer, it was gaining momentum. I took three big breaths and nudged Cambridge. "Remember your research?" I whispered. "In the library? What happened to all those other girls who ran away from fat camp?"

I couldn't see anything, but I felt Cambridge's shoulders shaking beside me. Oh no, Cambridge was losing it too. I patted her back, hoping to calm her down. Turned out she wasn't even crying. Cambridge was laughing like a hyena—a silently laughing hyena. Tears, happy ones, streamed down her face. "We totally set the precedent," she said, giggling. "Isn't that amazing?"

From: rgoodman@k5-12maryland.us.edu
To: Bethany Stern <bethanys@utopia.com>
Subject: Re: re: IF U WOKE UP WITH WINGS

Dear Bethany,

So Caleb and Cullen, my sons, are now five. They both have ADHD. I have tried and tried to read them the WAKE UP WITH WINGS book and they want nothing of it. Caleb only picks up books to shred them, and Cullen only wants to read about farting dogs.

All of it serves to remind me what great kids you and Jackie were. Jackie was always happy to be hula-hooping in a tutu. And you had this magnificent temper! You used to throw your diapers around and bang your fists on the ground and then, afterward, you'd be quiet as rain, flipping through books in the basement. On some level I always knew you'd become the storyteller of the family.

One last thing: I'd like to talk to Jackie. Do you have her number? I don't know what I want to say to her, only that, I don't know. She deserves better, I guess. I know she's in California, but I could call her cell.

Yours truly…Dad

34

#HASHTAG

PART OF ME wished Jackie still had her phone, because imagining their awkward conversation was so much fun.

Kudos on getting preggo, Jackie. Thanks, Dad. Sorry about the abortion. Sorry about your own stupid kids. How about coming over to swim in a giant inflatable pool? Let me just check my calendar, Dad. Oh yes, it seems that hell is set to freeze over, so I'll be right there, OK?

In the end, though, I ignored the e-mail. I wasn't in the mood for a renaissance with Richard Goodman, and I had more important problems to worry about—namely, being AWOL from Utopia. With each passing hour I'd become more nervous. Lawn mower motors were suddenly hovering helicopters. Noises in the hallway became approaching SWAT teams. When my phone rang, I nearly jumped out of my skin.

"I think it's the FBI," I told Cambridge, holding it far away from me. "I'm afraid to answer it."

Cambridge, who was taking all this very lightly, grabbed it. "Fat Camp Fugitives," she answered. "How may I assist you?" Silence. "Oh hey, Liliana. What's up?"

So maybe it wasn't the FBI, but Liliana didn't exactly have good news either. She told us that someone had seen us on campus yesterday, hence the AMBER Alert. Now Hank and Belinda were searching our room looking for clues. Liliana's brother, who had watched one too many episodes of *Bounty Hunters*, suggested his sister put them on the wrong trail. So she did. Liliana told the owners that we'd ordered plane tickets and were headed back East. She said it all confessional-like too, the way Gabe'd told her to. Liliana couldn't say for sure, but she thought it might've worked. "Even though it was his idea," she said, "I executed it. That's what really matters. A small token of your appreciation would be freakin' awesome, *verdad*?"

God bless crime television and our youngest roommate. In order to thank her, I ordered twelve long-stem chocolate roses from Olive's computer. I even made them promise to deliver them real late, so they'd get past Miss Marcia. I didn't know for sure if Liliana's plan had worked, but I was grateful for her effort. I mean, at the rate we were traveling up shit creek, any paddle would do.

"Cambridge?" I asked. We were back in the closet again. Olive's brownie customers averaged one every ten minutes. "Don't you have a bad feeling about all this?"

Cambridge pawed her way around the plants. "Not really," she said. "Liliana sent Hank and Belinda to the airport. We have a place to crash for the night. All we need now is dinner and we're set."

"How can you think about food at a time like this?"

Cambridge scratched her chin. "You're telling me you aren't hungry?"

"I don't think so."

From: rgoodman@k5-12maryland.us.edu
To: Bethany Stern <bethanys@utopia.com>
Subject: Re: re: re: IF U WOKE UP WITH WINGS

Dear Bethany,

I haven't heard back from you. Is it because you're so busy at Utopia? I bet you've met a friend, and you love the place now. What are your roommates like? The other campers? Perhaps to help pass the time, you'd like me to send some books to your e-reader. What authors do you prefer reading?

Oh, one more memory came to me recently. Right before your mother and I separated, a family moved in across the street. The dad was a religious man. I seem to remember the mom had a lot of birds. Doves, I think. The kid was a bit sneaky, always playing tricks. He was about your age. Maybe a year older. Was that TJ?

Just curious

~Dad

35

EXTRA LARGE THIN CRUST

I'D VENTURE THAT Olive earned at least a thousand dollars in the last three hours. Half the campus wanted to sample her product. Now that night had fallen, Olive checked her dimples in the mirror. She combed her hair into two Pippi Longstocking braids—flaunting her hairy armpits while doing it—and slid her feet into a pair of sandals. "Time to go to work," she sang out.

Cambridge made one last effort. "Please let us come with you."

"That's really funny," Olive responded, and stuffed a few more brownies into her Rastafarian purse. "This is a business matter. Besides, no one would let you in anyway. You don't have costumes."

Of course this only enticed Cambridge more. "Costumes?" she asked, trying to veil her excitement. "What if we make one?" she lawyered. "Then Baltimore and I will be disguised. No one will know a thing. We'll wear elaborate get-ups. We'll even paint our faces. This might be our only chance to attend a real-live college ... business matter." Cambridge cocked her head. "I mean, what's the big secret?"

A Post-it note helicoptered to the floor. Olive picked it up and stuck it back to the wall. "It's just not a good idea for you two to be there," Olive explained. "The students, well ... the kids left on campus fit into one of two categories: complete slackers or shameless overachievers. You put these kinds of extremes together, and it's total mayhem. Things could easily get out of hand."

Cambridge smirked. "We'd behave, Olive."

"This is California University of the Pacific," Olive snorted. "No one behaves."

"Five minutes?"

Olive shook her tangled mane. "Just sit here, eat your pizza, and watch TV."

"You sound like my nanny," Cambridge sneered, "minus the British accent."

Olive straightened the lap of her blue dress. "Promise me."

"I promise," said Cambridge, crossing her heart.

And then Olive was gone, her patchouli stench trapped in the room—just like us.

Now that we had the place to ourselves, we could direct our energy to more important matters—like designing an exit plan. Even though Cambridge assured me things were fine, this campus felt snugger than last year's pants. Had Hank and Belinda checked the airport yet? I wondered. Were they torturing Liliana? Either way, I sure hoped Cambridge had seen *Shawshank Redemption*, because I might need some help tunneling out of Poindexter with a spoon.

Yet our fate seemed the furthest thing from Cambridge's mind. Instead of planning our escape, Cambridge only wanted to discuss pizza. She wouldn't even consider a Greyhound ticket until after I ordered an extra-large thin crust with an obscene amount of toppings. Finally, I turned to her.

"Just so you know, Cambridge, Liliana's pretty sure they called our parents."

I watched her closely as I said this, but her face revealed nothing. I pressed, "What do you think your dad will do? You know, when they tell him?"

Cambridge petted a potted plant. "My dad will be cavalier about everything: very *I see. I see. I will discuss things with her mother and get back to you.*" She did the best impressions. "What about your dad, Bethany? What will he do?"

"They wouldn't bother telling him. My mom paid for it."

Cambridge's eyes widened. "You know what you should

do?" She stood up straight, dusted off her knees. "You should tell your father first, in one of your e-mails. Tell him before your mother does." She closed the closet door. "Play your parents against each other, see. Like all the divorced kids do. Tell him how awful Utopia is, and then he'll feel bad, Bethany. He might even sign you out! He'll blame it all on your mom. Then you won't even have to worry about getting busted, because you'll be free and clear!"

"I haven't seen my dad in a long time."

Cambridge stroked her chin. "So call in a favor."

"He doesn't extend favors."

"He's sent you fifty e-mails in the last two days. He must be feeling guilty about something. And that e-reader? With his diet recommendation."

"So?"

"So exchange it for something better." She twisted a lock around her finger. "What do you have to lose?"

Sure it sounded unlikely, but Cambridge had suggested it so convincingly. She did look a little loopy, rubbing her hands together like a mad scientist, but what can I tell you? I was caught up in a moment. There was something downright magical about the twilight leaking in the window, an enchanted forest growing in the closet, and my dreadlocked cohort imparting me with her wizardry. It was worth a shot, right?

Maybe I'd get lucky.

From: Bethany Stern <bethanys@utopia.com>
To: Richard Goodman rgoodman@k5-12maryland.us.
Subject: Re: re: re: re: IF U WOKE UP WITH WINGS

Dear Dad:

TJ? Yes, he was our neighbor. He was actually the magician @ ur twins' b-day party one year. U or Penny musta hired him. i was there too, tho I wasn't invited. U saw me but pretended u didn't.

As far as more book recs, i don't think that'll be necessary b/c I 4got to mention (wait 4 it. Wait 4 it.) I ran away from utopia. As in I am no longer @ fat camp. I "considered" returning for 20 secs and survey says... No TY, Richard Goodman.

The place is plum awful. The campers are shallow and mean. They bow down to Hollywood and lock up our phones. The owners beat and starve us and then contort our limbs into pretzel positions for fun. If you want to do anything then do this. Sign me out. Consider it my birthday present. It's much better than a rec for the forgiveness diet.

Anyway, utopia? Over and out…It's done…you should be grateful. They would have killed me there. Just need ur lil john hancock and we can put it to rest. Fax it over, rich. Do us all a favor. Help a daughter out. Please.

L8r, Bee

Ps Jackie's number is 4106958383. She'd love to hear from u.

36

TWEAKER

THIRTY MINUTES LATER, it arrived. Resting on the fore-arms of a dude—our handsome cardboard box. Cambridge paid the delivery guy, but he kept trying to peek behind us into Olive's room. He wore plasticky looking glasses and was obviously going for a rockabilly theme with his Elvis hair, cuffed jeans, and bowling shoes. There he stood, puffy pizza-warming bag hanging uselessly by his side. Then he introduced himself as Glo and said he was looking for Olive. "But I guess I'll just catch up with her later. Anyway," he said, finally turning away, "enjoy your pizza."

"Were you looking for a particular chocolate brownie?" asked Cambridge, nose in the Tupperware bin.

"No," said Glo, a little too quickly. "Well, who are you guys anyway?"

"Olive's cousins," said Cambridge. "And ours is a family business."

If I had to guess, I'd say Glo belonged to the *slacker* summer student category because he fell for this line like a common jack-ass. Glo said, "I see the resemblance. On second thought, I'd like to purchase two of these brownies." He walked in and closed the door behind him. "These are the brownies made with the, um, special ingredient, yes?"

Cambridge asked him, "Do we look like the kind of girls

who'd skimp on ingredients?"

I doubted Olive would want us to turn down a sale, so we collected his sixty-nine dollars, and Cambridge fished out two chocolate squares. I couldn't help but notice there were only two left. Weren't there a dozen or so before? "Mind if we follow you to the party?" Cambridge asked, presenting Glo with the treat. "We're supposed to meet our cousin there, but if you're headed over, we could just go together."

Glo scratched his head. "Well, OK," he said. "Let me just eat one first."

Cambridge shook the Tupperware bin and out dropped the last brownie. I thought she was about to pawn the last psychedelic square on this customer, only to my surprise, Cambridge didn't. Shocking me completely, Cambridge shoved the entire brownie in her mouth

"Tabitha!" I shouted. "What are you doing?"

She shushed me, spraying chocolate bits in the process. "According to *Medicinal Purposes of Psychotropic Botany*, I should be feeling something by now."

With a mouth full of brownie, Glo mumbled, "How many did you eat?"

"The book said a one-hundred-eighty-pound man should feel the effects after one hour. I weigh one eighty-eight, and it's been forty-five minutes."

Glo smiled chocolate-coated teeth. "Not more than one, I hope."

Cambridge appeared to be in deep thought. She opened the pizza box, and the smell of grease and pepperoni wafted out. "I'm not even hungry," she said, looking at our specially created-for-us pizza. "How strange."

On the front of Cambridge's tank top and scattered on Olive's sheets, I made out heaps of crumbs. I walked over to the bed, feeling the sheets in a blind, raging hope the crumbs were anthills. They weren't.

"How many brownies did you eat?"

Cambridge wouldn't look at me. "Your voice sounds funny," she said. "Are you under water?"

"Oh Jesus." I grabbed her face and turned it toward mine. Her pupils were as big as M&M's. "How many, Tabitha?"

"I've never done drugs. Not even pot. I've always wanted to."

"How many?"

"The book said to eat one until you feel something."

Glo tried not to laugh, "You don't get drug advice from a textbook."

"I didn't take the advice. I had three or four. Five?"

Getting off campus was proving more impossible with each passing second.

"You just ate five brownies?"

Cambridge counted on her fingers. "I believe you're right."

OK, Bethany, I told myself. *Don't freak.* It wasn't like I knew exactly what was in the brownies anyway. Maybe Olive really had infused them with a supplement. Ginseng. Gingko? Aside from her constant blinking and weird cheek biting, Cambridge looked messed up, yes, but not that bad. *Calm down,* I told myself. *I've seen worse.* My roommate stood up, a little wobbly, sure, but she did stand, walk to the mirror and look.

"I see dead people." *Oh God.* "You ready, Bee?"

"Ready for what? We're not going anywhere."

She clipped her hair back in a ponytail, missing half of it. "The party, silly. Glo here's our escort."

"Tabitha, we can't go. Someone could see us."

Cambridge blinked about a billion times. "Of course we can," she said easily. "It's our summer, Baltimore. We're here. We might as well." She fingered her dreads. "I want to go to a college party. Aren't you in the least bit curious?"

I could have lived with my curiosity. "We don't have costumes!" I exclaimed, as if that were the least of our worries.

Glo stood between us. He was shorter than us by a good margin. "You don't need costumes."

"Olive said it was a costume party," I argued. "A mandatory costumed affair."

Something odd flitted across his face. "Tell you what, you can change at the party."

Cambridge cleared her throat. Twice. "I believe I am starting to feel things now," she said academically. "Tingles and such. We should leave. Please come, Bethany. I don't want to go without you."

And before I could argue, before I could grab a slice of pizza mountainous with our toppings, she was pulling us out the door, down the stairwell, and out into a cool, cloudless night. Glo steered us toward a party he predicted would be righteous, man. Unforgettable.

37

COME AS YOU ARE

OUTSIDE, THE STARS were fierce and pointed. I had lots of time to observe them too, because Cambridge stopped every three feet to examine something. She described how the night sounded *wider* to her than ever before. Then Glo encouraged her to listen to the crickets. I didn't hear a thing, and I found Glo increasingly annoying.

"So the earth isn't moving?" asked Cambridge, staring at the cement.

"No, Cambridge. The earth is moving, but we can't feel it."

"I think I can," she replied, lying down on the path. She raked the pinpricked sky with her fingertips. "I definitely can."

Glo lay next to her. "There's Uranus," he said, snickering.

How did this guy get into college anyway?

"Are you mad at me, Bethany?" asked Cambridge, now propped on her elbow.

"No."

"Yes you are."

"I am not!"

But I was—a little.

I couldn't shake the feeling that behind every recycling bin or hidden inside one of the dark buildings towering alongside the walkway was a pissed-off Miss Marcia or Hollywood watching us through crosshairs. One wrong step, and we were toast. I wanted to be back in Olive's dorm room, not out here watching Cambridge and her Elvis sidekick log rolling down hills.

"Please don't be mad," she called, mid-tumble. "I just love brownies. So good they are."

The rare times TJ and I smoked pot, we ate boxes of Kraft macaroni and cheese and watched DVRed *American Envy*. Once TJ paused on The Levitator for so long, I feared his after-image would burn in the TV. Even the macaroni had gelatinized by the time we broke out of our inertia. My point is that was about as exciting as things got. Honeysuckle never spoke to me. I never saw tracers or doubted gravity. Cambridge's effects were more on par with crack or meth—not like I'd done them—but I'd never missed an episode of *My Drug Intervention* either. As she lagged behind, lighting the wrong ends of cigarettes and smoking them anyway, I should have been more worried than I was. She turned to me at one point with a fistful of honeysuckle and said, "They are trying to tell me something."

"You're frizzled, that's what they're saying."

"No," she said. "Something different. Something about sweetness."

According to our guide, Glo, the party was just beyond Polymer Park, the university football stadium. We had already cut across the field and started into the woods when the dirt gave way to cold sand. I could barely make out the sounds of tiny waves. No sooner did we clear the woods when I almost walked face first into a mountain of clothing: T-shirts, sweat socks, hippie dresses, shoes.

Glo crossed his arms. "Here's where you can change into your costumes," he said, smirking. "Your *birthday* costumes."

Faced with the Everest of fabric, I was sure I'd walked into a nightmare. *Impossible.* So impossible was the situation, I barely registered Glo's tangled chest hair next to me, his skinny white legs, his tube socks, and even his boxer shorts that he happened to be peeling off right now to publicize his pale white butt. And then he turned around. OMFG.

Before us stretched the mighty Lake Pacifica, which looked as big as the Chesapeake. Bonfires edged the shoreline and gathered around them were people. A lot of people. Maybe even a hundred people, and yes, my eyes did not deceive me. These students I mentioned, around the fires? Completely nude. Every last one of them. Including Glo. Butt naked.

I stood on the party's threshold and developed a keen interest in my flip-flops, not like they held my interest for long. I looked up. I had to look up. It was like a nudist colony had formed eight paces in front of me.

People really do frolic when they're naked, and all the fine folks celebrating the third of July, they frolicked with their glow sticks and body glitter and neon body paint. There were definitely a lot of Thespians because the crowd had the uncomplicated grace of nudity that could only come from spending time on stage. Boys held plastic cups of beer unselfconsciously, cell phones in the other hand, penises dangling. Long-legged girls stabbed at smoking logs, orange embers swirling dangerously close to their glitter-coated breasts. One guy, further back, contemplated the summer sky while he pissed in the sand. So many navels, armpits, the backsides of knees white as snow, butt-cracks. *Don't look. Don't look. Don't look.* So many penises.

As bodies bounced and jiggled near me, I wondered if these were the kinds of costume parties they threw in Ivy League universities everywhere. Well, community college never looked better for this girl.

While I didn't have a badge that read, *Hi, my name is: I DO NOT BELONG HERE*, I waited for someone to slap one on me. I tried to cultivate intention like, oh, I was supposed to discard my clothing in that pile? I didn't get the memo. But it was no use. I was a fat girl at a college party, which felt a lot like being a fat girl at a high school party. Only difference was everyone was naked. Not me. No way. I didn't even like swimming without a T-shirt. I should have prepared myself for all the bodies gyrating near me. I should have taken drugs. Maybe then I wouldn't care.

I turned around to whisper something like "Let's go" to Cambridge, whose prep school sensitivities must've been way compromised, but she was gone. So there I was, on the party's outskirts, wearing a hooded California University of the Pacific sweatshirt, short sweatpants with the football team's name, polymers, inscribed in an arc across my butt, and my everlasting flip-flops. I might as well have been wearing a snowsuit.

I picked up a red cup that a naked imp had abandoned on

a tree stump. Luckily some beer sloshed in it, so I chugged it down. Then, for the first time in my life, someone directed the words, "Take off your clothes," to me. I pretended not to hear them. I found a picnic table chained to a pole, climbed on top of it, and interviewed myself. *Would you do it for a thousand dollars, Bethany? No, Bethany, I would not. Would you do it for a steaming plate of crab and cream cheese dumplings? Shrimp lo mein? I would not, could not ... How about peanut butter Snickers pie? Well. With a side of moo-shoo pork? Forget it. What if TJ was here? No. And he wouldn't either.* He'd be next to me, fully-clothed, trying to convince me I wasn't the only person in the world who always felt like the only person in the world.

Sipping my lukewarm beer, I was aware of chemically altered eyes resting on my ensemble. Thankfully, further down the beach, I made out another person—also fully clothed—only this doofus wore jeans. OK, there were other people here who preferred clothing. Let the crowd go harass him then. At least my ankles were showing. Desperately wishing my beer would regenerate itself, I searched the throngs for Cambridge.

Someone had strung speakers in the trees and an ambient music played. Evidently I was supposed to be dancing. Cambridge, in her stupor, knew this because when I finally spotted her by the keg, she was dancing, nude, like her life depended on it.

I watched her for a while, amazed not so much by her nakedness but how well she wore it. Her arms swayed above her head as if rocking the moon to sleep. Her legs were strong and her shoulders broad; her waist curved in like a cello. It's a weird thing to see someone who's about your same height and weight, only they look better than you do. Watching her sweep her naked butt down, down, down to the sand, I could see she loved her body in a way I didn't love mine. Or couldn't. If she looked fat, I didn't notice, and I don't think anyone else did either. There had to be some heady algebraic formula for the number of pounds I'd have to shed versus an increase in confidence added with illegal substances before I'd dance naked in front of an audience. Mid-calculation, a forest sprite stepped right in front of me. It was Olive. She was naked, but that wasn't why I flinched. For some reason, I never imagined we'd run into her.

"What in the hell are you doing here," she asked and searched my eyes.

I willed myself to sound calm. "Hi?"

I guess it's hard to stay pissed off when you're standing there naked. Olive sat down next to me on a picnic bench. "What took you so long?" she asked, and smiled. She tilted her cup of beer into mine. "I was sixteen once too, you know. I never listened either."

I exhaled. Looking around, it was quite probable that Olive and I were the only sober people. "So what do you think?" she asked, waving toward the murky water, scores of naked students drinking, laughing, and dancing.

"It's something."

"You'd be less conspicuous if you took your clothes off," she observed. "Or at least dance. Just get out there and close your eyes."

I looked to see if Cambridge had her eyes closed—maybe that was her secret—but she wasn't there anymore. A hollow drumbeat sounded. "Where'd Cambridge go?" I asked Olive. "She was dancing there a second ago."

"I saw her too. With Glo."

I scanned the line at the keg. "She's really messed up."

"Messed up how?"

"She ate your brownies."

Olive's dimples creased. "She what?"

"You know, your supplement." I tried to say this as innocently as possible, but Olive knew Cambridge was not after a vitamin surge.

After my admission, Olive—sleek, small-breasted, and narrow-hipped—tensed. Everything about her was irate down to the metallic studs in her nipples. "Exactly how many brownies are we talking about?"

I noticed Cambridge finally. She was standing in the lake, black water up to her bellybutton, her large breasts skirting the water. She held something in her hands that, from my vantage point, looked like a toad. I approached her.

"What are you doing in the water?" I asked. "You shouldn't be swimming in your condition."

"Relax," she replied and gestured with the amphibian. "I'm a

Mermaiden and even won in a regatta." So now Cambridge was a mermaid. "Look!" she yelled. "He makes music." She squeezed the toad and out squeaked a strangled call. Glo stood next to her. He looked skinny and barrel-chested next to voluptuous Cambridge, whose breasts, as far as breasts were concerned, truly were spectacular. "I hear it too," said Glo. When he turned around, the moon illuminated his butt again, which was white and furry.

"Perhaps we are the only ones," she replied.

Glo gawked at Cambridge like Tampa Bay had, only his field of vision concentrated on her chest region.

"I love the way you look," he said to her breasts. "Turn around."

Cambridge pirouetted while Olive inched closer. "I need to know how many brownies you ate, Tabitha," said a suddenly serious Olive. "It's very important you tell me."

Cambridge ignored her. "Take off your clothes, Baltimore."

The water was now up to Olive's knees. "Tell me how many you had."

"I'm thinking of a number," Cambridge replied, "between one and twelve."

"Eight!" guessed Glo.

"Exactly!"

Out of nowhere, Glo kissed Cambridge. He just slopped one on her, his tongue slipping in and out like a reptile's.

"Oh God," said Olive, her voice tight with panic. "That's a toxic amount .I shouldn't have left them out. Why did I leave them out?"

I could see Olive clearly: the pink wheels of her nipples, the metal hoop in her bellybutton, and the parallel lines of her hips. She must have noticed the look on my face because she said, "Dammit! That's like three hundred dollars. You two owe me money."

"Owe you? What's that supposed to mean? What's in those things anyway?"

"It's a cannabis mushroom graft. A hybrid plant I've been experimenting with." She shook her head. "But you didn't hear that from me."

"Will she be OK though?" I asked.

Olive shrugged. "She should be in six to eight hours." We both looked at Cambridge, up to her neck in water, conversing with the toad. "She'll peak eventually, and when she does, you should keep an eye on her. Go to the hospital if she loses it."

"Loses what?" I asked no one because Olive was gone—wanting to be as far from us as possible.

Back in the water, the toad had escaped Cambridge's grip, and she and Glo dove under to locate him. As I watched their heads dunking and resurfacing, carried by some current I failed to see, I found myself confronting an age-old SAT question.

Person X is wasted and up to her teeth in ocean. Person Y stares at Person X's breasts like flotation devices. As X and Y drift further and further downstream, how long until Person Z gets off her fat butt and intersects their downward vector?

38

SEASICK

AFTER AN HOUR or so, it was clear Cambridge was so altered she couldn't swim out of a teardrop. I probably should have followed her earlier, but I didn't want to be a buzzkill.

After about thirty people asked me why I insisted on staying clothed, varying my answers—scurvy, venereal disease, I really am naked, you are just high—I tried to convince myself Cambridge would be OK. Five leftover cups of beer helped. In no time at all, we could leave this party and make our escape.

Obviously we'd missed the Greyhound I was hoping to take, but I'm sure there were hostels or shelters in San Francisco where we could stay until the next bus. Certainly there were other eastbound vehicles. Trains! I'd completely forgotten about trains. Maybe Glo even had a car, and he could take us to a station.

All I needed to do now was gather Cambridge and head back to Olive's room. Sober her up a bit. The pizza would help with that. I sure hoped it'd still be there. I missed it. All those toppings crowded together, wondering what happened to us. Discs of pepperoni touching Canadian bacon, mushrooms, green peppers ...

I was thinking about our forsaken thin crust pizza when I looked up and confronted Miss Marcia's eyes, blinking slowly at me, as if I were a hallucination. Miss Marcia, our Utopia counselor, wearing nothing but her freckles and Pacifica up to her knobby knees. Our eyes locked, and for a second, the moon, the party, even the pizza—everything disappeared. I was back in Utopia with her plastic clipboard, her penned notes on our files. Her breathy rasp on the power walk: "Faster girls, faster."

She didn't say anything because she, in addition to the guy next to her, looked rather, well, completely blotto. They swayed in the water, pulled by more than a current—that much was clear. She had the vacant look of someone either coming out of or going under anesthesia. Just to be sure, though, I uttered two words that took them both by surprise.

"Say cheese!"

Hollywood's violet cell phone flashed, and Miss Marcia's chemical romance was captured forever. My counselor tilted her head and muttered something to her companion. I don't even think she registered what'd just happened. Either way, she could go find Hank or Belinda, tell them she happened to be at a party, eating psychedelic brownies when she saw me, but in her condition I doubted she was up for it.

Right after her photo op, our counselor turned away, her penny-colored hair falling behind her. She waded out further into the lake with her boy. Miss Marcia was gifting me with a little time.

Lots of people who were not Cambridge floated bareassed in the water with their fun noodles. I walked down the beach, tiny waves uncurling over my flip-flops, searching for her. In the distance, tucked inside the woods, I saw a cabin. I walked faster and faster, knowing instinctively Cambridge was inside of it.

It turned out to be more of a large shed with oars, paddles, life jackets, and other nautical accessories jammed into corners and shelves. Several canoes hung from hooks. In the middle of the floor, a campfire burned, and around it several students contemplated the time/space continuum. One cross-eyed party-goer strummed a mandolin and, next to her, sat Cambridge and Glo—inside a canoe. Cambridge was attempting to paddle the canoe across the cement floor.

"I'm a Mermaiden!" she cheered.

As if it weren't evident enough, when I edged closer, I could see how wonky Cambridge looked. Her eyes were vacant and spacey, even her dreads looked limp. She leaned backward into Glo, but not flirtatiously, more like she'd collapse if he moved. Glo clutched her hair and straightened her, but she swayed again and fell backward into his lap.

"Cambridge!" I yelled. She looked up, but not quickly and not even in my direction.

The mandolin stopped. "Bethany!" She tapped Glo. "It's Bethany." Glo didn't look happy to see me. He didn't even look pleased Cambridge's head was in his groin again.

"This isn't fun anymore," she said from his crotch. She slid from Glo's lap and landed hard on the bottom of the canoe. "Something's wrong."

By the way she studied me, you could tell she was seeing triple.

This was what Olive had warned me about. She was peaking. Then she made a funny noise, crossed her eyes, and I knew what was coming. Seconds later, Cambridge turned a doomed shade of green and vomited all over the boat.

"Oops," she said. "I think I'm seasick."

Glo and his other cronies scampered away. Cambridge teetered over to her side, capsized, and barely missed her barf. Her head hit the floor. Then she threw up again and said, "This isn't great."

Next, the smell. I tried to ignore it as I pulled her up, draped her across my shoulders, and stumbled outside. As soon as my feet hit the dirt, my strength evaporated, and she fell onto the ground. While she roiled on the grass, I confronted the horrid fact that the kegs and campfires and clothing mountain were a thousand miles away. There was no way I could schlep her there, but what other choice did I have? I tried again, but stopped when I heard her retch. She threw up again, her eyes tearing. When she finished, she trembled, looking helpless and small. "My heart feels funny," she said, and touched a spot on her breast.

"Funny? What kind of funny?"

"Just off somehow."

This wasn't what I wanted to hear. Calling on strength probably honed at fat camp, I dragged Cambridge through the sand back to the keg lines, trees, and into what had now become a full-on drug-riddled, intensely naked college party. Music thumped from the trees. Games of Beer Pong competed on picnic tables. Girls wiggled like go-go dancers, and apparently the best way to deliver alcohol involved a handstand and someone unplugging the keg tap in your mouth. If Miss Marcia was around, I didn't see her and, at that point, I didn't care. I carried Cambridge toward a circle of guys pounding drums straddled between their hairy legs. I dropped her directly in the center. "She ate too many brownies," I said, breathing hard. "Please help me."

As usual, no one even looked at me. I wrenched the curly hair of a drummer. "Look at her," I said, so someone would. "She said her heart felt weird."

Drummer boy puzzled for about one second, then lit a hookah. "She seems fine to me," he said, talking through a huge inhalation. "She's just peaking." Swwooooosh, he exhaled. "Relax."

Everyone agreed with the stoner's assessment.

Except me.

Cambridge didn't look right. Her breathing was shallow, and every time I went to pull her up, she fell back down. I couldn't find Olive, and Glo was good as gone. I was so angry that when I said, "SOMEONE HELP ME!" it was loud. And I do mean LOUD. For a second, I was hopeful. No drumming. No strumming. Just my voice. "She's not peaking," I said, my teeth clenched. "She needs help."

Cambridge spit sand from her mouth. She flexed her fingers in front of her eyes like she was counting them. Still no one helped, and it was crystal-clear no one would.

I decided to drag her to the highway beyond the stadium, flag down an ambulance, or hitchhike to a hospital.

Pulling her still-naked body through the woods by her wrists, I made it as far as the stadium's turf—I still had to cross the damn field—when I decided I needed a new plan. My arms were weak. My legs felt like I'd done a billion squats, but I had no choice, I had to head back to campus—find an infirmary or something. When my fingers gave out from clenching her so tightly, I let her go and she landed face down in the field. I rolled her over, and she threw up. Again. Then her eyes drifted back in her head, and she made this choking sound. I tried to pick her up but wound up cursing her for being so heavy. This was a terrible time to wish for Google, but I couldn't help it. I wanted an Internet search, an app for drug interactions, slapped in her face. The first time, in an effort to wake her up. I was pissed. Pissed that she'd eaten all those brownies, livid that she was sick. My palm stung with the fact that this girl, my camp BFF, was dead weight. I screamed and dug my fingernails into her arms, pulling her up only to have her flop back down like a rag doll.

Get up. Get up. Get up.

You never know how you're going to react in a crisis, and if you told me I'd scrolled down the ICE contact on Hollywood's phone, I wouldn't have believed you. But that's exactly what I did. I located ICE and pushed send on the blinking lavender phone. I estimated the time to be about three o'clock in the morning.

"Hello," said a titanic voice.

"This is Bethany Stern. I, um, well. I go to camp with—"

"Yes?" Why did I feel like I was talking to Oz? "Are you calling from my daughter's phone? You're the one who stole it. You've got a lot of ner—"

"I need help. My friend Cambridge ate mushroom pot brownies with grafted acid in them, and she won't move." I realized I was sobbing. "Tell me what to do. Please. "

ICE Daddy Home sighed. "Is she breathing?" he asked calmly. Maybe everyone woke up pleasantly in Hollywood. Perhaps dreams were sweeter there. "Bethany, is it? Bethany. Can you tell if your friend is breathing?"

Why I never thought to check was a mystery. I knelt down and closed Cambridge's nostrils. Maybe there was a more artful way to discover if someone was breathing, but this was the only one I knew. She made a wheezing sound, and her mouth opened wide.

"Yes."

"Feel her pulse."

"For what?"

"For a pulse."

"I feel it."

"Good. What is it?" he asked.

"It's there."

"I mean, is it fast? Count it."

I guessed Daddy Home had heard about me from Holly-wood. Heard about my departure and fat camp revolt. "I can't count right now."

"Open her eyelids then. Do her eyeballs come down, Beth-any?"

"Yes."

"Can you see her pupils?"

"They're giant."

Then I heard this from Cambridge: "I'm sweating."

"She's sweating," I repeated to Hollywood's father.

Cambridge patted my arm like someone nearsighted pats a table for their glasses. "It's OK, Bee. It'll be OK. Is that your sister?"

"She says she's OK."

ICE Daddy Home sighed. "I think she's OK, Bethany."

"Are you sure?"

"Yes. Let her sleep."

"She won't die?" I asked.

"She won't die," he assured me.

"Did she peak?"

"Peak? I don't know, but she needs to sleep. Give her orange juice too."

"Well if that wasn't peaking I don't know what is." I paused. "She's fine now."

"OK."

"Thanks," I said, which must've sounded terrifically stupid.

"You're welcome."

"We aren't going to be doing anymore drugs this summer sir."

"That's good. Are they doing drugs at Utopia?"

"No. I mean. Not everyone. Sorry to wake you."

"Be careful, Bethany."

"I will."

"Thanks for calling."

"I'm sorry we stole Holl—I mean, your daughter's phone."

"No need to apologize. Amber can come on a little strong."

"I guess you're right."

"She has issues, you know. With food. She can't help being so—"

"Mean?" That came out of nowhere.

"You could say that. Good night, Bethany."

I hung up feeling like an ignoramus, but whatever, Cambridge was alive. She snored loudly beside me.

There were certain times in life when people—all people—required a cigarette. This moment, I resolved, removing one from the fanny pack encircling Cambridge's waist, qualified. I needed a break before I hauled Cambridge across campus. Lighting the soggy butt, I watched my hands quake. *OK,* I said to myself. *Now what?*

I sunk down on the edge of the football field, next to mud-covered Cambridge, and smoked. Hollywood's father sounded like a doctor. Then again, his knowledge of drugs had been impressive. I'd bet he was a rock star. Liliana had tried to convince us he was a famous actor, though. Maybe he played a surgeon on TV. He had that kind of voice—one that made people jump. *Scalpel! Scalpel!* It was a familiar voice, though. I swore I'd heard it before.

At the other end of the field, I saw someone walking toward campus. Dressed in jeans, a black T-shirt, and a skull cap, it must've been the other only clothed person at the party. It was definitely a guy, I could see that now, a bit on the scrawny side, but he'd have to do. Carrying Cambridge back by myself was impossible.

I screamed down toward the end zone, "Hey! You leaving?"

"Not exactly my scene," said the dude, not turning around, not stopping either.

"I could use a hand back here," I called. It felt like our sentences took a long time to get to one another. When he finally stopped and turned around, I had to do a double take. It was Gabe, Liliana's brother.

"Gabe?" I asked quietly.

It was really him, minus the skateboard. He jogged down the field so fast I hadn't even finished my cigarette when he barreled into me. "What happened here?" he asked.

I didn't know how to answer that. After so much nudity, you'd think I wouldn't notice Cambridge's anymore, but with Gabe there, it brought it forward. My first instinct was to cover Cambridge. I guess it was Gabe's too, because he pulled off his black hoodie to reveal his signature SPOOGE T-shirt which, I must mention, glowed in the dark. He knelt down next to Cambridge and eased one of her wilted arms into the sweatshirt. This was practical, but also sweet. I found myself staring at his hands.

Seeing him beneath our dorm window all those nights, I would not have guessed how skillfully he'd maneuver a naked girl. We dressed Cambridge, Gabe positioning her other arm inside his hoodie while I zipped it over her ample boobs. Even though I didn't ask him to, he donated his jeans and his shoes to the charity, tossing them to me in a denim lump. I knew the jeans wouldn't fit her, so once I got her legs in, I stretched the sweatshirt down to cover her stomach and crotch. Then Cambridge sat up, and in a wavery moonlight, hurled down the front of Gabe's sweatshirt.

Just barely, I saw a very Tabitha-like smirk on her face. "Pardon me," she said.

"Better out than in," offered Gabe, shivering a little in his gym shorts.

He lifted her beneath her armpits and draped one of her arms over his shoulder, and I stood beneath her other one. In shorts and SPOOGE T-shirt glowing ghoulishly, Gabe and I crossed the football field. We staggered along the path, Cambridge roiling between us, dry heaving every twenty feet. Gabe swiped his card at his dorm's back entrance, and, while still supporting Cambridge, held the door for me, and said, *"Despues de que usted, senorita."*

39

WATCH ME UNRAVEL

AS MORNING SPLINTERED the sky, Gabe flopped Cambridge on his bed, made a pile of T-shirts and boxers for himself on the floor, and now slept in the flannel nest. I studied all the boy stuff scattered about: Deodorant. Razor. Tennis shoes. Skateboard. How are boys so economical with their things? His room seemed so much less complicated than ours. And he fell asleep so quickly! Who does that?

I positioned the metal trash can next to Cambridge, prepared for more peaking, but she was through with that, apparently. She'd had a few moments I'd mistaken for lucidity, but they were followed by nonstop stupid talk or catatonic staring. It was hard to tell whether the drugs were working their way in or out of her system.

From Gabe's bed, Cambridge stared at the ceiling and swatted imaginary flies. I wondered how long she planned on being stoned. After five hours, it was getting old.

"Whose pants are these?" she asked, trying the zipper. She stretched out her body in an effort to zip them up, a move I knew all too well, but it wasn't happening. She sighed. "I'm surely ravenous."

"You're still not right, Cambridge. You need to sleep it off."

When she sat up, she looked like hell. Her lips were chapped, and her cheeks were smeared with dirt. We probably smelled like road kill. "You know what I could eat? Hawaiian pizza." Remembering the steaming box of yum we abandoned back in Olive's room, I grunted, "We ordered pizza and you left it."

She puzzled over this event obliterated from memory. "That's very uncharacteristic of me. On second thought, you know what I want? Breakfast. Like pancakes stacked in different sizes, homemade ones with chocolate chips in them. Some toast and scrambled eggs too."

This wouldn't have sounded so good had I not been so hungry myself. I was practically salivating while Cambridge mused, "Don't you just love when syrup gets on the bacon? Just a smidge?" She flung back her head. "God, what I wouldn't give for bacon now. Even Canadian bacon. Hey, didn't I have money?"

Great, I thought, noting that the fanny pack no longer circled her waist. "How will we eat without money?" Cambridge asked. "What's today? Wait." Clearly she'd injected espresso into her veins when I wasn't looking. "Is today the fifth? Is it? Don't I get a free breakfast at Denny's on my birthday?"

Gabe, who I assumed was sleeping, groaned, "*¡Dios!* Do you ever stop talking?"

"Today's your birthday?" I asked Cambridge.

"Today's the fourth," answered Gabe. He covered his head with a T-shirt. "Now go back to bed."

We should really let Gabe sleep. He lugged Cambridge across the entire campus and offered up his own bed. He didn't even look annoyed that two fat-camp escapees were in his dorm. In truth, he kind of seemed happy about it. The least we could do was stay quiet out of respect for the guy. So we did. For three whole minutes.

"Baltimore?"

"Shhh. Gabe is sleeping."

"Bethany?"

"What?"

"I'm so glad I met you."

I know that sounds trite, but coming from Cambridge, who was not prone to sentimentality, it was the nicest thing she'd ever said to me.

"Roger that."

"You saved my life. Do you remember?"

"I remember alright."

"The least I can do is buy you breakfast."

"Are you even sober?"

Cambridge stood up and wobbled a little, which basically answered my question. "Not quite," she said, "but breakfast would help."

Well, I reasoned, a girl had to eat.

40

NI MODO

WHO NEEDED DENNY'S when Copernicus Hall had its very own dining hall two flights down from Gabe's room? After tickling his neck and dripping Gatorade across his toes, Gabe woke up convinced that securing our breakfast was his civic duty. As soon as I saw the long, gleaming buffet in the center of Copernicus's dining room, I nearly took off running toward it. I knew we were pushing our luck grubbing out in the open like this, but it was very early, and, if you wanted to know the truth, I didn't care. Nothing could have stopped me from those buckets of food suspended over blue Sterno cans. Coffee. Bacon. Rapture.

All three of us sat together at a table still sticky with syrup.

"It might overwhelm me to go up there," Cambridge said, dropping her plate on top of mine. "Get me one of everything and pour syrup on the side. In all honesty, Bethany, I'm afraid my hallucinogenic trip won't ever end."

"It will end," said Gabe sagely. "Everything does."

While Cambridge talked herself down, I visited the buffet. God bless the fine CUP administrators who made breakfast at Copernicus possible. All that steam and deliciousness pooling around me. How I missed the silverware tidily rolled up in a napkin! The packets of jelly! Self-service toasters popping up chubby bagels! Waffles! Butter! And, and, and ... hallelujah—an omelet chef.

Under other circumstances, I'd be too nervous to eat in front
of a guy but, for whatever reason, Gabe didn't count. I was hungry and my cheddar-jack mushroom omelet sang to me.

Gabe's plate starred every item on the buffet drenched in
blueberry syrup. He beamed at the smorgasbord just like Liliana when someone mentioned chocolate. Come to think of it,
Gabe looked like a taller, skinnier version of his sister. He wore
his usual SPOOGE T-shirt—a drawing of two dogs humping on
the front and the words "Stolen Moments Tour 2011." His skin
was shiny, like he'd been misted in olive oil. His black, poker-
straight hair had been cut bluntly to his neck. I didn't remember
if Liliana had a dimple in the center of her chin, but her brother
did. It disappeared when he smiled, which he was doing now,
watching me. I felt my cheeks redden. Had I not noticed how
cute he was before?

"I must look awful," I said, opening my omelet like a gift.

"Not at all," he said. "*¡Comemos!*"

Liliana did not inherit the super-speedy metabolism her bro
had. Gabe ate like a robot sent on a mission to destroy everything on its plate. He slopped up eggs with toast and held his
fork awkwardly, like he wasn't sure what purpose it served. He
spattered ketchup indiscriminately. In record time, all three of
us, including slow-eater Cambridge, were done. By way of announcement, I guess, Gabe belched loud enough for people to
turn around. I almost called him out, but since he was the one
who swiped his meal card, I let it ride.

Thankfully, the stack of chocolate chip pancakes did Cambridge good, because she looked less narcotized. "How about
that party last night?" she asked, squeezing hazelnut creamer
in her coffee. "Were drums involved? And frogs? Were people
naked? I can't tell if I am having flashbacks or what."

Our champion brownie-consumer didn't recall her initiation
into the vomit hall of fame. She didn't remember Gabe dragging
her back to his dorm either. Gabe, who had the perfect opportunity to mention some other mortifying event, just said, "The
party wasn't all that memorable." Then he plucked some water-
melon off my plate, wrapped it in a napkin, and asked, shyly,
"It's cool if I take this to Liliana, right?"

Outside the dining hall's window, California University's main administrative building was cushioned by a glut of fog. If only the mist would do us the extraordinary favor of swallowing the entire campus as easily as I'd swallowed my delicious omelet, we could forget about our life on the run and stay in Copernicus forever.

I turned to Gabe. "That first day of camp when you drove by me, I noticed your ..." I paused. *What was that thing anyway?* "Your vehicle. Would you be willing to drive us somewhere?"

Whoever cut his long black hair must have chopped it with an axe. It was an odd contrast to his teeth, which were a little crooked. He covered his mouth when he spoke, like maybe he was self-conscious about them.

"Ah, *ni modo.* Drive you where?"

"San Francisco? Oakland? Baltimore?" I didn't think it mattered as long as it wasn't here. "Or maybe LA?" I asked him suddenly. "We'll go to the *American Envy* studios and wait for TJ. When he wins ..." Wait. That was the old Bethany. "Oh forget it. Never mind."

Gabe leaned back in his chair. He adjusted his skull cap, and I saw the part in his hair, a zigzag down the center of his scalp. "Your boyfriend's on *American Envy*?"

"He will be. He can levitate."

Cambridge kicked me under the table. "He's not her boyfriend."

Gabe leaned perilously further in the chair. "I think you guys are righteous on the one hand for leaving but then, on the other, you lack *cerebros.*" He tapped his head. "You need to approach this mathematically."

Cambridge smiled wryly. "Did you take the quantitative aptitude standardized test, Gabe?"

I looked down into my plate. I barely eked out a C in Algebra II.

"Of course I did."

"And what did you get?"

"*Perfecto.*" He polished his nails on his chest. "You?"

Cambridge rolled her eyes. "I missed a few."

Gabe put his hands up. "I'm only trying to shed some light on your quandary here," he replied. "I mean, say I drove you somewhere. Then what? Eventually you'll have to come back here."

"Yes," I said, "but eventually isn't now. Eventually might be never."

Gabe smiled then covered his teeth. "Statistically, ladies, eventually is *never* never."

Cambridge looked at Gabe. "I disagree with your math, Pythagoras. We need a ride. You in?"

Gabe opened his mouth in an effort, I guessed, to relate how dumb we were for running away with no plan and crappy math grades to boot. He'd probably present the idea that we should just go back to Utopia and suck it up, like two thousand other people hadn't suggested the same thing. Only no words came out of Gabe's mouth. His gaze skimmed the top of my head, toward the window behind us. When I turned around, I saw what had silenced him. A herd of joggers lumbered past. Two were holding their ribcages, breath coming out in white puffs, then I saw Atlanta, her face and big, poofy hair. Then Liliana filed past, half-walking, half-skipping, and there bringing up the rear of this motley crew, urging them to go faster, faster, was a girl in a white jogging suit. Her feet were clothed in ridiculous barefoot running socks. Not even sweating this July morning, her thin lips stretched into a smile. Hollywood.

Chariots of Fire didn't exactly pipe through the speakers, but it sure felt that time stretched like caramel when Hollywood stopped mid-stride and pivoted. Her hands were on her hips. I was aware of her heart-shaped face turning toward the window and Gabe's black hair whizzing out when he snapped around and yelled, "Duuuuuck." But it was too late. Recognition had already crossed her face. Before we dove under the table, I saw it. Her lips pulled together in a line to form, I was sure, the first letter of my name. In the cramped space under the table, I mouthed the word *please* to Gabe. Liliana's brother sighed and rolled his eyes. After an excruciating minute, he exited Copernicus through the kitchen with me and Cambridge following. He didn't stop until he got to the parking lot behind his dorm. There he waited by *ni modo* with his arms crossed. When Cambridge and I finally panted up the parking lot's hill, Gabe grabbed the pink flyer from the windshield of his truck and handed it to me.

"Better hurry," he said, opening his truck's door. "*Ustedes frigados.*"

I looked at the flyer, noting Cambridge's photo first and then my own, the words HAVE YOU SEEN .... I didn't need a translation. Oh, indeed. We were screwed.

41

GET AWAY

IN SPITE OF everything, I was the picture of positive thinking. I called on all those stupid business philosophies my mother's company always touted on their notepads. *When the going gets tough, Zyprexa gets tougher. Cetalphix: Helps you get a grip.* In a rare moment of strength, I thought, *Let them tack pink fliers around the globe. Let Hollywood throw phones at my shadow, because we've scored a ride.* I patted Gabe's truck. Our ship had come in.

Of course the ship was the color of rust and the driver's side window was cracked. And yes, Gabe had to climb in and open the passenger door by kicking it. Who needed side mirrors anyway? I'd overlook the many cosmetic flaws, provided it could drive.

Cambridge did not share my enthusiasm. "This is your car?" She whistled. "No way this heap is going anywhere."

"Funny, I said the same thing about you last night," Gabe shot back.

He was definitely related to Liliana. Same mouth.

Cambridge was wise to voice her concerns, though, because when we slid next to Gabe, it was obvious that the truck's interior parts were as decrepit as the rest of it. Even the insects behind Gabe's tires relaxed, because this truck wasn't going anywhere. Anyone could see it. Anyone, that is, except Gabe.

"It just takes a few times here," he said very patiently.

Sure, it turned *on*, but the truck retched as badly as Cambridge had last night. Gabe turned and returned the key, sweat dampening his brow, as *ni modo* farted black clouds of smoke. From the window that didn't roll up, I could see the pink *Have You Seen Us* flyers pinned beneath the windshield wiper of every Audi, Nissan, Volkswagen, Toyota, and Honda. Every vehicle appeared to be sticking out its tongue at us. Listening to Gabe's truck strain and hiccough, San Francisco seemed as far away as the moon.

Eventually Gabe got out, popped the hood, tugged some wires, and mumbled about plugs and oil, until Cambridge told him enough was enough. "We'll walk somewhere," she said. "Or take a bus."

"We don't have any money," I reminded her. "Or clothes."

Cambridge was still wearing Gabe's jeans that didn't zip. I was still dressed as a C.U.P. ambassador. Neither of us had showered.

When Gabe closed the hood, the truck rocked so hard I feared it'd collapse. He leaned on the no-doubt functioning Volkswagen parked in the spot next to us. "Stay with me tonight, and I'll try the truck in the morning." He picked the flyer from beneath the VW's windshield and crumpled it. "It's the fog, *sabes*. The engine is wet, that's all. I'll seal it with towels tonight and I promise," he looked at me, "I'll take you to your boyfriend tomorrow." His eyes were a dark-chocolate brown, the lids ringed in purple like he needed sleep.

"But Hollywood saw us."

"No she didn't," he replied. "And even if she did, there's nothing she can do."

Somehow I doubted that. But when the fog rolled into the parking lot, it didn't bring any other choices with it. Gabe was the first and only person to offer us a ride. Therefore, if we had an alternative to stuffing the hood with towels he swore were for this purpose, I sure wished I knew it.

After we finished sealing the engine, Cambridge and I sat on a concrete slab and smoked a cigarette. We watched Gabe gallop in and out of the rows of cars, plucking flyers from windshields and crumpling them. "That's some serious dedication,"

Cambridge said, pointing at our driver, his black and white vans blurred with purpose.

"He must be vested in having you spend another night in his dorm," I teased.

Cambridge squished her cigarette into the pavement. "Bethany, please. This one is all you."

I rubbed my stubbly, unshaved legs and pinched a mound of fat from my hip. "All me what? You're the showstopper," I said. "You should have seen yourself dancing with a fun noodle last night!"

She dragged on her cigarette. "Fun noodle? I thought you said his name was Glo." She scooched over, bumped me with her shoulder. "You could stop Gabe's show," she said, "if you wanted."

At that, I laughed good and hard. Obviously that brownie had permanently affected her brain.

From: richardgoodman@mdk-12.md.us.edu
To: Bethany Stern <bethanys@utopia.com>
Subject: TJ

Dear Bethany,

You don't *really* want me to fax over a signature, do you? Tell me that was a joke. You expect me to believe they actually beat you there? If you would call me, I'd be happy to discuss things with you.

Also, you mentioned the twin's birthday, so last night, I looked at pictures of their boys' birthday party. I most definitely remember the magician. He played punk music that was not appropriate. A dove crapped on the cake too. I thought his act was over-the-top until he turned his birds yellow using some kind of powder. My kids are still talking about it. What happened between you two?

I've wracked my brain over and over about Chuck E. Cheese's and even went through video footage from the party. I don't remember seeing you. I hope you believe me. Do you believe me?

I assume you're still at camp. Is there a number where I can reach you?

Can you at least let me know you're ok?

~Dad

42

WANTED

SOMEWHERE BETWEEN THE parking lot and Coperni-
cus, my positive thoughts curled up and died alongside Gabe's
truck. We'd been so close to freedom, only now, back in Gabe's
room, it seemed so impossibly far away. Obviously Gabe shared
a deep connection with his vehicle because he took its failures
personally. He'd looked a little humiliated trudging back to Copernicus Hall. We all did. It felt a little like walking to our own
execution.

Gabe had snatched a newspaper from the stairwell on our
way up, and now was reading at his desk. He made a funny noise
when he flipped it over.

"What?" I asked him.

He shook his head. "Nothing."

"I thought you were about to say that we were on the front
page or something."

He slipped the paper under his laptop. "You aren't on the
front page."

I exhaled. The last thing we needed was more media cover-
age of our fat camp exodus.

"You're on the last page," Gabe said, and tried—really, really
tried—not to smile.

When I leaned across the desk for the paper, he stopped me.
"It was nothing," he said. "A blurb. No one reads the campus

rag anyway. The front page was a series of warnings about illegal fireworks on campus and how five million people blow their
hands into the stratosphere because of them." He squinted. "You
guys were just this teeny, tiny blurb. In the back. Infinitesimal."

Cambridge fiddled with some of her hair beads. "Let's hear
it," she said.

"Better not." He nodded in my direction. "Bethany's white as
a ghost. Don't want her to freak on me—"

"Just read it!"

"Fine," he said, snapping the paper very professionally. He
cleared his throat. "It says here that Graham Michener, the university vice president, hopes students realize the gravity of the
situation at Utopia. And I quote," Gabe said, hooking his index
finger, " 'Any student who has information regarding these children will be compensated by CUP. This matter is of serious concern, and I ask all summer students living on or near campus to
treat it as such. The mothers were overwhelmingly distraught.
Tabitha is lactose intolerant, and Bethany's mother informed us
her daughter is,' " Gabe stopped. "I'm sorry," he said, cracking
up. He cleared his throat again. " 'Her daughter is unhappy and
prone to rages!' "

Cambridge leaned back on the bed. "Jesus Christ, I am not
lactose intolerant," she said.

Of course our pictures were in the paper too. They were the
same ones on the flyers, only these weren't black and white and
poorly copied. These were the photographs from our camp files:
me and Jackie standing in front of our row house and Cambridge alongside her horse. They were enlarged, full-colored,
and pixeled out the ass.

"And that picture!" Cambridge said, pointing to the small
square. "At least I don't look like that anymore." It was true. Her
hair was a gnarled mess now, and she'd abandoned makeup after we got to fat camp. She had a sort-of disguise. Not me. I even
wore the same flip-flops in my picture. Same hairstyle. Same
everything.

I didn't find any humor in the situation, which was why I
didn't get why Gabe and Cambridge laughed like fools. My life
disintegrated before my eyes while these two practically peed
themselves. "Cambridge? Didn't you hear it?" My heartbeat

raced loud in my ears. "Weren't you listening? We are wanted." My stomach knotted. "It's over!"

Cambridge stopped laughing, and the room got quiet. She moved closer to me on the bed. Gabe pitched the newspaper in the recycling bin and sat down on my other side.

"Calm down, Bethany," Cambridge said. "Take deep breaths." She petted my cheek. "Not every girl has the courage to walk out of fat camp," she said, and smiled. "We set the precedent!"

Gabe patted my knee. "Just sit tight until tomorrow."

Tomorrow? Was that when the giant net fell from the ceiling?

Gabe pulled off his SPOOGE shirt revealing a baby-blue T-shirt beneath it. He knelt in front of me. He had the look of a firefighter delivering the news that just before they rescued my cat, it had jumped into a river and drowned. "It's only the campus paper. No one cares. Besides," he said, "I've seen *CSIs* like this. They try to scare you into going back on your own. Utopia's avoiding the bad PR."

"That's true," echoed Cambridge. "The women's studies department would be all over this."

The two of them, I could see, were full of calculations.

Gabe tried to soothe the panic swelling in my chest. "Either way, I'll get you out of here tomorrow, Bethany. Let your boyfriend know you're coming to LA."

I detected a note of something in his voice. Doubt? Hurt? "He's not my boyfriend," I managed.

"Who else you e-mailing then?"

"Definitely not my boyfriend," I explained. What kind of loser did that make me, bouncing e-mails back and forth to my dad?

"Whoever you're e-mailing," Gabe said, "ask him for an air compressor and a few spark plugs." He yanked my ponytail. "And some sunshine."

And a miracle, I thought.

From: Bethany Stern <bethanys@utopia.com>
To: rgoodman@mdk12.library.us.edu
Subject: TJ

Dear Dad,

Nothing happened w/TJ. thats the short version. I don't have time to write the long b/c in other news: I'm still on the fly. my picture is on about a billion flyers around campus & I'm in the newspaper. People are searching 4 me. according to u, tho, I'm easily overlooked. So I'm not worried. Every eye's got a blind spot, dad.

You taught me that @ Chuck E Cheese.

when i get to back to Baltimore, if I ever get back to Baltimore, I'll be sure to stop over and swim. Or not. Definitely not.

Thanks for not believing me and thanks a lot for your signature.

~Bee

43

LULLABYE

BY LATE AFTERNOON, Cambridge, resting on Gabe's bed, complained that she'd been bitch-slapped with the world's worst hangover. Chin supported in one hand, she channel surfed, willing her droopy eyes open. Gabe, back at his laptop, searched the Internet for engine-drying remedies.

"You should relax," he said now, his back toward me. "Take a nap or something." He tapped at a picture of a truck on the computer's screen. "Lily told me you never slept. She said you snuck food from the mailroom every night."

My face burned. "Not true," I lied.

When Gabe turned around, I wanted to say something about his stupid band T-shirts and his polluting non-driving truck, but he lowered his voice and tilted his head, indicating he was verging on saying something important. "You should sleep now, Bethany." He threw a pillow over his shoulder. "It'll help keep those rages in check."

Oy. Couldn't my mom at least have pretended to be worried? Maybe I'd been kidnapped. Murdered. Why did everyone assume I ran away from Utopia because I was unhappy and angry?

Don't answer that.

"Rumors of my rage have been greatly exaggerated," I quipped. "And sleeping now would be the dumbest thing I could do." Of course, right after I said it, sleep became the only thing

I wanted. I wished Gabe would leave us alone so I could fling off my bra, loosen my sweatpants, and dream sweet pancake dreams. "I have to stay awake," I said drowsily. "What if they know we're here?"

Gabe gathered a fuzzy Southwestern blanket and draped it over me. "No one would believe I had two girls in my room. Besides, the truck will start tomorrow. I promise." He tucked the blanket around me. "Did you ever decide where you're going?"

Had we? I wondered. So bent on running away, I'd forgotten all about a destination. We'd missed that San Francisco bus by a day or so. There'd be other Greyhounds, of course. Other Amtraks. Why now, I wondered, on the brink of telling Gabe my mission to get back to Baltimore, did it sound so FUBARed? "I honestly have no idea," I admitted. "I was going to head back home, but now I don't know." I counted the tiles on Gabe's ceiling, blinked back the tears that had sprung out of nowhere. I guessed all those e-mails from my dad pushed everything forward. I guessed seeing Hollywood marathoning past Copernicus Dining Hall hadn't helped either. Suddenly, everything converged like some demented triangle from geometry class. How much crap I'd gotten myself into at Utopia. How much more crap waited for me at home. My head throbbed from unsuccessfully holding back the tears that slid down my cheeks. "It's hard to decide where to go. Every option looks pretty bleak."

Gabe had the courtesy to avoid looking at my tear-streaked face. "You could stay with me," he said to my feet, "for as long as you want."

I shook my head. He had nerd camp and his sister to look after. It seemed everyone had a place to be. Or a place they wanted to be. "I'll figure something out."

He rubbed his chin. "You could always go back to Utopia," he said. "I mean I know it's not exactly a paradise there, but I'd rather be building rockets than dealing with my parents at home. They would've had me working at Del Taco. And if Lili could spend her life at Utopia, she would. She only bitches about it because you do."

I felt a little guilty for bursting Liliana's bubble. Not everyone was sent to Utopia against her will, I had to remember that. Some people went gaga over California too. Hardly noticed the damp chill or the earthquakes.

Gabe leaned against the dorm's cinder block wall like he was weighing my options, sticking variables in for X and Y. He scratched his head. He wasn't what you'd call hot, but he was definitely handsome in a quiet way. It wasn't obvious at first, but the more you looked at him, the more you saw it, like those 3D posters. Something about him made me comfortable. Maybe it was because he had a sister. Or that his room was decorated with fantasy novels and sci-fi DVDs. I felt like I could tell him anything. "Maybe I'll go to San Francisco and redefine myself. Isn't that what everyone does in California?" I wiped away tears on the sleeve of my university sweatshirt. "I'll get my GED. Fill out some apps at Del Taco."

"You could," replied Gabe. He must've had his eyebrow pierced at some point, only now the hole had closed into a purple scab. A thin hoop hung on the lobe of each ear. "Or you could join a band."

"Evidently you've never heard my voice. I'm actually prohibited from singing in public places."

"Oh, come on," said Gabe, covering his mouth with his hand. "Let me hear it."

"I'm not kidding. I can't sing. At all."

"Well, keep in mind," said Gabe, grabbing his deodorant stick from the dresser, "the best ones never can." Then he closed his eyes and belted out some old-skool Nirvana, head banging à la grunge circa 1993. His voice was god-awful, it might even outsuck mine. I laughed through my tears and concluded that if Gabe and his paint-peeling voice attended Baltimore Magnet, we would hang. I could see us being friends. Hell, if I had wandered into another story, one where I'd showered and brushed my hair, one where I didn't happen to be a fat camp offender, I might've flirted with him. Of course in that story, I knew how to flirt too.

44

WHEN YOU PLAY WITH FIRE

EVEN THOUGH GABE'S singing voice could've roused coyotes in Nevada, Cambridge snored peacefully on the other bed. And, as afternoon wore on, my own eyelids grew heavier. *Well, maybe just for a few minutes*, I thought, drifting, drifting—and I was out too.

In my dream a police officer stood before me and yelled, "Miss Stern, I don't think you comprehend the gravity of your situation. I have a gun, and I'm not afraid to use it." I focused on his gun, wondering reasonably if it was made of licorice. The cop pulled the trigger. Pop, pop, pop. KA-BOOM.

I startled awake, feeling embarrassed. Had I screamed? Drooled on Gabe's pillow? Outside it was nearing dark. It had to be—

"Six thirty," said Gabe, reading my mind. "You slept six hours."

He was poised on the edge of his desk, feet in the chair, headphone wires looping around his neck. His chin rested on his fist like that famous sculpture of the dude thinking. I wondered how long he'd been staring at nothing. "Feel better?" he asked.

I nodded. I nearly inquired if his room had a gas leak, but unlike me, he appeared wide awake. He'd even showered.

I pointed at Cambridge next to me. "Looks like she's going for the record."

"She was up for a bit, but then fell back asleep."

Something that felt a lot like jealousy twisted my gut: that she'd been awake when I wasn't. As if sensing this, Gabe said, "She smoked a few cigarettes and launched firecrackers at campus security when they knocked on the door."

"What?"

"Joke." He patted the space beside him on the desk. Another pop, pop, pop. KA-BOOM. "Happy *Día de Independencia*, Bethany. Come see."

I sat next to him on the thankfully well-constructed desk. Outside his window, smoke trailed upward. "You picked a good time to run away because security's too distracted with illegal fireworks to even worry about you guys," he said knowingly. "This entire dorm is filled with future rocket scientists." A sizzle and a crackle rat-a-tat-tatted below. I was momentarily hopeful. If students ignored the hands-can-be-mutilated-for-life warning concerning fireworks, maybe Gabe was right, they'd also overlook our fat camp departure.

There in the trees I noticed firecracker cylinders smoldering. Amateurs. TJ could manipulate fire paper before he was ten, and these frat boys couldn't properly launch a bottle rocket. Gabe opened the desk drawer with his foot and removed a box of sparklers. He offered me one, lighting it with Cambridge's lighter.

"*¡Salud!*" he said, tapping his sparkler against mine. "They look like birthday candles, no?" He bit his lip. "Make a wish, Bethany."

With my bare feet swinging off his desk, I searched my mind for a request. "I wish I knew where to go or what to do. I wish the right option would—"

"One wish. Sheesh. Pick one."

The sparkler burned brightly. "I want this story to have a happy ending," I said, then huffed a breath. The sparkler sputtered but didn't go out. Gabe licked his fingers and extinguished the flame.

"You girls and your happy endings." He rubbed his chin. "You know my dad, a wise Indian chief, always asked me '*Hijo*, what do you do when you've dug yourself in a hole and there's no way out?'"

A few pyrotechnics whistled past the window. "If he was an Indian chief, why was he speaking Spanish?"

"Good question," replied Gabe, his dimple vanishing again when he smiled. "Most people usually fall for that, but I forgot you aren't most people." I looked at him, then instantly looked down. "It was actually in a movie, but the guy said 'If you're in a hole with no way out, your best bet isn't to run away.' *Entra más profundo*, see. You go in deeper."

Gabe paused as if to let the sheer sophistication wash over me. Instead, I observed that sometime during my nap, he'd abandoned the blue shirt and now sported a short-sleeved button down. It was newish looking. Kinda dressy. He'd changed into khaki shorts too, with an excess of pockets. On his knee I saw a scratch, raw and bloody. I wondered if he'd gotten it last night.

He fished out a piece of printer paper and folded it intricately. I studied his hands as he pressed down lines and angles, fashioning it into a rocket shape much like the airplanes he'd dispatched into our windows at Utopia. He slipped a sparkler into the plane's tail and lit it. Then he cast it out the window, where it performed a series of loopty loops and landed on another dorm's roof.

"You're good at that," I said.

"There's not a whole lot to do in New Mexico," he said. "You get creative."

I'd never known anyone who'd embraced boredom so philosophically. "Like Lili," he started. "She's a giant pain in my ass, but she can sew her face off. You should see her stuff."

I'd only seen Liliana's bedazzler work, which was quite artistic. I remembered the night she'd sewn the words BITE IT in a semicircle across the seat of my pants. "Your sister has serious *huevos*," I told Gabe, suddenly missing her.

Gabe flipped to a picture on his phone. It was Liliana, me, and Cambridge leaning out our dorm window. The light behind us was soft and yellow, all three of us smiling like we weren't hungry or pissed off.

"She covered for us at least twice," I informed Gabe. "If we ever get out of this mess, I want to do something super nice for her." *Nicer than the chocolate roses I'd sent her from Olive's dorm,* I thought.

Gabe tucked his phone in a drawer. "You could discover a cure for diabetes."

"If only I were smarter I would. Cambridge has a shot. Ask her."

His eyes searched mine. "I don't know about that," he said. "My money's on you, Bethany."

My molars ached in the way they usually do whenever anyone said something nice to me. A high-pitched firework whizzed past the dorm. Gabe cleared his throat.

"You know what else we do in New Mexico when we get bored?" A rocket launched a few windows down, penetrated a tree, shaking its leaves to the ground. He smiled crookedly. "We knock out."

Knock Out. Duh.

Gabe's room was pretty bare, but he did manage to bring the basic boy essential: a beloved PlayStation. Which meant he also brought Knock Out—also known as KO—the game that anyone with a Y chromosome played nonstop.

He looked positively jealous when he told me a few minutes later that I was welcome to play the game while he went to watch the fireworks with Liliana. He boasted he had the bloodiest un-cut KO version too, one that let you physically rip someone's head off. I looked at Liliana's brother now, bouncing around like a boxer, his sock tan noticeable on his Vans-less feet. He slid the special PlayStation glove on my hand with the enthusiasm of an engagement ring. "You can play as many games as you want," he said.

Not like I gave a fat hootenanny about Knock Out, but I liked how generously he offered it to me. Then I remembered how last night he'd handed over his shoes to Cambridge without question. How cold he must've been walking home in the dewy grass. By the time we'd gotten back, it was chilly enough to see my breath. Yet he'd looked happy dragging the stoned corpse that was Cambridge up the stairs. Now here we were in his room, lounging in his bed, Cambridge spiraled in his striped sheets, me getting ready to knock out Holyfield or some other doofus on his PlayStation. What a guy. What a sucker.

45

KNOCK OUT

EVEN THOUGH HE said he'd check out the fireworks with his sister, Gabe never left. I mean he packed up food for Liliana. He put on shoes. He played a few rounds of Knock Out, but leave he did not. Then, at around eight, it started raining. The fat drops spattered on his window, causing the smoking fireworks in the trees to sizzle out. Within minutes it drizzled then poured. The sound, like meat frying, echoed off the roof and walls of Copernicus Hall. Below his window, students hop-scotched around puddles.

Knowing this was a very, very bad sign for Operation Engine Dry, Gabe turned to the UniTV station for a weather report. Only instead of cartoon gray clouds, and a weather girl twirling an umbrella, we saw someone else. It was Hollywood. Highlighted hair, tank top with an American flag waving across her breasts— Miss Perfect herself. "Oh, I'm very concerned for my safety," she said into the microphone someone held in front of her. The wind picked up the ends of her hair and placed them back down, lovingly. "You heard what her mother said. She's unhappy and prone to rages." Hollywood paused. "Rages. As in she's violent. Look, we all just wanted to help her, but ..." She looked into the camera. "These dangerous girls are closer than you think. If you hear explosions, don't think Fourth of July." She moved a wad of gum from one side of her mouth to the other with her tongue. "Think Bethany Stern and Tabitha Nelson."

Gabe walked toward the TV and pointed a finger at our old dorm window. Just barely I made out Liliana's face. She was holding something, a piece of white paper, the teeny words "she's lying" almost indecipherable. The camera man might've seen it too because before Mount Hollywood erupted with more BS, we were back with the anchor lady and her stupid smile. "Thank you, Amber. Now let's check in with weather."

I barely heard the announcement—"Fireworks will be postponed due to an unseasonable rainstorm ..."—because my heart pumped in my ears. My hatred for Hollywood ignited my forehead and swooshed down to my feet. *I'm not violent*, I thought viciously. *If only I'd caught her phone. Bashed it over her skull. Rage? I'll show her rage.*

Watching me, a little nervously I might add, Gabe clicked off the television. "Forget her." Then he closed his laptop, silenced his phone. "Remember what I said earlier? *Entra más profun—*"

"Thanks, *sensei*," I replied, too harshly. "Wise advice."

The dorm was silent except for Cambridge's rhythmic snoring and the rain spattering outside. I'd hurt Gabe's feelings, I knew. He picked up his skateboard and spun its wheels quietly. His inky-black hair, parted in that zigzag, fell evenly against his jaw. At least he'd tried to help. No need to bite his head off. Sure, Liliana's sign was misspelled and hardly visible, but she'd tried too. They'd all tried.

I nudged Cambridge in the bed. "We've gone from campers to fugitives to terrorists in three hours. We should leave, Cambridge. Now!"

Zen as always, Cambridge folded her arms behind her head. "I don't want to go." She felt around the floor for her cigarettes, checked her pockets and then decided, I guessed, smoking was too much of an effort. "I think it'll all work out." Rain slithered down the panes; droplets tapped the roof. "Don't you want to know how it ends?" she asked, all innocence.

"It's going to end badly," I said. "*Very* badly. What more proof do you need?"

She looked from me to Gabe then back to me again. "I disagree."

On some level, like a molecular one, I knew I couldn't leave without either of them.

I sat down next to Gabe on his desk, and we stared at the sloppy, wet branches outside. "All this will be dry by tomorrow," said Gabe, "and we'll be driving to San Francisco. You'll see." I let myself believe him for a minute. Then Gabe scooched closer to me. "Hey, why do you let that girl get to you anyway?" he asked of Amber.

Because she's beautiful, I wanted to say. Because her clothes fit, and her boyfriend stands next to her in photos. Because her father answers her phone calls. Because girls like her make girls like me hate themselves.

"I don't know why," I said.

Gabe blew his bangs out of his face. "Not everyone goes for the Hollywood type, you know."

When his fingertips grazed mine, I flinched a little. He'd only been squishing the Knock Out glove into my hand. "What do you think?" he asked, beaming at his PlayStation. "Wanna play?"

46

#LUCKY

NO ONE EVER said you couldn't enjoy the moments before your life shot up in flames, right? So while I waited for more AMBER Alerts, Gabe and I played some prodigious rounds of Knock Out. Gabe (Martinez) taught me (Holyfield) how to punch, all knuckle and downward thrust. He taught me how to squint like a professional and how to hit first with your left and then cock back your right arm, your power arm, and let it fly. He threw out advice as often as he jabbed: *Only hit them in the head if it's clear. Try for soft tissue, it's easier on your hands. Not your knuckles, the space between your knuckles. Maintain your footwork. Good!* I tried to keep it all straight, and I must've because in round two, Gabe looked at me like I'd just sprouted wings.

"What?" I asked him. "What I'd do?"

"I can't believe it," he said, wide-eyed and amazed.

"WHAT?"

"You just knocked me out."

"For real?"

He indicated the screen where a ref was chopping his hand. Three. Two. One. "Beginner's luck," I said, and then an hour later, sweaty and out of breath, I knocked him out again.

Afterward we made popcorn, and Gabe dumped a macaroni and cheese flavor packet in the bag and shook it. Very ingenious.

Then he popped out a jar of peanut butter from his bookcase and, sitting next to me on the desk, we alternated sticking plastic spoons into it.

Whether it was because he thought we'd get away with everything or because we didn't, we laughed like it was our last night on Earth. Even Cambridge, who fell back asleep, chuckled in her dreams. We downloaded three hundred ringtones to Hollywood's phone and took countless shots of our middle fingers and once, for good measure, Gabe's butt. Then, around nine, when the rain tapered off, Gabe put his headphones on me and told me to close my eyes. I expected hip hop or rap or anything other than the obnoxious sound that sliced through the wires.

"It sounds like cat sex in a garbage can," I said. "How do you stand it?"

Gabe tensed. "That is sick *mierda* right there. You don't know what you're talking about."

He stared at the tablet like the problem was there. "Just close your eyes, Bethany. And listen." He placed his hands on the earbuds and gently pressed. Then he shuffled to a song that was kinda nice—slow and melancholy. I listened until a whiff of Cheetos forced my eyes open. When I did, Gabe's face was so close to mine, he could've counted my freckles. "Your face is purple," he said. "It's that god darn radio."

"What?" I screamed.

He lowered the volume and then, without backing up, he repeated what I'd misunderstood. "Your face is perfect," he said. "Like the golden ratio. One point six one eight. That's the ratio that nature mimics. The closer you get to it, the more it makes people, like, respond."

Was he seeing some kind of equation in my eyebrows?

He leaned away, removed the earbuds.

"I'm sorry I don't like SPOOGE," I said. I had no idea how to respond to Gabe's ... mathematical analysis? Observation? Flirting?

"I'm just saying that in spite of your substandard taste in music, Bethany, I find you ... well. Ever since the fountain. You know, the first time I saw you, I thought you were. I found your ratio ... dammit. I thought you were *linda*."

I absolutely positively could not look at him. "Who's Leenda?"

Gabe laughed and covered his mouth with his hand. "*Linda,* as in pretty." He looked down at his scratched-up knee, hesitated. "As in *boscocha.* As in *estoy loco para ti.*" He unlooped the wires from around my head and then, rather subtly, moved closer. The desk squeaked awkwardly. "Bethany, the first time I saw you I was like, here's a girl who gets it. *Linda,* as in beautiful."

All my life I had waited for someone to use the words *Bethany* and *beautiful* in the same sentence. ALL. MY. LIFE. Only it wasn't TJ. It was Liliana's brother?!

"You mean you don't think I'm fat?" I was beginning to feel a little dizzy.

"Are they mutually exclusive?"

"I don't know. Is that a math term?"

"In my mind, it is possible to be both beautiful and fat."

"And happy too?"

"Sure," said Gabe, easily. Outside, something crackled, followed by a boom so loud my spine rung. Must've been thunder.

"I like your world then," I said, and meant it.

From the corner of my eye a light flickered. *Perfect,* I thought, *the police are here to ruin this very intense moment.* Only when I turned toward the window, outside a dot burst into a million silver squiggles. They shimmered brightly, then dimmed. Not a chance these were police lights. They weren't illegal firecrackers either. These were the real deal.

"I guess they decided to do the fireworks even though it's raining," Gabe said, moving closer to me. Another blast and red and white strings blossomed behind him. With both our heads now tilted toward the sky, I could see Gabe's hair radiating light, his eyelashes sharpened into points. "In fact, I think it stopped raining."

In my estimation, the best part of fireworks was the interval between the first thump and the final explosion. Not the oh-ah moment that came afterward, but the electrical moment preceding it, when you thought, *I wonder what will happen next?* as a spark sprinted upward. It was during this tiny splinter of time, the seconds between contraction and detonation, when Gabe's blinking quickened; when he turned to me, and I was embarrassed to be caught watching him. I shifted my gaze away, concentrating on a patch of night erupting into a sugary web. He did not turn around to see the constellation behind him. Instead he tugged the plastic tips of my sweatshirt strings, pulled me closer, and kissed me. *Kissed me.*

At first our cheese-coated teeth collided sharply. Then, it was every kind of soft and sweet and wet and quiet. Our lips layered in each other's as tender as the rain collected in the sills. First his hand to my cheek, his other behind my neck pulling me closer, closer. I could have died.

Since it'd been a year since I'd kissed anyone, I'd forgotten how it went. Blood rushing to my head, a red flush prickling my neck and ears. Quiet parts inside me suddenly singing, tingling. His lips, softer than I would have imagined, swept mine. When I pulled back, Gabe's face was still there, eyes opening little by little. He leaned his forehead against mine, a bit self-consciously,. He swallowed. "I'm sorry," he said. "I just went for it."

"That's OK," I said, hating myself for receding. Why didn't I trust the moment?

"I've been waiting to do that for a long time."

"You just met me," I pointed out.

"Not true. I saw you get out of your minivan weeks ago."

"When I gave you directions?"

He nodded. "And told me Copernicus was dead."

"That made you want to kiss me?" I wondered what he'd found appealing about my big belly, busted flip-flops, and bad attitude. In my mind, my irrational and pathetic history repeated itself, starting with my birth and including pretty much everything after it. "But I'm so damaged," I said. How to explain my competitive mother and deadbeat dad and magician love and pretty sister and, and …

Gabe's lips fell like confetti on my forehead, my eyes, my neck. "No you're not," he said. "You're funny and smart." I shivered when his breath found my ear. "You knock me out."

His cheeks turned bright red. "Lili called it. She was all, 'mano, you're sweatin' Baltimore, and I realized my sister was right. The time frame? After the minivan and before right now. That's how long I've wanted to kiss you."

I tried to see what was right in front of my face—Gabe and

his zigzag part. His layered tees. The Velcro circles on the pockets of his shorts. Not a single deck of cards in his room. Gabe. With his finger beneath my chin, he lifted my face toward his. "I walked around this whole campus trying to find that party last night. I knew you'd be there. I waited there for hours, but never saw you. Then we both left at the same time. I heard you calling me across the football field." He laughed and twisted my sweatshirt string around his finger. "Even when Cambridge yacked all over my shirt, I swear it, Bethany, I was thinking, *Thank you, Dios. This is my lucky night.*"

We leaned back and watched the fireworks finale, my head on his chest, his hands in my hair, booms so powerful his cell phone trembled on the desk; chunks of color streaked past the window. We watched until the sky quieted to black, his hungry heart beating like a metronome. Me thinking: Cue the music, people. Close the curtain. Here's your happy ending.

47

THEN AGAIN, MAYBE NOT

BAD NEWS KNOCKED at six in the morning. Then bad news knocked again. Louder. Military-style. A knock that said, So long, folks. Thanks for playing.

I sat up quickly, leaned over and shook Cambridge, who had fallen off the bed last night and now slept on the floor. In a moment of terror, Gabe swung open his closet in an effort to hide us in there, I guessed, when a very familiar voice roared, "Do not make me kick this door down, young man."

Poor Gabe. The last thing he wanted was to be the guy with me when everything went to hell. But we all know how life works, so of course, Gabe was with me when it all blew up. Judging by the Spanish curses, he wasn't happy about it either. You might assume I was just as angry, and you'd be right. Gabe and I were supposed to be driving off into the, um, sunrise by now. But I knew this moment was coming. Hell, we all did.

KNOCK, KNOCK, KNOCK.

Might as well open the damn door myself.

Up close to it, I stopped. I stood there waiting for my X-ray vision to kick in.

"Bethany Mitzi Goodman Stern?" roared the voice from outside the door.

Must he be this loud? Did he have handcuffs? I hoped he didn't have handcuffs. I leaned my head on the door. He was awfully old-sounding for campus security—really familiar-sounding too.

"Is Tabitha Calliope Nelson with you?"

"Yes," I answered timidly.

"Open the door," he spat.

Cambridge stretched, her dreadlocks spilled down her back. "Just open the door for the clown, Bethany. Let's get it over with."

The man was shorter and fatter than I remembered. He dressed in clothes that someone not from California would consider Californian: flip-flops, long shorts, Hawaiian printed top, 49ers ball cap. Cambridge looked at me then back to our arrestor. "Who in the hell are you?" she asked.

The man stepped forward again. He appeared surprisingly soft, chubby. His shorts and shirt were wrinkled and his rimless glasses seemed fragile.

"You must be Tabitha Nelson," said the man, raising an eyebrow.

She clenched the blanket to her chin. "And you are ... ?"

Averting piles of clothing and popcorn bags, he slid in flip-flops across Gabe's floor. He bent down and put out his hand. "I'm Richard Goodman."

Cambridge coughed out a hello and shook his hand. Then the man looked right at me and said, "I'm Bethany's father."

He must've seen something funny in my expression, because he laughed a laugh I didn't remember forgetting. "Guess you weren't expecting me."

I hoped my voice worked. "You couldn't *fax* your signature?"

What dimension had I wandered into here? Last I checked, my father lived in Ellicott City. His wife, Penny, grew roses in terracotta pots and wore T-shirts with airbrushed pictures of her kids on them. How exactly did he get here? To Utopia?

Gabe looked just as confused. "This is your dad?" he asked.

"I'm the rent," my dad embarrassingly answered. "Bethany needed me."

Correction, I thought, *I needed your signature.* "Am I out of Utopia?" I asked, as images of broken shackles cropped up in my brain. "Am I free?"

My dad sat down backward in Gabe's chair, ready to reason. He'd gained twenty pounds since I'd last seen him. Maybe thirty. "Well, not exactly," he said. "You ladies are in serious hot water here."

"Why is that?" asked Cambridge

"You're both minors, for one."

Cambridge peeled a rubber band from her wrist. "Today happens to be my birthday," she said, and secured her ponytail. "My eighteenth birthday."

Now was probably not the best time to wish her happy birthday, but I did anyway. She winked then collapsed back on her pillow. She was off the hook.

When Richard Goodman's brown eyes zeroed in on me, I knew I wasn't. "But it's not your eighteenth birthday, right, Bethany?"

"Not like you were ever very good at remembering them," I said coolly.

My dad sighed. You could tell he was used to temper tantrums. "What do you say we take a little walk, Bethany? Talk things over?" He shook a greasy paper bag. "I brought bagels."

Question: What do you do when your father shows up at your door? With bagels? I didn't know either, so when I walked past the second guy to kiss me, I had no clue whether I was making a new mistake or correcting an old one. As my dad led me by the elbow past computer geeks peeking out their doors, down the stairwell, and out into the morning, my emotions flipped over and over like one of those calendars in a movie: Shock. Denial. Then humiliation. Much as it hurt to admit it, all the resentment that marched out so easily in my e-mails evaporated in Richard Goodman's presence.

In silence, we walked past the library, cut over the footbridge, and crossed the stadium's turf. We wound up at a picnic table by Lake Pacifica. No naked people swimming now, though. Only a crew team dragging equipment from the very boathouse Cambridge'd hurled in. My dad reached into the paper bag. "Do you like poppy?" he asked.

Only in that surreal moment, one I never could have imagined, I found I did not know.

48

DUNK

FOR SOME REASON I remembered my father being taller. Thinner. Younger. My dad, middle-aged, not ugly, but not especially memorable either. Do you remember what your librarian looked like the last time you visited your local branch?

My point exactly.

His face and arms were pale, like he didn't get outside too often. His hair occupied the spectrum between dark blond and brown; it was uneventful, and thinning around the temples. Behind glasses, his eyes were brown, and sad, like the eyes of most grown-ups and basset hounds everywhere.

Initially I'd thought we'd head directly to MontClaire Hall, where the fabled form awaited his signature. But it was barely sunrise. If a signature was what I wanted, then apparently a cross-campus tour and poppy seed bagel were a preliminary part of the bargain.

At the picnic table, my back faced the lake. My father sat opposite me, a bag of bagels between us. He surveyed the rowers tugging their vessels toward the water. "Did your mother ever tell you the story of how I rented a rowboat at the Inner Harbor when I proposed to her?"

I'd heard the story before, but I wanted to hear if he remembered it the same way she did. "It was so hot and I was so nervous, I passed out on the dock before we even got in the boat.

They had to carry me to Phillip's Crab House and rub ice cubes on my temples. And when I came to, your mom had already found the ring in my pocket and put it on."

Same story. Only in my mom's version, she told it like a cautionary tale.

"My overtures were always so grand and romantic in my imagination," he explained. "It's the execution that always tripped me up." That sure sounded familiar. I turned toward Pacifica, and we both regarded the crew boys balancing their skinny boats on their heads and wading into the water.

"Anyway," my dad said, placing another still-warm poppy seed in my hand, "it's good to see you, Bethany."

A knot rose in my throat.

"I did read all your e-mails, you know." I concentrated on the sound of paddles dipping behind me, boatmen shouting commands. "You have such a way with words."

Somehow the phrase "I know" crowded my mouth, but I locked it in.

"I wish I could go back and change everything between us."

"Well," I said reasonably, "you can't."

"True." He removed a tub of schmear from the bag. "But I could rescue you today," he said carefully. "I could sign you out. That has to count for something."

We have confirmation, I thought. *Richard Goodman just agreed to sign me out. I just received my get-out-of-fat-camp-five-and-a-half-weeks early card. Huzzah!* Only before I could stop it, my thoughts traveled to sleepy, smoky Cambridge and then to Gabe—his paper airplanes, his warm kisses. I wasn't sure why my emancipation didn't feel as good as I'd hoped, but I had an inkling it had to do with those two. "We can fly back to Baltimore tomorrow. Belinda and Hank will meet us at MontClaire at eight."

"What time is it now?" I asked.

He tilted his wrist. "Six."

"If we start walking now, we can make it to MontClaire in twenty minutes."

My plump librarian father looked a little disappointed that I wanted to speed up the process. Maybe he assumed I'd want to sit here shivering by the water, catching up on old times.

He shoved the schmear and bagel back in the paper bag, then he walked over to a skinny canoe facing down in the sand. He turned the boat over with his flip-flop, a move so natural I'd sworn he'd rehearsed it. "Or," he said. "I could row us to Mont-Claire Hall."

"Are you joking?"

Even though he smiled, he said, "No. It'd be a waste to come all the way to California University and not see the Pacific." He began sliding the boat toward the water.

"That's not the Pacific."

"What's one extra letter?"

My father yelled out in the general direction of the crew oaring on the lake. "Guys, my daughter will be a freshman here next fall. Mind if we test the waters?"

"Suit yourself," some delirious crew member yelled back. "There're life jackets in the shed."

"What are you doing?" I asked. My father, who had disappeared in the boathouse, must've been suffering from some deranged form of jetlag. He returned and began dragging the rowboat into the lake. You could see the determination on his face as he rolled up his shorts and tucked the ball cap low on his forehead. He adjusted his glasses. "I'm a Marylander," he said. "Sailing's in my blood."

"I'm pretty sure there's no sail on that thing."

"Humor me, Bethany." He shook the paddle. "You can eat your bagel, and I'll do all the work. We made it this far. Let's get some perspective from a schooner."

"A schooner?"

The boat rocked hypnotically on the tiny waves. "This," he said, "is a schooner."

He fitted the oars into their little holes, and made a painful animal noise before flinging himself inside the boat. He waved me toward him. "Come on."

I shook my head. Under no circumstance would I get in that boat. This went beyond the call of duty. I agreed to breakfast with the man, not some bonding experience that risked a heart attack, drowning, or hypothermia.

"Come on, Bethany."

I dug in my heels.

He shielded his eyes with his palm. "It's perfectly safe."
Somehow I knew he'd had this discussion with Caleb and Cullen
about a plate full of lima beans. "It will be fun," he urged. "It's
your last day in Utopia, after all."

I held the bagel bag and my flip-flops above my head and
waded up to my knees in the frigid water. My father steadied the
boat as I lumbered in. Balancing on the wooden slat that served
as a seat for people with a much smaller butt than my own, my
knees seemed to rest against my ears.

"It's California!" my father roared dorkfully. "The Pacifica!"

Please, God, I thought. *Don't say it.*

"I'm the king of the world!"

And ... he said it.

How we managed to squeeze more than four hundred
pounds into a boat as lean as a tampon was nothing short of a
nautical miracle. Some grace of buoyancy kept us afloat as my
dad rowed once, twice, thrice.

"Did you really think I'd try to talk you into going back to
Utopia?" Wheeze. Cough. "You made it sound like they were torturing you there. Jeez Louise."

Did he just say *Jeez Louise*? "Why else would you fly all
the way from Baltimore and knock on Gabe's door at six in the
morning?"

"Because I haven't seen you in a year."

"Two."

"Because you needed help."

"But how did you find me?"

"I got a tip."

"A tip? From who?"

"Whom."

I hesitated. "Whhooooooooooooommmmmmmmmmmm."

"I'm not at liberty to say." He held out his hand for a bagel.
When I dropped a pumpernickel in his palm, he made a face. I
exchanged it for an onion. "It doesn't matter. I'm here to sign
you out. End of story."

Rowing us farther away from the shore, I watched the campus wobble on the horizon. I feared if I moved, the boat would
topple over. So I sat there, still as marble. I wondered at exactly
what point my life had taken this turn, landing me here, rowing

a boat with my father.

Something about his presence unnerved me too. I wondered if my mom was behind it or Jackie or if he was a last ditch effort sent in by Hank and Belinda to reason with me. He'd mentioned the Costco pool earlier. The e-mails. And now he'd tracked me across the country. Why this sudden interest in me, I wondered, from the man so genuinely disinterested most of my life.

The stadium shrunk as my dad continued rowing. The oars squeaked and swooshed in rhythm. Mist unrolled down the edges of the footbridge. The campus was quiet save for the grunting crew ahead of us. The graceful curved backs of the campus hills appeared soft and inviting. If it wasn't for my dad and fat camp, I could see how you'd think this place was paradise.

"Well, this is going well," he said, then laughed that infernal laugh. "Couldn't ask for better scenery." He pondered the other boat ahead of us by at least a mile. "The crew team must practice this early every day. Can you imagine?"

I could not.

He sniffed deeply. "And that air. It's so humid back in Maryland. Everyone puts their trash out, and the whole neighborhood smells like rotten fruit, bananas, and car exhaust. It feels good out here. Nice." I wondered when he'd resume rowing. I really wanted to get this over with. He leaned carefully back in the vessel and examined the library building. Without looking at me, he said, "So that kid. Gabe. Is he like, well ..." He took a bite of bagel. "Should TJ be worried?"

"About what?" I snapped.

"Gabe. He seemed to like—"

"Why do you care?" It came out harsh, wicked. "I don't want to talk about Gabe, or TJ." I pulled another bagel from the sack. "Or the weather either." If he really was here to sign me out, then could we please get a move on it? If he expected me to sum up the last twelve or so years of my life, this wasn't the time or place.

We both watched the tiny waves with interest. The oars slapped the water. My dad started to say something, then he stopped. He tried again.

"I suppose it's best not to lie to each other, Bethany."

"So tell me why you're really here."

"I wanted to sign you out of camp, for one," he replied. "And ..." He tore apart the onion bagel. "I also wanted to talk about your forgiveness jar." He chewed thoughtfully. Swallowed. "The salad bar. When I said I didn't see you."

"You flew all the way here to tell me you never saw me that day?" He sure wanted to make a point, I guessed. "Fine, Dad. Can we move on?"

He rubbed the knife over the bagel without spreading any cream cheese. "I didn't fly three thousand miles to tell you I didn't see you." He folded his hands in his lap and twisted his gold watch so it faced him. "I flew across country to tell you that I did."

I knew it! I knew I hadn't been crazy. Even TJ'd picked up on it that day in February at Chuck E. Cheese's. So Richard Goodman flew all the way here to tell me he wasn't blind. He was fully sighted when he ignored me. When he ignored me. On purpose. Obviously my vindication didn't last long because of what trailed right behind it. My dad journeyed to California to tell me he saw me at Chuck E. Cheese's? To confirm what I never doubted? That he was too embarrassed to approach his fat daughter? Didn't want to introduce me (again) to his wife? His bratty kids? His Ellicott City neighbors?

Knowing I'd been right didn't make me feel better. It made me feel worse. The sharp truth skewered my heart like a kebab. I felt sick. So sick that when I dropped my bagel into the water, I didn't even care. My dad looked up quickly to say, "I'm so sorry."

A fury rose so fast it shocked me. The words "You are a fat bastard," tore out of my mouth. My temperature rocketed to hot, fueled by fiery, blistering rage. Like they were controlled by a higher power, I saw my hands—my own hands—dig out a bagel and hurl it at my dad. Then another one. I scooped up a mound of schmear and flung it. The plastic bottle of orange juice arced beautifully seconds before it splooshed over his shirt. Cream cheese slid down his glasses. Greasy bagel papers twisted violently in the air.

"I knew you saw me!" The entire crew probably heard me. I grabbed bagel after bagel, screaming the whole time. "And you ignored me?"

My dad barely moved. He did not even talk to me in a library voice and beg me to calm down. He did lean left and then right as bagel after bagel missiled past him. He appeared to actually listen while this voice shrilled, screamed like something alien, only to find out the cold, metallic voice belonged to me. He knew almost everything in my jar only to turn around and use it against me. My rage launched words like weapons of mass destruction; it spattered food everywhere until I was suddenly transported back to the minivan, somewhere in Ohio: Jackie driving, Doug hollering. Good Lord. Was it my destiny to be trapped in an eternal food fight?

I concentrated on the fog tiptoeing over the grassy dunes and willed my rage to fizzle. I watched the curious crew members in the boat ahead of us, and the occasional students on the path. I felt like such a fool. A complete 'tard. A raging shithead. Why had I tried the diet in the first place? Why did I write the e-mails? Why must I fall for everything?

When I veered hard to my right, the boat tipped just low enough for my dad to lose his balance. He faltered and lurched to his left before grabbing the edges of the boat. When I leaned a little further, panic lit his face in the half-second before he slid off the seat and fell in.

Let him drown, I thought.

His head surfaced starboard, his hat nowhere near it. "You ignored me because you were ashamed of me," I said. "I had all that pizza on my plate."

"No," he said, his voice watery.

As quickly and delicately as I could, I crouched on my knees and switched from my seat to his. I brought the oars to my chest just as I'd seen him do. I pushed. Nothing happened. I glanced back at the other crew team hoping they'd telepathically transmit their maritime knowledge, but the oars felt awkward in my hands. I cursed. Even rowing a boat was beyond me. "You ignored me because I was fat," I screamed at my father. I knew if I wasn't fat he would have hugged me at Chuck E. Cheese's, or better yet, invited me to the party in the first place. If I wasn't fat, I would be better. Nicer. Prettier. TJ would want to sleep with me. Hollywood wouldn't chuck phones at my face, and I WOULD KNOW HOW TO ROW A BOAT. I just wanted to start over. I just wanted to wake up and be someone new.

Sopping wet, my father managed to look surprised. His ball cap floated next to him among bagel detritus. "What? That had nothing to do with it."

And he went on. Treading water, he shouted words I never heard. I pulled one oar out of the ring, dunked it in the water and pulled. Sploosh. My dad reached for the boat, nearly gripped it, just before I managed to move it. One stroke. Other Side. Two strokes. Switch. One stroke. It was a lot harder than it looked, but by some miracle of the universe, I rowed my way back to the shore.

At the picnic table, my hands were bleeding and raw. Splinters buried themselves in my palms. As I rubbed my aching shoulder, my dad emerged from the water like a lagoon creature. Soaked to the bone, he adjusted his bent glasses, which were laced with kelp. He zigzagged across the sand, water streaming from his pockets. He stood in front of me, breathing so heavily he barely got the words out. "I see you still have your temper," he said.

Why that struck me as insanely funny, I couldn't tell you. But I laughed harder and harder as he edged closer and closer. And when he sat down next to me, water puddling by our feet, that was when I cried. Not hot, raging tears, but shameful ones. Humiliated tears. Sad tears. I leaned into his cold, wet Hawaiian-printed shirt. He wrapped his arms around me, rubbed my back, and told me it would be OK.

"I was in Chuck E. Cheese's with my kids and wife when suddenly my own daughter walks in, and I don't even know her. I don't even know you, Bethany. I let that happen. I was ashamed of myself, not you."

"Then why recommend a diet book?" I asked his chest. "Why suggest The Forgiveness Diet?"

"Not because I wanted you to lose weight. Look at me," he said, grabbing my wrists. "Look at me. I recommended the book because I wanted you to forgive me."

I looked into his face and said, "Well, I don't."

"I guess I deserve that," he said. He aimed his now-ruined watch into the garbage pail. "You reminded me of so much in your e-mail. All that anger. You reminded me of me." His voice wavered with emotion. "Of the person I used to be before I became an asshole." Behind his cheese-smeared glasses, his eyes, shiny with tears, threatened to spill.

Watching him, I saw for the first time what my mom'd been saying for years. We looked alike. Something about the slant of the nose, shape of the mouth, an uncanny ability to sit for lengths of time without getting bored. "You had no problems being an asshole before. Why the shift now?"

When my father smiled, his teeth were straight and close like mine. "Because of this," he said and withdrew a slip of paper from his water-logged wallet. It read:

I forgive myself for being a terrible father.

"I swear it must've blown right out of my jar," he said, staring at it curiously. "Caleb found it in the sandbox. He kept saying he didn't understand because he thought I was a good father. I always read them stories and watched their soccer games and swim classes and hosted parties at Chuck E. Cheese's." He stopped. A muscle in his jaw worked. "But it wasn't about Caleb and Cullen. It was about Jackie. It was about you."

The sun reached its warm fingers through the fog. Smells of warm pavement, sunscreen, and wet grass transported me to other summers when things weren't this complicated. Listening to my dad, I tried to hold on to my anger, but found it was a lot like holding on to a bird. It quivered in front of us, held steady, then took flight. He crumpled up his forgivelet and flicked it into the Pacifica. His wet hand covered mine. "I have a getaway car, you know. I rented it at the airport."

I could hardly believe my ears. "Even though I just dunked you," I asked, "you'll still sign me out?"

He pointed to the parking garage behind the stadium. "Anywhere you want to go, I'll take you."

49

FINDING FORTUNES

TURNED OUT THE Honda Fit he rented at the airport wasn't the getaway car I'd imagined. So instead of heading for the hills, we discovered the college town just outside CUP's gate. With his hands stationed obediently at the ten and two o'clock positions, my father chauffeured me past smoke shops, tattoo parlors, bookstores, and smoothie stands. We passed a record shop where silver musical notes swung in the window. I thought of Gabe, his obsession with the SPOOGE band, his kiss last night, how the place we left things off seemed both full and empty of promise.

My father braked at a yellow light and a flock of cyclists wheeled past. Then on the corner of Steinbeck Street and Quark Avenue, we spotted one lone Chinese restaurant ambitious enough to comfort us. Blessed be the sign that read OPEN.

The restaurant with red velvet walls prepared food so savory my tastebuds shivered in ecstasy. Pulling apart the seams of dough protecting a dumpling's insides, I realized the last time I'd eaten Chinese food was with TJ, the night before I left for Utopia. How different life seemed to me now, in this pastel town, tie-dye sheets hanging out of storefronts like laundry. Inside the restaurant, customers ordered off a chalkboard and sat at cafeteria-style tables. Me and my father shared a table with eleven strangers. Richard Goodman was a slow and deliberate eater who made a lot of "mmmmm" noises. In front of him were two cups of soup: one egg drop, one wonton, and a plate overflowing with crab dumplings, spareribs, fried noodles, and several other dishes I couldn't identify. Despite the early hour, the restaurant was loud and chaotic. Ferns hung from the ceiling, and three different televisions blared Asian music videos. Even though we could throw a stone at the campus from where we were sitting, Utopia felt about a billion miles away.

My dad's glasses sat cockeyed on his face and his shirt, which had somewhat dried, was smeared with dirt. Despite all that, he looked about as happy to be eating as I did. No paternity test needed here, folks. We both ate with elbows on the table and a look of concentration on our face. Dunking an egg roll in duck sauce, he started, "So I know about Jackie. And I know about Doug. I know what you meant when you mentioned Chuck E. Cheese's." He peeled off a layer of egg roll skin, just like I did. "But I still don't know what happened between you and TJ." Another dunk in duck sauce. "Would this be a good time to tell me about it?"

Actually the timing couldn't have been worse: food sizzling behind us, ancient gumball machines turning at the hands of toddlers, the chatter of strangers next to us. In spite of all this, I found I couldn't keep my secret locked up anymore. Must've been the sticky restaurant, everything coated in oil making it too slippery to hold back. Either way, there was no stopping it.

I told him about TJ, our neighbor. How he was so quiet you'd look up and there'd he be: in the driveway, inside my room, outside on the porch holding up his knuckles like he was on the verge of knocking. Told him about his doves, the patient way he'd trained them to perform. Obviously TJ was handsome, but it was more than that. He was mysterious, moody. I often felt we mortals weren't enough for him. He was above it. Above everything. No wonder he wanted to float so badly.

"After our first kiss, we um," I stopped and studied my egg roll. How could I tell him these things? I took a big breath. "I mean there was more kissing, here and there. But he never sought me out, you know. It was always my idea. It was me initiating things."

My dad listened as though an exam would follow. He scooped

fluffy rice into his bowl. "So you decided to lose weight?"

"Yes. Last summer. I stopped eating." Just the mention of last summer made my hands tremble. "Every time I sat at the table, I would think: *If you eat this food, he will never touch you. He will never love you.* So stupid for me to think about prom, but I did. *If you eat this, no prom dress.* It was like a game, see. I would wobble to the refrigerator, find the strength to open it, only to close it and then chew gum in my room. Mom was proud that I wanted to look normal. Jackie worried she might've had to evaluate her role as the pretty one, but TJ didn't say anything."

A giant shrimp dangled from my father's chopsticks. "It's a delicate thing to mention weight to a girl. Maybe he was nervous."

I went on, wanting to get the whole story out before I changed my mind.

"So one night he told me to come over. He asked me to wear a black dress. I thought it was because he'd noticed that I'd lost a few pounds and he wanted to, you know"—I cast my eyes downward—"commemorate the night. So I bought a black dress at H&M and it was grown-up—not the kind of dress Mom would have let me out of the house in. Underneath I wore some oh, never mind, some nice garments. I put on makeup and perfume. I looked in the mirror and was like, *Bring it.*"

My dad, who never used to drink, waved two fingers at the guy behind the counter and ordered a shot of sake. On a Sunday. At ten in the morning. One minute later, he'd downed two of them, eyes tearing as he swallowed hard. "Go on," he urged.

"I went over to TJ's in a raincoat even though it was hot and muggy. Once I was in his room I took it off it and he goes, 'Dang, girl. Where you going like that?'"

My dad cleared his throat like he wanted to interrupt, or maybe stop me. I'm sure it was uncomfortable for him to hear it, but not as awkward as I felt saying it. I didn't stop. I had to keep telling it.

"That night, in his room, TJ sprinkled the stupid powder on my dress like he did on the doves at your kids' birthday party. The powder is a microorganism that eats the dye in fabric. He only asked me to wear a dress so he could rehearse a stupid magic trick," I explained. "That's what it was about. The powder only worked on black material."

"So then what happened?" he asked. "After he changed your dress?"

I sighed. "TJ must've seen my disappointment because he spun me around and told me how lovely I looked in yellow, which was bullshit. And because I've known him so long I felt this, I don't know, resignation when I sat down on his bed. Not on my part, but his."

The Chinese restaurant faded, and suddenly I was back in Baltimore, sitting on the bed between TJ and his resignation. "That night I ignored his resignation and obviously TJ did too because, he kissed me first, which he almost never did. A long, lingering kiss with a crescendo that weakened my knees. And I was like, *hallelujah*. I just needed to lose weight. That's all it took. And when he asked me if I'd like to lie down, I was all, *You bet your ass*. TJ adjusted a pillow under my head. Then he kissed my neck and my shoulders. Then he took off his glasses, which I found strange. I mean, wouldn't he want to see me better? He said, 'I want to look at you,' as he dropped his glasses on the nightstand."

I didn't mention how TJ slowly untied my dress's knot behind my neck, lifted the now-yellow dress over my head, and straightened my hair out. My iridescent bra and panties were like something you'd find in the bottom of the ocean. He had stared at them. *You my girl, Bee.* He'd said it with like, emotion.

"I was his girl," I told my dad now. "Or so I thought."

Was it completely inappropriate to be telling this story to my dad? Probably. But it had to be told, and I guess he was destined to hear it. He lifted rice in and out of his bowl like his life depended on it. He concentrated more on the task than my face. If he looked directly at me, I'm not sure I could've gone on.

"When you say he seemed resigned," he gently reminded me, "what did he do next?"

What happened afterward was that TJ lay on top of me and traced his fingertips on my stomach, which was still blubbery, yes, but less blubbery. Then he fumbled with my green bra and mentioned how he could get out of a straitjacket, but couldn't unhook a bra. So I led his hands to the front, because it was one of the front clasps, and unsnapped it. My face grew hot

just remembering it. I didn't tell my father how as TJ kissed
my breasts, caressed them, my only thought was, *This must
never stop*. Left out all those details, obviously, especially the
part about how when TJ looped his thumbs around my underwear, I thought: *This is it. I'm ready*. I knew it'd be TJ I'd give
myself to eventually. Of course I'd never have imagined the six
shots of cranberry vodka beforehand, but my dad didn't need
to know that either. Just like he didn't need to know that when
I told TJ I loved him, confessed that I'd always loved him, it'd
been an accident. The words had edged up my throat and para-
chuted out before I could stop them. I'd never said the words
to anyone. *Never*. Not even my mom. Not my sister. Never my
dad. Of course once TJ'd heard them, he recoiled as if he'd been
punched in the face.

I looked at my father. "I accidentally told him I loved him."

"Accidentally?"

"Then TJ stopped and said, 'I can't do this.' "

He tilted his head. "He stopped?"

My chin trembled. Then tears flooded my eyes. "He found
me too repulsive." A busser slapped a pyramid of dishes into a
gray bucket. "He touches dirty coins and stupid birds and sticky
kids. But not me. I was too gross. Too fat."

"Well," said my father. He chose his words carefully. "Maybe
he wasn't ready or he was afraid he'd disappoint you."

I clarified. "No, we never even got that far. He said ... well ...
he wasn't feeling it. You know. Down there."

Did everyone just get really quiet?

"He's how old?" asked my dad. "TJ? When this happened?"
His face, I could see now, was as red as the velvet walls.

"Seventeen," I said through tears.

"You say this boy loves you? Or used to?"

"I don't know," I cried. Releasing my secret in the middle
of a Chinese restaurant suddenly seemed like a dumb idea. "All
the times you hear about the awful things boys do to girls but it
was me." My voice was definitely too loud. "I wanted it. I wanted
him. Only he didn't want me.

"After our attempt, TJ pushed off me and gathered my dingy
dress. He offered to walk me home, but I refused. After dry heaving in the bushes, I went back to my house and woke Jackie who

said, 'Try again in another twenty pounds.' " I cut the dress into pieces and tossed them in the garbage. I made a sundae. Then an omelet. I ate and ate and ate. Then I ate some more. I swore you could hear my stomach stretching. The next morning TJ ran into my house. I thought at first he was going to apologize, to tell me he'd made a mistake. But it was the doves. Someone had stolen them. TJ showed me their cage outside, door flung open and everything. He dragged me all around Baltimore, far into Towson, Harford County too, hanging flyers. We posted ads on Craigslist. We never talked about anything again. The doves eventually came back. Just like my weight."

My dad sprinkled dried noodles into his soup. "Have you considered that TJ might be gay? I mean statistically magicians, um ..."

I shook my head. "Impossible. TJ's dad would disown him if he thought was gay."

"All the more reason to keep it a secret, yes?"

He stirred his soup and continued. "Supposing he is gay, it doesn't make what happened that night any easier, does it?" He slid a plate of spareribs to me, but I couldn't eat. "You can't make people love you, Bethany. Sounds basic, but most of life's lessons are. I mean, if he didn't like you heavier, then losing weight probably wouldn't change it." Tears skidded down my cheeks faster than I could catch them. "There's always a person who can break your heart and will. Then there's the person who every one meets, usually when they least expect it. That's the person who knows just how to break your heart, only they wouldn't dare."

I nodded my head like what he said made sense, but it didn't. It all sounded like the crap on my mom's notepads. I guess he saw the doubt on my face, so he shut up. Then he reached into his pocket. When I first saw the handkerchief he'd pulled out, I thought it was a magic trick, one of those endless cords that kept untangling. Turned out to be a real one, though.

My dad said plainly, "TJ was a dumbass."

I wiped my eyes on the handkerchief. "A dumbass for not sleeping with me?"

His face reddened. "Not for that. For letting you go. For not holding on. For watching the best thing that ever happened to him walk away." He tossed me a fortune cookie. "That's why he's a dumbass. And you know what?"

"What?"

"I am too. For the same reasons."

I still don't know whether it was the words of Confucius inside my cookie—Forget Injury, Never Forget Kindness—or it was the words of my dad. All I can say is that when I finished telling my story, the whole story, for the first time, I felt exactly like I had earlier on the lake. Not the moment the shoreline appeared far in the distance and I thought, *There's no way I can do it*. Not that moment. The one just before it. The moment I plunged the oars deep in the water and thought, *Well, who knows. Maybe I can. Maybe I can do anything.*

50

SCHOOLED

BACK IN THE car, my entire body melted into the passenger seat like I'd just finished a triathlon. The college town now swarmed with students, who lounged at café tables, talking on their phones or reading on their e-readers. My dad wanted to see every inch of the place, so we toured bookstores and cafés. He bought shot glasses and sweatshirts and polymer pennants and key chains.

Finally, at a gas station on the outskirts of town, my dad threw the car keys at me. "I just thought of the greatest gift I could give you."

"No more gifts. Really."

Beneath the gas station lights, I noticed his head was badly sunburned. "Get out," he said.

"What?"

"I'm serious, Bethany. Get out of the car."

Somewhat reluctantly, I got out of the car.

"Now get in."

I must have looked confused.

"Get in the driver's side, Bethany."

"I can't."

"Bethany Mitzi Goodman Stern, get in the damn car."

I crawled onto the driver's seat, and he climbed onto the passenger seat.

"Good. Now turn the key."

"But I'm not legal," I said.

"Like I'm going to believe you are at all concerned with legalities."

"But I don't know how to drive."

"I'll teach you."

"No," I argued. Everything about the car felt wrong. I was so used to the other side of driving, the passenger side. The normal side. Here the steering wheel seemed intrusive and all these buttons? Did each one have a function? How was I supposed to find a proper radio station and drive at the same time? What's worse was this car was a manual transmission, which meant it had like eighty gears. "No," I spat again.

"No?" my dad repeated, looking shocked. "Why not?"

"Because it's stupid," I said, knowing I sounded like a five-year-old. "Because it's a stick shift."

"I can teach you stick shift."

"Because I'm afraid," I admitted.

If you wanted to know the truth, the whole driving process kind of freaked me out. I marveled at how easily people took to it. Let's get behind the wheel of a three-ton machine and drive on roads with *thousands* of other people. What fun! Let's have faith that all three hundred million Americans will actually stop at a red octagon.

"First you turn the key," said my father.

I put the key in the ignition and turned. Nothing happened.

"Rule Number One: You need to press the clutch in all the way in order for a manual transmission to start."

"Oh."

"No big deal. Try again."

"So which one is the clutch?"

"Good question. Try each one. The one that works when you turn the key is the clutch."

This was the way he taught—like someone who had spent way too much time in a classroom. Or a library. If the brake doesn't make you stop, then well, that isn't the brake. I started the car twice, but it seized every time I let off the clutch. On about the tenth time, I kept the engine idling. Progress.

"How do you turn on the headlights?"

"Try every switch."

"Clearly those are the windshield wipers."

"Clearly."

"Is it always so jerky? So rocky?"

"In the beginning," he said. "It always is in the beginning."

I took to driving the way I took to every sport: awkwardly and with much hesitation. My dad wouldn't give up, though. Maybe he thought I was the next Danica Patrick. I'm sure all hopes were dashed when it took me *two hours* to circle the gas station. I only mistook the brake for the clutch about fifty times, but my teacher was patient.

"You," he lied, "are a goddamned natural."

I kept waiting for him to tell me, "That's enough for one day." I kept waiting for the sigh, the hiss whenever the car bucked like a bronco, but he only said, "Gently, now." I thought he was crazy when he suggested practicing more in the huge parking lot across from campus, but he was serious.

He never gripped his seat or pumped an imaginary brake like my mom whenever Jackie drove. He turned off the radio, told me to listen to the engine's RPMs. Feel the car. "No better place," he said, "for learning to drive."

I couldn't help but believe him. I mean teeter-tottering on the edge of the gas station, I had to cross two lanes of traffic in order to get to the parking lot across the street. My heart beat loudly in my ears. *Don't stall. Don't stall. Don't stall.* And when I did, students honked, cyclists screamed, but there was my dad beside me. "Screw them," he said. "They should be grateful. Just look at this view."

The town, all pink and white light, windy and cool, arranged itself before us. Eventually I found my footing and pitched the Fit forward into the parking lot, where we practiced until dusk.

"How about you drive me back to MontClaire?"

"Are you kidding?"

"You can do it."

"I can't."

"You can!"

"I can't!"

My dad, locked in some kind of standoff with me, finally relented. "We did a lot for a day," he said. "That can be enough."

So we switched places, and I tried to observe everything he did on the way back. How artfully my father drove: avoiding pedestrians and dog walkers and scooters and people in wheelchairs and professors juggling papers, and boyfriends and girlfriends and freshmen and juniors and old people and fat people and daughters and fathers. He didn't drive too fast or too slow. He crested hills then switchbacked down the campus's frilly streets, in neutral, but not riding the brake. He dodged live squirrels and gum wrappers and even distracted savants who crossed the street before looking. Through all of it, I found that this was something I admired about him—how easily he drove. How unafraid of it he was.

When we arrived back at MontClaire Hall, it was evening. I sat in the car with my dad not wanting to turn the engine off, wanting him to keep going, to keep driving. "I'll come get you at seven tomorrow morning," he said. "Pack up your stuff tonight, and say goodbye to everyone." My dad reached across my lap. "And before I forget, I have something for you." He opened the glove compartment. "Happy birthday."

I touched the rectangle-shaped box. "A book, Dad. Really?" I was scared to open it and see the title: *How to Stop Being a Teenager. Why Fat Girls Always Lose. Don't Fall For A Magician.*

"Not a book," my dad disclosed.

I tore off the wrapping paper and was relieved to find a stationery set: little yellow envelopes and pale lilac paper, feathery pens and rubber stamps. "On the off chance you wanted to stay at Utopia," my dad started, "I was hoping you'd write me letters. Old-fashioned letters. It's an artform, you know, and so many of your generation don't do it, but I like your letters. They sting like hell, but they're good. So good. " He stopped. "But since you're leaving tomorrow, you can write letters to your friends— Cambridge and that guy, Gabe. I'm sure they'd appreciate that. Camp friendships often last a lifetime, you know."

"Thanks," I said, hoping he was right.

I trekked back to MontClaire Hall, stationery secured under my arm, listening to my dad shift effortlessly from one gear to the next.

51

I'll WRITE

WALKING BACK TO MontClaire Hall, I planned my exit speech. It went a little something like this: "Later!" On second thought, maybe I'd opt for a more Cambridge route. Professional. Like, "I'm sorry, Hank and Belinda, but I decided against losing weight with this establishment. I'll be leaving in the morning and, in no time at all, this two-bit operation will be shut down."

On the brief walk from the fountain to MontClaire Hall, I reveled in what felt like a small victory. I'd learned to drive and ditched Utopia all in the span of a day. And then I opened the door.

Inside MontClaire Hall, almost every single camper had gathered. Tampa Bay wearing his Miami Heat hat sat next to Atlanta and her Bumpit bouffant. The little campers, Chicago and Houston, were there. Even Gabe had made an appearance. There he stood by the rusty fan, crossing his arms, tapping his shoe on his skateboard. By the looks of him, he was pissed about something.

"Did you send my sister chocolate?" It wasn't an inquiry. It was an accusation. "Did you send her twelve chocolate roses, Bethany?"

All I could concentrate on was my heart, which was sure to leap from my chest. "That's perfect, Bethany. Of all people, you knew she couldn't eat that. I mean, what the hell were you thinking?" Again he didn't wait for a response. "Well she got them. And she ate them. Are you happy now?" His voice cracked. "She's in the hospital in a coma."

His shoes squeaked when he turned around and hightailed out of the room. The door had one of those air compressor things on it to keep from slamming, but rest assured, Gabe slammed it anyway. When I rasped a lame, "I didn't mean to hurt her," the only ones who heard me were the campers left in the common room. And they didn't believe me either. "Will she be alright?" I asked quietly.

Atlanta pondered her manicure. "Maybe. She passed out cold in the room until her brother found her. The paramedics left about a half-hour ago. She peed her pants." I could see her fillings when she yawned. "Tragic."

I ran upstairs to my old dorm room. Though I'd hoped to find Liliana bedazzling on her bed, I didn't. The dorm was silent. And I didn't know whether it was because I'd been gone for two days or because Liliana wasn't in it, but it felt strange being there. Spooky. It looked emptier than I'd remembered it. My bottom bunk remained disheveled, sheets pulling up to reveal a corner of vinyl mattress. Liliana's bed was unmade too, her bedazzler resting on her desk. Next to it sat a narrow cardboard box tied in a gold ribbon. I approached it slowly, the way you would a bomb. I lifted the lid and saw one chocolate rose left inside, a white one because she hated white chocolate. The card was still stuck to the cover: *As promised, Bee*

I settled on Liliana's bed, which had the same blueberry smell she gave off sometimes. I fondled the box's ribbon, inspected her bedazzler. I opened the desk drawer and found her knitting needles and crochet hook. *Could it be possible*, a voice inside me asked, *that I put my roommate in a coma?* Noting the glucose monitor on the bottom of the bed, and the little paper slips tossed haphazardly, I knew it was more than possible—it was inevitable. Liliana, my thirteen-year-old roommate, whose blue braces glittered whenever she smiled, was unconscious as a result of the chocolate roses some insensitive asshole had sent her. That *I* sent her. In addition to being an insensitive asshole, I think that also made me an accomplice. Maybe even a murderer?

Forget it, Bethany, I said to myself, dismissing my thoughts. *You have an exit.*

My dad said he'd pick me up tomorrow morning. All I needed to do was what he suggested. Open the closet, throw my stuff in the duffle bag, and walk out. How could I face Liliana? How could I face Gabe? Simple: I couldn't. I had to leave.

When I heard a sharp tap against the window, I nearly dove under the bed. I was sure it was Gabe looking for revenge. I finally found enough courage to peek out, and I saw Cambridge pacing the path below.

"I've been waiting for you all day. What happened with your dad?" she asked.

"Everything was fine with my dad. It just went to hell the minute I got back."

"What happened?"

I steeled myself. "Remember, when we were in Olive's room, and Liliana wanted a token of appreciation for covering for us?"

"And?"

"I sent her chocolate roses. Twelve of them." My throat closed, and I barely got the words out. "She's in some kind of sugar shock now. A coma."

"Damn," Cambridge replied, pulling her hair into a ponytail. "Is she in the hospital or what?"

"It's my fault, Cambridge."

"You didn't mean to hurt her, Bethany. You know how she is about chocolate."

"She could die, Tabitha."

Cambridge stood up straight. "We can go visit her. We'll find out where she is."

"I'm sure she hates me," I cried.

When she saw my tears, Cambridge said, "Don't be like that, Bethany. Her sugar levels probably went crazy. Look, I care about her too, and I know they'll get it straightened out." She brushed dirt off her feet. "Liliana is so tough."

I wanted to agree with her, but couldn't. Underneath all his anger, Gabe had seemed uncertain about his sister, and that uncertainty scared me.

"Why don't you just come with me," she said again. "We'll go to the hospital together. I just signed myself out, by the way. Left

my stuff and everything," Cambridge said, trying not to smile.
"I considered it an eighteenth birthday present to myself. And
get this? Belinda and Hank wanted an exit weight and would
you believe I lost five pounds? I think it was all that vomiting.
Anyway, I've been staying at Olive's." She waved me toward her
again. "Are you coming or what? Let's go."

I didn't look at her when I said the following: "My dad
booked me a flight for tomorrow morning."

An expression I couldn't identify swept across Cambridge's
face. For the first time this summer, I'd surprised her. "What?
You're going back to Baltimore? With your dad? But what ..."
She pursed her lips. "What about everything here? What about
Gabe?"

"After poisoning his sister, he'll be glad to see me go."

"And Liliana?"

I shook my head.

"What about me, Baltimore. Us? Our adventure?"

Like I had another choice. "I have to go, Tabitha."

Cambridge and her perfectly timed debates. "Do you?" Her
sharp dings. "Do you really, Bethany?"

I swallowed the cantaloupe-sized lump in my throat. "I'll
write you letters," I said.

She swirled her neck. "I won't open them." Then she turned
to go, but whipped back around and said, "I thought you were
brave, but you're not. You're a. You're a ..." Even in her anger,
she had grace. "You're a coward, Bethany."

She was the only person on this earth to call me on my own
shit. I would miss her to pieces.

52

WAKE-UP CALL

LATER THAT NIGHT I called the university hospital, but they could only tell me Liliana was stable, which sounded better than unstable, but not as good as cured. For the first time in three weeks I spent the night alone. In a few hours, I'd showered, done laundry, and relinquished Hollywood's cell phone on the bathroom counter for her to find in the morning.

I wondered how to fill the four hours until morning, so I made Liliana's bed and attempted to knit. Then I drafted a letter on my new stationery.

Dear Gabe & Liliana,
Please forgive me for sending you chocolate, liliana—it was beyond stupid, it was borderline homicidal. Thank you for being a great roomie and for being so hip and fashionable. I don't blame you if you hate me but maybe you'll get over it one day.
Gabe, for the record, you are the only person who didn't make me feel like a freak. thank you for not only looking at me, but for liking what you saw. I'm sorry I let you both down.
I tore it up and tried again:
L + G,
I'm sorry about the chocolate. I wouldn't expect you to 4give me, but if u do pls email me bumblingbee@yeehaw.net I'm glad I met you both.

I stuffed it inside a yellow envelope and left it on Liliana's desk.

I stared out the window and waited for sunrise, but night stretched on like elastic. I thought of all of the other gifts I could've sent Liliana. A fruit basket. Flowers. Gift Card. But no, I had to go with chocolate. When I heard a buzzing, I checked my bra because I was so used to having the cell phone there. By the third vibration, I remembered I'd left it on the bathroom counter. "Bee?"

"Hey." My voice sounded gritty, tired.

"Guess what? I'm in Los Angeles. On *American Envy*. I made the top twenty."

"Wow." My enthusiasm was there, yes, but TJ must've heard something dampening it.

"You'll watch me, right?" He paused. "Right?"

"Of course," I said. "When's it on?"

"Final cut airs in two weeks. I'm so nervous, Bee."

"You won't get cut."

"I don't know. My stomach is all in knots. The doves are being sketchy. The levitating trick is complex. I mean, I've messed it up before. I feel like I need to raise the stakes too. I've thought about disappearing."

"You always hated vanishing."

"I'm getting better, I think. I'm trying."

It was weird to hear him sounding so vulnerable. He actually seemed nervous. "You won't get cut, TJ," I said. For the first time in I don't know how long, the silence between us was uncomfortable.

"What's up with you?" he asked. "How's camp?"

Where to begin ... I ran away? I almost drowned my dad? Nearly killed my roommate and screwed up the only chance with a guy who actually liked me?

"Everything's fine, TJ," I said, surprised by how much I wanted to end the conversation. "I'll watch you on Sunday."

A few months ago, that conversation would've played and replayed in my mind until I could've recited it, but tonight I found I didn't have the energy. Maybe TJ would win *American Envy*. No amount of levitating or disappearing or magic tricks could bring Liliana out of a coma.

I was about to delete the number from the call history and return the phone to the bathroom counter when I felt the air shift. "Good thing I have unlimited calling," said Hollywood, who now stood in front of me. She tapped her purple slippers impatiently. "Or I'd send you the bill."

53

SHOULDA

UNLESS YOU COUNT the morning she jogged past us at Copernicus, not to mention her debut on UniTV, this was the first time Hollywood and I had occupied the same room. Lowering her arm like a drawbridge and opening her fingers one by one, she waited for me to deposit the phone into her hand. I knew if I did, she'd probably leave my room and that would be the end of it. Yet I didn't let the phone go. Instead, I tightened my grip. "By the way," I replied pissfully, "I signed you up for twenty ringtone clubs and tweets from Walmart."

"Funny." She wiggled her fingers with irritation. "Give me my phone."

What was taking me so long? Why did I hold on tighter?

Hollywood groaned at the inconvenience. "You can steal it again, Bethany, but I'll find you just as easily as last time. GPS is great for locating fat girls. Too bad you were so close when the little Latina passed out. Maybe you could've helped."

So it was her. She was the anonymous tip that led my dad straight to me. She'd tracked me on the phone! Shocked, my fingers loosened, and the next thing I knew, Hollywood had reunited with her violet phone. She smiled victoriously.

"I should have known it was you," I said, my teeth clenched. "Of course you would be the one to rat us out."

She laughed. "Oh, I'd have thought Cambridge would've figured it out long before you. Or maybe she knew all along." Standing there, she looked so ridiculous in her nightgown. So dainty. "I didn't rat you out either," she clarified. "I simply revealed your coordinates. Personally, I'm glad you left. Things were much better without you."

I didn't know why that stung so badly. Was it because I felt everyone had been telling me that same thing over and over again? Like everyone's lives could officially begin the minute I left—like a surprise party in reverse? At her words, something in me recoiled. And then, as if it only gathering strength, that same thing lunged.

"When I talked to your dad, he told me you have these problems. Problems with food. I saw it on your file too. What kinds of prob—"

Hollywood paused. "You're lying."

"No, me and your dad had a lovely conversation on your phone. He gave me great advice. He did mention these problems, though. He seemed very concerned."

"You're making it up." She was turning red. "My dad doesn't speak to people like you."

"Sure he does. He seemed nice. You must've inherited your personality from your mother. Anyway, your dad's got this fantastic voice too, and we got along just fine. Like this," and I held up two crossed fingers.

"You should really stop making stuff up."

I'm sure Hollywood wanted to make a big exit with her phone, but she couldn't bring herself to do it. I had her hooked now.

"I'm not lying," I said.

"Why don't you just go back to Baltimore?"

This entire conversation leading up to this point had taken place with me sitting on the bed and Hollywood standing. Here was when I stood. In front of her. "Maybe I will go back to Baltimore," I said. "But before I do, there's something I want to do first."

I flexed my hand. "Something I should've done on weigh day."

Hollywood looked confused as I moved even closer to her, close enough I could've touched the spaghetti straps of her nightgown. "The one thing I should have done all along."

"Done wh—?"

She never saw it coming because I never saw it coming. In seconds, the fingers of my left hand bent into a white-knuckled fist, and I punched her. Punched her exactly the way Gabe had instructed during Knock Out. The first jab? That was what Gabe called a rangefinder. I found the range, alright. Then I crossed over with the fist of my right hand and decked Captain Thin in the jaw. That was, Gabe had told me, the power shot. And shot full of power it was. My jab cross was enviable, stellar. Religious. Thumb between my index finger, slightly tucked, Holyfield-style. All knuckle and downward thrust crashing into her jaw. "I should have done that," I said. "I should have knocked you out." Then I ripped the phone from her hand, walked into the bathroom, and slammed it in the toilet. Then I flushed it.

Then everything got quiet. The phone didn't go down, only floated in a circle on the water's surface. Plink, went the faucet. Plink. Plink. So quiet. Very quiet and, I was almost giddy because I thought I'd gotten away with it. Gotten away with everything. Fat camp. Dunking my dad. Liliana's coma. Punching Hollywood. Flushing her phone. Practically cocky, I rotated on my flip-flops and took one step toward my dorm room.

I was ready for more. I wanted a classic ViewTube girl fight now. Everything had come down to this moment, and I burned for it. I was hungry for the violence of it. I would do everything I should've done on weigh day ... twice. Now this was my ending! Only when I walked back into my dorm, Hollywood was still on the floor. Shouldn't she be regenerating like the tail of a lizard or something? Why was she was holding her face and groaning? I guessed I'd hit her harder than I realized. She was balled into a fetal position, and I could see her lace panties under her night-gown, a birthmark behind her calf. Dammit, Amber! I was just getting started! I watched her ribcage lift up and down with each breath. "You fat bitch," she wheezed. "You fat bitch."

I decided to make her get up. I knelt down and grabbed a handful of hair. I double wrapped it around my wrist like a rope, her head jerking as if I'd snapped her neck. Her tresses felt waxy and thick, like doll hair shedding between my fingers.

"Call me something else," I said. "Say my name."

I yanked that hair until she yelped.

"Don't, Bethany," she cried, not a warning either. A plea. "Don't pull it off." Her one hand tightened around my wrist, but it was limp. Her strength was evaporating. I jerked my hand again, and that was when I saw her hair shift. Shift like normal hair wouldn't. "Please. Don't," she cried.

I tugged again. Tears leaked from her eyes. "Don't pull it off. It's a wig. It's glued. It will tear my scalp. Please."

I thought of her hair dryer whinnies at five in the morning and her ever-present Speedo bathing cap. *A wig? Why? Cancer?*

Tears somersaulted down her cheeks. I saw the tendons in her neck thrumming with blood when she stood up on trembling legs, supported herself on the desk, and rubbed the butt cheek I'd knocked her on. "Just go," she sobbed. "Just leave."

"You have cancer?" I asked. Slivers of Amber's blond hair dripped from my fingers; her fair skin was trapped under my nails. "Is it leukemia?"

She rolled her green eyes. "Just go, Bethany. Go back to Baltimore."

From: ellenstern@zyprexapharm.com
To: Bethany Stern <bethanys@utopia.com>
Subject: The best you

Dear Bethany,

I've spoken with Hank and Belinda and they've informed me that you have decided to leave Utopia. Against my wishes, Dick has agreed to pick you up and bring you back to Maryland. Before you arrive, however, I thought you should know a few things.

You might think when you come back here, you'll talk me into paying for your gym membership again or starting some new fad diet. I want you to know that's not possible. I'm sure you think it's about the money, but it's not.

Our problems are attached to us like tails. You can run away from Utopia, but all the problems you created there will follow you here—just like all the problems you created here followed you there. Wherever you go, Bethany, there you are.

So if you come back to Maryland early, know that I have a long list of issues ready for you to confront. Also know that TJ has left for LA, so you can't run to his house either. Also know that Jackie won't be home until the end of the summer, so it will just be me and you. I encourage you to think things through before continuing with your decision to run away (once again) when things start to get uncomfortable.

Love, Mom

54

REPRESENT

I WAS RELIEVED to see daylight. Finally I could put this disastrous summer behind me. I grabbed my duffle bag and took one last look around my dorm. The closer I got to the door, though, the heavier I felt. I tried again, but it seemed as though I were wading through quicksand. I dropped my duffle bag to lighten my load. Only I still couldn't lift one leg in front of the other. I sat down on Liliana's bed, convincing myself I was tired. Maybe that was the reason why walking out the door seemed impossible. I tried again and again, but the same thing happened. My heart thumped, and my legs refused to move. *Just one foot in front of the other*, I told myself. One step closer to the door was another step closer to Baltimore.

And a step further from Liliana, Cambridge, and ... Gabe.

Who said that?

Your conscience.

Oh great. You. Look, I'm trying to leave.

Are you sure you want to run away? Again?

What kind of guilt trip is this? Don't you know how long I've waited to be free from fat camp? Carb counting? Pilates?

About as long as you've waited for a friend—a real one; about as long as you've waited for someone to believe in you or a guy to kiss you ... first.

Damn that italic voice for being right. I'd been waiting my

whole life for a real friend and now that I had three of them I was getting ready to leave? Run away like I always did? Pretend this summer never happened? There was just no pretending that I'd go home and my life would return to whatever normal existed before. I couldn't keep up the illusion that the life I was returning to was normal or fun or anything other than a suckfest. Why had it taken my fist colliding with Hollywood's jaw to make that point? I didn't know. I just knew my days of running away were over. I set down my duffle bag once and for all and waited for my conscience to tell me what to do next. But it was done with the lesson, apparently, because all was quiet. Where was my echo in the universe that let everyone know nothing would ever be the same?

Including me?

55

DON'T H8

MY FATHER PULLED into the circular drive at seven. He got out of the rented Fit a few minutes later and stared at MontClaire Hall, trying to guess which window was mine. He absently flicked coins in the fountain, scrolling through his cell phone for my number, which he didn't have. I knew this was my one and only chance to legitimately leave Utopia, so maybe I should've at least gone down there by the mermaid fountain, thrown my own penny in the mix, and reconsidered. He must've assumed I'd overslept or forgotten. At seven thirty, I folded a piece of his stationery into the perfect airplane and aimed it out my window. It landed by his shoe. He read the words, I DECIDED TO STAY. Two minutes later, he looked up and smiled and climbed into the Fit.

After my father drove off, I unpacked my belongings and opened the closet to reveal Liliana's bedazzled and feathery clothing. Each studded item contained a memory. Her favorite Hello Kitty shirt hung next to her rhinestone sweats. All of it made me miss her. Cambridge's abandoned clothes were stacked neatly in her drawer. It was hard to believe that a few weeks ago, Cambridge had been the type of girl to fold everything and stack it crisply. It felt weird without either of them in the room, but I knew I had to unpack. That was step one. Once I finished that, it was time for step two.

Hollywood's room looked a lot softer than mine. They'd set up a lamp on the floor that gave off a soft glow. I didn't barge inside, but I didn't exactly knock either. Hollywood was standing by her dresser, back to me, writing something. A red scratch bore down one side of her face, and I noted two purple splotch-es maturing into the shape of my knuckles. Seeing her injuries contrast her fair skin made me feel awful. She hadn't heard me come in and hadn't yet realized I was behind her. It wasn't un-til I was close enough to touch her that I understood she was filling her forgiveness jar, the same one she'd brought into our room our first day of fat camp. She folded a piece of paper and dropped it into a vase. I couldn't stop myself from saying, "The diet is a scam. It doesn't work."

She jumped when she heard my voice. Then she pretended she hadn't. "I know," she said and dropped the paper in anyway. "I know."

"I mean, it didn't work for me," I clarified. "But I never bought the book. I only saw it on TV." What a stupid thing to admit. "That was probably my first mistake," I said, "believing what I saw on TV."

Hollywood flinched when she smiled. I guessed it hurt. "My dad's been telling since I was two or three that nothing you see on TV is real. But I'd think, *I see you on TV and you're real.* It always messed with me."

So I guessed Liliana had been right. Hollywood's dad really was a famous actor. "Well," I went on, "it's not like you need a diet anyway. You're not even fat." I never understood why Hollywood enrolled at Utopia. She wore, at most, maybe a size ten. Probably an eight. "Are you here to lose weight or for some other reason?"

She didn't say anything. We were eye-locked in the mirror over her dresser. During that eye-lock or maybe before, proba-bly when I yanked her wig, I figured Hollywood was doing things to make herself thin. Bad things. Things that made her hair fall out. If anyone had food issues worse than my own, it was defi-nitely this girl. "Last year," I confessed, "I used to chew food and spit it out. I promised myself it was different than throwing up. It was just tasting. I'd suck chips and crackers until they were powdery. I couldn't swallow them though. That was my rule. I was hungry all the time." Our eyes were still locked in the mirror. "It worked too. I lost weight." I finally looked down. "I gained it back though."

I'd just wanted to taste food, see—not eat it. Knew I couldn't eat it. It became a game almost. How much food could I not eat? Of course, if I'd accidentally swallowed something, I'd tell myself how stupid I was. I'd think about bringing the food back up, but I never did. Even then I'd seen how quickly these things could spin out of control. None of it lasted long because the one person I'd wanted to notice me never did.

I'd never told anybody these things before, but somehow I knew my secret would be safe with Hollywood. I told her how my mom told me I was allergic to sugar for years until, in third grade, I licked the frosting off some birthday cake and nothing happened. When I told my mom that I must've outgrown my sugar allergy, she didn't look happy at my discovery. So I went back to pretending to be grateful for her specially made-for-me salads and acting like I was happy to have my failures broadcast around the dinner table. Only later, back in my room, I'd feast on cookies and puddings, going to sleep with sugary sweetness coating my teeth. I was probably ten years old.

"I guess we all have problems," Hollywood replied, her wavering voice betraying her. Even with her swollen jaw, she still had the looks of a cat—something very feline about her green eyes and triangular face. "I think you have a big problem, Amber. Is that why your hair fell out, and why you're so thin?"

"I am not thin."

"Is it because you make yourself sick?"

"I'm just thin compared to you. I have a disease that makes my hair weak. It's not like I'm bald."

"Are you bulimic, Amber?"

"No." Her nervous laughter was a fence between us. Her eyes narrowed. "What exactly did my father tell you?"

Everything I needed to know was written across her face. "Nothing," I said. "Forget it."

And I didn't realize we'd been whispering until she stopped whispering and yelled, "What did he say? Did he tell you who he is?" she cried. She threw a brush, and it knocked into her forgiveness bucket. The papers spilled across the dresser. "It's his job, you know." She raised her voice another notch. "It's his job to criticize."

Atlanta, her roommate, stirred in her bed. "What is going on?" She looked at Hollywood's face. "Oh my God!" she exclaimed. "What happened?"

"Nothing," I said. "We were just having a discussion."

Atlanta sat up in her bed. "What happened, Amber?"

Hollywood looked uncertain. Her usual bitchiness seemed lost. With her free hand, she steadied her wig like I might rip it off. Turning to me, Hollywood said, "It's nothing."

I mimed zipping my lips. She pulled me by the elbow out of Atlanta's earshot.

"I used to make myself throw up, OK? But it's been three months, OK? That's how long since I, you know—and I haven't since I've been here. So stop. I'm better. Get it? I only did it because I was afraid."

"Afraid?"

"Afraid of looking like you."

Hollywood could pack a punch, alright. That one hit me between the ribs. Words so brutal my eyes watered. As far as I knew, I'd never been anyone's worst-case scenario before. "That's not what I meant," she said, backpedaling.

"Oh, I think it is." I sat down at her desk. Did I really want to stay here? Stay knowing I'd pissed off every friend I'd ever had? Share a bathroom with this witch? I knew Hollywood was bulimic, but damn if she didn't have a doctorate in cruelty. I thought of her file, her photograph, how her hair had probably been real then, wind-knotted and wild by the Pacific. I didn't even try to stop myself from saying, "I'm not going home." I took a breath. "I'm coming back to Utopia."

Amber searched my face. "What? You can't come back like nothing happened."

"Why not?"

"Because you made a decision." Her teeth, I could see now, were too perfect. Fake.

"Well, I changed my mind."

Hollywood sighed. "Do you really think you can convince Hank and Belinda to let you stay, after all that's happened?"

Hank and Belinda! I thought with alarm. *I probably should have talked to them earlier.*

"No," I told Hollywood. "But you can." I got up and walked over to her. I tugged her hair, gently this time. "Why don't you give your dad a call, Amber?"

56

LEVERAGE

DID I REALLY think Miss Marcia would let me back on her team? After ditching her on a power walk? Not likely. Good thing I had leverage with our counselor. All I had to do was show her the photo I'd snapped during her psychedelic trip. You know, on the phone I THREW IN THE TOILET! There went my leverage. Looked like I'd have to go with the honest approach. I walked down to Miss Marcia's dorm room. "I think I want to come back to Utopia," I said. "I was hoping the picture I snapped of you might change your mind about me, but I accidentally flushed the phone down the toilet. Sorry."

The redheaded counselor wore tie-dyed pajamas and eye-glasses. "Oh," she said in her much-too-loud-for-morning voice. "You don't need to blackmail me. I always liked you, but I thought you hated it here."

I certainly wasn't about to win "camper of the year" or any-thing, but hate is a strong word. "I want Liliana to get better," I said, "and me too." It was much easier to say this to my flip-flops. "I need to figure this whole madness out."

Despite having the loudest voice of anyone I knew, Miss Marcia was a thinking woman. When she took to her desk chair to ponder things, she did so quietly. Finally, she asked, "You know what I think would help Liliana the most?"

"What?"

"New leadership. I think there needs to be some changes at Utopia."

I nodded in strong agreement. Miss Marcia knew a thing or two about camp dynamics, for sure. She continued, "The emphasis needs to shift from weight loss to weight management. Weight confidence. Finding the right weight for your body and accepting it. Maintaining it." She rubbed her hands together. "It doesn't help seeing skinny people all the time and thinking they're brilliant because they can button their pants."

Miss Marcia was nothing short of a genius.

She stroked her chin. "Kids need someone they can identify with, not someone trying to squeeze into a prom dress. They need to see someone who's struggled. Someone who didn't necessarily want to change but had to. Someone smart and irreverent and funny."

Funny is good, I thought.

"So," said Miss Marcia, "are you up for it?"

"Of course," I said. Absolutely! Things definitely needed to change at Utopia, and all the innovations Miss Marcia mentioned were good ones. I watched her open her closet and remove a T-shirt adorned with the words "Captain Thin." Fabulous. A new captain. That was exactly the kind of thing Utopia needed. Our redheaded counselor smiled a toothy grin. "So, Baltimore?"

"Yes?"

"Guess what?"

"What?"

"You're the new captain."

"What?"

Each word was like a slap to the face. *You. Are. The. New. Captain*, she repeated.

"Good one, Marsh." I began to sweat. "Did you have a few brownies for breakfast?"

She balled up the pink shirt and threw it at me. "You're funny," she said. "You're irreverent. You've struggled, and people will relate to you."

"I'm fat." I waved the shirt. "This says 'Captain Thin.' "

"So what?"

"I hate exercising."

"You're inspirational. I've made up my mind, Bethany. You

can come back to Utopia, but I think you should be captain. It would make Liliana proud. Plus, Hank and Belinda will want some sign of commitment after all the trouble you caused."

"But what about—"

"No buts," said our counselor. "It's all you."

Just then Hollywood walked into Miss Marcia's room. I'd never been more relieved to see her. Surely she would not let Miss Marcia dethrone her. I'd bet once the former captain saw the pink shirt in my hand, she'd fight me for it. No one was more attached to being Captain Thin than Hollywood. "So you're Captain Thin now?" she asked, not even meanly.

"No," I said. "I don't want to be. I mean you're good at it. You were born for this kind of thing. Please," I said, trying to pawn off the T-shirt, "take it."

Hollywood hid her hands behind her back. "I don't want it," she said. "*You* can wake everyone up for power walk. Thank God."

"What? You don't want your job?"

"No way," said Hollywood. "I quit."

You've got to be kidding me! How does one walk into a room and walk out fifteen minutes later as Captain Thin? Even Batman had a choice. I threw the shirt on Miss Marcia's bed and prayed to God that Hollywood hadn't called her dad.

"Tell me your dad said no."

Hollywood nodded toward Miss Marcia. "He said yes. You were technically never signed out to begin with. My dad talked to Belinda and Hank anyway. They think you're just the kind of change we need around here. You're totally back in," she said and punched my arm, "Captain."

57

QUEEN BEE

A few hours later, Hank, Belinda, Miss Marcia, and I were gathered around a table in the common room trying to keep an open mind. They were there to listen as Miss Marcia and I addressed some of Utopia's problems. It was like some serious United Nations negotiations in that room, but, eventually, we compromised. For example, we would no longer have guest speakers whose only claim to fame is that they were not fat. The girls would have the omelet chef every other day and, as captain, I got to institute a policy.

Now I stood in the mailroom, Hollywood next to me, about to implement what I believed would be the best fat camp rule of all time. I stood among the same desks and chemistry posters, the same file cabinet and mail slots. The only thing missing was Cambridge. I sure wished she'd been beside me instead of Hollywood, who looked a little confused. She gazed at the scissors I held in my hand. "Bethany?" she asked. "What are you doing with those?"

It was late afternoon and hot in the mailroom. Someone had propped the window open with a chemistry textbook. The sounds of laughter and far away music drifted in.

"I'm implementing my change," I told Hollywood.

She raised an eyebrow. "And Hank and Belinda. They approved of this?"

"Yes," I said, "reluctantly."

"Are you sure?"

I looked at the deluxe Electrolux scale positioned in the corner. "I'm sure."

Amber sat down behind a desk and sighed. "Go ahead then."

Like a scene in a B-horror flick, I cocked my arm back and thrust the scissors into the scale's LED display. It split open like flesh. I did it again. And again. The scale's black screen bled to an oily green. I jumped up and down on the platform, hoping to destroy its springs. Hollywood watched me, disgusted at first, like I was stabbing a bunny. Then she said the strangest thing. She said, "Let me help you."

Downright medieval in her chunky sandals, Hollywood jumped on the platform too. She strangled the machine's long neck until it snapped in half. With hair falling in points around her sweaty face, she grabbed the metal piece and thwacked it on a desk. She tore it apart like an Uma Thurman in *Kill Bill*. I didn't ask who she imagined the scale to be as she cracked it over the radiator a few times. For all I knew her fantasy included my face at its center, so why ruin it for everyone? I just went on liberating tiny corkscrews and silver batteries and other debris like a butcher. Once the scale's innards and plastic shreds flew around the mailroom, we called it quits. All in all, it was a sad, crazy, pissed-off but quasi beautiful moment.

We collapsed on desk chairs and composed ourselves. I scratched my ankle with my flip-flop. "I wish we could do that to the salad bar next," I said.

Amber laughed, a lilting chuckle that filled the room like light. "Too bad you only got to make one suggestion."

Obviously the salad bar would stay. But the scale? The scale would go. Correction: The scale did go. Correction: The scale went.

"Please open your notebooks and take note of Bethany's rule: No more Weigh Days, people. That is all."

58

MY FELLOW UTOPIANS

NEEDLESS TO SAY, my transformation from fat camp fugitive to team captain wasn't easy. It proved most difficult for the other campers who were now ordered to listen to me. In the few days that followed, no one took me seriously. If you're ever bored, try rousing twenty-three sleeping trolls at six o'clock every morning. Good times. Want to cultivate self-loathing? Ask a group of tweens if they want to swim laps ... for fun. Then try telling them that after they swim laps and eat salad, they won't be getting weighed.

In no time at all I could see why Hollywood resigned. The Captain Thin gig kinda blew.

Adding even more suck to a suckful situation, I didn't have anyone around to distract me either. I hadn't heard from Cambridge at all. I swore I saw her walking around campus one time, but it must've been a mirage. I'd assumed she'd flown back to Boston by now. Maybe she'd rediscovered her preppy self and went back to being perfect. Being in the dorm room alone made her absence unbearable, especially at night when I reclined on the bottom bunk and tried to convince myself she didn't hate me. Liliana probably hated me too, but since she was in the hospital with IVs sticking out everywhere, she couldn't exactly verify it. I called every day to check on her, but the nurse only confirmed that although she was getting better, she still had diabetes.

Then there was Gabe.

I thought about him constantly and even went as far as folding the most intricate airplane, walking down to Copernicus and then, at the last minute, talking myself out of sailing it through his window. I had a feeling he needed time to think things through. *Entra más profundo* and all.

The good news was that Hank, Belinda, and Miss Marcia really did change a few things around at Utopia, so it didn't suck half as much as it used to. For instance, since I'd eighty-sixed public weigh days, Sundays took on new meaning. Instead of getting publicly humiliated on the scale, Hank and Belinda decided that campers should do fun things—like eat. The owners instituted a Don't Ask, Don't Tell policy. That meant Monday through Saturday, we counted calories. We monitored protein. They drew food pyramids on white boards and read our weight loss journals. Monday through Saturday the salad bar reigned. Guest speakers now included a chemistry student who broke down the equation of an actual calorie and a nutritionist who spoke for thirty minutes about the difference between fast and slow carbohydrates. Tuesday and Thursdays consisted of tag-team therapy sessions where Hank and Belinda channeled their inner Dr. Drew.

However.

On Sunday they left us alone. Campers could roam the campus, visit the gym, and if they accidentally wandered into a cinnamon bun along the way, Hank and Belinda only asked you not to brag about it. Then, on Sunday evenings, Hank and Belinda promised that campers would take part in activities that did not involve sweating or sports bras or scales.

After five days as Captain Thin, it was now Sunday, our first ever official unweighed weigh day. Hank and Belinda decided that they'd host an evening barbecue by the lake where campers were encouraged to dress "clashfully." It was a far cry from the naked hippie orgy a few nights ago, but what can I tell you, most of the campers wouldn't be into naked hippies anyway. I showed up late and was glad to see that the younger campers had spray-painted their hair and wore plaids and polka dots, a few had polished their nails different colors, and many wore unpaired flip-flops, etc. The boys wore their boxers outside their shorts or they showed up in drag. I was counted on to participate so I wore my Captain Thin shirt inside out and put on (CUP) underwear outside my shorts. My hair was crazy green and turquoise and I'd bedazzled my flip-flops with studs. Liliana would have been impressed.

From the looks of things, Hank and Belinda had kept their promise because chicken hot dogs, turkey burgers, and sugar free s'mores were distributed generously. I sat at a picnic table and watched the younger campers charge in and out of the water. If it was hard for them being away from home, you couldn't tell now. They looked like they were having a great time with their silly costumes and temporary tattoos inking their arms and legs. This was a moment when being team captain did not entirely suck. The kids let their guard down and romped up and down the shoreline, oblivious to their jiggling bellies or double chins. When I glanced further down the shoreline, I made out the shape of a figure sitting on a log. I knew immediately by the hooded sweatshirt and slant of the shoulders that it was Gabe. I felt suddenly embarrassed in my blue/green hair and underwear outside my shorts. I expected he would say something cruel or, fueled by his hatred, interrupt our evening. How dare we have fun when his sister was so sick? But our eyes found each other's and held steady. His stare was not friendly, true, but underneath the coolness was something else. Maybe it was surprise—seeing me out there with all these Utopians. But it felt different than that. It was almost as if he'd been waiting for me. A few minutes later, squishing marshmallows between graham crackers around a campfire, I looked up and he was gone.

59

ACCEPTANCE SPEECH

LIFE AS CAPTAIN Thin got a little better each day. However, morning power walk was a different story. Everyone was all nicey-nice until six thirty rolled around and suddenly it was, *Bethany, who? Power walk, what? I never agreed to that.* Even Hollywood was over it. As much as I tried to motivate everyone—as much as I wore my Captain Thin shirt with pride, no one budged. It was dead silence until breakfast. This eventually led me back to my too-empty and too-quiet dorm room. Not so much as a paper airplane floated through my window. These were the times—in the quiet, early morning—when I really wanted to eat. Instead I leaned back on the bottom bunk, lifted my legs, and tapped my feet on Cambridge's mattress above me. I wrote e-mails to my dad. I read books on my e-reader. I tried to figure out how to get everyone out of bed.

Finally Miss Marcia had had enough of everyone's power walk avoidance and called an emergency meeting. In the common room, after twenty minutes of her loud interrogations, it came out that the older campers didn't trust me. Hell, they didn't even like me. Tampa Bay shot me a dirty look and said, "Why power walk with Baltimore? She obviously doesn't know anything about losing weight."

"No," I said, in spite of the fact that the question was directed at Miss Marcia. "But I know a boatload about getting fat." The campers arranged on the floor were silent—probably because truer words were never spoken. I spent my whole life gaining weight; it just might've been the one thing I was indisputably good at. "I know even more about ignoring the problem or pretending there isn't one in the first place. I get an A-plus in running away. But then Liliana got sick."

Liliana's coma had scared me to the core, but looking around at the faces gathered in MontClaire Hall, it hadn't affected everyone in the same way.

"Go ahead," urged Miss Marcia. "Maybe you should explain why you came back to camp."

I knew this conversation was unavoidable. "I wanted a new ending," I told the campers now. I did not falter when I'd said it and, for the campers in back who weren't paying attention, I said it again. "I wanted my ending." My volume rivaled Miss Marcia's. "Not the one you wanted," I said to Houston with the blue streak in her hair. "Or the one you thought I should have," I said to Hollywood. "I didn't want Liliana's ending either," I said, directing my strong words to Miss Marcia, "but mine." My eyes fell on each one of them. "I don't even know I'll be without this one thing everyone sees, the only thing I ever see, but," I said, and I could see Hollywood nodding her head, "I can't wait to find out."

"What about the scale?" whined Houston. "How will we know if we've made progress?"

"There are other ways to measure your worth," I shot back.

Tampa Bay crossed his arms. "You came back for an ending?" I could tell he was angry that I hadn't brought Tabitha with me. "A new ending?" He said the words doubtfully.

"Yes," I spat. "I wasn't aware it determined whether or not you got your butt out of bed in the morning for a walk."

And then I dropped it and hoped to holy hell that they got it because I didn't feel like saying it again. *Please,* I thought, watching them smack their gum and tap their fingers, *please get it. Please get that as much as dieting and power walking sucks, sometimes being fat sucks too.* Didn't they know what it felt like to have a perfect stranger offer advice just because they happened to notice your dress size? *You'd be so pretty if ... You'd be perfect if ...* And the diets! What we're willing to try—throwing

up, spitting out, tossing secrets in a fishbowl. All of us banking
on the unlikely possibility that we could wake up, unzip our old
skin, and find something shiny and beautiful inside. Something
no one ever expected.

"I totally get it," said Hollywood. Maybe the other campers
who yawned and chewed their fingernails didn't, but Hollywood
definitely got it. Scanning the other twenty or so blank stares, I
experienced profound sympathy for every high school teacher
in America.

"So do we have to power walk or not?" That was posited
from Atlanta and her energetic hair.

"Yes," I said. "You need to walk."

I didn't have time to dwell on the groans that followed because just then, MontClaire Hall's front door beeped and clicked.
When it swung open, Liliana Delgado stood behind it. There she
stood beside Gabe, pale and limp in her *Mornings Suck* night-
shirt and leggings. A barcoded hospital bracelet circled her wrist.

"I'm really dead," she said. "Funny how hell looks just like
Utopia, no?"

She offered some version of a smile. Her voice was scratchy;
her skin washed out. "I'm sorry, Liliana," I blurted in front of
everyone. I guessed I should've gone with "hello" first, but I
wanted to get the apology out and over with. When she saw me,
her mouth fell open.

"Baltimore? *¿Qué estás haciendo?*"

I'm sure I looked like I was about to deliver a PowerPoint
presentation standing up in front of everyone like that. "I wasn't
sure you'd come back," I said.

She flashed a blue-braces smile and spread her fingers into
the Vulcan salute. "I'll live long and prosper so long as I follow
these guidelines." In front of me, Liliana fanned about a thousand pamphlets across the sofa table. *Living With Type I Diabetes. Cooking With Diabetes. Eating Out With Diabetes. You and
Your Diabetes. Learning to Control Diabetes.*"

The other campers inferred that our meeting was adjourned
and made their way out of the common room. That left me, Liliana, and Gabe, and about twenty tons of awkward.

Of course Gabe had the look of a trapped animal. He observed the ceiling, his checkered Vans, anywhere but me. We

waited for the clumsy moment to pass. It didn't.

"What're you doing here anyway?" Liliana asked, collapsing on the sofa. Tape gathered in the crooks of her elbows. "Where's Cambridge?"

I looked to Gabe for support, sympathy. I don't know why I looked to Gabe, but once I did I regretted it. It was as if knives flew out of his gaze and pinned me to the wall.

"Actually, Liliana, I'm kind of the captain now."

"Impossible."

"It's true. I think Cambridge went back to Boston. I wanted to stay and well, I'm sorry. I wanted to stay with you. Make an effort. "

A weird noise came from Gabe.

His sister glared at him. "*'Mano*, it's not her fault."

"Yes it is," he said. "She bought the chocolate."

"Well, I ate it."

"*Todo lo que*," said Gabe, rolling his eyes. "I'm out." And then he left, shutting the door a little too hard.

After her brother left, Liliana stated the obvious. "He's a bit of a grudge holder." She tapped me with her elbow. "He'll get over it. In no time, he'll be all butterflies and ocean mist just like a douche commercial, *verdad*?"

"What about you?" I asked. "Are you a grudge holder? Would you ever forgive someone who accidentally put you in a coma?"

Liliana pretended to consider it. She rubbed her chin. "I know you didn't do it on purpose," she said. "It's part of this disease. I can't eat whatever I want. I don't know why that's so hard for me to get." She propped her feet on the coffee table. "I think I need to take care of myself instead of waiting for my brother to do it for me. It's time for me to face the facts about my pancreas."

"I know the feeling," I replied. My pancreas might be OK, but I had my own facts to face.

"What about Cambridge? She didn't return with you?"

"No."

Liliana tilted her head. "Surprising."

I'm glad I wasn't the only person who thought so.

"Anyway," Liliana said. She stood up a little wobbly. "I can't speak for *'mano*, but I can forgive you. I mean I do forgive you.

¡Te perdono, bruja!"

Back upstairs I watched Liliana bedazzle shorts like old times. She looked paler, weaker, and thinner, but her blue braces still sparkled like sapphires whenever she cursed at the machine, which had taken to firing stones where she hadn't intended them. I tried talking to her about a medical plan, but she wasn't having it. She only wanted to discuss who wore what at the Teen Choice Awards and how if you're gonna wear eye makeup then you sure as shit better learn how to apply it correctly. When I dug out the box from Amazon under my bed and handed it to her, she jumped back a little.

"This is not chocolate," I assured her.

"You didn't need to get me anything," she said, unwrapping the box.

I'd wanted to get her a gift though. A real one. I cashed out my PayPal and ordered her a gently used super-deluxe PS Singer 3500 sewing machine, which Liliana now separated from a swarm of Styrofoam peanuts. When she realized what it was, that little smartass got emotional. Liliana centered it on her desk. "This beats chocolate," she said, her eyes glazed with tears. *"Gracias."*

"Cry all you want, but I'm still getting you out of bed for power walking tomorrow."

"Good luck with that."

From: osbournecfo@forgivenessdietllc.com
To: Bethany Stern <bethanys@utopia.com>
Subject: forgive me

Dear Ms. Stern,

I apologize for the delay in getting back to you … I regret that your efforts with THE FORGIVENESS DIET have not been met with success. I personally read all fifty-three of your e-mails. I was particularly fond of the one wherein you expressly wished for me to contract pubic lice. The one in which you threatened to shove me in a potato sack alongside two hundred copies of my book and cast me off a bridge was also particularly moving.

While everyone who has ever written me wants a response, you were the only one who really demanded one. I suppose that's why I'm sending you this now.

I'm fairly certain you never purchased my book because most of the hate mail comes from people who threw secrets in a bucket and waited for the magic. If you'd read the book, you'd know that the bucket is only a fraction of it.

Eight years ago I woke up and did something I'd never done before. I walked to breakfast. It was less than a block away and, at well over three hundred pounds, I wasn't sure I'd make it. I did. I decided then and there that if I wanted to eat breakfast the next day, I needed to walk there again. It was my new rule. It was always breakfast, you see, because the day was still young. By afternoon we've already settled into ourselves, accepted our limitations. But in the morning, you can be anybody. You can be the guy who walks to breakfast.

I began by picking restaurants close by. Then they got further away. First five blocks. Then two miles. Then five. At first I walked. Then I ran. I lost two hundred pounds. It took four years.

You, like the millions of people who write me every day, want to know my secret. The problem is there is no secret, Bethany. That has been the hardest part for people to accept. After losing so much weight, I am consistently surprised not by how my life has changed, but by how much it hasn't.

My forgiveness journey began less conspicuously. I never intended to forgive anyone, it just happened that way. I just started forgiving damn near everybody: the panting jogger training for a marathon I'd see every morning, the cigarette-smoking teenager walking the dog, the guys who yelled "Fattie!" out the window of their parents' car, the girls who threw trash at me, the waitresses who eyed my pancakes disdainfully. And the stretch marks—oh the stretch marks, all silvery and purple. You can't have growth without them, you know. Anyway, I forgave them all. What a thing of beauty, this life. What a thing of beauty you are too. If only you could see it.

My commercial was a stroke of marketing genius that promised something it could not deliver. I never questioned its ethicality. I never questioned the money that poured down the greedy throat of my bank account either. For that, among many other transgressions, I hope you will forgive me. We all make mistakes, Bethany. Even me. Even you.

In short, if you would like to lose weight, I suggest you walk to breakfast. Likewise, if people have not always treated you fairly, I suggest you forgive them. The bucket (and the book) is purely optional.

Sincerely,

Michael Osbourne, Author, *The Forgiveness Diet*

60

STROKE

THE NEXT MORNING I gave the omelet chef twenty bucks. I posted a note in MontClaire's dining hall: *If you want to eat go to the boathouse.* That was more than a mile away! That'd get the campers' apathetic butts walking! Thirty minutes later, every single camper queued, paper plate extended, waiting for their omelet. Thank you, Mr. Osbourne of Forgiveness Diet fame. Problem solved.

If speed walking toward a Western omelet was the only exercise required of us, things might have been grand. Only our counselor must've spent the night pondering things too, because while we were eating, she slid a boat from the boathouse. Then, securing a bathing cap over her blazing red hair, she stripped down to her bathing suit. A man resembling a Greek god climbed in the boat beside her. Watching them, everyone's plastic forks paused.

Marcia's toes curled around the boat's edge, and she screamed, "If you want to get back to campus, you'll need to row there. We have too many factions on our team. You need to remember we're united. Today I'm instituting a sport that will unify you. It's called *crew*." Her voice seriously shook the birds out of trees. "And Courtney here will teach you how to do it."

I did not like the sound of this. The last "crew" I participated in involved squeezing into that pencil-thin boat with my dad.

Miss Marcia joined hands with Courtney, who teeter-tottered on his own vessel. In a sexy British accent, Courtney informed us, "From here forward, if you want breakfast, you need to walk here. If you want to get back to campus in time for lunch, you'll need to row there. This bloody boat will be the best thing that ever happened to you." And I guess because they were standing by Lake Pacifica, Miss Marcia in her bikini, Courtney's six-pack abdomen firm and steady—not to mention that the walk back to MontClaire Hall was super long—we believed them.

There were five boats of campers, though our boat only had four crew members. The first lesson Courtney imparted was that five was better than four. A four-person crew meant we'd have to work harder. If a camper didn't show up for crew, they would not get to eat breakfast. What Courtney deemed worse than skipping the most important meal of the day was that your team or *crew* lost an oarsman. That meant they lost drag, which you'd assume was a good thing because heavy people create a lot of drag. However, fat people were strong. A crew would overlook drag because strength eclipsed it—at least on canoes, which were to be called shells or sculls. Courtney explained all this in his please-stop-fantasizing-about-me voice. He was perfect looking, almost as if he were chiseled from rock. Believe it or not, I found learning about the sport of crew easy. It wasn't like field hockey or softball with a ton of rules to keep track of. According to our fearless leader, in rowing you had a coxswain (Miss Marcia), who told you when to stroke. The oars acted as a lever to propel you across the water. To steer, you either held the oars forward or backward on one side (starboard) or the other (port). The object was to get to your destination faster than the other rowers, or, in our case, faster than the day before. Courtney's accent made it all seem very civilized. He invoked physics and mathematical words about fulcrums and angles, which I sure wished I'd listened to by the time we tried to execute them.

Learning on the shore was much easier than practice in the water. We sat in those boats, packed like sardines, and agreed that even though he was gorgeous, Courtney had to die. Rowing a boat was simply not what you'd expect. It was really fricking hard. Calluses surfaced on our hands. Splinters stuck between our fingers.

After the two-hour "lesson" provided by Courtney (now called wanker) and another two hours on the water, we finally made it across the lake. We were supposed to row *back* to the boathouse, but that was not about to happen. Leaving those minions of hell behind us, we staggered on legs that shimmied like mousse, past Olive's drug-growing dormitory, past Copernicus. I tried not to think about any of the memories I had there, but failed miserably. To add insult to my injuries, when Gabe visited our window later that night, he only wanted to talk to his sister.

"He'll get over it," Liliana told me again after her brother wheeled off. Because of the rowing pain, we rubbed Bengay on our muscles. Our room smelled like a geriatric ward. "He likes you too much to stay away."

I didn't really believe her, but I tried to put it out of my mind. Just like I had to stow Chinese food, Milk Duds, Red Bulls, gingerbread lattes, macaroni, and everything else I missed, I had to pack away Gabe too. I stuffed him next to Cambridge in one of those magician boxes and threw away the key.

I decided I'd keep myself busy speed walking to breakfast, paddling a boat to the point of exhaustion, and smearing Bengay on my muscles at night. I also began planning diabetic meals swiped from Liliana's hospital pamphlets. I scavenged for recipes on the Internet. A med student measured Liliana's blood sugar religiously. I gave up vending machines. I quit soda completely. Not once did I step on a scale.

61

REUNION

IF YOU WANT to know the truth, power walking to breakfast soon became the easiest part of our day. Crew left us breathless, wasted, but you couldn't deny the results. We'd been doing it about five days when Liliana demanded, "Look at my butt! *¡Miras!* Does it look different to you because it feels different to me. Firmer, no?" Oddly enough her butt *did* look different, better. Maybe those lines in my legs were calf muscles? Then, one morning after our omelets, Miss Marcia dropped a bomb. She announced that in spite of the fact that we only had a few weeks left of camp, Utopia would be getting a new camper. Everyone looked around anxiously. Why would anyone join fat camp *now*?

Miss Marcia continued, "And because we have one crew team with only four members, we figured a new Utopian would even things out." Since I happened to be a member of that crew, I felt a bit relieved. *Let's hope this new girl knows her way around a lake.*

"Does she even know how to row?" Hollywood asked.

Miss Marcia smiled big in her neon-green bikini. "Actually," our counselor started, "our new camper is a champion crew woman."

I felt giddy. A champion? That meant she was fast! And capable! We could row this lake in minutes!

Miss Marcia cleared her throat. "She went to a prestigious

boarding school back East and managed to maintain a 4.2 GPA all the while preserving a coveted oarswoman spot on the Mermaidens, a highly ranked New England team. In fact, *Who's Crew* wrote an article about her."

Well bring her out, we all thought impatiently. *Make this girl the coxswain!* Miss Marcia waved at the boathouse and about twenty other campers nearly fell off the picnic tables when the three-time rowing champion turned out to be Tabitha Calliope Nelson.

Cambridge (*Cambridge!*) walked out of the boathouse in her navy-blue bathing suit, dragging a scull behind her. Head down and determined, her dreadlocks captured in a rubber band, she looked nothing shy of an athlete. With a signal from Miss Marcia, Cambridge ran right past us, out into the water, and lifted herself up in the boat so artfully, we all gasped. She grabbed hold of the oars and rowed into the lake like some goddamn poetry. It was a beautiful sight, so natural and graceful she looked. Even though she was heavy, she seemed comfortably suited to the boat, the oars almost an extension of her arms. In the time it took for us campers to accumulate fifty splinters and row twenty feet, Cambridge had oared to the footbridge and back. Tampa Bay ran straight out into the water to greet her. She walked right past him, though, toward me.

"Is there anything you can't do?" I asked her.

"Drive a car," she countered and pulled me into a hug.

Around us the other campers prepared the boats for crew.

"Is it true?" I asked her. "Are you really a camper again?"

Cambridge nodded her head. "I've been staying with Olive, and I can't take one more minute of the rock-'n'-roll lifestyle. Too many brownies. Too many cigarettes and check this out." She turned around and I saw a very new-looking tattoo: a tree branch that curved upward toward her shoulder blades. One spindly branch climbed up to her neck and, just beneath her hair, a white cocoon dangled with an iridescent butterfly wing pushing out of it.

I traced it with my finger. Parts of it were still red and puffy. "When will she finish it?" Only the bottom half of the butterfly wing had been inked in turquoise and yellow.

"I think I might keep it this way. It reminds me that nothing's ever perfect."

Typical Cambridge. Always viewing imperfections as accomplishments. After I examined her tattoo, she examined me. She scanned my bedazzled shorts and frumpy black hoodie. She pulled one of her dreadlocks.

"I heard you whooped Hollywood's ass. You're quite the fighter."

I shrugged. "Who knew, right?"

"I did." She looked down at her bare feet. "Well, I had a feeling anyway," she said. "Remember when you knocked out Gabe?"

I felt a little sad when I heard his name. "Yeah."

Changing the subject, I offered, "We changed some stuff around here too. No more weigh days. And Sundays are free. You can eat whatever you want." I didn't mean to sound so desperately happy, but come on, I missed her. Liliana had returned safely. Even Hollywood had demolished a scale. But Cambridge? She belonged here. Not at Utopia necessarily, but with me. We rolled like that.

She extracted her old keycard from her pocket. "I kept my keycard the whole time," she said. "I guess I always knew you'd go back, which meant I'd go back."

I held out my hand to her. "We have the omelet chef every other morning. You can even have seconds." I wiggled my fingers. "There's an espresso machine too," I sang out enticingly.

With that, she dropped her hand in mine. And that was how Cambridge came back into my life. Easily. Like she was meant to be there because—hello?—she was. We walked right over to the boat that already held Liliana, Hollywood, and Tampa Bay. She rowed across the lake again, not even breaking a sweat. Now, I realized, we were a crew. Finally, our team was complete.

62

A PROUD SPONSOR

NOW MANY OF us gathered in the common room waiting for the show to start. Centered on my lap was a gigantic bowl of popcorn misted with—because it was Sunday—light butter. As I prepared myself to see TJ's national television debut, Cambridge, who sat on my left, warned me not to freak out and Liliana, on my right, told me to go right ahead.

I'd been thinking about it all day. How exactly do you mentally prepare to see your first love on *American Envy*? I had no idea. All I knew was I wanted the show to start right now while, at the same time, wished the season would get canceled. *Envy* didn't start until eight, but by seven, I'd claimed my spot in front of the TV in the common room. By seven thirty, I broke out in a cold sweat, and by seven forty-five, I worried I might pass out. Today was Sunday, our second official unweighed weigh day and since its new season began tonight, Belinda and Hank decided an *American Envy* party would be a good way to commemorate the evening.

The common room was unusually quiet. I sat on the sofa between Liliana and Cambridge, the other campers dispersed around the carpet and chairs. An irritating scratching sound rose up, and Liliana elbowed me. "I told you he'd be back. The cause of the sound had been a certain skateboarder ollying around MontClaire Hall's common room. Gabe jumped off the board and flopped on Liliana's lap. "Move over," he said.

"Plant your butt cheeks on someone else, 'mano. Bethany's boyfriend's about to be on TV."

Cambridge moved over and patted the sofa. "Here," she said. "There's room."

I waited for Gabe to say something insulting, or apologetic, or even ordinary, but he didn't. Instead we watched the Aluma Wallet commercial like we hadn't seen it three hundred times before. Then, as soon as the commercial ended, the screen went black. It was time *for American Envy.*

DO YOU NEED TO LOSE WEIGHT?

Jesus Christ, I thought. *Not this again.*

HAVE YOU TRIED EVERY DIET AND FAILED?

I did not want to watch this commercial right now. At fat camp. In front of everyone. I heard Cambridge's gentle laugh followed by, "Is this the one your dad recommended?"

I ignored her. A more awkward moment never existed. I tried to tune out the lady in the giant sunhat sipping her drink. I tried to ignore the overflowing forgiveness buckets and prismatic scraps of paper. I even tried to ignore the 1-800 number that flashed below Michael Osbourne. Instead I waited for Gabe to nudge me, as TJ had, to tell me to give it a try. I waited for the campers to boast of their success. But Gabe didn't nudge me, and none of the campers bragged about their weight loss on the forgiveness plan. Instead we all watched the infomercial with the same eyes we'd always had only, for some reason, we saw it differently this time. The stupid surfer looked orange with his spray-on tan. The music seemed artificial. Even the voice sounded computer enhanced. I couldn't help but think of Michael Osbourne's e-mail too and his own weight loss story—how he'd lost two hundred pounds over four years and how it had been a journey with mistakes, just as mine would be. And how he'd said forgiveness came at the end of the journey, not the beginning. That's what I was thinking about as the surfer (an actor no doubt) swam out into the ocean and the lady twirled in her gold bikini.

YES, the voice intoned, IT'S ABOUT FORGIVENESS.

Nobody said anything during the commercial, which was way too long and ridiculously cheesy. Not one of us wrote down the number either. But by the end of it, Gabe leaned into me. Our outer thighs pressed into each other's.

63

DOVES

ON THE TV, Timothy Tinsel fiddled with his earpiece. "Welcome to season five. I'm Timothy Tinsel, host of *American Envy*." The generic pop music twitted and stills of the three judges appeared: Apple Bitterstein crying over a cat whisperer in season two; Eugene Gold smirking at tap dancers in season three; Tyra Lyra Stevens swooning as a singer serenaded her. In seconds, we were back with Timothy. "Let's give our viewers at home a peek at the talented and the not-so-talented our producers uncovered this summer."

Footage of contortionists and rappers montaged across the screen. I refused to be distracted. Everything about Utopia, MontClaire Hall, and California disintegrated. "We are down to twenty of the most promising stars in America. They are with us tonight. And guess what?" He pointed a finger at the camera. "You'll meet them when we get back." I wanted to reach into the guts of the television and speed things up. Beside me, Gabe sat perfectly still. I chewed my popcorn thoughtfully and tried to pretend these were normal circumstances. In no time we were back with Tinsel. The show contained a lot of fluff, and I think we were getting a little impatient. Finally dead last in the lineup, TJ walked out on stage rocking a tuxedo like he had invented it.

My heart stopped.

"My name is Toby Jacobson and I'm from Baltimore, Maryland."

"How old are you Toby?" asked Apple Bitterstein, lips like cloud puffs.

"I'll be nineteen in October."

Halloween, I thought.

"Well you're certainly dressed to impress," said Tyra Lyra, practically drooling.

Rumor had it she dated contestants. "So tell us, Mr. Jacobson, why do you think you'll be *American Envy's* next winner?"

Black-Conversed, clean-shaven TJ, his hat dipped down over one eye and his skinny tie arranged perfectly, was flawless. Back at Utopia, I sweated like a farm animal and tried to remember to breathe. On that Los Angeles stage, there was not even a kink in TJ's voice.

"I used to live in Las Vegas. My dad was a Blackjack dealer at Monte Carlo, so we saw shows for free. I saw David Copperfield when I was four and learned how to palm objects at five. I knew I'd become a magician. Even when my father gave up Vegas for Baltimore and Blackjack for Jesus, I kept on with magic." He cleared his throat. "I did my card tricks on my friend, Bethany. I studied Yigal Mesika, Dan Sperry, Paul Vigil, David Blaine, Criss Angel, and Copperfield. Any chance I got, I saw them perform. I incorporated doves four years ago and when someone stole them last year, I almost gave up." My hands shook when he mentioned the birds. "They came back though," he said, and from his sleeve the two creamy doves erupted in the air.

Eugene Gold, the meanest judge, leaned forward. "We've seen your impressive work with coins and cards. You wowed our producers in Baltimore, but you aren't in Baltimore anymore." He cracked his knuckles and folded his hands on the judges' table. "There are only twenty left, Mr. Jacobson. What do you have that they don't?"

From his other sleeve, TJ plucked out a feather. He flicked it in the air then blew underneath it. *Not that one*, I thought. He'd pretend to swallow the feather then blow it out his ear. He needed more than elementary school tricks for these judges. Much to my surprise, though, TJ had enhanced the sleight because when the camera panned the auditorium, about a million feathers, white and silky, rained down. He must've rigged the ceiling somehow. Feathers billowed on folding seats and aisles, an endless supply.

"I have more skill than they do," said my neighbor, honestly. "More patience."

He snapped and the feathers stopped, a few falling to rest on the judges' table.

Gold raised a finger in the air. "You never mentioned Penn & Teller. Certainly they were influential." The judge blew plumage from his upper lip. "Feathers from the ceiling? That's classic Penn & Teller one hundred percent."

I willed TJ not to lose it.

"Penn & Teller are spoilers," TJ stated calmly. "They're comedians. I'm an illusionist, and I only work alone. I can assure you, Mr. Gold, the feather trick is mine." Two doves flew from the rafters and landed on TJ's shoulders. Slowly the birds changed from white to yellow. They extended their intricate wings, championing their new sunny color.

Ignoring TJ's condensed theory about illusionists versus comedians, the judge continued. "Ten of you will leave tonight. Convince me you shouldn't be one of them."

The judges moaned. Eugene was a bastard.

TJ nodded at someone, and instantly his music choice pelted out. Trent Reznor. I can't tell you how many times we argued about his music. I found it distracting. TJ said that was the point. He needed dramatic, operatic, industrial. Listening to it now, pulsing cruelly like my own sloppy heartbeat, I realized he was right—the music was perfect. "You like to push people, Eugene," said TJ. "I've always liked that about you."

The judges fidgeted nervously; Mr. Gold cocked his head.

"Mr. Jacobson? Are you levitating?"

Looking genuinely surprised, TJ replied, "I believe I am."

This was the Balducci levitation TJ had tried to capture in my basement two months ago. Basically you rest one foot on the other and stand at an angle. He certainly did his homework because there were more than a few inches between his feet and the stage. He really did appear to hover. Gold shook his head and folded his arms across his chest. Something about magicians made the judge cynical. TJ used to say he was harder on illusionists than anyone else. On the stage now, unaffected by the judge's doubt, TJ continued.

While effortlessly performing a Balducci levitation, TJ flicked a red handkerchief from his pocket and patted it like pizza dough. He spun it on his finger and, when he moved away, the handkerchief stayed, orbiting in the air. He did that with two more handkerchiefs, a white one and a black one, until the three spun obediently before him. Then, while they were still spinning no less, he positioned them, adjusting the red one first, the black a little lower, one in the middle like, like steps! Yes, as far apart as steps, twirling rectangles of color. Next, he lifted a foot as if to stand on the first red handkerchief. He tested it convincingly, balancing one foot at a time, all extensively choreographed. Then he climbed up, settling both feet down, rocking slightly. The scarf looked solid, airtight, but how? How could you stand on a scarf in midair? The judges, in addition to all of MontClaire Hall, watched, speechless. Climbing the second scarf and finally ascending to the third, red handkerchief TJ now balanced himself five feet off the stage. He tore off his hat, and spun it directly to the judges' table. The yellow doves chased it, landing on Gold's shoulders. Eugene laughed, put his hands up. "OK, Toby Jacobson. You've convinced me. You can stay."

All three judges stood and applauded. Five feet off the stage, still standing on the red handkerchief, TJ smiled. Then, surprising us all, he stepped off the handkerchief and bowed. It all happened so fast it took a few seconds to register that when he bowed his feet rested on ... nothing. Nothing. TJ levitated, five feet off the ground.

This was too much for Tyra Lyra. She climbed the stairs in her stilettos and crossed her arms. She lifted his jacket and shook it out. "How are you doing it?"

She placed her hands on her hips. "I want to know how you're doing it."

TJ's Conversed feet began precisely where her head ended. The camera zeroed in on his face, which, I noticed for the first time, wasn't sporting glasses.

"Most everyone trusts their eyes to do their seeing. That's their first mistake."

Tyra Lyra sighed. "So what am I seeing wrong here?" She opened and closed her mascara-coated eyes. "What should I be seeing?"

TJ wiggled his fingers above the host and a filmy powder dusted her dress. "For starters, you'd see that yellow's not your color."

Tyra Lyra huffed. "My dress is black, Mr. Jacobson."

"You sure about that?" asked TJ, crossing his arms. Then darkness swallowed the stage and TJ, still hovering, began to disappear. Not in a dramatic flash either, but slowly. First his feet vanished, then his legs. His limbs became particlelike, comprised of dots until eventually, he faded like a memory.

A very pale and frightened Tyra Lyra lumbered down the steps in her now-yellow dress. She touched the fabric. "Hope this changes back," she said.

Eugene Gold, one yellow dove on each shoulder, looked at the stage like TJ was still on it. "I don't know about your dress, Tyra, but I have a feeling nothing will ever be the same after that kid."

Every last one of us campers blanched. *Feeling*? Eugene Gold didn't have feelings. The persnickety judge had never said that before—about anyone. People truly believed he was a robot because his criticisms were so concise. "There's an energy there," Gold continued. "Something rare and extraordinary."

Hollywood, who sat Indian style on the floor, verbalized what we were all thinking, "He's never said that before." Then she looked at me. "That TJ guy is going to take it. Your boyfriend's about to win *Envy*."

"Maybe," I replied, knowing it was possible. "But he's still not my boyfriend."

Slowly reeling me back to Utopia was Gabe, beside me on the sofa, inching closer. Closer. "Just so you're aware," he whispered in my ear, his gentle fingers closing around mine, "I can't compete with that."

64

FLOAT LIKE A BUTTERFLY

AFTER TJ'S DEBUT on *American Envy*, Gabe and I found our way back to each other. The next night we were fighting in Copernicus Hall like old times. I didn't realize how much I'd missed him until I was back in his room, making fists inside the PlayStation glove and listening to him go on about jabs and punches. Our K/O fights were brutal. Neither of us held back—at least not in the video game version. Outside of the game was a different story. Even though he went on and on about Knock Out, rocket camp, and calculus, he never mentioned SPOOGE again. Never put his earbuds on me and well, you know—went for it. There were a few close calls, lulls in our conversations, or times when I felt his eyes on me a beat too long, but these moments were short-lived, and eventually he'd power up the PlayStation and we'd punch each other's lights out.

All that tension went straight to our game, because we went from K/O level two to level eighteen in two days. Finally, after I'd won the belt and had his avatar crying in the ring's corner, Gabe did a little research and Fed-Exed about three new games to his dorm. Opening the padded envelope, he grinned at me and said, "*Entra más profundo.*"

That night we stayed up for a long time trying the games. My favorite one was Femme Fatal, a black market import he'd acquired from Japan. The game was nothing short of badass.

Girls shouted insulting things at us in Japanese then cried when you punched them. Gabe didn't even care that his avatar wore a bikini and cursed whenever she broke a nail. These girls were tough, and Gabe got his junk handed to him more than once.

We played nonstop for hours, and I probably would have kept going had Gabe not checked his phone and said, "I can tell just by looking at you that you love this, but you're two hours late for curfew." Not one to use the word "love" alongside any cardiovascular activity, I was surprised that he was right. I was a smelly, sweaty, sore-muscled fool by the end of the night but, at last, I'd found a sport I didn't entirely suck at. We played every night and after about a week, I found myself looking forward to seeing Gabe, yes, but also to fighting. Gabe took it upon himself to teach me lessons before the fights. His dorm room turned into a boxing appreciation course. Surfing ViewTube and Cineflix, we watched clips of kickboxers like Iron Mike and Semmy Schlit and Ramon Dekkers. Then we watched the female boxers: Laila Ali, Christy Martin, and Lucia Rijker. Gabe froze the computer shots of cross-jabs, knockouts, uppercuts, and rabbit punches. Then we stood in front of the mirror behind his closet door and practiced those moves. When we stumbled across an old Ali and Foreman fight on ViewTube, I knew I was witnessing something magical. It was like Cambridge rowing that boat or Liliana on her sewing machine or Jackie and the hula hoop she once kept spinning for six hours. It was something you couldn't manu-facture or imitate or even articulate. It was pure, unobstructed, awesome.

From: ellenstern@zyprexapharm.com
To: Bethany Stern <bethanys@utopia.com>
Subject: The best you

Dear Bethany,

I'm glad you decided to go back to camp. I don't know if your father had any-thing to do with that decision, but if he did, I'm glad for it. Hank and Belinda told me how much progress you've made and what a great captain you are. They say you are an inspiration.

I'm glad things are working out at Utopia. I always knew you would accom-plish great things. You have always been the bigger person in our house, and I don't mean the heaviest one either.

Speaking of great things, yesterday I went to a workshop at Zyprexa Pharm. They were revealing a new slogan. Zyprexa: Finding the best in you. During the whole presentation, I thought of you. I think you encountered the best in you this summer. And you didn't even need Zyprexa!

I am proud of you, Bethany. Enjoy these last few weeks in California. I'm jeal-ous. It's so hot here and the snowball stand closed early last week.

Jackie will be there to pick you up. It will be great to have you both home.

Love,

Mom

65

GOING NOWHERE

TWO WEEKS LEFT on the fat camp clock and things finally came together. Only when the curtain's about to close is it all rainbows and unicorns. Olive volunteered to plant a garden outside MontClaire Hall so tempting we had no choice but to call it Eden. Not that anything would bloom in our last few weeks, but next spring, should anyone want them, there'd be oranges and herbs, onions, tomatoes, and peppers. The omelet chef was ecstatic. As for the rest of us, Miss Marcia's intuition about rowing was right. With the exception of Cambridge, our hatred of crew definitely united us. Every day we tried to get out of it, tossing excuses to Miss Marcia nonstop. *The water's too choppy. It's too foggy. This sport is elitist!* And every day, before our omelets were even digested, Miss Marcia blew the whistle and we sloshed through the water, scrambled inside our sculls, while the coxswain (Hollywood) screamed STROKE, STROKE, STROKE obscenely in our ears.

Once in a while, there came a spectacular moment in crew. Like when we all rowed together in a rhythm, for instance. It didn't feel like any one person was pulling more weight than the other; it was pure machination. The other thing in crew was you sat backward, so you never saw your finish line getting closer. You only observed your starting point get smaller and smaller. Nearly every single morning, somewhere out on Lake Pacifica between start and finish, I wasn't Bethany anymore. I wasn't fat or skinny. There were no secrets. There was only crew: our unified breathing, the boat, wet oars dipping in and out, the horizon arching her back. That sensation lasted only a minute, but it was a long minute. And a good one. When we banked on shore, sore and shaky, the football stadium was microscopic. It was pretty empowering to see how far we'd come.

Crew made every other sport look like ping-pong. Even Hollywood complained about it in spite of the fact that it burned an insane amount of calories all the while being low-impact. After mutilating the scale and swearing to me she was "over" her eating disorder, Hollywood managed to keep herself skinny. One morning during crew, Liliana forgot she was on a boat because when a cramp gripped her calf, she stood up and tried to walk it off. In seconds, our boat biffed. We floundered in the icy water, cursing Liliana, her muscle, and the boat. Clumsily, we flipped the shell over and pulled our sopping wet selves inside. Hollywood—up to her neck in ice cold water—couldn't do it. She attempted to haul herself, but it was like her arms quit working. Her teeth chattered, and her skin turned blue. She cursed up a storm—eff this and eff that—blaming the slippery boat and the current, but you could see she was too weak. No matter how hard she tried, no matter how much we steadied the boat for her, she could not lift herself in. Finally, Tabitha and I grabbed her under her arms and lugged her in the boat. In doing that, I couldn't help but notice how her ribcage pointed through her T-shirt. Once aboard, she collapsed on the coxswain's bench, looking gray as a wad of gum. Sure Hollywood had moments of bitchiness, especially when she acted all superior. But considering she was bald, not to mention her inability to lift her own self out of water, I could see her skinniness was a burden too. She could have it. We waded on our boat, the other teams long finished, waiting for her to catch her breath. She might be skinny, but she still couldn't haul her ass out of a lake. As for the rest of our heavyset team, we were doing a bang-up job of saving ourselves.

Once we learned how to move our bodies, we learned how to feed them. Hank and Belinda invited culinary arts majors to give us some cooking lessons. This was not your everyday college

Top Ramen 101 either. These students imparted wisdom. For instance, we all learned how to poach salmon, whip up a mean dill and pesto salad, stuff chicken breasts with wild rice, and turn chick peas into hummus. Shocking us all, Tampa Bay got really into it. Now he prepared elaborate healthy meals for all the campers, watching Cambridge closely as she sampled them.

Most nights after dinner, Gabe and I went off to fight. He never made a full-on move on me, and, after a while, I just assumed he wouldn't. Camp was ending soon anyway. Now was not a good time for getting hot and bothered. We had boxing for that.

Late at night, we'd walk back to MontClaire Hall, taking the most indirect route. Usually we'd stop at the parking lot and visit *ni modo*. One night, standing beneath a streetlight next to his busted-up truck, Gabe held the driver's side door open for me. "Bethany, let's drive across country."

And we did.

Alright. So we didn't actually drive across the country. We only pretended to drive across the country, and pretending to drive is a lot easier than actual driving.

"Can you see it?" Gabe asked, pointing toward Copernicus Hall. "It's the Golden Gate bridge."

I shielded my forehead with my palm. "It's rather tall."

"And the hills, Bethany. Feel the butterflies in your stomach?"

"I do," I said, "so quit riding the brake."

"I am not riding the brake."

"Indeed you are."

Gabe raised an eyebrow and slid next to me. "You think you can do better?"

"I doubt I could do worse."

"You drive then," he said. "Show me how it's done." So I shoved my butt in his face as I shifted into the cockpit of *ni modo*. I was sure glad we were pretending because, once there, I felt about twenty feet off the ground. The bent, rusted hood stretched for miles. I turned the key and, of course, nothing happened.

"Hear that?" he asked.

I acted as if the cricket chirps were engine noise. "Churns

like a dream." Then, all business, I gave him my tour of San Francisco, which involved barking sea lions, glittery hills, and everything else I'd learned from watching *Dragon Fight*.

"Keep your eyes on the road, Bethany. And make sure you signal," reminded Gabe, who taught a lot like my dad. So I kept my eyes on the road and made sure I signaled. And I must've impressed him with my mock-driving abilities, because after that first night, I fake-drove Gabe everywhere. We faux-drove to New Mexico, where he admired the mountain chains, sagebrush, and rock formations, all the while telling me to check my mirrors and blind spot. He named the wide Indian reservations and remarked on the sky.

"You've never seen a sunset like that, now have you?"

"No," I said, eyes peeled. "I believe these New Mexico sunsets are enchanting."

"They are purple. Purple like—"

"An eggplant?"

"Not quite as dark."

"A bruise?"

"Yes! A fresh one."

"I see the bruised sunset of which you speak." I sighed. "It's lovely."

"Bethany, you have quite a way with words."

"So I've been told." I slammed the brake to avoid imaginary tumbleweed. "Stop looking at me while I drive."

"I can't."

How cheesy to drive around Oregon, Arizona, and Texas without actually using the motor, without leaving the parking space! Only with Gabe you could be supremely ridiculous, and he went along. This guy's imagination rivaled mine. Whether it was video-gaming or pretend-driving, we somehow managed to create a fantasy world together. I'd never done that before. With anyone. I was always willing to step into TJ's world, but he never quite managed to step into mine. Not Gabe. It was like in a cartoon, when the character would draw a little door on the wall when you needed to escape. Only Gabe walked right through with me.

Sometimes, when we were make-believe driving, he'd jerk the steering wheel and warn I was headed straight for a wild buffalo or a baby stroller. Then we'd pretend to park in Baltimore like a rich Roland Park couple. "That gown is beautiful, Miss Stern. Blue is your color."

"It's yellow."

"I meant yellow. I'm colorblind. Either way, it's ravishing."

Sometimes Liliana and Cambridge and even Tampa Bay piled in the truck's bed and joined us as we drove to the National Air and Space Museum in DC, but mostly they didn't. Mostly it was just me and Gabe who liked going nowhere.

66

GUILTY

WITH ONLY TEN days left of camp, a canopy of stars above us, Gabe wanted to see Los Angeles. So while I navigated highways with more lanes than a music clef, Gabe pointed out the sites. Then Gabe grabbed the wheel and said, "Turn here. It's the Hollywood sign." I did as he instructed, and together we looked through his cracked windshield, pausing to take in the landmark's magnificence.

"Wonder what it's made of," Gabe said.

"Silicon," I posited. He laughed and covered his mouth with his hand.

The night was warm and damp. Bugs swarmed in the streetlights of the parking lot and tapped against the windshield. He directed me toward the view of a Toyota Prius parked next to us.

"I just wanted to let you know," Gabe said to the Toyota Prius, "that I'm not going to kiss you. I'm not going to kiss you in front of this Hollywood sign."

I didn't know why he was suddenly narrating. Or why he felt obliged to point out why he wasn't kissing me. I also didn't understand why he was sharing this with the Toyota Prius all the while moving closer to me.

"I'm not going to kiss you because I have feelings for you, *verdad*. And with your camp ending and my final project coming up, well ..."

Fine, I thought. *Let's not state the obvious, dude. We're just driving.*

Then he looked at me. "And Hollywood, right? How crazy would it be to make a move, you know, here. In the middle of the city."

Colossally crazy. And if he was so adamantly opposed to our kissing then why was he leaning in? Why was he parting his lips in that anticipatory way? If he wasn't going to kiss me then what was with all the flitting butterfly wings in my stomach? Why did I swallow my gum?!

"I can't kiss you because you're not the kind of girl that I only want to kiss once. You're the kind of girl I want to keep kissing. The kind of girl I want to put my hands all over. The kind of girl I could fall ..."

And then we were kissing. Not soft and sweet kisses. No way. The making-up-for-lost-time kissing. The I-can't-get-close-enough-to-you kissing. The I-want-to-turn-myself-inside-out kissing. "I'm not going to take off your shirt," he said as he took off my shirt. The look of reverence as he totally stared at my bra was priceless. And then we kissed some more even though he kept saying we weren't. His hands were not in my hair either. My hands were not on his chest. They did not slide along his smooth stomach. Nor did they burrow into his pockets. Searching. Feeling.

OMFG.

I did not feel anything.

"I'm so glad we're not making out," Gabe said.

"This is neither the time or place," I replied.

"That Hollywood sign is an atrocity."

"A nuisance."

There in his truck, next to the Toyota Prius aka Hollywood sign, I lifted my arms and he peeled off my sports bra. Things slowed down then lost their urgency. He stared at my naked breasts so long I'd thought they'd hypnotized him. Then he held my face in his hands and began to kiss me again, slowly. Softly. He lingered over my lips. He kissed my mouth and my neck. He kissed my throat, groaned softly in my ear. "I am not in love with you tonight," he said. "I am not in love with you here next to the Hollywood sign." I could only listen as he told me how much he didn't love me. How he hadn't loved me since he first saw me by the mermaid fountain with trash in my hair. How even when Liliana got sick, he was pissed, but it did not affect his not-love. And I believed him. He really didn't love me. In fact, I'd bet he practically choked on his not-love for me. And I wanted to tell him that I didn't love him either but right then, leaning back as he pulled me forward, I felt something skitter down my shoulder. Something tiptoeing almost, like the blades of a pinwheel. Gabe stopped, searched the torn pleather seats and raised a weathered Kleenex.

I took the tissue from him. "Where did you find this?"

"I think it came out of your bra."

My bra? Why did I have a piece of tissue in my bra?

We uncrumpled it slowly, carefully, as if it were a treasure map. Then by the light of the moon and streetlamp, I could see what it was. A tattered napkin. The words, the purple ink and the handwriting were all mine. It read, *I forgive the doves for flying back.*

I jolted upright; my hand went for my heart, but landed on my boob. I covered myself with my sports bra. "How did you get this?" I yelled, though I hadn't meant to.

"It just appeared. I don't know," Gabe said confusedly.

"But that's TJ's trick," I said. "Where did you find it?"

Gabe held up his hands defensively. "I swear it came out of nowhere."

I turned it this way and that. Leaned in closer to the windshield, which we'd steamed up pretty thick. How had it gotten here? Was it carried by the wind? Tangled in my bra? Was it TJ? Had he planted it somehow? I knew Gabe was waiting for an explanation, but I couldn't talk. Silence had gripped like a boa constrictor, squeezing me for every word. If it weren't for this truck and the fact that my door refused to open, I would've taken off running.

Sitting in silence for what felt like hours, Gabe finally took his index finger to the steamy windshield, where he wrote the following two words: *Tell me.*

I rolled the forgivelet between my fingers. And despite the fact that I had every reason not to, I told him anyway. I told Gabe everything.

"It was me," I said. "I let the doves out. I let TJ's doves out."

Of all of the contents of my forgiveness bucket, this one had been the hardest to write. The one secret I felt sure I'd take to the grave. "No one stole them, Gabe," I continued. "I opened the cage door myself and said, 'fly.' I never thought they'd come back. The whole time we searched the city and nearby counties, I never said a word about it." My one secret, the only one left, fluttered between Gabe and me like wings.

Well, there went that.

When he reached across me, I thought for sure it was to open my door and push me out. His hand stopped and floated over mine for a spell. Then it dropped, and his fingers closed over mine.

"All that rage, *verdad*?" He brushed away my tears with his fingertips. "Like your mom was saying in the newspaper, all that rage had to come out. He hurt you. So you hurt him back. It's basic Isaac Newton." He took the paper from my hand, rolled it in a ball, and flicked it out the window.

I stared at him curiously.

"I mean those doves?" he continued. "That's your basic rocketry principle number three."

His breath was wintery when he leaned in close. He smiled, his bottom teeth crooked. "All effort comes back. Every action has an opposite and equal reaction."

"Is this what you guys talk about in math camp?"

"Listen." He positioned his face directly in front of mine. "It all comes back. That's the way the universe works. You call it magic. I call it physics. It's what happens when two things collide. One lets go, and the other holds on."

"But the birds," I said, remembering them balanced on the phone wire. "The birds flew back. Both of them."

"Exactly," shouted Gabe. "You let go. They came back. Physics."

We sat out there until dew slipped into his truck's various cracks and wept on the dashboard. Next to me, *Señor* Einstein went on about billiard balls and asteroids and equal reactions. Even though I'd be late for crew, I let the professor have his lesson about force and mass and other equations of the heart. Oddly enough, the more he informed, the more it made sense.

And the more it made sense, the more I let go. I fell for Gabe the way you fall through space: feet off the ground, eyes closed, and totally independent of gravity. I didn't know if Sir Isaac Newton had even half the swagger Gabe did, but if he did then look out. All that talk about science and rockets. Thrust and control. Actions and reactions. It did things to me. Made me tremble all over. Made me row that scull later that morning in some kind of frenzy all the while thinking about bowling ... seventh-period study hall ... dissecting fetal pigs ... Disney movies with talking cats ... yodeling ... dodge ball ... citing sources ... anything, anything, anything, but ...

Gabe.

67

HASTA

A FEW DAYS later, we were climbing Mount McKinley in Alaska. I mean, in the parking lot. Gabe pointed at the white Mazda Protégé next to us, "Check out that iceberg."

"Are there icebergs in Alaska?"

"It's an avalanche. *¡Dios!* It's crumbling, Bethany! Floor it! Floor it!"

Panicked, I went, "The truck won't start. We're doomed."

"Step on the gas! *Entonces vuelte a llave. ¡La llave!*"

So I stepped on the gas. And I turned the key and you know what? The engine started. True story.

I must have screamed for fifteen straight seconds.

"The beast is alive," shouted Gabe "*¡Sabes! ¡Sabes! ¡Lo vive!* Let's take her out, Bethany."

This world seemed huge in a vehicle that actually drove! Should we see the real Hollywood? Las Vegas? Seattle? Before I talked myself out of it, I reversed Gabe's truck (expertly I might add), drove it around the parking lot, then returned it to its original space.

"I don't like driving," I said. "It scares me."

Gabe touched my hand. "It's only scary at first."

I shook my head. "I kinda just want to stay here," I said and, conveniently, the truck stalled.

"Yeah. Me too."

"I mean with you."

"*Hay ver*," Gabe said, looking at me sideways. "*Entra más profundo*, eh?"

"*Sí*."

Camp ended so soon. Gabe had finished his final project, as he was expected to do. Liliana was managing her diabetes. Cambridge had a tattoo and a headful of dreadlocks. And, except for one minor infraction, I managed to stay at Utopia for—give or take a day or two—eight weeks.

Now our last moments together could've been measured in hours, and still no one wanted to have a conversation about it. Cambridge went on oaring every morning. Liliana sewed like she'd never have to pack up the Singer Deluxe. Even now, in his truck, Gabe totally avoided the conversation and hopped out of his window, opened the door for me, and said, "Let's take a walk," like nothing would change.

We wandered past the library and the gym, pointing out memories to each other. We held hands and ignored the mathematic certainty that Maryland and New Mexico were nowhere near each other. We sipped chai lattes with skim until we found ourselves by the lake. Trees criss-crossed above us, the wind sailed in and out of leaves. "Hey," said Gabe, pointing at something wobbling on the water, "isn't that Tabitha?"

I was a little surprised to see her out there in the water, but there was no mistaking all that hair. She rowed Utopia's own Tampa Bay in a canoe. She must've broken into the boathouse and thieved the boat and oars. The couple was about forty strokes from where Gabe and I stood. I wanted to call out to her, but, at the last minute, I changed my mind. This turned out to be a good decision, because when Cambridge stood up on the boat's wooden seat, she happened to be naked. Full-frontal Tabitha Nelson. I guess she decided to take her bra off with Tampa Bay after all.

Beside me Gabe kept quiet—luckily. Maybe he was embarrassed. Maybe he didn't want to interrupt Tampa Bay's romantic gondola ride. I'd like to think that Gabe was quiet because he knew that this was how I wanted to remember Cambridge: naked, fierce, jumping off a boat into freezing water. Water splashed when Tampa Bay jumped in after her. The boat, now empty, bobbed on the surface. Cambridge dove under just as Tampa Bay reached for her.

Poor Simon. He hadn't yet learned how unsentimental Cambridge was, how slippery. He would try to hold on to her, but there was no way. How depressing it was to realize how exceptionally lame and dull my life was before she strutted into it. Yet as much as I fretted over Gabe's pending absence in my life, I didn't worry over Cambridge's. I knew that beautiful girl with the giant boobs skinny-dipping before me would always be in my life. Always. You think I'm being young or hokey or optimistic. Nope. It was like a law that Newton forgot to mention.

Cradled by the water's waves, she floated on her back and watched morning fracture the dark skyline. That's what I mean. Something about that girl made everything within a fifty-billion-mile radius—even the frickin' sun—sparkle harder.

Gabe and I tiptoed away from the scene and wandered back to MontClaire Hall. We sat by the fountain out front until finally I couldn't take it anymore. I had to ask him the question.

"So what's going to happen? When camp ends?"

"I imagine we'll get certificates or something."

I groaned. "I mean between me and you. Us."

Gabe sighed. "I have this feeling we'll see each other again. After camp. "

"Maybe at the reunion," I huffed, "but not anytime soon. I mean, should we just shake hands or something? Make it anticlimactic? That might be the best thing considering I live in Baltimore, and you live in Albuquerque."

He kissed my cheek. "If only the map were arranged alphabetically."

"Gabe!" Why did everything have to follow an equation? "You'll probably never see me again."

"I will see you again."

For a mathematician, this guy sure left a lot to chance.

"How?"

Gabe scooched closer to me, wrapped his hoodie around my shoulders. "I didn't want to tell you, but you are such a shit about surprises, so I'll just let you in on it. Tomorrow I'm giving you the most Delilah-Rogers-romance-novel ending you ever imagined. *Verdad*? Remember when you made that wish back in my room on the Fourth of July?"

I nodded.

"Well I'm gonna give you what you wished for. Your happy ending. Liliana helped me plan it. She sewed you a dress too. Something fancy. I'm going to pick you up in *ni modo*. I might even clean it out first too. And then I'm going to drive you—really drive you—to Half Moon Bay, where I will serenade you with my sensual voice. I'm gonna put some clam shells in your hair and build one of those romantic fires and I'm going to ... I'm going to ..."

"What?"

"Put on my glasses."

"You don't wear them."

"I'm going to borrow *mi abuela's* bifocals so I can get a good, close look at you."

"And that's when you'll say goodbye?" I whispered.

"Yeah," he said. "Only it's gonna be better than that."

I tried to memorize everything about him—his brown eyes that looked full and wet; his two side teeth that overlapped each other; his olive skin; the SPOOGE T-shirt I'd come to know personally; the pale moons of his fingernails; the wallet chain in his back pocket; the shell of his ear; his zigzag hair part; the stubble of his sideburns; his smell; his rocket principles; his voice.

"That's what I'm gonna do," he said, then stood up to go. "It's gonna be perfect."

ENTER A NEW DESTINATION

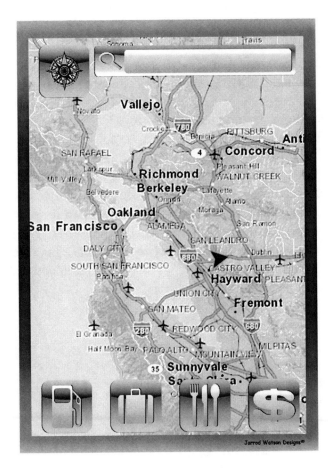

68

BEGINNING'S END

LILIANA MADE MY dress from the bathroom shower curtain and bath mat. She bedazzled the uneven hem and sewed rhinestones along the sleeves. Truth be told, I looked like a regurgitated octopus. The dress was ugly. So very, very ugly. And when I came out to model it, I was afraid everyone was crying because I looked so hideous.

"It's OK," I consoled Liliana. "It's your first design. You'll get better at it."

But she told me she was crying because I looked so beautiful. Then Cambridge got weepy because, she said, even though I resembled a toilet brush, she still thought I was awesome. And then I started crying—crying because Liliana's braces were as radiant as the morning sun. And Cambridge's arms were lean and strong. It was the last day of fat camp, people. So I wore the dress, right? I totally wore the dress.

In addition to it being the last day of fat camp, it was also International Freshman Orientation Day here at the CUP. Cambridge informed us of this as, outside the window, a dozen coach buses leaned around MontClaire's circular drive. Apparently the university brought the foreign students in early.

An entire army of international freshmen were unloaded. One after another, buses dumped the students onto the damp grass below our window. It was sunny and a Northern California version of warm outside. Seeing the college freshmen trickle off the buses reminded me that fall was around the corner. On the trees, the tippy-tops of leaves were beginning to yellow and the smell of pencil shavings and ink cartridges lingered in hallways. Soon enough I'd be shoving a label in a red plastic divider. In nineteen days, I'd be in homeroom. *Stern? Bethany?*

69

SELFIES

CAMBRIDGE SPREAD OUR curtains wider. "Let's come back next year," she said. "I'll give my dad another quiet summer with his mistress." Outside, one soon-to-be-student narrated into a digital camera. Another freshman unlatched a guitar case and strummed a chord we barely heard.

"I think my mom might doubt the camp's effectiveness," I said.

Liliana tugged at the waistband of my rubbery dress. "She won't," she said.

Below us, we watched international students open laptops and chat on cell phones. They towed luggage across the lawn and smoked cigarettes nervously in the shade.

"There's always college," offered Cambridge. "You could come back here in two years." She elbowed me. "Earn yourself a boxing scholarship." This was so unlikely, even Cambridge couldn't say it without cracking up. "So maybe a literature one. There is a romantic period, you know." My roommate, who had walked into the common room eight weeks ago with a hair weave, attempted to tie back her dreadlocks now. With all the bling and beads and knots she had in there, she couldn't squeeze her mane into the ponytail holder, so she relented. "You never know, Bethany. Anything's possible."

I considered what it might be like to enroll at California University of the Pacific as an actual college student, attending classes and stumbling around the museumlike campus. It was a little foggy for my taste, sure, but it was scenic and spacious. There was room to grow. And who knew, maybe with TJ gone, I'd do my homework for once. College? It was a possibility. Either way, as the international freshmen walked single file to the Student Union Complex, the clock chimed nine times. My fat camp days were officially over.

We left our dorm, and I ventured outside. Campers stood under trees, on stairs, looking thinner, for the most part, and exhausted. Not a single one of us looked the same. Hank, Belinda, and Miss Marcia had a proper farewell for us last night. They didn't weigh us, but we did put on the outfits we arrived in eight weeks ago. Almost everyone of us, including me, had to hold the shorts to keep them from falling down. I stood with Hank and Belinda and shook every camper's hand. When Hank announced, "Bethany Thern, you were the beth captain we ever had," no one argued with him.

Outside now, the only camper missing was Hollywood, which figured because the first car that circled MontClaire Hall was an industrial-sized, pimped-out, stretch Hummer limousine that no doubt belonged to whatever family member was tasked with picking her up. It stopped gracefully in front of the mermaid fountain, a motor so oiled we barely heard it. After all this time, I still knew nothing of Hollywood's dad except he was punctual—and rich and overwhelmingly important enough to get me back into Utopia in less than five minutes. While Hollywood presumably packed up her gear inside MontClaire, we collectively watched the limo's dark window ease down. An elegant-looking hand appeared then waved.

"I know whose hand that is," said Liliana beside me.

"Really?"

"*¡Esto! ¡Esto!* Look at the license plate."

AMRCNVY

"What does that mean?"

Liliana jumped up and down, pointing and gasping. "It's Eugene Gold. It's Eugene Gold."

Suddenly Mr. Gold's head peered out and smiled at Liliana, an obvious fan. Liliana spread her fingers into a V and Mr. Gold smirked. He looked in my direction and yelled, "Nice dress." Liliana practically keeled over. I guessed Amber's dad really was influential, considering he was Eugene Gold, America's most heart-less judge. For the second time this summer, I didn't envy Hol-lywood at all. A dad like that? No, thanks. I'll stick with mine.

Speaking of mine, Richard Goodman had taken to e-mailing me almost every day. His e-mails were funny and always included doz-ens and dozens of book recommendations—none of which involved weight loss. As a super-nifty librarian, he had access to advanced read-ers copies of e-books too, which meant I got to read Delilah Rogers on my e-reader before anyone else did. He also forwarded me classics. Still convinced I was the storyteller he never could be, he recommend-ed Steinbeck, Toni Morrison, Hunter S. Thompson, Thomas Hardy, Ralph Ellison, and Margaret Atwood and the like regularly. These fat tomes piled on my e-reader's virtual bookshelf by the day.

Finally, Hollywood walked out in a high-powered suit and heels. You'd never guess she spent the summer at fat camp. She pointed her phone at the three of us. "I want to remember the girls next door," she said. The camera clicked. Her big sunglasses made her head look freakishly small. She took them off to hug me—yes, hug me—and I noticed again how thin she was. When she kissed me on both cheeks, I smelled her perfume. "Subscribe to my feed and follow my blog," she said. "I'll friend you too." Me and Hollywood as *friends*? I wasn't sure when that happened, but if I had to guess, it more than likely occurred on scale demolition day. If I wished anything for her, it was only that when she got home, she destroyed her scale. That we all did.

"Let me introduce you to my dad," Hollywood said, and waved us over to the limo. After eight entire weeks in California, my one and only celebrity-spotting consisted of Eugene Gold.

The *American Envy* judge looked exactly the same in real life as on television, only shorter. Same stubbled chin. Same green eyes. Same infectious grin. Starstruck, the only thing I remem-bered to do was thank him for saving Cambridge's life.

"No worries," he said, and he brought me into a hug. "I used to do a lot of drugs too," he confessed. "I'm glad your friend turned out OK." Cambridge assured him she was off the psychotropics and offered gratitude again for teaching me how to take a pulse.

"Well, ladies," he said, opening the door for his daughter, "looks like this place did wonders for you." He reached inside the immense limo and came out with a tangled bouquet of yellow roses. Hollywood accepted them then folded her skinny self into the car, waving the whole time like Miss America.

Amber Gold. Amber Gold. Amber Gold. It was no use. She'd always be Hollywood to me.

70

THE 101

EVEN THOUGH JACKIE hated to wait, I'd have to make her wait. I didn't care for how long either. I barely heard a peep from her all summer, so if she thought she could just show up and carry me off, well, she could think again. I had plans. Gabe was supposed to pick me up an hour ago, but he got tied up trying to get his truck to start. This had delayed things. Now it was afternoon, and all the campers were gone except me and Cambridge and Liliana. Jackie wasn't here yet either, but when she got here, I'd decided, she'd have to wait some more. In my mind, I rehearsed what I'd say.

You see, Jackie, there's the guy and well. I'm waiting for my happy ending. We can't leave because this guy I met, well, my boy ...

I was concentrating so thoroughly that when a Honda Odyssey chugged up the drive, I hardly noticed it. Considering it had a giant surfboard attached to the roof rack, I didn't give it a second thought. As the van approached, it started to look familiar. It was a little worn-out, sure, but it was definitely ours. After a series of stomach flip-flops, I fought the urge to run.

The three of us were sitting on the steps of MontClaire Hall. "That's my sister," I said to Cambridge and Liliana. Together we watched Jackie pull into the circular drive and kill the engine. Ever so slowly, her door screeched open.

I knew I should be preparing to greet her, to offer one of the ten thousand apologies I needed to make on the endless ride from California to Baltimore. I should have been translating the words "I'm sorry" into every language known to man. Instead I steeled myself to tell her that things were running a bit behind schedule. *So, OK, Jackie. Don't get mad, but there's this guy, and he wants to go to the beach before I leave ...*

"Look at you," said Jackie, walking toward me. "You look completely different."

The new highlights in Jackie's hair dazzled like a crown. Instead of *I'm sorry* or *you'll have to wait*, "Nice hair," were my first words. I separated from my friends and walked closer to the van.

"You like, huh?" When she flipped her head over, I could see her bikini string, a baby pink, tied behind her neck. "They highlighted underneath too."

When she righted herself, her face was positively beautiful.

I looked at the van and barely made out Doug's profile behind the tinted glass. *I knew they'd get back together.*

"San Francisco has salons better than Towson," said Jackie. "The one I went to, Xanadu, did my color chart, and I'm a spring. All this time I thought I was a fall, and what do you know? I can wear pink and it's fine. I've been working at a dance school wearing a pink leotard. Lipstick? Pink as petals. Boots, too."

Given our hellbent road trip, complete with the silent treatment starting in Ohio and ending in Utopia, I'd forgotten about Jackie's usual nonstop chatter. Her ability to sing everything from one topic to the next, tra-la-la-la, like a bird. Like my mom. She touched my cheek, and I pulled back.

"Wait, you're working at a dance studio?"

Freckles clustered across Jackie's nose and cheeks. So unfairly, God graced her with a beauty mark above her lip. "All summer." She paused, counting on her fingers. "Seven weeks yesterday." I cocked my head. A *job*?

"Here's what happened," she began. "Remember I told you about the butterflies? The cocoon in the car?" I nodded and she continued. "Right after that, we were on the 101. I pulled over on the shoulder, and San Francisco was in the distance, you know. All foggy. So weirdly, though, the mist opened up right in front of the Bay Bridge." She lifted my duffle bag, popped the trunk. "And I just knew it was over for me and Doug. So I told him so."

I could not stop staring at this new Jackie, who was really the old Jackie. The old Jackie who talked my ear off, peed when she laughed too hard, never remembered which side the gas tank was on, and took ballet lessons long after I gave up. There was no reason for this except aliens. Aliens had abducted the new Jackie and put my old sister back.

"I wish I'd known it was over before, like a year ago, but I hadn't known then the way I knew it on the 101. So I gave him my phone to call for a taxi or whatever. I told him to keep it. Then, when I got to San Francisco, things started, I don't know, happening. I met a friend who needed a roommate, and then the old roommate was leaving her job."

"You left Doug on the 101?"

"Pretty much. He did make it back to Baltimore though. I saw it on my phone bill."

We loaded the Odyssey. Beach sand and seashells littered the back.

"But Doug," I said.

She inhaled. Breathe, my mom had always told her. Breathe when you're telling a story.

"I was getting to that." Picking up a pink seashell from the trunk, she studied its pearl underbelly. Jackie cleared her throat. "After your forgiveness jar, I was just hanging on to him. It was stupid." Her eyes filled. "Anyway, it's over. He flew back weeks ago." She pulled a curl of my hair and lengthened it. "True story."

Jackie wore dark jeans and tall, pink furry boots. Her shirt was too tight and dotted with coffee stains. She looked wild again, colorful. She dragged a finger along my arm. "Nice dress," she said, eyeing my ensemble. "It's different. Hey. Are these your friends?" She waved to Cambridge and Liliana, still sitting on the stoop. "Hi, I'm Jackie."

Before she headed over to Cambridge and Liliana, I stopped her. "Jackie," I began. "I need you to wait here for a bit. There's this guy and—"

"A guy? TJ?"

"No," I replied.

A sly smile brightened her face. "That's fine," she said. "But I need to tell you something first." She pulled in a big breath. "I got an apartment in the city. I'm not going back to Baltimore. I'm staying in California."

By *staying* did she mean relocating temporarily? Did she mean extending her visit for a week? A month. "For how long?"

Jackie folded her arms across her chest. "Indefinitely."

"What?" Somehow in all my imaginings of fat camp finales, this ending never figured in. Not for one minute did I picture returning to a Baltimore without Jackie in it. "For real, Jackie? Does Mom know about this?"

"She knows I'm staying in California and no, she's not happy about it, but I can't go back there."

My mind refused to process this. "You can't just stay here. What about home?" I realized I was whining. "What about me?"

We both inherited our dad's cratered chin, and hers trembled now. She reached her hands inside her purse, a tiny round thing about the size of a canteen. She pulled out a set of keys.

"You are the proud owner of," Jackie said and plopped her ringly-dingly keychain in my hand, "a very used minivan. Mom's minivan. Then my minivan. Now yours. Take it. I don't need it. In the city, the BART goes everywhere." Her pewter Virgo figurine, the photoscopes from Rehoboth, a tiny Old Bay spice shaker, and a photo of Doug in a heart weighed two tons in my hand. "I need to stay." She closed her eyes and kissed my forehead. "I'm sorry."

Even though I held real-live keys that fit into a real-live ignition, I didn't care. This was not the plan. Gabe was supposed to drive me to the beach, say goodbye, and then, predictably, I would drive home *with my sister*. Dammit, this was not my happy ending!

"You can't just *stay* here. Mom is going to plotz, Jackie. Get in the van. Come on." When I grabbed my sister's elbow, she froze. The expression on her face told me everything I needed to know "It's not an option, Bee. I've rented an apartment. I have a patio." She looked at me, and the tears spilled out. "And a washing machine in the basement. The whole complex is pink as an Easter egg. You would love it."

She squeezed my hand around the keychain. "*Dad* is going

to drive you back to Baltimore. The van will make it there. Don't underestimate it because it's old," she said. "Dad just changed the oil and got new brake pads and filled it with premium gas. He'll drive it home, and once you get your license, it will be yours."

Oddly enough, I wasn't thinking about the fact that I had a car, a fifteen-year-old Honda Odyssey minivan, but whatever. That's not where my mind was. My mind was stuck on the word *dad,* how it had fallen out of Jackie's mouth so casually, and that was when I knew that it wasn't Doug's profile behind the window. It was my father's.

His door opened. "Hi, Bee," he said and laughed. He wore an orange Alcatraz shirt and shorts. California must have rubbed off on him, because he'd threaded a cloth rainbow belt through his belt loops. He seemed to have lost a few pounds too. "I'm really gonna miss it here," he said and stretched like a lion in the sunlight. "But we'll be back, right? To visit Jackie? To surf?"

This was not the life I left. My dad never mentioned California. He did not wear rainbow belts. My sister's hair was never highlighted, and the minivan never guzzled premium gasoline.

"So Dad found me after you decided to stay at Utopia. He hung with me in San Francisco for a bit and helped me move into my own place. He surfed in the mornings and got pretty OK at it."

My dad? On a surfboard? Was that what the gigantic board with the word INSIGHT angled down its fin was about? Someone freakin' pinch me.

My dad petted the surfboard. "You keep the van, and I keep the board."

"What about your kids?" I asked. "Caleb and, and—"

"Cullen. They're fine. Penny got a nanny."

I was reeling, dizzy. Around me the earth danced with wavy lines like in a movie right before a dream sequence. I looked to my sister and then my dad. This must be what it felt like. What it felt like to faint—to fall backward into space. Swaying, knees buckling, my brain stuttered and shifted. Suddenly it was 2003. Jackie was nine. I was five. We were in the basement of our old house in Silver Springs. It was snowing outside. See the striped hula hoop orbiting Jackie like a planet's ring? She could twirl that thing for hours. My dad and I were eating cheese and crackers on the sofa because Mom wasn't home to complain about crumbs. We watched Jackie twirl her way to the bookshelf. There she removed her favorite book the way a doctor might remove a rib. Eight-year-old Jackie stretched her *please* out like taffy. My dad had read this book approximately ten thousand times, but each time it was new. Every voice was just right. Every nuance executed. He cracked the spine. Cleared his throat. The snow clicked against the window ...

"Hey," I said, to both of them. The world tilted then righted itself. "Remember that book about the caterpillar that won't stop eating?"

Jackie smiled through her tears. My dad got that cloudy look like he was remembering it too. I had no idea why that memory came to me. Maybe it was because Jackie still looked like a little girl when she cried, pitted chin quivering. "I'll come back and visit, but I just can't do it," she said and wiped her eyes with the back of her hand. "I can't go back there, Bethany. I'm sorry." I was pretty sure, though, I remembered this because this summer, Jackie had woken up with wings.

It took every ounce of strength not to grab a tangle of my sister's newly colored hair and shove her in the minivan and demand my father drive her back to Baltimore. I wouldn't do it. I couldn't do it. If I did, she'd get back together with Doug. Doug would grow weed in his mom's basement until someone, out of concern for Jackie, offered him a job. I didn't know when Jackie figured this out, but she did. So when she turned from me, I didn't stop her. When she walked away, I let her go. It was Miss Marcia who offered her a ride back to San Francisco, and before Jackie had even closed the car door, I knew she wouldn't be coming back to Baltimore for a long, long time.

71

YIELD

I WATCHED MISS Marcia's car until I had to squint my eyes. Then it disappeared. Of everything I had to let go of this summer, my sister would be the hardest. I looked to the minivan, *my* minivan, where Richard Goodman was tightening the straps that secured his surfboard.

"I promise to hurry back to Maryland," he yelled to me. "It should take us about a week to get there. I brought you some books we could listen to. It might actually be fun. You ready to go?"

My roommates, both seated on the steps behind me, must have suspected a change of plan. Why did Jackie walk off with Miss Marcia, and why wasn't I following her? Exactly who was this old guy in an Alcatraz shirt sitting on top of the car anyway?

From the roof, my dad unfolded a map that spanned the width of his arms. "Haven't driven across the country in twenty-five years," he said. "This should be an adventure."

I didn't share his enthusiasm. To complicate matters, Gabe was now two hours late, and I was beginning to worry. "Do you think you can wait here for a bit," I asked my dad. "I haven't said goodbye to Gabe yet, and I want to."

My father checked the tires and blabbed about thermostats and air filters and said something that sounded like, *Go on and take your time. There's no hurry.* And he started to say something about southern routes versus northern routes—only I didn't hear the rest because all of a sudden there was this explosion, a sonic boom so frickin' loud it rattled the minivan. Then, in the distance, a black column of smoke began to rise.

Liliana shouted, "His truck! I think Gabe's truck's on fire."

The three of us took off. Not power walking either. Running. We sprinted over hills and dodged pedestrians. All three of us charged toward Copernicus, fueled by some mad instinct; we huffed past buildings and park benches until we crested the hill that led to the parking lot behind Copernicus.

Once there, a few spectators gathered around the fallout, coughing into their hands and assessing the damage of nearby cars. Everything smelled burnt.

"*Está muerto*," Gabe muttered. He was sitting on a concrete parking block, head in his hands. "*Perfecto*."

"Barbecue," Liliana remarked, still panting. She stepped closer and looked directly into the black pit of *ni modo*. "I've been telling you this whole time that the truck is done. There goes that plan. Do you think Mom will—"

"Shut up, Liliana."

Careful to avoid looking at it, I walked past the truck as if it were a campfire and sat down next to Gabe. He held out a cylindrical rocket. "Here, Bethany," he said. "It survived the fire."

"What is it?" I asked, coughing a little into my dress.

"It's my final project."

I studied the nose cone and fins and his name, *Gabriel Delgado*, penned along the body tube. "What's it do?"

Gabe laughed and covered his mouth. "When launched very high into the air, it flies. Like most model rockets."

"Thanks," I said, both flattered and confused. I gestured behind me. "I'm sorry about your truck."

Gabe leaned into me. "I guess you don't have to be a rocket scientist to figure out this was bound to happen." He removed a black bandana from his pocket and tied it around his head. His face was smeared with grease. "Too bad it happened today."

"Hey," screamed Liliana. "I know your truck is ablaze, 'mano, but did you see Bethany's dress?"

"I did," he deadpanned. "It's something."

Cambridge, who'd been inspecting the fallout, laughed. "I'd

bet it's flame retardant too."

Gabe whispered so Liliana wouldn't hear. "You do realize that dress is a little unusual. Or is that a secret?"

"It's a secret," I replied.

Gabe rubbed his eyes. "Scientifically speaking, you are the only woman on Earth who could wear such a dress and still look hot." I felt my face flush. Together we watched his charcoaled truck pollute the otherwise lovely afternoon. "I had it all planned, *verdad*," he started. "I was going to tell you that I wanted to see you again. And FaceTime with you. And text you and have like a long-distance relationship. Then Liliana told me to launch the rocket right at sunset and confess how madly I don't love you." Smoke gripped him for a second and he coughed. When he looked up his eyes were tearing. "Which is to say that I do love you, Bethany. I'm sorry your happy ending went up in flames."

So maybe to Newton and other untrained eyes, the situation looked pretty hopeless. His dying truck dead. The unlaunched model rocket. The endless miles between Maryland and New Mexico. But I couldn't help thinking about Michael Osbourne and The Forgiveness Diet e-mail I'd read a thousand times. Beauty didn't live in what was perfect. It lived in what wasn't. It settled in the flaws. Gabe's crooked smile. His black pirate do-rag. The worn hem of his shorts. The way our teeth scraped when we kissed. Beauty was in the long journey to find it too, like my journey: complete with miles of silence, gum-caked forgivelets, pissed-off siblings, black eyes, and toasted truck engines.

"I love you too," I said.

"Really?" He tilted his head. "Even though my plan backfired and my truck died and, and—" I pressed my finger to his lips. "But your ending, Bethany?"

"*Esto es esto,*" I said, breathing the words into his mouth. "This is it. Here's my happy ending."

Even though our walk back to MontClaire Hall took a long time, my father did not look annoyed. In fact, he barely looked up from the book he was reading on the lawn. When he saw us arrive, he inserted a blade of grass to mark his page, closed the book, and said, "Must've been some explosion." He stood up and brushed the grass off his behind. "You ready to go now, Bethany?"

Leave? Now?

My dad walked closer. "Traffic might be bad. We need to think about getting on the road, Bee."

I wasn't in a hurry. I would have plowed through another eight weeks of fat camp just to have Gabe, Liliana, and Cambridge a little bit longer. "My friends need a ride. I can't just leave them here."

My father suddenly stopped. "What?"

"They need a lift. Gabe's truck died."

He touched his rainbow belt. "A ride to where, Bethany?"

"New Mexico," said Gabe and Liliana in unison.

My dad's lips twitched. "That's funny, guys."

"Technically," reasoned Cambridge, "it's on your way."

My father checked his watch and lifted an index finger. "I have a better idea. How about I drive you to the airport? That seems like a compromise. Surely there will be a flight for you."

Gabe, Cambridge, and Liliana stared at their feet. Obviously this was not the ending any of us had predicted, but what other choice did we have? Sensing our disappointment, my dad looked at the minivan and crossed his arms. "Goodbyes are never easy. I understand that. But you guys have the e-mail and the texting and the Skype. Never mind actual letter writing." He directed this to Gabe: "Bethany can write one hell of a letter, you know. You guys will all keep in touch. In the meantime, we really need to hit the road. I'll take you to the airport."

No one moved. Liliana put her arm around me and then Gabe. "*Padre*, this is an emergency. We need to get back to Albuquerque, and I've never been on a plane in my life." Cambridge sighed. "Are you sure you won't reconsider?" she asked. "I have a few bucks for gas."

My father did not look remotely conflicted by his decision. "The airport, Tabitha. That's my final offer.

Relentless Cambridge. "It's really a beautiful drive across country, you know. I can point out all the historical landmarks. Just think how guilty you'd feel if all of our flights crashed too. Driving us is the much safer choice."

Out came Richard Goodman's librarian voice. Equitable. Agreeable. Diplomatic. "It's a nice idea," my dad started, "but I can't take responsibility for all of you. It's just impossible. You guys are kids. What if something happens? What if ...."

I didn't know what else he said because I walked away. I walked toward the minivan, Jackie's keychain a weight in my hand. "What if ...," I said, and I could feel their eyes behind me. "What if I ..." Then, before I lost my nerve, I unlocked the door. "What if *I* drove, Dad?" After flinging open the door, I climbed into the driver's seat like I'd done it a million times before. Like a pro. "What if I drove the minivan," I said again, and pointed at my father, "and you, you sat in the back? You could help if I needed it. Shut up if I didn't. Like a guardian."

Stationed in the driver's seat, key still in my hand, I saw them all on the lawn, four faces drawn in disbelief. "I need sixty hours for my permit. Who says I can't blow them out in one week?"

Of course they knew how I felt about driving—I could see it in their shocked expressions. But now was not the time for questions. Now was the time for action. I slid the key into the ignition, and the minivan roared to life.

Cambridge was the first to move. She picked up her luggage and stepped closer. Then Gabe and Liliana followed.

"We'll stop along the way," I told them, rolling down my window. "Sightseeing. That kind of thing."

Gabe opened the passenger side door and laid his model rocket and backpack on the floor. Then he climbed in. Liliana and Cambridge piled in the middle seat. My dad, however, still stood on the lawn, waiting. He shook his head.

Inside the van, every single one of us was quiet, watching him. He passed his book from one hand to the other, scratched his chin. Of course we were all waiting for the stubborn *No* to eject from his mouth. Waiting for his tantrum—or mine. I was waiting for the outright refusal. After all, I was afraid to drive, terrified of it; they all knew it. My dad knew it. Only to my surprise, he took one step closer. Then another. "I'll fill up the tank," he said. "Check the air pressure in the tires. I have audio books too. Kerouac. Márquez. Toni." A few seconds later, he was outside my window. "You can give your friends a lift, but you'll need to do the bulk of the driving," he said. "*All* of the driving in fact." His face was framed by the square of the window. "I can't let you do this alone. I'm sorry."

It's not easy to be a father, I decided. But it was a job and my dad met all the requirements. It wasn't easy to marry a woman like my mom either, a woman so talented you couldn't possibly forget. Of course if you did, she'd be there to remind you. It must all-out suck to be smart enough to get into optometry school only to discover the eye was about as interesting as the dust balls collecting in your library. How classically FUBARed to learn your two daughters were worse for the wear when you walked out. And how fundamentally catastrophic to realize that you were headed home to ADHD twins and a wife who would never be the same now that your two other children had crashed their way back into your world. So I guess that was why I tapped the button on my armrest, and the van's back door eased open.

"This bus is departing," I told him. "Come on in." He looked mystified at first, incredulous. But then came the smile. He didn't hesitate.

"To the airport, Cambridge?" I asked.

"Not a chance, Captain," she replied, pulling her hair back into a ponytail.

"How about you, Dad?"

"I believe I'd prefer a more scenic route," he explained and cracked his window from the back bench.

"Gabe? Liliana? You want in on the next flight to Albuquerque."

"I thought this was the next flight to Albuquerque," Gabe observed.

Meanwhile, my dad and Liliana were already chattering about mountain passes, prairies, and desert skies. All the things they'd never seen but wanted to. Gabe tapped me with his elbow. "You got this," he said, and pointed east. "Just head thatta way."

I yielded to the traffic in the circle, but the other drivers encouraged me with a wave. I shifted into drive just as Cambridge opened a navigator app on her phone. I eased off the brake, and we moved forward. Forward. A little more gas and we accelerated around the circular drive. We rocketed past the mermaid fountain spitting her trickle of water. I thought of my dad's coins corralled in the bottom and how watching him that day, weeks ago, up in my dorm, I'd assumed he'd wished for something noble, like the return of all overdue library books, or universal literacy, or that his kids, Cullen and Caleb, would quit the violin. Now, however, I was pretty sure he wished for me. His daughter. How did I know?

With Utopia shrinking behind us, the road unrolling ahead, I felt my throat swell, amplify like something was stuck in there—a new song or the tight fist of a flower. Whatever it was, it was ready to climb out. And that was what my dad had been talking about. What he knew all along. It was a story. My story.

And this is how it begins.

FIN

ACKNOWLEDGMENTS

First and foremost, thank you to Josh, Judy and Jill Ruden for providing me with space when I needed it and plenty of distraction when I didn't. Living with a writer is pure hell. I can hardly stand myself. How you put up with me is nothing short of a miracle. I love you all. I promise not to write another book. Oh, and thanks for knowing when I'm lying.

Thanks also to my family (especially Marlene, Tim, Wendy, Esther, Paul, Cami, Tom & Elizabeth) who generously provided both fodder and encouragement. I also would like to acknowledge Albert, Judy, Carolyn and Lenora who died before seeing this book, but would not have been surprised by its publication either. Thanks also to Josh's family who not only encouraged me, but sometimes financed me.

Because I could never write during nap time, thank you to the long list of childcare providers who took wonderful care of my children while I wrote. Thank you to The Children's House and Juliet Romero and to Dr. G, who told me it was ok to listen to the voices in my head.

I am eternally grateful to Ellen Dworksky's writing group and for my friendships with writerly friends. We are of the same tribe and I could not imagine life without you-- and hopefully will never have to. Thank you also to Whitney, Dylan, Priscilla, and Rebecca.

Thank you to early readers like Chris Eboch, Suzanne Morgan Williams, KL Going, Miriam Gershow, Mike Mullen, Donna Cooner, and Alisa Valdes and to industry professionals like Wendy Sherman, Kim Perel and Kenneth Wright.

Finally, thanks to Joe Coccaro for being the grumpy old editor that every book needs. I could not have asked for better. Thank you to John Koehler for calling me personally, "I'd like to sign up for fat camp." You not only are a fighter, Koehler Books, you are a champion. Finally, a big mwah to my agent, Antonella Iannarino, a rock star who's even brighter than the moon moon moon.